FLICKERS OF FORTUNE

46. ASCENDING

S. R. CRONIN

Cover design by Deranged Doctor Design
Original Editing by Joel Handley

This book is a work of fiction and, with the exception of news
items, public figures, and cultural information, the events,
characters and institutions in it are imaginary, as are the
organizations d^4 and y^1. No individual character, organization, or
group of people included as part of the fictional narrative is
intended to represent any real person or group.

A version of this book was published in 2015 under the title d^4. It
was designed for an electronic reader and included numerous links
to photographs, articles and music. A later iteration was published
in paperback. In Flickers of Fortune, all text supplementing those
links has been removed, and the story has been shortened and
updated.

Dedication

This book is dedicated to the quiet energy source that is my middle child. She is imagination in motion, charging into the future. I love her for the way she believes she can do anything and I thank her for the times she's reminded me I can, too. May her touch with tomorrow always sparkle with a web of possibilities, and may the best of those come true.

The future is a funny thing because it takes only a second to become the past. This novel is a tribute to those who look to tomorrow and must watch their predictions disintegrate into reality. Here's to the planners and predictors, the science fiction writers and weather forecasters, and all pretend, hopeful and real psychics of every flavor. May their prophecies steer us towards kindness, and may their visions converge on a long and happy life for this marvelous creature we call humanity.

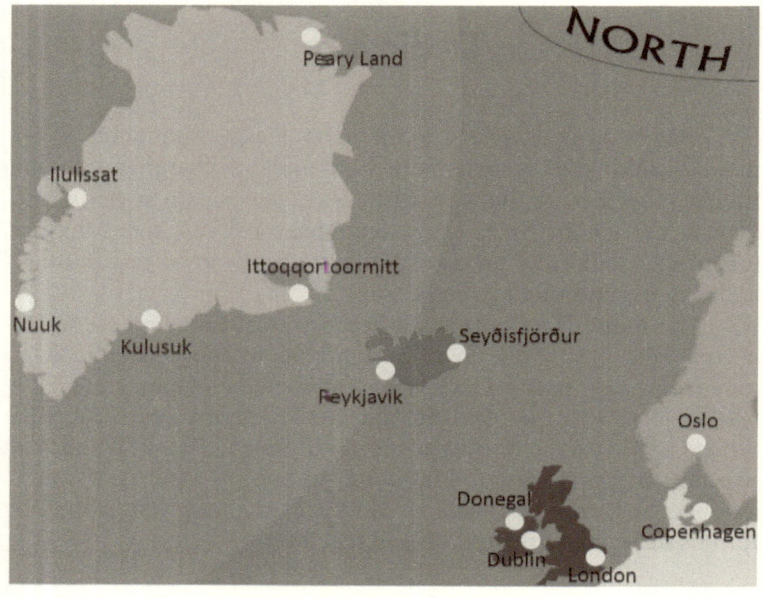

This map of the North Atlantic is approximately to scale and only shows cities and regions that play a role in this story.

The Past

1. Childhood Fights

"Why? Why would you hit your brother over the head?"

Ariel's mother looked more surprised than annoyed as she stared at her five-year-old daughter clenching a heavy three-ring binder in her small hands. Ariel glared back at her mommy with all the defiance she could muster. Her seven-year-old brother Zane was crying and rubbing his skull.

"He told me to," Ariel said. "He did."

"I don't believe that."

"He was kicking over my blocks. I told him three times to stop and he didn't."

"Zane? You kicked over what she was building?" The boy fidgeted while he looked at the floor.

"Then he said 'make me.'" Ariel's bright red hair bobbed up and down for emphasis. Her icy blue eyes bored into Zane with disapproval. "So I did."

Her mother stifled a laugh and Ariel wondered why this was funny.

"Okay. Zane, I guess in a way you did tell her to do it." Ariel tensed as her mommy turned to her. Hitting other people was high on the list of things she wasn't supposed to do.

"You're not in trouble, not this time," her mother said. "I don't want you hurting people, but if someone is doing something bad, well, then you stop them. Like you did."

Oh. It was okay this time?

Mommy reached out to pat her shoulder and as the large fingers brushed against her small neck, Ariel felt her mother's words circle around in her mind. *You stop them.*

Her mother's touch set off the weird thing in her head. It was a twirling feeling, like the one she got when she spun around too fast on the monkey swing, only her body didn't turn. The inside of her head did, like everything had been one way and now it was different even though nothing in the room changed.

Ariel shrugged. Adults must have ways of dealing with this because they never mentioned the problem. Ariel knew the feeling would pass if she went outside to play. When she got older, she'd figure out why this happened.

******

Baldur grew slowly, and at twelve years old he was embarrassed because his younger brother was now taller and stronger. As the first touches of spring began shattering Iceland's long winter, ten-year-old Oskar began to lord his new physical superiority over the older brother who'd once ruled his world. Baldur was lucky he was quicker and smarter than Oskar, or as the long summer days took hold, he'd have endured more frequent beatings than he got.

Once school was out, Oskar never tired of taking advantage of Baldur's slight stature, and Baldur realized this had become more than a little brother's revenge. Yes, Baldur had enjoyed skirmishing with Oskar, and okay, he'd enjoyed winning the skirmishes too. But he couldn't remember ever enjoying hurting Oskar the way Oskar seemed to enjoy hurting him.

Mother intervened a few times when Oskar's beatings took a turn towards brutal, and Baldur saw growing concern in her eyes. He was hopeful the adults would keep the situation under control. Then his father surprised everyone by telling his mother to stay out of her sons' fights.

"They're boys. Baldur needs to learn to take care of himself. You make him weak every time you step in." The criticism in his father's voice was clear.

Very well. The adults were going to be of no help, as usual.

Baldur was a logical boy. He knew he couldn't make his pale, slight body grow faster, and he could think of no way to make Oskar less cruel. So he'd have to learn to fight better, even though it annoyed him, because that was exactly what his father intended.

He vowed not to ask his father for help. If the old man hoped his son would turn to him for instruction in self-defense, Baldur would let the fool see how wrong he was.

Baldur scoured the library for volumes on martial arts and fighting techniques. He liked to read anything, and he studied well. Some books were in Icelandic, others were in Danish, Norwegian or even English, so he worked to read all the languages better. Being a bright boy had its advantages.

He learned the human body's vital points and drew diagrams of where to punch. By autumn, he was sneaking out of bed and spending hours in the barn, engulfed in layers of thermal underwear, practicing kicks and punches by the flickering light of an oil lamp. If his teeth chattered, he worked harder, until his pale blond hair was soaked in sweat.

His parents must have heard him leave the house, but they never checked on him. It was only a matter of time before Oskar snuck out to find him, and discovered him in the barn.

On a clear night in October, Baldur heard his brother coming. It was time to let the lunkhead know the power structure had changed again. Baldur yelled out insults to Oskar then ran up to the loft, giving Oskar the impression he was trying to hide. A surprise ambush would add to his advantage.

Oskar fell over Baldur's outstretched leg as he came up the last step, and as Baldur straddled him and raised his arm for a decisive punch, he placed his left hand against Oskar's collarbone and his fingers brushed against his brother's bare throat.

The quick whirly thing in his head happened like it always did when he touched someone skin to skin. Baldur didn't question it, he assumed it was an artifact of human contact, too normal to mention. After all, no one talked about swallowing or exhaling.

The flicker of what was coming was always followed in a second or two by the happening itself, then the phenomenon was gone. It was useless and sometimes annoying. He figured it was why people didn't touch each other much.

Only this time, the flicker wasn't what Baldur expected. It wasn't Baldur delivering the punch. It was Oskar biting into his left wrist, drawing a spurt of blood before Baldur could do what he'd planned. Baldur jerked his arm away before the painful reality could follow the image, and then in outright anger he swung his fist harder than ever into his brother's nose.

The blood spurting everywhere was Oskar's, and Baldur wondered if his father would be proud of him or angry. It didn't matter. Oskar was holding his nose in pain and eying him with a new level of hatred.

Baldur realized two things. First, he was going to have to be careful around his brother for the rest of his life. Second, the flickers could be useful if something surprising was about to happen.

Why hadn't someone mentioned *that* before? Why didn't others use this more to their advantage? Or maybe they did. Baldur had a lot of questions, but straddling his angry, bleeding brother was not the time to sort them out. When he got older, he'd figure out why this happened.

2009

2. Grown-up Issues

As a child, Ariel figured everybody knew about the past and the future. They all talked about their memories. These fragments of what happened yesterday or years ago were brought back at will, or sometimes popped up randomly. Everyone managed the intrusion, even at inconvenient times.

Young Ariel figured people had the same knowledge of the future because they talked like they did. Adults, especially those on the news shows her mother watched, went on about what was likely to happen tomorrow exactly like they knew it was so. The way she did.

When Ariel was ten, she figured out these people were only guessing and had been all along. Ariel was angry at being misled. Why had grown-ups pretended they knew something when they didn't? She considered asking her parents, but by the time she was ten she'd decided they didn't know much either.

In seventh grade, Ariel figured out why no one admitted they were guessing about the future. It never occurred to them they could be doing anything else. There was a word for Ariel's future memories. They were called premonitions and sensible people didn't believe in them. Sensible people considered memories of the future to be superstitious nonsense.

Ariel was an analytical child. She figured if she told her parents she could remember the future, she'd get in trouble. Kids got grounded for making things up.

The biggest problem was she couldn't prove anything because her forward memories were unreliable. They had a fuzziness to them because nothing from the future was ever certain. It made sense inside, but she didn't know how to explain it to anyone else.

Now, at twenty-one, she was still trying to figure it out. It had become her deepest secret.

Having her own vocabulary helped. She had memories and premories. Memories could be set off by anything, and came with pictures, smells, sounds, and knowledge. Like, she didn't just see an image of a rock gorge in her mind. She smelled the dust and knew it was the Grand Canyon where she'd been in 2001. Memories were complex. They changed a little as items were forgotten or new ones recalled. They were never complete.

Premories were never complete either and they also came with knowledge. No visions of standing by a rock gorge and wondering where it was. Knowing this was the Grand Canyon was as clear in a premory as it was in a memory.

However, she couldn't will premories out of nowhere. They were mostly set off by touch. Skin-to-skin contact was the strongest trigger. Touching objects or touching someone through clothing sometimes worked, but it took intent on her part. She figured that was good, because she was always touching something.

As a teenager, she avoided physical contact with people, except of course for some sexual experimentation. Others got the impression she was cold, but nothing was further from the truth. Ariel had a warm heart and cared a great deal for the people she was close to. She just preferred not to touch them.

Once she left for college, her premories became more frequent and less voluntary. She'd grab a door handle and random knowledge about a stranger's best or worst experience next week would pop into her mind. It was annoying. She started to wear gloves. She guessed the onslaught of information was brought on by being on her own for the first time. Maybe her subconscious was trying to help her? If so, it wasn't working so well.

Liquor, however, did help. Ariel knew if she partied tonight, she'd shut the premories out until morning. It wasn't a good solution, but sometimes you just had to make it to tomorrow.

******

As a new professor at a small engineering school in Denmark, Carl was happy to have an office of his own. Part Inuit, he'd grown up in far off Greenland, and after the crowded quarters he'd shared all his life, this little office meant a lot.

He repaid the university by having ample office hours to meet with all the undergrads struggling with the difficult aeronautical engineering courses. The man who stood outside of his office today, however, was too old to be a normal student and too young to be a normal student's parent. Curious, Carl motioned him inside.

He spoke English with a heavy Irish accent, and the desperation in his eyes made Carl wonder if the man was stable. The high quality of his clothes, shoes and briefcase argued against insanity, even though Carl knew it shouldn't. The wealthy had their share of crazy people too.

This visitor had an uncommon knowledge of aeronautics, and he wanted to help fund private space exploration. That alone didn't indicate a loose grip on reality; many people shared that dream. However, this man went as far as insisting the future of the human race lay in permanent settlements off Earth and he wanted to know what *he* could do to help put humans into space. Carl tried to answer with as much gentleness in his voice as he could.

Cost and timing were both enormous. Even a well-informed layman didn't understand the obstacles. No one had that kind of money, or wanted to spend the decades needed.

"Find another passion," Carl said. "There are plenty of worthwhile endeavors for a man with money who wants to make the world better. Any one of them will produce more tangible results."

"Yes, but not one of those results will matter. Not after 2352. How can a person know this, and not do something?"

Carl froze in his chair. For a minute, he questioned his own sanity instead.

"What did you say?"

Carl had a cousin more Inuit than he, who claimed to see the future. Many Inuit did and Carl, with his more Danish upbringing, had been taught to take such claims with a grain of salt.

This boy was his age and they became best friends at family gatherings. The boy's visions were always of events at least decades away. Carl loved science fiction and as a child he'd read nothing but stories of rocket ships and robots. He'd listen to his cousin and join in, adding his own ideas from whatever he was reading. For years, at every wedding and funeral, the two boys would sneak off and collaborate on a shared vision of the future that was half prophecy and half comic books and pulp fiction.

Then one day in their early teens, his cousin informed him he'd become certain the human race would soon be extinct. They argued about it, with a passion only the young can have for a dispute so philosophical. Carl believed humans would one day be so far flung across the galaxy that even the sun going supernova would not put an end to his species. But his cousin remained adamant. It would all end in the year 2352.

Carl retorted that the boy was full of shit and it was about time someone told him so. After Carl's outburst, the two of them stopped sharing anything. The next time they met, Carl apologized, but the fun had gone out of their friendship. Teen activities began to keep Carl away from family events, and the boys lost touch.

Carl stared at his visitor. Could the cousin be playing some trick on him? More likely his own mind had substituted the wrong year.

"You're sure this happens in *exactly* 2352?"

The visitor nodded. "I'm positive. There are many variations, but it's always that year, no matter how it goes."

Carl scooted his chair forward, to better hear the man.

"You're the second person to mention this particular year to me. Please, tell me more."

******

Ariel and her best friend Laura headed over to the frat party already lightly buzzed, thanks to a pre-party cocktail shared with friends in the sorority. Instead of having its usual soothing effect, tonight the alcohol was making Ariel agitated. It was probably because she'd made the mistake of opening a care package from her mom, and the connection was strong enough to get her started.

Damn. The images in her head kept getting clearer, clamoring for her attention like inmates who see a jailor in the distance.

"Are you okay?" Laura asked as they walked through the crowded university courtyard. Usually quiet, Laura got more solicitous when she drank. "You seem kind of off tonight."

"Yeah, I feel kind of off. You think maybe there was something else in that drink?"

Laura shook her head. "No. I feel fine. I didn't have as much as you did though."

"I'll be okay. Damn. I left my phone back in the room. Oh well." Ariel shook it off with a determined laugh. "Come on. Let's go have some fun."

Only the party wasn't fun, at least not for Ariel. The harder she tried to enjoy herself, the more overwhelmed she became. She couldn't get the images to solidify or even slow down, and she couldn't get herself to ignore them.

A dangerous possibility was emerging and it concerned her family. Mom, Dad, thirteen-year-old sister Teddie and older brother Zane swam in and out of her focus, the mélange of video clips repeating in her head until she started to see a pattern.

This wasn't normal. She usually saw how much fun something was going to be. Or not. Or if a pair of shoes she admired was likely to go on sale or if a girl down the hall would pass her math test. *Let's face it. I see stupid stuff. Ignore it, pay attention, believe it or not. It never matters.*

Her knowledge of the future always came with a vague sense of likelihood—*real likely, sort of likely, outside chance.* Ariel tended to assign fractions, like one out of three, even though she knew she was guessing. Usually she saw several outcomes, and, if she tried, she could get to the possibilities out on the fringe. Weird options lived out there. She knew enough to ignore them.

Tonight, for some reason, fringe possibilities were turning into high probabilities. There was a good chance her mother was going to die. Next weekend. Drown, in fact. Drown? Her mother hated the water and could barely swim. No way she would drown.

Ariel made her way outside, pushing past those who tried to talk to her. She walked far enough away from the frat house to find silence and took a few deep breaths.

Water. Ninety-percent chance her mother, Lola Zeitman, would hear rushing water while she fought for air. Wait. Weren't mom and dad going canoeing next weekend? Yeah, on some creek up in Arkansas. Were creeks deep enough to drown in? Ariel concentrated. The premory was filled with heavy rains and rivers swollen from storms. Shit It looked like she knew something she couldn't ignore.

Her heart started to pound. She had to call her parents and talk them out of going on this trip. She'd tell them whatever she needed to, as long as they believed her and stayed home.

As Ariel thought about the phone call, she got dizzier. She sat on the curb and tried to clear her head. These days she understood disorientation meant new possibilities were being incorporated into the premory, and some of those new outcomes came from actions she was about to take.

As she tried to sort out which possibilities were tied to what, she saw filmy threads linking one behavior to several, but not all, outcomes. She noticed the same end result could be achieved by a variety of ways. The strength of the cord was related to the strength of the causality, right?

So her visions weren't a line, they were a web. The past, present and future touched in an intricate spider's creation in which some actions mattered little and some were key to countless outcomes. Everything could be achieved many ways and any action could produce several results. Ariel stared in delight at the clarity of the revelation.

Life and time, and cause and effect, were so much more complex than she'd known. Tonight's premonition was more complicated than any Ariel had experienced, probably because it was so much more important than anything from before. She studied it more.

If her mother went on the river, there was a ninety-percentish chance she'd get trapped under a canoe, but less than a forty-percent chance she'd die. It was more likely she'd find a way out, although Ariel couldn't see how. If she didn't die, then there was nearly a one-hundred-percent chance dad would try to rescue mom as she flailed her way downstream without a life jacket. What happened to her mom's life jacket? Never mind.

Once it went this way, there was a twenty-percentish chance dad would die trying to pull mom out of the raging river. What the hell were her parents doing in this river anyway? Didn't they have more sense than this?

Apparently her family had never skirted disaster so closely, or she'd have dealt with this situation before. Ariel started walking home as she tried to clear her head. She had to get back to the sorority and get her phone.

But the sparkling threads began rotating in her mind as she moved, giving her a three-dimensional look at the vision. It came with the most compelling certainty she'd ever experienced with a premory. Look over here. Her mother needed to be in that river, she needed to almost drown, because then and only then would something wonderful happen over there. Not just to her mother, either, because it appeared the results of the time in the river were great for lots of people. The canoe accident was a nexus point, one of the big shining loci that mattered far more than most things did.

She looked further. Her dad had to wade out into the water because it caused him to learn something important, and he needed that knowledge over in another other part of the web. If he lived, which he probably would, he'd be different from then on. That difference would not only save his own life, it would save other lives, too. Her dad was going to be quite a hero someday, but only if he waded out there and lived through it.

Ariel's walk brought her home, and as she made her way to her room she was glad it was Friday night and the sorority house was empty. She could feel tears running down her cheeks at the enormity of the choice she was about to make.

Thanks to unusually heavy rains, her parents were poised to acquire a destiny, a chance for making a positive difference in the world. Yet this future happened only if Ariel didn't make a phone call home. She had to sit tight for a week and let it unfold, as though her gift of seeing the future never existed.

Ariel thought of how awful it would be if it turned out poorly. She looked for the worst-case images in the fleeting, floating mirage. Like headlights on a car at night, her vision only seemed to penetrate so far into the gloom ahead. Now, she studied the furthest she could see with a new urgency. If she did nothing, there were possible outcomes that were very sad. However, there was no mistaking the fact that her interference would introduce a higher probability of a worse outcome down the road. She was sure.

Either you believe in a gift of prophecy or you don't. If you don't believe, why call people and get them upset? And if you do? Damn that care package from mom. Ariel knew her best course of action was to pretend like this whole stream of information had never made it into her consciousness.

She got up and pulled a beer out of the mini-fridge hidden under Laura's bed and chugged it down, wondering how many more she was going to need to get through an entire week of this.

She didn't get to ponder it for long. The complex premory left her exhausted, and in less than a minute she was sound asleep on her bed.

Touching the Sky to Save the World

3. Winter

Distance from her family and their misadventures was one reason getting a job in London was perfect for Ariel. Sure, going to Europe was exciting, but she hadn't taken the job for fun, or even for resume building.

The canoeing accident nearly three years ago left Ariel worried about her ability to do the right thing when the safety of those she loved was an issue. Yes, the horrible weekend ended well, but she didn't want to be around for the next catastrophe. Not because she didn't love them, but because she did.

She put water on the stove to boil pasta for dinner and pulled dishes out of the small cupboard. It helped that she enjoyed what she was learning in London. When she finished her master's degree last spring studying the technology used for trading stocks, she expected to work on Wall Street. Ultra-Low Latency Ltd. of London had found her instead.

Ullow was training her to be a support engineer. The position used both her social skills and her flair for understanding how computers moved massive amounts of data. She'd caught on well and knew they were happy with her.

These first six months had been a lot about her company's specialized hardware, while her social life revolved around people she barely knew. That was so much easier. If she brushed against a man's hand, or picked up a pen used by another woman, she got a fleeting glimpse of a future she could ignore.

Learning better coping techniques helped too. Now that she was free from the grind of studying and had some money, she took yoga classes at least twice a week. She enrolled in self-defense training. All the breathing, stretching, kicking and punching worked to keep her calm.

She'd be done with Ullow's introductory training soon, and hoped to be assigned to the company's personalized consulting services. It would be a promotion. She'd touched enough things around the office to know odds were better than even she'd get her wish.

She popped red sauce in the microwave and poured herself a glass of Chianti. Yes, wine still took the edge off of the premories, so why not make it an Italian theme night? Too bad there wasn't a guy to join her for dinner. That would have made it worth lighting candles.

"You want me to move out of London? But I've only been here six months!" Ariel heard the shrillness in her voice, and knew she was being unreasonable. The company was within its rights to ask her to transfer if she wanted this opportunity. It was just such a surprise, and Ariel didn't deal well with surprises. They almost never happened.

If she'd paid more attention to gossip, she'd have known. Last week everyone was whispering about Gloria, a support engineer Ariel met at a few social events. Clyde, known around the office as Gloria's asshole boyfriend, surprised everyone by proposing to Gloria after she accepted a transfer to the Dublin office. Everyone guessed a few too many brews, and Clyde's growing realization he'd be having sex far less often, combined to overcome his dislike of commitment. Gloria responded with a happy yes and decided she had to stay in London.

Now Ullow needed someone in Dublin next week and nobody wanted to go. Not that Dublin didn't have its charms, but the office was located in one of the least charming parts of town. All of Ullow's glamorous wining and dining was done in London, where the perks were better and the chance to impress management was higher. Of the few clients who were handled there, rumor had it none of them would enhance a young engineer's career.

Ariel picked up a wink when co-workers spoke of these customers. There seemed to be an understanding that the Irish would find ways to bend rules where the British would not. Work that raised eyebrows in London was diverted westward, where eyebrows were, by custom, less likely to raise.

Ariel understood she was expected to go without complaint, but she didn't like being forced into this move. She tried to make her voice more pleasant as she reached for the manila folder the HR man had been trying to hand her.

As she took out the contents, she must have brushed against something once handled by Gloria, because she knew there was a fifty-fifty chance Clyde wouldn't even go through with the wedding. It didn't matter. As she handled more papers she got more information. The more she learned, the more surprised she was.

Before today, there'd been nothing spectacular in her near future. Now, she was probably going to Ireland where she'd meet people and learn things that would change her forever.

"I'd really like to think about it." She said it as calmly as she could while she crinkled the papers between her thumb and index finger, trying to learn more.

"We'd like to get the paperwork started before the end of the week," the man from HR said. "Tomorrow is Friday."

"Right. Let me take this information home and I'll give you my answer in the morning."

As she stepped outside for air, she had a pretty good idea of what her answer would be. The nice man from HR hadn't noticed her placing her hand against the wall after handling his manila folder, and he had no way of knowing it was to steady herself against a kaleidoscope of new visions rushing at her while a tiny percent probability turned into an almost certainty.

"Holy crap."

Ariel muttered it as she made her way out of the building, her eyes half closed as she tried to calm her mind.

"Holy crap."

She sat down on the cold concrete steps to steady herself.

"Holy crap." She couldn't quit saying it.

What Clyde didn't know, couldn't know, would never know, was that in making his proposal he probably affected the fate of the world. Many weeks from now, Ariel was likely to discover she had a chance to play a role in the survival of the human race. She couldn't see how, she couldn't see when, and as the flashes of little specks of her most distant visions whirled their way through her brain, all she got with any clarity was that her going to Ireland mattered. A lot.

Yes, she ought to accept the transfer.

HR handled the paperwork and logistics in record time, and early the next week Ariel looked around her apartment wondering where to start.

At least I don't have much to pack.

She tried to be positive as she stuffed the contents of her sock drawer into a bag. London's cold fog and drizzle hadn't lifted since the first of the year. Maybe the weather in Ireland would be better.

The next morning, she dragged her things out through the cold mist to the waiting cab. Monday morning traffic was heavy and they sat on the entrance ramp for twenty minutes, listening to honking horns. The cab finally inched forward as the mist turned into a hard rain. Ariel touched the chilly glass of the back seat window only to know there would be a steady parade of disgruntled passengers in this cab staring out at the cold rain over the next few weeks.

As her plane took off from Gatwick Airport, she watched the grey fog outside her window turn darker and denser. Then finally, the aircraft broke free of the gloom. Tendrils of grey reached upwards out of the clouds as though trying to pull the plane back to earth, but it kept rising. Soon, nothing but a bright blue sky surrounded it.

Ariel put her hand tight against the Plexiglas and smiled. It felt for a second like she was touching the sky.

4. Blue Blouses

"So they finally talked someone into coming here." Eoin Finn barely looked up from his monitor as he typed away with staccato strokes. Ariel stood in the doorway of her new boss's office, waiting to be invited in, but Eoin kept his fingers moving as if he wished this interruption would go away.

She stared at him. When he finally looked up he seemed surprised to find an attractive young woman glaring at him.

"Oh. I take it back. The London office has been unusually helpful this time, now, haven't they? You'll do nicely." When she continued to stand there, he added "Glad to have you here. Now go on. Get settled in."

Ariel gave him a shrug back and headed to her desk. So, this constituted an Irish welcome.

Ariel had been told her new boss Eoin handled all local sales efforts as well as Ullow's three Dublin clients. He was reputed to be a workaholic loner with mediocre people skills, and she wasn't inclined to disagree. Ullow's upper management recognized Eoin was worn out from handling too many responsibilities, so Ariel's position was created.

Later, when Ariel was fooling around with her email, Eoin came by, and seemed more relaxed.

"Didn't mean to be short; I don't interrupt so well. Here. Read through these briefs I made when I began this job." He laid four files on her desk. "They contain my confidential take on our three clients, and I'm trusting you not to quote me. Trust from me is important. Here's another folder on all of our other best prospects in Dublin."

Ariel peaked inside of one folder and saw pages of notes hand-written in an extremely neat and tiny script.

"You don't need to know every detail of what these guys are doing. I'll be the first to admit they're a prickly lot, and I think each of them likes to handle their business here because we're more inclined to let them be that way. So get the big picture. Your main job is to assure each one *they* are our number one priority. Tell them you hang out with the people writing their code and it's going splendidly. Tell them this often. Note additional requests and pass those on to me. I'll take it from there."

The man had dark brown hair, but his face was fair and heavily freckled in the way of many Irish. Ariel guessed he was in his early forties, but his upturned nose probably made him look younger. He squinted back at her, studying her reddish hair and blue eyes as if he had just noticed them.

"You part Irish? Better yet, you like Guinness? Around here, either one helps and both would be great."

Ariel laughed. "I'm a quarter Irish on my mom's side. I love Guinness, too, but I think I got that from my dad. His side is Dutch and Scottish."

"Well, we won't hold your dad against you. Buy a round for clients any time you can. I'm guessing this will be easy for you, and it ought to free me up to get some real work done."

Ariel hesitated. She didn't get the feeling her new boss welcomed questions.

"It is okay if I get to know more about the coding, right? You know, find out what the programmers *are* working on?"

Eoin shrugged. "If you like. Trust me, it's boring stuff." He turned to leave, then paused. "You're not one of those women who goes around digging into every little thing, are you?"

Ariel stared at him as he walked away. *No, I guess I'm not.* She picked up the top folder and began to leaf through it.

The first profile was of Cillian McGrane, heir to a pharmaceutical manufacturing conglomerate in Ireland and a man who invested his own considerable wealth as a hobby. Across the top of the page Eoin had handwritten in red marker: "DO NOT quote me or copy this." Ariel had to smile.

Eoin described Cillian as a man with a lot of inherited wealth and not a great deal of maturity. Along with a strong attachment to social drinking and pretty women, he had what amounted to a gambling problem. Ariel looked at the photograph. Cillian carried himself like the kind of charmer who knew he looked good. She checked his age. Forty-three.

Eoin's notes went on to describe how Cillian's interest in race horses had diminished over the years and he'd turned to the stock market for his thrills. Unfortunately, the markets of the previous decade weren't kind to him, and he now used high frequency trading to ensure his wins exceeded his losses. Ullow's job was to see that it was so.

Ariel thought she knew the type. He wanted to think there was risk in what he was doing, and he was defying the odds by winning. Never tell him his software made winning a nearly sure thing, or he'd no longer want to play the game.

The second client, Baldur Hákonarson, was a professional Icelandic investor from Reykjavik whose firm handled many of the wealthiest inhabitants of the small island nation. The firm had some international clients as well. Ariel had a vague memory of Iceland declaring bankruptcy during the financial meltdown of 2008. Hadn't Iceland's richest lost everything then? Judging from the size of this portfolio, apparently not.

Baldur was described as a private man, well respected in the financial community in spite of his relative youth. His company carried the enigmatic name d^4.

His photograph showed a handsome pale blond man with thinning hair and a slender build, in a beautifully tailored suit. Eoin's information said Baldur was turning thirty-one this month, but Ariel thought his thin almost white hair and slight build made one think of someone older. She supposed he used that illusion to his advantage.

According to Eoin, Baldur had impeccable credentials in the financial world. He'd run his small firm for two years, but his reputation came from his consistent success with investments before he entered the world of HFT, or high frequency trading. Eoin noted Baldur's concerns were that the techniques Ullow offered were legal and reliable. In other words, this man not only wouldn't mind a sure thing, he'd prefer one.

Finally, there was Mikkel Nygaard. A Greenlander. People really lived in Greenland? A few quick keystrokes let Ariel discover sixty-thousand people did. Fishing and a little tourism were the main industries, but a fair amount of the population lived in Greenland's far north, hunting and living off the land.

Mikkel was described as Danish with some Inuit ancestry, and Eoin had noted that intermarriage between the two groups was common in Greenland. Mikkel's tiny firm was headquartered in Nuuk, Greenland's capital of sixteen-thousand people. At only twenty-eight, he was the youngest and the newest to the financial scene. His company was less than two years old, and he had no previous history in the world of investing.

Like Baldur, he managed other people's money and a lot of it. Unlike Baldur, he handled only one account, which Eoin noted Mikkel was hell-bent on growing by any means available. What was this man investing? Maybe a pension fund? Hell, he could be handling the retirement savings of his entire country. Besides fishing and escorting around a few tourists, what went on in Greenland? Ariel thought she ought to learn more.

Mikkel was also described as unusually private. Eoin went so far as to refer to him as a man who didn't like to be asked any questions ever, about anything.

Ariel studied Mikkel's picture. He was an attractive young man as well, but his longish light brown hair, jeans and flannel shirt would have made him out of place in any part of the financial world. He looked like he was posing in an ad for high-end camping equipment.

Ariel wondered which of these three men, if any, would be the one to steer her in a direction with the far-reaching consequences she'd seen. Ever since that quick and confusing premory about Clyde's marriage proposal, she'd tried to see more of this future with no success. Her vision had gone back to the mundane events of the next few weeks. Now that she had names and photographs of her clients, though, maybe she could do better.

She sat at her desk and concentrated, trying to see something. What came to her were glimpses of her first meeting with each man. Those glimpses gave no clue to what lay beyond, except an eighty-percent chance she'd be wearing a blue blouse all three times. Great.

She tried again, this time touching the three folders in turn, knowing how the right contact could set off the premories. But now the distant edges of her visions only flickered with too many tiny snippets, like a television showroom at the other end of the mall with each set turned to a different channel. Her brain either couldn't or wouldn't bring a single premory into focus in her consciousness.

Very well. I'll wait. Guess I'll go shopping for some more blue blouses. They do look good with my eyes.

******

Siarnaq held the blue of the sky deep within his memory, and he brought it out in the heart of winter to cheer his soul. There was much about this frozen time of year to bring him joy, this time when the ice was solid and his dogsled could take him and his small machines and tools easily from village to village in the weeks during which the dark never ended. The People, the Kalaallit, became more friendly in the winter, letting their inner warmth more than fill the void left by the missing sun.

Yet, Siarnaq was one of those few who felt sad as the days wore on without even the faintest glimmer of twilight, and holding on to the memory of the summer solstice was how he coped. Maybe it was that same dab of Danish ancestry that had given him his unusual height. Or maybe the sorrow came from knowing the things only he knew.

As a young man who could repair engines and fix the electronic devices of the modern world, he was welcomed everywhere; for the little conveniences of the others had made their way into the furthest corners of his beloved Kalaallit Nunaat, now so commonly called Greenland. Siarnaq knew that one who could move about skillfully on the ice and yet who understood radios, batteries and diesel generators could write his own ticket as the people became increasingly dependent on these luxuries. Yet dependence was not what Siarnaq wished.

His sense of gloom at the height of winter was mild compared to the sorrow caused by his other curse. Many of the People had a sense of the future, it was true. Would the ice come early, would the fishing be good? Half of the population seemed to lay claim to predicting these important events by one means or another. Some even foresaw more unusual events: deaths, disease, or unexpected visitors from elsewhere.

Only Siarnaq seemed to be burdened with seeing the far future, that of generations past the end of his own life. He had no idea what the fishing would be like tomorrow, or if he would ever marry and if so, whom. These were questions he would have appreciated answers to, but that information would not come.

No, he only knew that the Inuit population keeping the old ways was likely to decline and become more modern with every generation. Any sensible person could guess that, of course. Siarnaq's curse was seeing it happen in his head and, of all the seers of the Kalaallit, knowing why the trend was so disastrous.

One day, generations from now, The People, his people, would play an important role as humanity faced extinction. Siarnaq knew this with the same certainty he knew where the nose was on his face. The children needed to stay in the villages. The adults had to resist becoming too dependent on modern conveniences. Siarnaq believed his visions were given to him so he could be part of making this future happen. His people could ill afford to eschew every contraption, as they fought to retain their way of life in a modern world that would not leave them alone. So, Siarnaq decided his role must be to embrace the machine and help his people achieve a balance in its use.

At a young age, he left his village, studied the ways of the outsiders, and became adept at repairing their things. Now, he traveled throughout his homeland, using his knowledge even as he taught his people the importance of not needing these conveniences. For surely, he reasoned, he could reach them better as an ally than as a naysayer.

"Use this to improve but never to replace the old ways," he told them, chiefs and children alike. Siarnaq figured his message of self-sufficiency was best delivered by the person who brought or fixed the modern device to begin with.

Another who knew the things Siarnaq knew might give up, engulfed by the hopelessness of it. However, Siarnaq intended to ensure his people would fulfill their destiny when the time came — their sad destiny, for their lot in the end would be to prolong the final elimination of humanity for a few more dozen generations. Yet, if that was all the Kalaallit could provide, it was better than nothing. He would see to it those generations would have their lives.

******

Baldur Hákonarson was the first of the three to make time to meet Ariel, his new personal support engineer from Ullow. At least Ariel assumed he'd made time, because his executive assistant sent Eoin an invite for Ariel to present an update to Baldur's board of directors a week after she started. Eoin accepted and cc'd Ariel. So that was how this was going to work.

A week later, she arrived at 10 a.m. in Reykjavik to a night sky adorned with a faint glimmer of grey light in the south. She was met by a limo driver, and by 11 a.m. she was setting up her presentation in front of three well-dressed older businessmen and one older woman in a suit showing her to be of equal stature. The small boardroom was on the top floor of a modern office building, and a beautiful, low-angle sunrise was now erupting through the glass windows off to the south.

Her audience had little to say to her, other than to assure her they all understood English. Good thing, as her Icelandic was limited to halló, their rather easy-to-remember greeting.

As the four of them chatted in Icelandic, they cast appraising looks her way, and she realized how young and inexpensively dressed she must appear. A minute or two later, a man with thin hair so blonde it was almost white entered the room.

"Baldur," he offered, turning eyes on her that were bluer than her own. She realized he was the only one who'd introduced himself. His greeting reminded her of the Icelandic custom of using first names only, even in the most formal situations. "Do not *ever* call him Mr. Hákonarson," Eoin had emphasized before she left.

"I'm happy to be here and looking forward to adding to the growth of your company, Baldur," she said with all the confidence she could muster. His face told her he was surprised by the implication she could possibly make any difference.

"So you've enjoyed your, what, three days so far in this new assignment?"

"Yes, well, I'm getting up to speed fast." She was irritated at how he'd gone straight to her inexperience. "It's quite like the projects I worked on over in London."

"I see. Well, I suspect we're a more demanding group." He gave his board members a knowing smile. They nodded and chuckled in agreement, leaving Ariel with the feeling of being on the other side of a joke she didn't get.

She tried to regain her composure, moving back to the front of the room and speaking as she flipped through her slides. It went fine, but she had the impression nobody was listening. It was a formality, something to put into a report. She guessed the meaningful stuff happened between Balder and Eoin, and maybe the hardware experts and programmers. That annoyed her. She was no ornament. Maybe for the next meeting she'd get their attention by learning a few words of Icelandic.

"Thank you," Baldur said in a bored voice when she finished. "We appreciate you making the trip. I'll send the video to the other six guiding members of d^4 who live outside of Iceland and couldn't join us."

The board members were gathering up their coats and hats. Baldur reached for his briefcase, then he stopped and reached out to shake her hand. She pulled back without thinking.

He was surprised by her reaction. Then something odd flashed across his face, a look of understanding. "I wanted to say farewell. I realize I didn't greet you properly when I came in."

"I'm sorry. I can be a little jumpy sometimes." Ariel reached out and took his hand firmly, striving for a business-like shake, but a millisecond after the touch, the premories started.

Her initial flash of fear gave way to curiosity. Ariel was overwhelmed by images much larger than those she was used to. Close-up and huge, like murals on wall, with her so near she couldn't make out the picture. Amidst the blur she sensed the immediate future, and saw herself pulling her own hand away in confusion. As she tried to steady herself, lest she become engulfed in the intensity of the sensation, she pulled her hand back as she had seen herself do a second before.

Holy shit. She'd never in her life had something so immediate come at her, and she fought to regain her composure. As her gaze met Baldur's eyes, she could have sworn he looked bothered as well, and appeared to be struggling to regain his composure, too.

"I'm glad I met you," he said. With that he turned and left the conference room like he needed to use the restroom or had remembered an important call he had to make. Ariel watched him go in silence, as the remaining board members left talking to each other, oblivious to the drama that had occurred.

There was no question Baldur had set off the most unusual premories Ariel ever experienced. Was it because the man would play an important role in her life? What if he had her curse? No, she must have imagined his response. Finding another person with precognitions was incredibly unlikely, for if there were others like her, the world would be so different.

She needed to get a grip. Do her job. Become familiar with Baldur's professional needs and do her best to see her firm met them. Also, she needed to avoid touching him again.

5. St. Brigid's Day

Cillian McGrane needed another beer. The lovely lady with upswept brown hair standing next to him preferred more champagne. Ariel flipped through the mental images she remembered from the files, and identified the woman as Nell Gallagher, a part-time actress from Donegal who was one of several women often seen at Cillian's side. Cillian had one ex-wife in heavily Catholic Ireland and Ariel guessed he didn't intend to have a second.

Nell looked up and recognized Ariel as well.

"Cillian. Isn't this the new girl from your stock company, the one handling all your mumbo jumbo money making?" She said it in the friendliest of ways, implying no objection to mumbo jumbo money making. Cillian turned to Ariel.

"I do believe it is."

"Thanks for the invitation, Mr. McGrane," Ariel said.

"Please, I'm Cillian, with a hard 'k' sound for you foreigners. Mr. McGrane is my stuffy ol' da." He smiled to soften his rebuke. "I'm more than a wee bit cut in the country, and wasn't sure you'd brave the drive alone." He gestured towards the windows. "The sun is out, so it's a lovely afternoon for St. Brigid's Day now, isn't it? Oh yes, Ground Hog Day to you. Either way, nicer to meet here than at some boring meeting."

Ariel nodded, thinking of the awkward presentation in the d^4 boardroom.

"Better yet, when you come to my party, you get to taste what the money you help make goes for." He gave her a conspiratorial wink. "Try the lobster wrapped in bacon."

His phone buzzed in his pocket.

"Damn thing never lets me be." He pulled the offending gadget out to glare at the name of the interrupter. His face softened as he read it. "Oh, sorry. I have to take this." He looked at Nell and waggled his fingers towards Ariel. "Would you mind, dear..."

"Of course not." Nell turned to Ariel as Cillian headed off. "Let me show you the stables. It's a short walk and they're quite remarkable."

Ariel had never understood the fascination some people had for horses and she couldn't imagine any stable remarkable enough to make her want to put up with smelling all that horse shit. But she had enough social skills to know that would be a poor response.

"Sure." She smiled and off the two women went.

"Cillian has become a big fan of your company. I worry he's placing too much faith in you." Nell said it lightly as they walked but Ariel picked up on the woman's protectiveness.

"There's always risk to investing in stocks. We reduce it considerably though. I trust Cillian has financial advisors who push him to keep his portfolio diversified?"

"Oh he does." Nell nodded as she made her way down the stone path in stylish boots that complimented her skirt and glittery sweater. "The more he wins with you guys, though, the more he tries to override their advice. So what is it you do exactly? You send his transactions faster than the speed of light so they beat out everyone else's?"

Ariel winced. Okay, so science wasn't Nell's strong suit.

"Nothing travels faster than light." She worked hard to keep condescension out of her voice as her own foot wobbled on a loose cobblestone in her tiny heels. She wished she'd chosen something more substantial than the silly sparkly cocktail dress she'd managed to find on sale last week when she'd been invited to this party. "Electronic information travels near the speed of light. It's, like, about a second for information to get to the moon, which is three-hundred-thousand miles away." *Too many facts.* "My point is; our hardware minimizes the path the information has to travel. A shorter path gets our customer's stock order in quicker."

"That doesn't make sense. It takes a whole hundredth of a second for information to go from Dublin to New York, because that's about three thousand miles. Cillian ought to be losing every time he places an order because he lives so far away."

"Perfect analysis." Ariel was impressed this woman could do math in her head while walking. "But Cillian isn't making the decisions. Our software thinks for him and issues buy and sell orders faster than any human could. Our hardware lives on Wall Street, and next door to the London Stock Exchange. You're right, milliseconds matter and we make Cillian faster every way we can."

"Oh." Nell seemed surprised to find the mumbo-jumbo was so simple. "What happens when everybody starts using your company and they're all super-fast?"

"Well, you need a certain amount of capital to use what we offer."

"I see. You have to be rich to get richer?"

"Basically. Making people more successful isn't exactly running a soup kitchen. I'm a good person, but this pays my bills."

"Hey, I meant no offense. I party with a man who shows off the money you make for him, so I'm not throwing rocks here."

They were at the door to the stable. Nell paused.

"Aren't we going in?"

"I don't see why." Nell laughed. "I'd hate to see you step in horseshit in those little shoes of yours and I don't think you particularly like horses. I just wanted the chance to visit. Let's head back to the party and I'll introduce you to Cillian's financial advisors. You can sweet-talk them."

Ariel agreed, and made a mental note not to underestimate Nell Gallagher.

In late January, Mikkel Nygaard came to Dublin for the purpose of meeting Ariel. Of the three men, he seemed to be the most irritated at having been handed off to a newcomer. He met privately with Eoin first.

"Not to worry, lass," Eoin had assured her the day before. "I expect he'll want to complain to me privately before he meets you. This one doesn't have much of a sense of humor. Well, neither does Baldur, but Mikkel, he takes his money even more seriously. I'll make it clear nothing has changed for him. When you meet him, let him see how sharp you are, then let him figure out how he's going to get even better service from us."

Right. Act intelligent. Ariel was more nervous than she wanted to let on as she sat across the wooden table from Mikkel in one of the small conference rooms.

She supposed he looked more or less Danish, with medium-brown shaggy hair that would have benefitted from a stylist. His body seemed used to physical activity, and Ariel got a sense of solid strength from him His dress was barely more businesslike than the flannel shirt and jeans worn in his photo, leaving her certain this wasn't a man who wanted to spend his time in the world of high finance. His dark brown eyes gave evidence of his Inuit heritage. Ariel studied those eyes, thinking she had never seen irises that close to being black.

His dark eyes bored back into hers.

"What do you think about the specific order-handling treatment that successful HFT techniques rely on?" He asked it with no introduction or greeting.

"I think some rules have to be in place to decide which stock orders to handle first. The current system isn't perfect, but it gets the job done. It benefits high frequency traders like us, but the savvy can and will find a way to take advantage of any protocols, and you can't run a market without rules."

Mikkel was watching her. "So you've thought about this."

"Yes. It *is* what I do for a living."

The implications of the instantaneous fluctuations in the stock market had fascinated Ariel since she first learned of them. "I have reservations about some of the boutique order types being offered by some electronic exchanges, but given they exist, I'll use them to help my own customers make money."

"That's good to hear." Mikkel stood up, indicating he'd concluded his business. "Good. You know your stuff. I won't object to including you as part of the team. Tell Eoin I'll play nice as long as Ullow abides by my rules."

He offered his hand, perhaps to soften his words and his abrupt departure, but Ariel was taking no chances on touching another client. She turned away as though she didn't notice.

"Fine. I'll let Eoin know I don't object to being on your team, either." She said it as she rose to walk out of the door. Mikkel raised a single eyebrow, and looked amused as she left.

Later, Ariel thought about her handshake with Baldur and her reaction to Mikkel offering his hand. She shouldn't have ignored it. Not only was it rude, but maybe she should be touching more people involved with her future, not less. If they all set off the same reaction, that would be good to know. If her dealings with Baldur, and Baldur alone, were significant, then it would help to know that as well.

Why? What's the point here?

Ariel avoided philosophical questions, thinking life should be simple, direct and fun. But okay. She could think her way through this. She sat down at the tiny kitchen table to make a list. She did like making lists.

Priorities. She wrote it across the top in big, bold blue letters.

1. Stay alive.

It came without hesitation.

That's not as dumb as it sounds. It's my top priority. I ought to find another self-defense class here and I definitely need a yoga studio.

2. Enjoy my life.

Ariel smiled as she wrote this one. For as long as she could remember, she'd wanted to be normal and have fun. She envied those who didn't know the cotton candy or the roller coaster ride would bring a tummy ache

Her smile faded as she considered the flash of premory when she was handed the packet about her assignment in Dublin. She'd seen something about saving the human race. Saving it? From what?

3. Figure out how humanity is at risk.

She stared at her own words. *What if I don't like the answer?* She picked up the pen.

4. Make the survival of the human race more likely.

She wrote it in big strong letters, then realized she was out of priorities.

Should saving my species be listed ahead of staying alive? Or least ahead of having fun?

She shrugged and got up to grab a carton of eggs out of the refrigerator. It was an omelet for dinner again tonight. As she broke the shells and dropped the eggs into a little plastic bowl, she decided she'd had enough philosophy for one evening.

Tomorrow, she'd go on a campaign to reach out and touch people.

"Slumming today?" Jake asked.

Jake was a senior coder in the group, and considered the coordinator for Baldur's project. He was one of those tall, chubby men with dark curly hair and a gentle way about him that made the comparison to a teddy bear inevitable. Ariel had already established a friendly working relationship with him, even though he'd pointed out more than once that Ariel spent too little time with the programmers.

"Just wondering if you guys will ever finish what you're working on," Ariel teased him back. She wanted to ask him more questions about his work, but Eoin continued to discourage their interaction in myriad little ways.

"Of course we won't." Jake played along. "Will Microsoft ever stop releasing new operating systems? Will Google stop reinventing itself? Programming is long-term job security, baby. Better than building roads because you never run out of a place to put new software."

Ariel gave him an appreciative smile back. She liked Jake for his sense of humor and for the fact that he seemed impervious to office politics.

"Do you have a time to talk about Baldur's latest request for modifications?" As Ariel asked the question, she reached out in what she hoped was a sisterly way and touched Jake's arm. "Because I really am trying to be of some use here, both to our company and our customer."

Jake nodded, apparently impressed by Ariel's sincerity.

"Okay. I'll let the front office people in on some of the secrets." He winked. "As you know, Baldur is mostly concerned with tools for making faster changes to his parameters. Seriously, one minute he wants the defaults to go one way and two minutes later he wants them to do something else, and then three minutes later he wants it to go back to the way it was. It's insane, because no one has worthwhile information on stocks that changes that fast."

"So why does he care?"

Jake gestured for Ariel to have a seat in his office as he got up to close his door. He lowered his voice.

33

"At first I thought he liked fooling around with the software for entertainment, but he's spending too much money on these changes. He doesn't seem like the kind of guy who thinks play time is all that important."

Ariel had to agree. "Do you think he's delusional? Like, he's convinced himself he needs to make changes that fast."

Jake nodded. "I figured he was maybe, you know, harmless crazy. One of those weird smart guys who's lost touch. So I looked into his trading history. We've got all sorts of records, so we can run tests using real data. I thought I'd establish how this stuff he's asking for is frivolous, in case we couldn't meet his demands down the road. Kind of a CYA thing."

"I'd be careful. I don't think Eoin would like the idea of you proving a big client is asking for things he doesn't need."

"I know. I didn't tell Eoin. Look, if you want me to stop talking now, I will. I don't want to put you in a compromising position."

"It's okay. Everyone does a little probing on their own. I've got no problem with where you're going."

"That's just it. I'm not going there. I thought I was, but the truth is weirder. Baldur isn't asking for tools he doesn't need."

Jake took a deep breath, like he was trying to decide if he should go on.

"Don't you smoke?" Ariel asked.

"Yeah. Want to join me outside while I have a cigarette?"

Ariel nodded. This no longer seemed like the sort of conversation to hold in the office, and she was starting to have a funny feeling about how this tied in with the close-up visions she'd had when she touched Baldur's hand. A cigarette would probably help Jake and fresh air would definitely help her.

Once they were outside, Jake resumed.

"I ran tests using what Baldur tried to do against what he could have done if he had the tools he wanted. I looked at the same kind of information for Cillian and for two other clients from London. Here's the thing. If I improve the speed at which Cillian and the other clients make parameter changes, it doesn't benefit them. But, Baldur would have done substantially better if he had the tools he wanted."

"Really? Is he getting some kind of insider information?"

"Not that fast, he isn't. Besides, his parameters deal with trends. It's like he has a minute-to-minute sense of what whole segments of the market will do. He still needs us, our machines and our software, to make the trades, but the faster he can direct the software, the better he does. We give him more speed and he starts to beat out everyone else past any statistical probability."

Ariel's funny feeling about Baldur was growing. "Jake, do you believe somebody can, I don't know, sense the future?"

"You mean be psychic? No, I don't. Or I didn't. But facts are facts. I don't know how else to explain what this man can do."

Ariel tried to make light of it. "In this case, it's some speedy crystal ball, isn't it? I don't think any psychic claims to predict things that fast."

She tried to redirect the conversation. "Should we be giving Baldur tools to beat out everyone else?"

Jake shrugged. "I don't see that it's Ullow's job to penalize Baldur for being good. Just because I don't know how he does it, doesn't mean it's unethical." Jake looked uncomfortable. "I haven't shared this information with anyone else. Could we keep this between us, at least until I figure out more about what I've figured out?" Jake gave Ariel the same friendly brush back on the arm. "Please?"

"Of course. Thanks Jake. I can do my job better if I know more, even if I don't understand it either. If you figure out how he manages this, I'd love an update."

As she headed back inside, she knew two things. The first was Jake's touch set off no alarms. The second was

next week Jake's wife would probably surprise him by bringing home a new puppy. A really cute one, too.

******

Siarnaq watched in amazement as the three parallel dog sleds moved in careful unison over the ice. As he squinted at their oversized, unfamiliar cargo he thought he had never seen anything like it. The drivers struggled to keep the sleds moving at the same pace as they hurried something unknown through the darkness to their destination.

It was large and shiny. It straddled all three of the sleds, hanging a dozen feet or so off of both edges. Certainly it was made by humans, and it was doubtful the people involved were Inuit. So much metal, so much craftsmanship—this thing had to have been made using many massive machines of the others.

The deep of winter was the time for such travel. In the nearly continual night, the well frozen ice provided an easy path in a world without a single road connecting one town with another. Along the Western coast of Greenland, the Inuit enjoyed the freedom provided by their seasonal frozen highways.

This group had chosen the middle of a moonless night for their oddly synchronized journey. The better to avoid attention. Siarnaq appeared to be the only traveler close enough to watch the mysterious cargo make its way.

He shook his head as the trio of sleds moved off into the distance. To a man concerned with keeping life as free from outside influence as possble, this giant metal contraption being slid along in the night was not a good thing.

Siarnaq knew people who knew people. Someone would have information about something so bizarre. He'd learn where this thing came from, and see that it was returned.

6. First Daylight

Ariel spent a few days digesting the conversation with Jake. He was a smart guy with no agenda. If he thought Baldur could see what the next few minutes would bring, then Baldur probably could. It explained the odd interchange she had with Baldur, too.

Ariel realized she was most likely to precalled events happening in a week or more. Occurrences only hours away, or over a year away, weren't ever there. She'd certainly never had a premory of something minutes into the future, or decades from now. It seemed a rather arbitrary window.

So what if Baldur was like her, but saw ahead through a different gap? Maybe he could predict events seconds to minutes ahead, but no further. That explained his love of making quick stock trades, and the horribly close-up images she hadn't been able to decipher when she touched him. Was she seeing her own immediate future?

Ariel considered how she precalled. She never saw the future through another's eyes, but always through her own. Many of her premories centered around other people, but they were always of what she'd see and hear if she was present.

So had Baldur experienced her frequency when they touched? Had her visions of what might come to pass in the weeks ahead enticed him with their distant possibilities? What if he'd had premories through her eyes? Ariel spent the rest of the morning bothered by the possibility.

By afternoon, she forced herself to focus on her other clients. It was time to make friends. How could she possibly get to know a couple of prickly rich guys better?

"You want to take *me* out to lunch?" Nell was surprised. "Shouldn't you be taking out Cillian, dear? I don't dish on my friends, and I can eat a surprisingly expensive meal."

"How about a little general background on the McGrane family? Nothing I couldn't learn elsewhere, but you save me some time. In exchange for the best Mediterranean food in town."

"Oh well now, someone has done her homework." Nell laughed. "Is my love of *dolmades* that legendary?"

Ariel demurred with a laugh of her own. Of course she'd gotten intel. She made a mental note to call the restaurant ahead of time to make sure the stuffed grape leaves Nell loved were freshly made. She was betting no one could refrain from interjecting a morsel of personal knowledge into a tale told while happily eating their favorite food.

Baldur's personal assistant was named Hulda, and Ariel struggled to put a face with the name. They hadn't interacted much during Ariel's visit but she recalled a pleasant blonde woman, mid-forties, who was quiet and efficient. Maybe a little meek. Her hair was worn simple and long, like a teenaged girl.

"I was hoping to learn more about d⁴," Ariel explained. "Especially the members I wasn't able to meet." She was lucky Hulda spoke English well enough to converse over the phone.

Hulda told her the contact information for d⁴'s board was confidential, as they preferred communication only by invitation. Surely Ariel understood.

Ariel changed tactic. "Maybe if I come to Iceland for other business, I could drop by your office and take some of Baldur's staff out for lunch?"

"Baldur outsources the bookkeeping. You people are his IT department. Most days I'm the only staff here and I eat my lunch at my desk. But thank you for the invitation."

"Maybe I could come on a day when the accountants are already there for a meeting?" Ariel wasn't going to give up easily.

"We don't have meetings, miss. Baldur's contractors come in when he needs them." She hesitated. "Baldur does have a lawyer, and he fills in for Baldur sometimes. Perhaps if you're in town, you'd like to take Ulfur to lunch?"

Okay, this was news. Even Eoin's impressive intelligence on Baldur had not mentioned Ulfur.

"That would be perfect. How do I reach Ulfur?"

"I'll connect you."

Eoin was a fidgety man. Ariel had already noticed he seldom let employees into his office, and as Ariel stood in his doorway, she marveled at how spotless it was. There was one cup to hold his pencils and one to hold his pens, and not one writing implement was in the wrong place.

"You need something, Zeitman? Or you just feeling lonely today?" He stopped typing and looked up from his computer screen, pretending to be annoyed, but now that she knew him better she didn't think he was.

"We didn't talk about how much I can spend," she answered. "I mean, I know I can do lunches and stuff, but what if I want to develop a relationship with some of the underlings at these companies."

"Why? And like who?"

"Well, Cillian has a financial advisor who doesn't particularly like us."

"Yeah, yeah. Doyle worked for Cillian's father and now he lives in fear of Cillian squandering the family fortune. He may be right. Doyle doesn't like investing, but he does appreciate how we protect the McGrane money better than the horses did. You'll never win him over more than that. Nothing to be gained there."

Eoin stood up and started to fiddle with some papers on his bookshelf. It was a gesture of dismissing her, and Ariel knew it. "Who else do you want to wine and dine?" he asked when she didn't leave.

"Ulfur, Baldur's right-hand man."

"Who the fuck is Ulfur?" Eoin pronounced it fook, the way all the Irish did. It had the effect of making the word seem less obscene. The Irish seemed to know it too, as they said fook far more frequently than Ariel had ever heard its counterpart used in an American office.

"According to Hulda, he's Baldur's lawyer. She declined my offer to take her to lunch, but she was nice enough to suggest I take Ulfur instead."

"You actually invited a secretary out for a business lunch?" Eoin turned to face her as he stood, now giving her his full attention.

"Yeah." Ariel knew the few women in her field routinely socialized with the other women in the office, blurring the lines between management, technical professionals and support staff. She'd forgotten men didn't have the same behind-the-scenes egalitarianism working in their favor.

"Well done, Zeitman. You learned something I didn't know. There's a guy named Ulfur. So now you want another ticket to Reykjavik? For lunch?"

"I was thinking of something bigger, actually. I thought if I could find a similar back-up in Mikkel's group, maybe I could put together an appreciation event for the experts behind the scenes in all three companies. Ulfur, Doyle and what's his name. It might be more fun if it was a group. Would Ullow foot the bill for some sort of outing?"

"You want to take these guys walrus hunting for the weekend?" Eoin laughed. "Realistically, Ariel, all three of these clients don't like to mix much; I'm not sure they'd be so keen to have their seconds mixing either. What's more, you're not the ideal candidate to host a little male bonding."

He sighed, and to his credit he looked like he was trying to handle this with care. "I suppose, if you came up with the right activity, something appealing, then these guys might want to go, and you could build a little goodwill for Ullow. I'll give you a teeny bit of rope to run with this one."

A lone programmer at Ullow handled Cillian's requests, because they tended to be fewer than those of his counterparts. It didn't surprise Ariel that Cillian was unenthused about software silently making him money while he slept, even if he was happy to have the profit. Cillian liked to devote his business-related energy to experimenting with inputs to improve the outcome. Cillian wanted to drive, not travel on autopilot. His personal programmer's main job was to give Cillian knobs he could turn without hurting himself.

"It's a stupid job, but it pays well," Brendan confessed to Ariel. As the only other ginger in the office, the two of them shared a bond. Brendan's carrot top tended more towards a wavy bright orange blond, a combination made all the more striking because it set above a rather long, narrow and serious face.

"I give him things to change so he feels he is trying something new. Sometimes he does better than he was, and he goes off and rides his horses to celebrate and then goes to his favorite bar and buys everyone a drink. Other times, he does worse and quits in disgust. He goes for a horseback ride to clear his head and then drinks at his favorite bar. His software returns to making him money once he stops playing."

"How well does Cillian understand this?"

"He knows we protect him, he's not stupid. He does have a gambler's heart though, and believes deep down he'll come up with something magic, in spite of my safeguards, and make a huge fortune. That's what keeps him interested."

"Why doesn't he fire us and do whatever he pleases?"

Brendan looked uncomfortable. "He can't. Ullow actually works for Doyle. It's part of the agreement that transferred the family wealth to Cillian. Doyle has managed the McGrane fortune since Cillian's dad began to amass it back in the seventies."

"Does Eoin know about this? I mean making changes to entertain Cillian?"

"Eoin is the one who insists I do it. Every month or two Eoin, Doyle and I go over plans. My job is to produce a new release often enough that Cillian doesn't lose interest and take up a more expensive hobby. I make a lot of graphical changes."

"I'm sure you do," Ariel said as she reached out and touched Brendan lightly on the arm, ignoring the several mundane images brought on by the touch. "I don't fault you for it," she added as she left Brendan's office.

After she made her way onto the elevator, it occurred to her how many of those mundane images involved Brendan spending time with Cillian, laughing and talking like they were the best of friends. It seemed odd behavior for Brendon, given his role in Cillian's life.

******

41

February is the month for celebrating the return of the sun in the northernmost reaches of Greenland. In Qaanaaq, on the far northwestern coast, the sun rose for the first time on Feb 14. As an honored visitor, Siarnaq was included in the festivities as families gathered for songs and shared coffee and cakes to celebrate the first daylight of the new year.

He asked his questions about the strange large machines being moved on a moonless night in winter, but the locals had no idea what he was talking about and teased him saying he was seeing things. Later a woman from the Eastern side of Greenland approach him. She'd spoken to her kin over there, and heard of the machines Siarnaq described. They came from Canada and were being moved over the ice, to somewhere further north than her remote town of Ittoqqortoormitt.

"There is nothing north of Ittoqqortoormitt." It was Siarnaq's turn to laugh.

"There's the National Park," the woman said. "Those from Ittoqqortoormitt hunt in the park. They say a man of Greenland is responsible for this. Not one of the People, but an engineer who went to Copenhagen."

Siarnaq felt the tightness in his chest. There were not many who could be so described, and a cousin who'd hurt him deeply over a decade ago was one of those few.

"Is he an older man? A young one? Do you know anything about him?"

"He is young. They say he left Greenland a few years ago to study rocket ships. Now he's building one up near those weather stations in Peary Land, where it's so dry there is no ice or snow. No one can imagine why."

Siarnaq thanked the woman. He was sure he knew who the man was.

Long ago, Siarnaq played childhood games with his cousin Carl. They shared secrets and dreams, and then Carl became an enemy by telling Siarnaq his gift of prophecy was fake. Carl cemented his status with a casual apology followed by years of absence at family events.

Siarnaq had composed many angry, hurt diatribes in his head to this unfeeling cousin. Even now, as a grown man, the memory stung. However, the pain was overshadowed by discovering Carl was the one working to bring machinery to the far north where it least belonged.

Siarnaq left that day with a new mission. He'd not only work to keep his people sufficiently free from the modern ways, but now he'd do everything in his power to thwart his heartless cousin, too.

******

Ariel had met with the two Ullow programmers assigned to Mikkel's project several times, because their unique situation involved her more. Both were eager young men with a slight build, brown hair and cherubic faces sprinkled with freckles. They weren't that hard to tell apart, but to her ongoing embarrassment Ariel couldn't seem to remember which one was Fergus and which was Ronan.

She knew Mikkel didn't like changes to his software, and he wouldn't have wanted modifications if it weren't for his competitiveness with one of Ullow's other customers, Baldur. The rivalry appeared to be one way.

Baldur competed against the world-wide investing community and behaved like he had an insurmountable advantage. Ariel now suspected he did.

Mikkel, on the other hand, made it clear his main goal was to do as well or better than Baldur. This struck Ariel as unnecessarily personal, and it was awkward for Ullow. They continually improved their own software for all of their clients, of course, and they also contracted to make user-specific modifications that were the property of whoever paid for them.

It was the grey area in between that caused problems. A company could request an enhancement and partly pay for its development in order to speed up progress. In return, that company would get to beta test it for a while, which meant they benefitted from its features before its official release. Baldur's company often pushed for improvements this way, and they seemed content with the slight advantage this bought them.

It was Mikkel who wasn't content when that happened. He asked Fergus and Ronan to develop whatever improvements were being made for Baldur. Then he'd pay his share so he could test those improvements too. Fergus and Ronan, both just out of university, were put in the awkward role of working as corporate spies in their own company. Ariel had already gotten involved twice.

Eoin had coached the lads, as he called them, to split the difference, sometimes mirroring the work being done for Baldur and sometimes letting Baldur have his advantage. This tightrope act had worked so far, but it made Ariel nervous. Along with Brendan's ongoing efforts to write entertainment software for Cillian, she was starting to understand why Eoin had discouraged her from looking behind the scenes.

"Have you ever talked to anyone else from Mikkel's company besides Mikkel?" she asked Fergus and Ronan one afternoon as she wandered by on a fact-finding walk.

They looked at each other. "Nope."

Ariel squinted at the two young men, who both seemed about eighteen years old. "Not a secretary, not a personal assistant, not even a fill-in when he's on vacation."

"Nope," the one she thought was Fergus repeated. "We don't talk to him that much, really."

"Don't think he's ever gone on vacation in the year we've been here," added the one who must have been Ronan.

"Do you have anything but a cell phone number for him?"

"Oh yes. Cell phone coverage isn't that good in Greenland. He has a landline."

Now they were getting somewhere. "What happens when you call the land line and he's not there?"

"It rings and rings," Fergus offered.

"Or we get the answering service," Ronan added. "She's a nice lady. She handles the phone for every business in Nuuk, I think. She doesn't always pick up but when she does, she's real pleasant about it."

"Who has an answering service these days?"

"All the people with landlines in Nuuk," Eoin replied from the doorway behind her. Ariel jumped.

"I did some looking around for you, Ariel. I agree. For all the money the man handles, it's odd Mikkel has no staff. No lawyer, no accountants, no one in human resources to hire them. Baldur is a master of outsourcing, but Mikkel seems to be a master do-it-yourselfer."

"You want me to drop this idea of taking out our clients direct reports?"

"Not at all. Up to now I've let my client's private business stay private, but your curiosity is starting to rub off. I want you to plan a vacation to Nuuk. It's a small town; you ought to be able to find out where Mikkel keeps his people. Don't be obvious. Go see the northern lights and ride a dog sled. You need to get more acquainted with the north anyway."

She looked at him, puzzled.

"Go on. You've got a nice direct way about you, so go meet the lady who runs the answering service. I bet you come back from Nuuk knowing more about Mikkel Nygaard than anyone here does. As a reward, I won't ask questions about your expense report next month."

As Eoin left, Ronan gave a little whistle. "Wow. No questions about your expense report for a whole month?"

"I've always wanted to go to Greenland," Fergus added.

"It's February," Ariel said. "I bet you wanted to go in July."

7. A Good Deal of Warmth

"One of the best times to experience winter in Greenland is during March, when the sun begins to provides a good deal of warmth." Or so the site dedicated to travel in Greenland assured her. Given the temperature dropped to twenty below zero in March, Ariel wondered what constituted a good deal of warmth to a Greenlander.

Then again, the idea of riding on a dog sled, racing over the frigid ice while she looked up at the northern lights, had a certain appeal. She opted for a three-night tour out of Reykjavik that would take her to Nuuk and another popular town further north. The stopover in Iceland would give her the chance to visit the mysteriously empty offices of d⁴, meet Ulfur, and bring Hulda a better sandwich for the lunch she took at her desk.

Nell's idea of lunch involved a nice bottle of wine and lots of her things à la carte. She held up her end of the bargain though, eliminating the small talk and going straight to what Ariel needed to know.

"Cillian's an old friend from college." Nell settled into her chair and took her first sip of wine. "We went to university together two decades ago. When I first met him, he'd just fallen in love with Lara, his ex. I got to be friends with her too.

"What happened to Lara?"

"It's complicated. I'd say Lara started to grow up and remind Cillian of his parents."

"Cillian wasn't fond of his parents?"

Nell let out a sharp laugh. "That would be an understatement. His mom was one those fussy women, and old man McGrane was a dour man from a well-off Irish family. The kind that preferred tea to whiskey, you know. He wanted to grow an empire and found a way, once he moved into manufacturing pharmaceuticals. Cillian and his sister were raised to behave. Then sis fell in love with an unemployed factory worker, and basically ran away from home. Cillian took up partying and fell in love with Lara."

"His parents objected to falling in love?"

"Lara wasn't what they had in mind. They wanted someone with a family pedigree. They tolerated her. Once she had children of her own, she grew up a little and Cillian felt like he had three adults pushing him around. He asserted his independence one of the few ways he could. With his penis."

"Ugh. Lara wouldn't forgive?"

"Why would she? She was smart enough to see it would keep happening. I think she loved Cillian too much to stay and let it play out. She made a new life."

"A happy ending for her?"

"Don't know. Cillian's parents wanted custody of the grandkids. They got the marriage annulled, which made the kiddos technically bastards. That really pissed Lara off. Soon after, she and the kids disappeared. Police looked into foul play, but most people think Lara had the good sense to go far away. No one has heard from her since."

"How did Cillian handle it?"

"He pretended not to care. He was in his mid-thirties by then. Gambling, drinking, and womanizing; doing everything his dad hated. A couple of years later Mrs. McGrane died, Cillian's dad retreated into a deep depression, and Cillian had responsibilities whether he liked it or not. By then he'd run up a lot of debts with his horses and he needed to start taking better care of the family money."

"Yet you've stayed friends with him through all this?"

"He's got a good heart, and I always could see his side, even when he was at his worst. Besides, I never had expectations of him. With a man like Cillian, that makes all the difference."

"Nice summary. See, you did save me a lot of time."

"Thanks, I have a way with words." Nell licked a piece of hummus off of her fingers. "This stuff is so good." She stood up and put her hand on Ariel's shoulder. "I'm headed to the loo, dear. Just so you know, this is all public knowledge."

As Nell made her way to the restroom, Ariel scrutinized the premory Nell's touch had left behind. In it, a teenaged boy was hurrying down the street, nervous he'd be discovered. He wore old jeans and a dirty t-shirt saying something rude. He was working as a courier. He kept his head down. There was danger involved.

It seemed pretty random until Ariel realized the teenaged boy was Nell. Was this a role she'd play on stage somewhere? Why cast a forty-something woman for the part?

Nell returned before Ariel could make sense of the scene, and she continued her story without a prompt. Ariel kept quiet, hoping what came next wouldn't be common knowledge.

"Old Mr. McGrane isn't right enough in the head to manage anything these days. I understand he has lucid periods, during which he checks on his realm and dictates his wishes. The rest of the time, he sits upstairs at the estate and stares out a window. He won't do therapy, and the drugs, which his company makes, leave him as depressed and less alert. Monitoring Cillian is now Doyle's job. Doyle has the old man's power of attorney and controls the family fortune, but his instructions are to let Cillian behave as if the money is his own. That is, as long as Cillian behaves."

"So Doyle is his babysitter," Ariel said.

"Yup. And Cillian McGrane is his dad's biggest disappointment. He was created to grow the McGrane empire, and all he wants to do is enjoy it."

"I think Cillian McGrane's got more sense than I thought," Ariel said. She picked up the check the waiter left and her eyes widened.

"What *was* that wine?"

"A 2010 Château La Nerthe Chateauneuf-du-Pape. Worth every penny, don't you think?"

Ariel considered how much she'd learned over lunch, and agreed.

The work portion of the trip would all be at the end, so Ariel tried to enjoy the beginning of her vacation. She packed a few good books and her warmest clothes, and delighted in a window seat as she watched the late afternoon sun set on her way into Iceland. The giant Vatnajökull glacier gleamed beneath her when the plane dipped below the clouds and Ariel thought she'd never seen anything so beautiful as the various shades of blues glistening off of the ice in the light of low winter sun.

She joined her group at the Reykjavik airport for the evening flight on to Nuuk. The small band of mostly Icelandic travelers was quiet, but friendly, and she felt thankful to live in a time and place where a woman could travel alone without problems. Nuuk was a quick stopover, and the next morning they boarded the pint-sized plane for Ilulissat, the main tourist destination in Greenland.

Ariel stepped off the plane to her first view of the barren rocks mottled with bright colored lichens that make up the tundra. She'd never set foot inside of the Arctic Circle before. Tiny flickers and flashes erupted as her boot touched the ground.

My premonitions are stronger here. The cold dry air? The earth's magnetic field? There had to be a reason.

While they were waiting for the luggage, Ariel wandered off, looking for a bathroom. She turned into an office and noticed a man's legs sticking out from under a desk.

"Are you okay?" She felt like she should say something.

She heard him chuckle. "No, I'm in serious need of somebody to grab the other end of this wire. One man doing a two man job." Ariel saw that he was trying to get a computer cable to go through a small hole in the top of the desk.

"Let me help." She came over, pulled the cord through and plugged it into the monitor where it was clearly intended to go.

"Thanks," he said as he wriggled out from under the desk. He noticed she'd connected the cable. "A helpful tourist *and* one that knows how to connect hardware."

"I can manage more than plugging in a monitor." She laughed. "IT training here, though I don't use it enough these days. I'm Ariel and I'm looking for a ladies' room."

"You came all the way to the arctic to find a place to pee?"

She rolled her eyes and when he held out his hand she took it without thinking.

"Siarnaq," he said and Ariel saw a small spark in the air before their hands touched.

Then for a few seconds, neither of them could have said a word if they had wanted to.

Ariel saw the flickers of the distant future going wild in the corners of her brain, like far off flashing lights. He let go of her hand.

"You're a seer." He said it like it was fact. He studied her red hair, fair skin and blue eyes. She wasn't of the People, or at least if she had Inuit ancestors they were few indeed. Had he ever met a seer who wasn't mostly Inuit? He didn't think so.

"You get visions of the future, too?" Ariel's heart was beating harder. She'd never expected to be asking this question.

The Inuit man laughed. "The world is full of seers."

I had no idea that would be so good to know.

"You have a lot to learn about your gift. You're with the tour group?" She nodded, not trusting herself to speak. "Today, they give you time to shop and sightsee. Let's go get a cup of coffee."

Siarnaq was younger than she first thought, a young man in his twenties wearing older men's clothes. A look around showed him to be taller than most Inuit, and he spoke English well. Seated across from him at a booth in a little coffee shop, Ariel was waking up to the fact that he was cute, in spite of a bad haircut, and clothes that would have looked out of style twenty years ago.

They'd established that each of them saw movies in their own heads, like memories but of the future. Siarnaq came from a culture seeped in magic, and viewed his gift with no particular awe. He'd studied and traveled some, enough to understand why Ariel would be more uncomfortable in her society.

"So it's hard for you, too, knowing how it all will end? Is that why you came to Greenland? To see where mankind makes its final stand?"

Ariel shook her head in confusion. "What are you talking about? I don't know how anything is going to end. Do you? I almost never see anything past the next several months."

She thought back to the odd premonitions when she was asked to transfer to Ireland. "There was one exception. It was about my own future in a few months, but it gave me a hint of something awful for the whole human race. I've been trying to learn more ever since. It didn't necessarily mean the end to everything, though, at least I don't think it did."

"We're not so alike after all." He was the one who understood it first. "I *only* see after my lifetime, to places that are decades, maybe centuries from now. I can't be sure. I see a lot of one thing, and it's the slow end of humanity. It follows me everywhere. But not you? You get to see your own future! What I wouldn't give…"

"It's not as useful as you'd think," Ariel said. "Although it definitely beats what you've got. Talk about depressing."

"When I touched you today, I got visions that were close up and blurry, like I'd never seen before. They were from my own life."

She started to tell Siarnaq about her experience with Baldur, but got as far as opening her mouth when she decided to wait. She was only guessing about Baldur, and this exchange was complicated enough.

"So we must be tuned to different frequencies!" Siarnaq was pleased with his discovery. "You understand science. You understand radios."

"I studied them in school; I don't remember much."

"Well, I work a lot with them. They're an important part of communication in my world. Do you know how long a radio wave is?"

"Long. Like maybe feet."

"You people still know what AM radio is?"

Ariel rolled her eyes. "Yeah. It's the stations you turn to for sports."

Siarnaq pointed out the window. "The waves for AM radio are from here to that building down the road."

"Really?"

"Your FM radio waves? More like just from me to you."

Ariel got the analogy. "So I'm an FM radio seeing things more closely and you're an AM radio seeing things further away. How cool is this? Are there other kinds like us, but in other frequencies?"

"I don't know." Siarnaq shrugged. "Lots of Inuit tell the future, but most use tools for their fortune-telling, and no one seems as sure about their predictions as I am." His eyes showed his sorrow. "It's a horrible burden, this knowing the human race will end so soon. We Inuit will do our part," he assured her. "I will see to it."

"I think we ought to work towards humanity bouncing back." Ariel was disturbed by the extent to which Siarnaq had latched on to the gloomiest outcome possible.

"What do you mean? You think my vision is wrong?"

"Of course not." Ariel didn't understand the problem. "But surely you've seen several futures? Even I, with my short-term information, know there are always a variety of outcomes. One may be more likely but still..."

"What do *you* mean? The future is the future. You see what will be. There is no maybe this or maybe that. There is what is. You can't change that."

"Okay." Ariel saw the problem. "You think the future is fixed?"

"Of course it is. Why wouldn't it be?" Siarnaq was deciding this girl wasn't as smart as she had seemed. "The present and past are fixed. The future is no different. Besides, how could people see the future if there wasn't one to see?"

Ariel took a breath. Then she took another sip of her coffee.

"I promise you, close up at my frequency, I see several possible futures all the time. It's how the future works. You might ask me to coffee or not. I might say yes; I might say no. I pick. You pick. With each pick, the possibilities shift a little." Ariel stopped talking and gave the matter some thought. "Maybe, I don't know, maybe the far future is fixed. Maybe you're right and all the little things we choose don't matter in the end. That would be kind of sad, but it's possible. If you only see one final outcome, then we're screwed."

Siarnaq was listening intently, and there was hint of a smile on his face.

"You think I'm funny?"

"No, I think I'm funny. I'm wondering why I never considered tomorrow could be different than yesterday. Perhaps you're the one who's right. You, an outsider, have taught me something of use about the world."

Ariel suspected this was a high compliment.

"Maybe I have seen different outcomes, but because I didn't understand, I forced them all into being parts of one story. I thought all the other visions were of what came before, when in fact some of them may have been what came instead."

"Can you tell me more about what does happen?" she asked.

"I don't know specifics, and I think it's because my people don't either. I always see through them. Contact and supplies from outside of Greenland stop within a few weeks. Then our contact with Nuuk and the other southern towns stops. Curious Inuit leave the far north to report back on what has happened. They never return. We get messages by radio, telling the people they must stay put and not send any more people south. We do this and we survive. We think we are all that is left of humanity, but that may not be true. There are not many of us, and we do okay for a while, but we've lost much of our ability to get by. We grow less, over generations, until that is that."

The sorrow in Siarnaq's expression settled into the grooves worn into this skin by reliving this ending many times before.

"So you work to bring radio communication to all of Greenland, so it will be there when it is needed?"

"That too. More importantly, I bring modern ways and yet warn my people not to depend too much on them. I want my people's children to survive for as long as they can."

Ariel hesitated. She didn't want to argue with this newfound friend and yet she couldn't resist pointing out an inconsistency when she saw one.

"Then at some level you do believe you can change the future? Otherwise, why bring radios? Why try to keep your people self-sufficient?"

Siarnaq had to laugh at her logic. "You are right. I think I can cheat the future a little, so I try to nudge the inevitable. The big things are fixed, but a mere man can be forgiven for trying to make small changes."

It made sense to Ariel. "Seeing so far ahead, I understand how it would feel that way. Big events, etched in stone. Seeing the way I do, I feel like everyone makes so much difference all the time it makes me dizzy."

"So you feel people are too powerful?"

She nodded. "It bothers me as much as feeling powerless bothers you."

They were ready to part as friends, kindred spirits who'd found each other against all odds and had a brief moment of understanding. Ariel intended to go rejoin her group. She would have, too, if Siarnaq hadn't reached out to take her hand as they both stood to leave.

Even his brief touch reignited the splatter of visions she'd felt earlier, and she worked to steady the dizziness. While the giddy feeling was uncomfortable to Ariel, it seemed to intrigue Siarnaq, and he held on to her hand for several seconds.

"May I?" he asked as he pushed up her sleeve and ran his other hand up her arm.

It wasn't like being touched by anyone else. The contact between new skin, and more skin, set off more images, as Ariel felt her own natural frequency start to piggyback onto the wavelength of Siarnaq's visions. Her day-to-day clarity began to form around his far future events and the more skin contact she made with the man the clearer the melding of their two visions was becoming. He let go of her and took a step away. It stopped.

She took a step forward, pushed up his sleeve and placed the whole inside of her lower arm against his. The combined visions came back stronger. He gave her a curious smile. People in the small diner were starting to stare. This wasn't the ideal place for a science experiment. Ariel hesitated only a second.

"Let's go outside," she said. Then, as they put on coats and walked out into the below zero dusk, she realized outdoors was not going to be any better.

"Would you like to come back to my room?" He nodded. They both knew. At that point, they couldn't walk away without finding out more.

Ariel didn't consider herself promiscuous. She'd never invited a man she'd just met back to her hotel room. As they walked, she reminded herself this didn't have to end with sex, even though she was pretty sure it would. If it didn't, wouldn't the two of them always wonder what would have happened if it had?

They lay together on the bed, huddled under covers in an otherwise cold room, without a stich of clothing between them. Ariel let her senses go as she touched him with all the skin she could manage. She realized she'd always held back from men, not wanting to learn too much as their bodies touched. Now, she opened up her senses and let the input come in waves as she felt his body shudder as he did the same. Later she'd realize there had been little foreplay. The quiet touch of their skin from head to toe had been all the enticement either of them had needed.

Ariel held her breath as she felt the day-to-day lives of dozens of hardy souls as they struggled with their pain and enjoyed their pleasures. Little decisions made big differences in their cold harsh world, like they did in Ariel's own life. Marriages, births, travel, and deaths ran through her head, and she guessed Siarnaq was enjoying a similar show as her day-to-day awareness superimposed itself on his world.

When she and Siarnaq finally tired of the stories of others, they moved their bodies to reach all the closeness they could achieve. It was gentle and friendly, not a burst of passion but a final embrace of understanding as two souls shared without holding back.

He had tears in his eyes afterwards, and Ariel felt certain the encounter must have meant as much to him as it had to her.

"I'm glad we found each other," she said, pulling her clothes back on. He surprised her when he answered.

"I'm glad I found you. You are more than you realize. Thank you for letting me see that."

She didn't know how to reply. "Do you think we'll see each other again?" She reached for his hand as she asked the question, and was puzzled by the lack of input. Were her senses worn out? Maybe this ability could become exhausted.

He nodded his head. "There are nice outcomes where that occurs. You didn't see them?"

"No, I mostly saw your people, living and thriving. Everything I saw came from their future."

"Not me. For once, I didn't see past my lifetime at all. I saw my own tomorrows, and many of them will be good." He reached out and touched her hair. "Thank you, lady with the sunset hair. You've cheered me more than you know, and odds are high this will happen for us at least once more. I will look forward to it."

He hugged her long and hard before he left.

8. Treats

Ariel finished the two days of touring with only part of her in the present. Some of her lived with the Inuit of the tomorrow, sharing their joys and sorrows as she begged them to find ways to thrive. A bit of her remained under the blankets in a cold, small hotel room, reliving the memory of her skin rubbing against that of another with an eagerness experienced for the first time.

Sunday night, the rest of her tour group bade her farewell as they left for the airport to return home. Their smiles told her they'd heard of her dalliance with a local man earlier in the trip, and assumed she was staying on in Nuuk to continue the romance. *No secrets in small towns.*

Luckily, in this part of the world no one felt obliged to stone her to death for her behavior. Rather, they seemed to find the sexual activity of a healthy young woman to be normal and even charming. As to small towns and secrets, she'd be counting on that phenomenon tomorrow as she sought out information on Mikkel.

The answering service was open early the next day, and the owner waved at her as she spoke into her headphones. It was a busy Monday morning in Nuuk, as call after call interrupted Ariel's attempt to make an introduction. Finally, the woman got tired of it as well, and plopped a child who couldn't have been more than six into her chair, sticking headphones onto the little girl with instructions in Danish.

"English?" Ariel asked.

"Some." The woman looked at her child. "She tells them to call back. It's okay."

Ariel discovered the woman had involved the little girl because she assumed Ariel wanted to set up service. Once she learned otherwise, the woman lost interest in the conversation.

"Please. I was hoping you could tell me about your customer Mikkel Nygaard. I'm trying to find contact information for him."

"He pays his bills, that's all I know. You have his phone number. You want his email address?" She was pausing to be polite, but nothing could have been further from a cozy chat.

"I have his email and phone number already."

"Then what do you need? He answers emails." The woman was dismissing her, and the little girl started to cry in frustration as two phones rang as once. As the woman pulled the head phones off the crying child, Ariel had an idea.

"Let me take her across the street and buy her a soda. It's my thank you, for bothering you."

The woman nodded, and gestured for them to go while she put one phone line on hold. Ariel took the child's hand and couldn't help thinking of all the child molesters promising candy she'd been taught to fear since birth. Different dynamics in a world in which there were few strangers, and not a single road leading out of town.

When she brought the child back, the woman was friendlier and phone lines were quieter.

"I'm looking for Mikkel's employees. I'm in sales and he's a customer and I want to do something nice for his staff. He seems like the sort who'd say don't bother, so I thought I'd pick up some pastries and take them there. Only I can't find any office in town with his company's name. Can you help?"

The woman running the answering service shook her head in amusement. "You sales people. Nobody works for him. He does everything from his home. He travels a lot, all over Greenland and everywhere else. He's got fancy college degrees and works making parts for airplanes, I think."

She looked at Ariel hopefully. At first Ariel was confused, but it came to her.

"Would you like me to go get you a pastry? I mean, that's what I came here to do, and it looks to me like you pretty much are this guy's staff."

"The hotel down the street has coffee and makes good cakes."

"What's their best?"

"I like the coconut."

Ariel smiled. "I'll be back with two pieces."

Ah, Chateauneuf-du-Pape for lunch and now coconut cake for breakfast. Treats do keep the world running.

Ariel's flight was delayed into Reykjavik, and she got to her hotel too late to do anything but order room service. Bored, she decided to try some online research on Mikkel and his business. She could have done this sooner, but internet snooping seemed so invasive. She'd never bothered to look into the personal lives of her clients over in London.

Now, however, she had mysteries to solve. She started to type. It didn't surprise her Mikkel had no obvious internet footprint, but Ariel was determined and detail-oriented. The information came.

Nygaard was a popular name, but Mikkel Nygaard was not. The offhand comment about fancy degrees led her to Dr. Carl M. Nygaard of Greenland, who had studied aeronautical engineering. It sure sounded like the degree in airplanes she'd heard about.

Dr. Nygaard had finished a Ph.D. program with impressive speed, and become an associate professor at a small university in Copenhagen. He taught introductory engineering and was liked by his students, according to the school's outdated faculty rating system.

Why would a young professor in engineering become obsessed with making money? And use his middle name?

Ariel's eyes were tired. She rubbed them, pulling the hotel bathrobe around her. It was time to get under the covers and get some sleep. Tomorrow would be a big day visiting with Baldur's staff.

Hulda had taken the day off, but had set up Ariel's appointment with Ulfur as promised. Ariel arrived hoping he could be enticed into conversation over coffee, or beer, and would provide insight into Baldur and his secretive company. That's probably why it took several minutes before Ariel understood exactly what Ulfur's job was.

He introduced himself as Baldur's attorney, but after several adept deflections of her questions, she realized he was a professional at not giving answers. If someone wanted to know about d^4, they were sent to Ulfur, because not providing information was Ulfur's job. It looked like he was worth every penny.

He was a small, pudgy man in his late fifties, and he spoke perfect English as he sat on the other side of a wide desk.

"I know that to Americans the Scandinavians can appear reserved or even unfriendly. I assure you nothing could be further from the truth. We are the nicest of people, but have a different cultural style." He said it like he'd explained it a hundred times before, and Ariel guessed he had.

"Oh, no, everyone was perfectly nice to me. I'm not here to complain. I just didn't get much of an impression of what d^4 is like behind the brochure. I thought I'd be a more effective liaison if I learned more. That's all. What a shame Hulda is off today."

"Yes, she hated to miss you. A visit was a good idea," Ulfur said it in the most agreeable fashion. "I'm happy to help instead, of course. Ask me anything."

To Ariel's frustration, Ulfur stayed on the other side of his desk, ruling out any casual touch. Ariel placed both hands on the wood, but picked up nothing. So she concentrated on talk instead. Fifteen minutes later, she'd tried every question she could think of. Ulfur answered every one of them, yet Ariel didn't know any more than when she walked in the door.

Ulfur was in the process of showing her out when Baldur arrived. Ulfur raised an eyebrow when he saw his boss dressed in designer jeans and a fashionable but casual top.

"I heard our new Ullow rep might drop by today." Baldur spoke in a friendlier tone than Ariel had heard him use during her last visit. "I'm off today, but had to come get something, so thought I'd say hello." Then in response to Ulfur's questioning look he added, "Run along to your meeting, Ulfur. I'll see Ariel out."

Once Ulfur took his leave, Baldur gave Ariel a long appraising gaze. It took in every square inch of her body and would have been considered harassment in most circles. She stood her ground and stared at him while he looked.

She wondered if physical contact with him would allow her to see the short-term future the way closeness with Siarnaq had opened up distant tomorrows. If so, she could confirm right now what Jake suspected about Baldur. How much physical contact with this man was she willing to make?

Baldur seemed to be having similar thoughts of his own, and there was an eagerness in his eyes as he took a step toward her. She could have sworn she saw a visible electric spark jump between them as he reached for her hand.

It's stronger here, too. Not as much as in Greenland, but stronger than what I'm used to.

She reached for Baldur as well. As they held each other's hands without speaking, the close-up images returned. This time, they focused, then became clearer as he circled her body with both of his arms and held her tight. As he leaned down for a kiss she saw images of him removing her clothes, and she knew this was the most likely near future. Was she really going to do this?

It wasn't the only possibility. He paused, stepping back and loosening their embrace.

"I had no idea someone like you existed." He seemed so happy at the discovery. "You're my greatest wish come true." He touched her hair like he couldn't believe his good fortune. "You're even pretty. Not that it would be necessary, but it is nice."

"This is amazing," Ariel agreed, trying to find her way in an awkward conversation. "The way the touch works. We need to learn more about it." She reached out the bare inside of her arm in invitation. "Do you want to know more?"

He laughed, and for the second time Ariel got the feeling there was a joke she didn't quite understand. "Much more, my little flame-haired oracle. I will want to know everything."

Okay. I suppose I want to know everything too.

As he placed the inside of his lower arm against hers, she saw another near future, one where she backed off from him and ran from his office. What the hell?

"With what I will learn from you, elskan, I'll own the world." He murmured it like it was a sensual remark. Maybe it was to him? "Every man, woman and child on the planet will work for me, one way or another." His eyes narrowed in pleasure at the thought, and the passion went out of the moment for Ariel.

"Why would you want that?" It was the first thing that popped out. "I mean, owning the world is crazy. I thought we could exchange information. Help each other."

He looked at her in pity. "Humans don't help each other." He said it like she was a silly child. "We pretend to, so we can get what we want."

He took a step towards her and as his fingers touched her wrist she had a flash of him trying to force himself on her. She turned and ran for the door, the way she had in the premory that flashed in her mind seconds before.

Only as it happened for real, he yelled after her. "Go. I see ahead too, you know. Next time you won't want to run off." His laugh echoed in her mind for hours afterward, as she replayed the scene over in her head all the way back to Dublin.

Ariel anticipated a call from Mikkel after her thinly disguised snooping expedition, but she was surprised at how fast it came and how pissed he was.

"I wanted to do something nice for your staff," she stammered, a bit taken aback. It wasn't the whole truth, but it was some of it, and it should have mitigated the unwarranted hostility.

"Doing something nice for my staff is not in our agreement. You are not to come to Nuuk. You are not to ask questions about me. You *are* to provide me with tools to make money. I require absolutely nothing else from you. Do you understand?"

"I do, although I think it's time somebody mentioned you don't own Greenland. I can visit any time I like for personal reasons having nothing to do with you."

Mikkel's voice softened a bit. "Of course you can. Look, you appear to be an intelligent woman. Holding three clients by the hand is not a good use of your talents. I suggest you ask Eoin for more responsibilities or a transfer back to London."

The man had a point about her workload.

"I'll pass along your input," she said, allowing snippiness to creep into her voice. "Speaking of job assignments matching a person's talents, Dr. Carl M. Nygaard has an impressive educational background easily discovered by anyone who looks for it." Ariel was annoyed enough to charge ahead. "I have to wonder why someone who got a Ph.D. in engineering is now so obsessed with making money."

"I see. So my requests for privacy have gone unheeded in more than one arena." His voice was cold again.

"Why would a man of science not expect those around him to be curious? Why would a reasonable man be so angry when my motivation clearly includes being of assistance to you?"

"It's complicated," he said. "You have no idea what I'm up against, and I'd like to keep it that way. My arrangement with Ullow is simple. I contact you or Eoin if I need anything. Otherwise, I don't want to hear from you." She could tell he tried to say it in as reasonable a tone as he could manage.

"Works fine for me." She hit the end call button.

So he wanted her to stay out of Greenland. Ariel had to smile. The giant frozen island offered more fun than expected. She thought of Siarnaq next to her, stretched out skin-to-skin along the full length of her body as they kept each other warm under the many blankets. She pulled up a calendar to consider her options.

******

Cillian and Nell were each enjoying a Guinness as they sat in front of a peat fire. Peat, once burned out of necessity on a cold island lacking in trees, had now become a trendy way to celebrate Ireland's roots. The two of them inhaled the oily aroma of dirt, smoke and something else no one, not even an Irish poet, had been able to describe well.

"So, will this new girl be a problem?" Cillian asked.

"Not intentionally," Nell said. "She's bright, she'd as soon do what's right, and she's got no allegiances to any of the players in this mess."

"Eoin should never have asked London to send over a new person. He knows not one of his customers wanted someone poking their nose into things. I'd have complained if it wouldn't have been so out of character."

"I wouldn't worry about her. I gave her your full public bio. She bought into the part about your strict parents and your runaway sister and your racing horses, and I added a few personal tidbits I was proud of."

"Good call. How did she respond?"

"Like you'd expect. You're a pretty sympathetic character. Everything I told her *is* true, it's just not the whole truth. Now that she thinks she knows the dirt, there's no reason to dig deeper. Brendan tells me he's been working to the same end in the office, and she believes he designs bells and whistles for you to play with. She thinks it's a stupid waste of time, but accepts it."

"I agree the young woman has a good heart," Cillian said. "But I'm worried about how curious she is. She could cause us trouble without meaning to." Cillian took a long slow sip of his brew. "We should consider filling her in on more."

"Let's not rush. Brendan is doing a great job keeping an eye on her."

"So are you. Some days I just want this all to be over, to stop worrying and go find my kids and know they're okay."

"I know. But as long as your dad and Doyle have their icy fingers on your fortune, you've got to play this game."

"Preferably without the self-pity." Cillian finished the last swallow of his beer and stood up. "How about a brisk ride to clear the head."

"Sure." Nell always did what she could to keep Cillian's spirits up.

******

Eoin liked his new employee, even if he wasn't used to females like her. His own wife was a sweet woman with little interest in the outside world. Her growing children were everything to her. Eoin would be the first to admit he didn't understand women like Ariel, driven to work outside the home, getting by well into their twenties without a bloke to care for them. But she was hardworking and he was happy enough to have her on his staff. It made this whole incident with Mikkel so unfortunate.

The email was blistering. Ariel's thinly disguised vacation to Nuuk violated an understanding between them, Mikkel claimed, and any further transgressions would result in him insisting Ariel be removed from the project.

Eoin was dismayed Mikkel had taken this so poorly. He was baffled by Mikkel's extreme insistence on privacy, too, and he wanted answers. He figured giving curious Ariel a little freedom to snoop was a safe way to learn more.

Yes, he'd known Mikkel would be irritated, but Eoin planned to blame Ariel, maintaining harmony by chastising her in front of Mikkel while letting her know later she'd done nothing wrong. Sort of a public swat on the butt with no harm done. That, and a brief apology to Mikkel along the lines of "you know how women are, always sticking their nose into other people's business" should have sufficed.

The worst of it was she'd come back with no information, or at least none she was willing to share. Eoin knew he wasn't the greatest at reading people, but he did better when dealing with those who weren't all that different from him. Ariel seemed troubled, and her claims to have learned nothing rang incomplete.

Eoin already had made the mistake of letting curiosity nudge him into learning more about a secretive client. Two years earlier, Baldur had been every bit as angry at Eoin's snooping, and had vacillated between demanding Eoin be sent packing and electing to take Eoin fully into his confidence. Eoin had pushed for the latter, and for two years now, Eoin had lived with the consequences of that deal.

It had been a bargain with the devil. If you keep my secrets, then your company can keep my money. London leaned heavily on Eoin to make matters with Baldur work, so Eoin had kept Baldur's secrets since.

He wondered if Ariel had sold her soul now as well. If so, what were the secrets she'd be keeping? Could Mikkel possibly be doing anything worse than Baldur?

April 2012

9. Never Happened

Ariel was curious about most things. Why was the sky blue and what was dirt anyway? Why did people have to sleep? She liked quick information and questions with answers. As she typed her current quandary into a search engine, she wasn't sure if this one had an answer or not.

"Why do people want to make more money than they can spend?"

Ariel understood wanting to be wealthy. Who wouldn't like to travel and buy whatever clothes struck your fancy? What Ariel didn't get was wanting to be worth four hundred million instead of three. At some point, didn't all the houses and expensive vacations roll together? Why were men like Mikkel and Baldur hell-bent on taking a huge fortune and growing it? Somebody out there had to have worthwhile thoughts on the subject.

People did. Inquiries led her to a well maintained site for discussing wealth. It seemed to be asking the same question. Ariel skimmed through various threads.

Wait a minute. This was maintained by the group called y^1, headed by her brother's friend Toby. Ariel had heard about Toby and his passion for understanding money.

Ariel tried searching the site for comments about Cillian. He was barely mentioned. She typed in Mikkel's name. Nothing came back. Okay, what about Baldur? Whoa. The name Baldur Hákonarson got eight-hundred some hits. Now this guy got talked about.

Ariel began clicking, but the links were to conversations held in chat rooms for members only. Damn. Looked like she needed to become a member.

She found the page to join, but it was full of essay questions. There had to be an easier way. Surely Zane could fix it so she could join without filling out all that information.

She glanced at the clock. It was still too early to call Chicago, but the perfect time for calling her sister. Teddie was a junior in high school and an exchange student in India. When Ariel had said goodbye to her last June, she'd caught flickers of futures in which her little sister discovered some psychic ability of her own. Ariel spent months last fall wondering if her sister would learn to see the future, too. Whenever she tried to learn more, though, all she saw was a ghostly image of Teddie. It frightened her.

Then her sister had called last December, embarrassed as she explained she'd developed an interest in an odd topic but couldn't get off campus to shop. When Ariel visited India for Christmas, would she please bring along any books she could find on out-of-body experiences?

Ariel had understood what was going on. The ghostly images meant Teddie was learning to use astral projection. Ariel was delighted she and her little sister, different in so many ways, were going to have the possession of secret talents in common.

Ariel remembered how she'd set off to have some fun peeking into the strange little book stores tucked away in the dodgier parts of London. As she picked up the first book, she'd had a strong premory of being dismayed to learn how her paying for the book with a credit card had caused problems for Teddie.

Baffled, Ariel had checked her wallet, found enough cash, and used it. Over the next couple of days, she amassed a collection of books on out-of-body experiences and bought them all without leaving any internet footprint.

Teddie was delighted to get the books at Christmas, and Ariel had pretty much forgotten about the odd premonition when she bought them. Now, as she reached for her phone to call Teddie, it came flooding back with a new urgency.

She had to be careful. Contacting Teddie put her at risk all of the sudden. Ariel put the phone down. She'd wait to call until she knew more.

******

Siarnaq enjoyed the encounter with the American girl more than he'd enjoyed anything in a long time. His people took comfort in the pleasures of sex, using its warmth and joy as a countermeasure against the harshness of their lives. Yet he had never experienced the type of closeness he did with this stranger, this woman who had a gift so much like his own.

With her skin pressing against his, his visions had merged with hers as he held an awareness of his own life for the first time. He saw good times in his future. He saw the difference he could make regarding the habits of his own people. Most comforting of all, he saw she was right about probabilities. It was easier to see when one looked at the near term. Nothing was ever for sure. This sunset-haired girl had given him the gift of hope, and now he thanked her every day for it.

But every gift has its curse, as Siarnaq knew. Along with the joys of knowing came information he'd rather not possess. Probable sorrows awaited him, and some of them involved Ariel. Failure to make his people more self-sufficient remained a possibility, no matter what he did. Worst of all, while lying in her arms, he'd learned she knew the man who was working to undo the things Siarnaq was trying to accomplish.

Not wanting to spoil their time together, Siarnaq kept quiet about his distressing visions of Carl Nygaard, his cousin and his childhood friend. Carl was forcing the modern world into the corners of Kalaallit Nunaat. Why would his better educated cousin, part Inuit himself, be hell-bent on putting technology right where it was least needed? It made no sense.

His beautiful new friend wrote him to suggest she come visit again in a few weeks. Would he like to see her? Was she joking? He could think of nothing he would like better. It was true, he hoped as he lay next to her he could learn more about what Carl was up to. But if not that, then simply lying next to her would be more than joy enough.

******

Ariel's brother Zane was happy to pass along Toby's phone number in Hawaii, and Ariel waited for a good time to call her brother's friend who lived ten time zones away. A relaxed voice greeted her once they connected. He was having morning coffee; she was having an evening drink.

"The membership requirement is there to keep discussions civil and intelligent. Of course I'm willing to assume Zane's sister can manage that."

"I hope so." Ariel laughed. "I was intimidated by all the stuff I had to write. I don't do essay questions."

"Well, they're there so existing members can get to know you, but they can be waived. Maybe you'll fill out some of it later. You do understand y[1] is an online organization that analyzes and discusses the flow of money, right? Why the sudden interest in economics? I thought you worked with computers."

"I do. But I work with computers that handle stock trades. My company provides hardware and software for high frequency trading. You know, buying and selling the same stocks within milliseconds to capitalize on tiny fluctuations in a stock price."

There was a long silence on the other end of the line.

"I know what high frequency trading is. Ariel, I'm not sure I can let you in after all. At least not until I know more about you. My members count on me and the other moderators to protect their ability to speak safely."

"I'm no threat to anybody," Ariel was a little surprised at the sudden lack of cooperation from her own brother's friend.

"Probably not, but some in your industry are. The whole site has been lit up lately about a perceived threat to the world's financial stability. Many members believe it's created by your industry. That's not to say those you work with are all bad people or automatically excluded from our discussion boards, but I have to be more careful with someone in your field."

Ariel pushed back.

"I ended up on your website because I was researching my company's clients. Two of them seem to be of little interest to your members, but the third is a big topic of conversation. I can't get to the information about Baldur unless I'm a member myself."

More silence. "Baldur is your *client*?"

"Is that a bad thing?" Ariel didn't know how to respond.

"You know, Ariel, I've got some business in Europe coming up. If this can wait a couple of weeks, could we meet and talk in person?"

"Of course. Let me know when you're coming. I'll look forward to it."

"Yeah," Toby said. "Me too. In the meantime, could you pretend we didn't have this conversation?"

Ariel shrugged. "Sure. No problem."

As she walked home from the bus stop the next day, Ariel tried to recall what Zane had told her about Toby. She'd last seen Zane over Christmas, when the whole family had met in Darjeeling. London had been particularly dreary last December, and she'd looked forward to the trip, even though she knew being in the same hotel with her parents, brother and sister would bring images of their futures flooding into her head.

The trip had been far different than Ariel hoped. Trauma crept back into the Zeitman's lives as Teddie's best friend was kidnapped in Darjeeling a few days before the family arrived. Everyone had been in shock. The incident had left Ariel wondering if she could have prevented the kidnapping. Should she keep better tabs on everyone she knew? Was life always going to be this way, filled with trying to strike a balance between knowing too little and knowing too much?

It was now April and Teddie's friend still hadn't been found. Before she left Darjeeling, though, Ariel had picked up signs the outcome was likely to be good. She hoped this happy ending was coming soon.

She and Zane had talked a lot during that visit. She'd learned more about his long distance relationship with a young man living in Hawaii, and how Zane's career plans were evolving. Both narratives were full of praise for Toby, who'd helped him in various ways. By the time Ariel made it the front door of her building she'd decided anyone her brother admired so much had to be worth trusting.

The noise in the barely lit hallway inside the front door startled her as she opened it. It was a man's cough, made to alert her to his presence. She turned and saw a balding Scottish-looking man in his late fifties standing in the shadows, holding a white canoe paddle with a yellow top. It looked like the one her mother kept in her bedroom, a relic of an outdoor adventure from long ago.

"I'm a friend of your mum's. I've been in touch with her by telepathy." He nodded at the canoe paddle. "I brought this to prove it."

What?

An hour later she and the man named Tom had finished a pot of tea and Ariel had a throbbing headache. She let the man into her apartment once he convinced her he knew her mother from an escapade a few years ago in Nigeria. Mrs. Zeitman traveled for her work and, as part professional and part hippie, her mom had made many odd friends over the years. Accepting a man claiming to be a telepath as her mom's buddy wasn't difficult.

Tom's story moved into the hard-to-believe, however, when he told Ariel her own mother had telepathic abilities and was a member of a large group with psychic tendencies.

"Mom never told me this because?" a skeptical Ariel asked, even as she realized how idiotic the question was.

"I don't think your mum ever intended to tell anyone in your family, dear, except for your dad of course."

"So my dad knows my mom is a telepath and he's, like, okay with this?"

Tom's smile had a trace of sadness. "What are his options? Look, your mum would never have sent me with a message like this, except she can't risk contacting you and she needs your help."

"My mom's in some kind of trouble?"

"No, she's fine. Your sister Teddie is in danger, and your mum needs you to go to India at the end of this month, under the pretense of visiting Teddie for her seventeenth birthday. She'll be recovering from some minor surgery I'll try to explain. Your family's communication is being monitored by the people who kidnapped your sister's friend. What a nasty bit of business, that. So your mum sent me because…"

"Because you're a telepath and nobody could trace her communications with you," Ariel finished the sentence for him, and she was pretty sure that was when the headache started.

By the time Tom left, Ariel supposed she'd accepted his story. It explained her odd premonition yesterday about the need for caution in contacting Teddie.

Was is so unexpected her mother would have a skill as unusual as Ariel's own? It explained why Ariel had always been so cautious around her mom, so careful not to think about the future. On some deep level, hadn't she always suspected her mother would somehow be able to "tell"?

She supposed she had.

Ariel assured Tom she already knew about Teddie's fascination with out-of-body experiences and assumed her sister had that ability. Tom promised to pass word of Ariel's cooperation back to the Zeitman household in Texas.

"It'd be best if you could act like you spontaneously decided to go have a holiday with your sister. You know, like you have no idea about your mum and no clue about what your sister is up to, and like this whole conversation with me never happened."

"Not to worry. I'm getting practice in that arena."

Tom gave her a quizzical look, and Ariel watched with fascination as the man's eyes went strangely blank for a second or two.

"Did you just try to read my mind? Isn't that illegal or something?"

The soft, almost sad smile crossed the man's face for a second time. "No, but it is considered bad manners. I seldom do it, but I know how much your mum would like assurances you're safe and well."

Another uncomfortable thought occurred to Ariel. "Does my mom???"

"No, she doesn't," Tom said. "Except for the lightest, most noninvasive touch once in a while to make sure you're okay. She's one of the most ethical telepaths I know, and on the whole we're a bloody decent group. All that empathy, you know. So no worries, your secrets are safe with me. But please Ariel, be careful if you're going to start in with a dangerous crowd yourself."

"I'll be careful. I promise. Do me a favor and assure my folks I'm fine. Remember, Tom, we never had *any* of this conversation."

"Right. We never did."

The next question was whether she could get herself to Greenland before she left for India. Maybe she could combine the trips and save money. Why not? She'd spend a weekend with Siarnaq, if the dates worked for him, and head from there to a birthday visit with Teddie.

Siarnaq was delighted about the possibility, and offered to make her travel easier by meeting her in the small East Greenland town of Kulusuk, only a short flight from Iceland. It was perfect. Ariel booked travel on to Darjeeling, thinking it sounded like a great way to greet the spring.

May 2012

10. Springtime On the Road

The weekend with Siarnaq was too short. Ariel was surprised how she and a man from such a different culture could share so much in common. They laughed at the same things, and it was often a humor born of knowing what one hadn't wished to know. Siarnaq didn't understand social networking or traffic jams or Asian Fusion restaurants, but he understood Ariel. She wrapped herself in that joy and wore it like a cloak for two glorious days.

By Sunday afternoon they were both sad and uneasy about the future. Travel to Greenland was far from cheap and Siarnaq lacked the means to come to Dublin. Ariel had precalled enough to know this probably wasn't their last encounter, but a lot of different of stormy possibilities lay ahead. Siarnaq had the same information. A few hours before Ariel's plane left, they faced each other and talked.

"Along with the joy you've shown me, I've learned much that is sad," he said.

"Me too. There are so many outcomes between us, I can't focus on one long enough to understand it, but few bode well for us as a couple." She had to laugh. "I suppose you don't have to be precognitive to figure that one out."

He looked at the floor. "I can't leave my world and you know it. I saw one scenario in which you tried to convince me to, and I left you in anger. I saw another in which you decided you could live as an Inuit. You didn't last long. But, I don't think this means we can't be together again."

S. R. Cronin

"I agree. I saw ways it happens. We've both seen other, more disturbing options, though. I see a strong chance you get angry at someone I know."

"I'm already angry at someone you know. I didn't say anything because I didn't want it to taint our time together. I had a childhood friend, a cousin, who I told about my visions. When I shared the big ending for everyone, and how I was going to help the Inuit stay self-sufficient, I thought he'd be proud to know me. Instead he told me I was full of shit. After that, we stopped talking."

"That must have hard on you. You're still angry at him?"

"Not really. Kids say stupid things like that. But he must be someone you know, because when I touch you I get information about him."

"I don't know a lot of people from Greenland..." Ariel was getting a quick idea of where this was going.

"But you do know my cousin Carl?"

Ariel nodded. "Yes. He goes by Mikkel Nygaard now, and he's one of my clients—my least friendly client, to be honest. We've already had one run-in and he told me to stay out of Greenland."

"Well, he's nastier than you think. I have no idea why, but he's working to undo what I once told him I'd be doing."

"He's encouraging the Inuit to adopt modern ways? Why?"

"I don't know. Thanks to you I've gotten premonitions of him moving lots of machinery to the far north. I've already seen one of his sleds, although at the time I didn't know what it was. Now I've seen visions of him teaching Inuit to work with his contraptions. Why would he do this?"

"I wish I understood premories better," Ariel said. "When I'm touching you I see lives from the far future, and when I'm near you or touch things you touch, I get them about you. There's never been anything about Mikkel, though. The truth is I know little about him. Do you want me to try to find out more?"

"No! I want you to stay as far away from him as possible."

"Hey, you understand I have to deal with him for work right?" Ariel's tone was heavier than she intended, filled with shades of "don't tell me what to do." She backed off. "I'll stay out of the mess between the two of you, though."

"Thanks." Siarnaq said no more.

74

"Let's stay in touch," Ariel added, working to soften her voice. "I'll keep my ears open. If I do learn anything useful about Mikkel, I'll tell you."

Ariel hugged Siarnaq goodbye, feeling sadder than she expected. On the plane, she stared at Greenland's white coastline until it was nothing more than a tiny dot on her horizon.

Forty-eight hours later, Ariel looked down at her sleeping sister. Teddie's face was pale and clammy. Ariel reached out to touch her, hoping to learn of the most likely outcomes to her sister's troubling situation. She withdrew her hand, startled, as Teddie opened her eyes wide. Ariel searched for something reassuring to say.

"Hey. Thought maybe you could use a friendly face."

"Isn't my family was supposed to stay away from me?" Teddie whispered it in a scratchy voice.

"Mom and Dad decided your sister in Ireland could come visit you for your seventeenth birthday. Not suspicious, right? I hear you've had some sort of surgery, though, so you're not exactly ready to party."

Others heard their voices and came into the room, and Ariel stepped away from Teddie's side, realizing her opportunity had passed. Maybe she'd try again later. Then again, maybe not.

The next morning Ariel sipped coffee as she visited with Teddie's adult friend Amy, who ran an aid organization for human trafficking victims. Amy was part of the group trying to ensure Teddie's safety and find her friends. She was a short, almost stocky American woman in brightly colored clothes who seemed to have a warm heart and a fondness for Teddie. Ariel's admiration for the woman grew as they talked.

"So you think these people really go flitting around on some plane of light and energy that mirrors this world?" Ariel asked.

Amy shrugged. "It's hard to explain any other way."

"Wow. That's a kick. And my little sister does this?"

Amy shrugged a second time and laughed. "Apparently she does it rather well."

Teddie poked her head full of black curls into the dining room, and when she saw her sister talking to Amy she joined them.

"So how did mom find a way to tell you about this?"

"She didn't. Apparently some creep you've pissed off has our whole family under radio silence, and we can't talk about anything that involves you. I did find out mom sold the magazine article she's been writing and it's going to come out in a couple of months."

"She told me. We talk about things like that, because if we didn't it would seem suspicious. How did you get drafted to come here?"

"Mom sent someone from London to talk to me in person. Honestly, I felt bad I hadn't thought of visiting you."

"Did this guy happen to mention how he communicated with our mother?" Teddie was clearly trying to feel her way through this. Ariel wanted to reassure her.

"Yep, I've been read in. My mother is a telepath with a bunch of telepath friends, and my little sister goes around snooping on people." When Teddie started to object to being called a snoop, Ariel raised her hand laughing. "I'm kidding Teddie. I'm envious. It sounds like an incredibly cool thing to be able to do."

Ariel realized how much she'd like to share with Teddie her own visions of the future and the cool things her own brain did. But Teddie didn't need to be distracted by anything right now, she needed to heal. Someone else came into the dining room and that removed even the slightest temptation.

Over the next few days Ariel did what she could to provide her sister with comfort while trying her best not to get in the way. Spring flowers were sprouting in the garden, and Ariel spent hours out there in her sweats, doing yoga and practicing the Tai Chi routines she'd begun to learn in Dublin. She also spent time wondering if knowledge of Teddie's future would help her sister or harm her. If only there was some way to tell.

If she did talk to Teddie about this, how would she explain what she knew? Given the talents of this group, calling it hunch wouldn't suffice. With two telepaths in the house, were her talents already known?

Ariel thought not. She was pretty sure her own mother had no idea, and mom was supposed to be a good telepath. Perhaps a combination of preoccupation, the telepath's code of respect for other's privacy, and good old fashioned not seeing what one didn't expect had worked in Ariel's favor.

Was there anything helpful Ariel could do if she knew more about Teddie's situation? What would she do if she discovered the most likely outcomes were awful? Could she even go back to Dublin and tend to her own growing troubles if she found out her sister wouldn't survive this ordeal?

She decided to go with a quick touch as she was leaving. If she found something useful, she'd tell her sister as she walked out the door, avoiding questions from others. If she learned something awful, well, at least she could get out of there fast.

The day before she left, Ariel was allowed to go over to Amy's office to use the internet to take care of business and travel matters. She went back to the y^1 site to solidify the questions she had for her brother's friend Toby. She searched harder for anything she could access about Baldur.

She found speculation that his entire board of directors participated, and had been selected for their ability to do so. *Participated? In what?* Ariel assumed the group consisted of rich people bringing money to the table. But if Baldur's wealth was the minimum standard, there were thousands who could qualify based on money. This conversation implied d^4 was a closed community with a special entry requirement most investors failed to meet. Could Baldur have amassed a group of high frequency seers?

Maybe the gift Ariel thought made her so unique wasn't rare at all. Maybe plenty of others had it, and they'd figured out ways to benefit from it far more than she had.

She closed the window and moved on. Her inbox was overflowing and her social sites had so many notifications she'd never get through them. She hunted for what was important.

It looked like Toby had written her a few days ago, asking if she could meet in Frankfurt any time soon. Well, she could. Everybody flew through Frankfurt, and she had a layover there tomorrow night. She wrote back to set up the meeting, anxious to get back to a world where she could make a difference.

That night when Ariel got up to pee, she saw her sister sleeping on the couch and altered her plan. She wouldn't get a more private chance to take that quick look at Teddie's future. She tiptoed over, reached down and placed the back of her hand against her little sister's cheek.

She knew.

Teddie would figure out how to do what needed to be done. She *was* figuring it out, and it was best to let her be. Ariel sighed with relief. Go Teddie.

"Thanks for coming. I really appreciate it," her sister said the next morning, black curls bobbing around as she looked up from a group of photos lying in front of her.

"Hey, I could get into this whole spy secret mission thing." Ariel wanted to give her sister a hug, but it was better not to complicate her exit with more information. She gave her a grinning thumbs-up instead as she said her goodbyes all around. *Keep it light.*

"Next year, we'll do some real celebrating, okay?" She waved to them all as she walked through the door.

******

Siarnaq stopped short of telling Ariel everything he learned about Mikkel when he touched her. Ariel's job mattered to her, and she was teeming with information about people from work. Lying by her side, Siarnaq had seen near-futures for Ariel's boss, co-workers and clients. Much of it made no sense, as he didn't know the people. However, one story stuck out.

An Icelandic man, thin and very blond, was part of Ariel's world. He worked with money; in fact, he lived for money. Siarnaq had been unable to tell why. He'd seen a future in which the man became annoyed at a rival investor from Greenland. The Icelander became determined to put a stop to this Greenlander's activities.

Ariel was right when she said knowledge came with the visions. Siarnaq hadn't thought about it before, but he did more than see. He knew things, too. Not everything, but some relevant details, like those attached to a memory.

The result was Siarnaq knew the Greenlander was Mikkel Nygaard. The Icelander was called Baldur and soon he'd be looking for ways to stop his competitor. Once he began looking, Siarnaq would find a way to be there, to offer Baldur his services.

******

Toby waived to Ariel from across the hotel bar in Frankfurt. He was a handsome, well-tanned man of around fifty.

"You look like your pictures," he said as he gestured for her to have a seat. "Can I buy you a drink?"

"Absolutely. Thanks for meeting me."

"No problem. If you don't mind my saying so, your family does have a penchant for getting into trouble."

"And for getting out of it. At least so far."

"Let's hope that continues," Toby said. "You've got a tiger by the tail here. How much do you know about y^1?"

"It's an online organization of people who talk about money and philosophy. Zane loves that stuff. Wealth distribution, the human need to be rewarded versus the need for kindness. I wouldn't think too many serious investors frequent your website."

Toby looked thoughtful. "Some do. Making money from money has practical implications for the wellbeing of humanity, and a number of those who do it want to discuss the topic."

Ariel didn't respond, and Toby waited as well.

"Is Baldur a member of your group?"

"No, he's not. If he's aware of us, he considers us irrelevant."

"Would you let him join if he wanted to?" Ariel asked because it looked like Toby had offered all the information he was going to without coaxing.

"No, I don't think so. We're a private group. We can pick and choose our members. Respectful participation is the main requirement, but there are others."

"What requirements would Baldur violate, assuming he's capable of respectful discussion?"

Toby smiled slightly. "I suppose he's capable of that. We also require members not join for the purpose of furthering their own self-serving agenda. Some would argue that humans are incapable of doing anything but furthering their own agendas. I happen to disagree."

"So do I." Ariel hadn't thought about it much, but as she said it she realized it was true. "Would you care to know who the last person was who told me humans are always selfish?"

"I'm going to go out on limb and guess it was Baldur. Was he trying to recruit you?"

"I'm not sure what he was trying to do." Ariel was glad to deflect the question. "Listen, I oversee his account for a firm that furnishes the hardware and writes the software he uses for high frequency trading. I'm not required to like him or his business practices, only to see his work gets done on time. Is there any problem with you telling me why your group talks about him so much and yet wouldn't let him join?"

"Probably not. Okay, y[1] members don't all agree on much, but if a small group had an unknown capability that would allow them to suck the wealth of the world away from everyone else, we all think that would be wrong. We'd fight it. Luckily, the gods of chance rule the universe. No one keeps winning at the craps table forever, so we spend time talking about how much of an advantage is too much of one."

"You think Baldur has an advantage in investing?" Ariel thought of her co-worker Jake and his theories.

"Lots of people have advantages in investing. I think Baldur has way more than that. He's able to statistically remove chance. Several y[1] members fear Baldur could amass most of the wealth of the world in a few decades. Many of us are trying to figure out what needs to be changed to keep his company from owning everything in our lifetimes.

Ariel grimaced. "You blame my company?"

"Of course not. Ullow has dozens of clients, and they're all making money. However, they're making a little less than they used to, in spite of your company's efforts. It's incremental, but changes in fractions of a percent are the name of the game. He's smart, this Baldur. We're worried by the time governing bodies wise up, d[4] will be too powerful to stop."

"What do you expect me to do? I can't spy on him for you."

Toby said nothing.

"I mean, I've signed agreements and stuff. I could go to jail."

Toby continued to say nothing. Ariel realized he was giving her time to process what he'd told her.

"Take over the world? Seriously? How sure are you people?"

"If it would help you make a decision, I'll let you read all the discussions for yourself. Your company is doing nothing wrong. There are ethical issues with the inherent unfairness of high frequency trading, but that's nothing compared to what d[4] is doing."

"So I get to be a member?"

"No. Not only is it a bad idea for you to be a member, it's a bad idea for anyone to know we met or you read this stuff. So, here."

He shoved sheets of printouts into her hands, and as he did, she had a quick premory of him assuring his cohorts that Ariel Zeitman was on their side. There was a ninety-percent chance of that happening after she read this stuff.

"This information is *that* compelling?" Toby gave her an odd look.

"You read it and you tell me. No wait. Don't tell me anything. We shouldn't communicate directly again, for your safety. Your brother is our best contact. Let him know what you think after you read this. He can tell me."

"Okay," Ariel said. "I could be joining your cause. Zane will be in touch."

S. R. Cronin

11. The Cassandras
of the World

Baldur stared out of his office window, considering black swans. Not real ones, of course, but the theory. As a man schooled in economics, he knew how an event outside the realm of normal expectations could produce big consequences and appear obvious in hindsight. World War I, the rise of the internet and the 911 attacks on the U.S. all came to mind. Baldur worried he had two potential black swans facing him now and the last thing he needed was unexpected consequences.

The first swan had red hair and was more of a shock than a surprise.

It had taken Baldur two whole years to find ten investors with a skill like his own. In the turmoil of 2009, they left telltale marks in their day-trading records. He was Icelandic, so he began his search in his home country, where he found four worthy candidates. His calculations showed he needed several more, so d^4 went international.

None of the ten he ended up with understood their own capabilities when he found them. Certainly none grasped the implications for what they could accomplish if they banded together. Baldur taught them to be better and d^4 became the first investment company that couldn't lose.

Baldur considered the existence of others like him to have been predictable. Nature almost never has a one and only. Yet through all the searching for others, he'd never considered someone could see further into the future. Seeing the immediate made sense to him. After all, the next few seconds were fairly well determined.

This girl, however, one of his black swans, saw the messier world of next week and next month. Her fragments were hard to interpret, based on what he'd seen with her touch. He supposed they'd be even harder to act upon. How did she survive with all those possibilities coming at her? Such a gift would have driven a weaker individual insane.

Maybe that was why he'd never met another like her. Maybe the others were all bonkers and locked away.

At any rate, her existence was a threat. Last time they met, she must have picked up on his skills as easily as he'd discovered hers. Apparently, touch could do that.

Baldur knew his own gift was related to skin contact, but touch through electronic means like his keyboard worked as well as touching other humans or their things. It didn't surprise him; touch was nothing more than electromagnetic signals. But it was lucky. He hardly could walk around a stock exchange running his hands over everyone.

Given the nature of their encounters, Baldur was pretty sure Ariel's gift worked by touch as well.

After their first meeting, he should have pretended nothing happened. Then he could have pushed her company to transfer her back to London and, with time, she'd have thought she imagined the whole thing. It would have been the most logical solution.

Instead, he'd done the opposite, showing up during her meeting with Ulfur, hoping to learn more by using all the skin contact he could arrange. Why? Because for once, acting logically didn't sound like nearly as much fun.

Unfortunately, the second encounter didn't go the way he hoped. Her touch set off receptors he didn't realize he possessed. He was drawn to her body and what she could do and know. He felt the power of what he could become if he was linked with her, and he craved that power with a frightening intensity. Worse yet, he was certain she'd seen the yearning in his eyes and heard it in his voice.

He should have pretended it was sexual. She would have believed it; women liked to think they were insanely desirable. But no, drunk with lust for what she could give him, he'd made dumb boasts.

Now, she was wary, maybe even scared. Sooner or later she'd see him in her future, and realize what d^4 was really about. Then she'd feel compelled to stop him or to warn others. The black swan would have changed history.

Of course, the Cassandras of the world had a poor record of being believed, but Baldur couldn't take that chance. Once scrutiny of a such a successful small investment company began, others would do statistical analysis and verify this Cassandra was on to something. Rules would be passed to slow him down or stop him. Fines could be levied to take away what he had. He could be prohibited from trading at all.

Was there any way this black swan could be used to his advantage?

Baldur considered. High frequency trading done under the radar made money in small increments. It was lots and lots of small increments, but it was still a slow process.

Ariel's visions would be perfect for trading in futures and options that took weeks to months to mature but paid bigger money. She could be the best asset in the world, he realized with a growing hunger. If it went well, in a matter of months he could accomplish what he'd expected to spend years achieving. Could she be persuaded to work with him? Why not? He could promise her the moon.

That brought him to his second problem, his other black swan. Was it even possible to have two of them at once?

He was certain no unknown investor out there of any significance possessed his skills. Yet another man, this Mikkel Nygaard fellow, had piggy backed on Baldur's successes and was managing to cut ever so slightly into Baldur's gradual increase in profits.

Eoin had already explained to Baldur how Mikkel was hell-bent on keeping up with d^4 and wanted whatever tools Baldur had. Baldur had found the hero worship to be flattering, and he'd accepted Eoin's advice to humor Mikkel. So he had a puppy who wanted to imitate him. What was the harm?

Recent analysis, however, showed Mikkel was a surprisingly effective puppy. He and his one-man company had amassed more than Baldur realized. This success of anyone outside of d^4 hadn't been predicted. His first black swan could perhaps be turned to his advantage, but this imitator could not. Enough was enough. Baldur made a call to Eoin to set up a meeting. It was time to put a stop to Mikkel's success.

******

Some days Mikkel was tired of the secrecy, and tired of being misunderstood. He was by nature an honest man, one with a generous heart that preferred to see the good in people. He thought he was horribly suited to his current role, with its ongoing lies and the requirement he be looking over his shoulder at every turn.

He would never have chosen this life, of course, if his expertise hadn't been so perfect and the need hadn't been so dire. Damn his cousin Siarnaq. Damn the cold winter nights he'd spent looking at stars and dreaming of space. Damn the northern lights with their dancing magnetism that inspired his love of physics. And damn the damn Irishman who'd walked into his office talking about the annihilation of the human race in 2352.

From that day on, the Irishman's visions had become a life's work for Mikkel. He'd left the comfortable world of Professor Carl Nygaard and embraced the chance to save his species. As Mikkel, he ran a stealth operation involving dozens of scientists, psychologists, engineers and manufacturers who stayed hidden as they planned one of the most daring missions of all time.

Mikkel had learned to be a better administrator, and even something of a leader. Surprisingly, it was his almost off-handed decision early on to handle the fundraising that caused him more grief than anything. The decision was a matter of efficiency, and of preserving secrecy. Back in 2009 the small group had no manpower to spare.

Yet the role of investor for Mikkel Nygaard had become his public persona, and over the past three years an ongoing rivalry with a fellow investor had taken on a surprising importance. Now it seemed like the effectiveness of Mikkel the financial wizard was more vital to humanity's survival than all of Dr. Nygaard's contributions to putting the human race into space.

Mikkel understood the fine line he walked. Most decisions remained inconsequential and yet the rare innocuous one could turn out to have far reaching consequences. His psychic Irishman was of no use in predicting day-to-day outcomes of anything, but the man had an uncanny ability to tell when some small act of Mikkel's had a chance of disturbing the far future.

The choice to hide what they were doing was one such event. The secrecy was an added burden, and it seemed to Mikkel to be an unnecessary one. But the Irishman had been adamant. Go public with this space program now and its odds of serving its ultimate function dropped to almost zero.

Now the psychic had weighed in on another decision. The red-haired computer girl who was becoming a nuisance would turn out to be more than that. She'd injected herself into important decisions with far reaching consequences. The young woman needed to be given more information. An introduction to the situation she'd walked into would be arranged.

******

These days Baldur didn't need his visions for avoiding his brother's fists, or anyone else's. He used them for stock trades and little else. Occasionally a flash of something surprised him, and he avoided a minor car accident or bite of unpleasant food. It was mildly useful.

When the phone rang, he reached for it, then stopped. He was too busy to take random calls. Let them leave a message.

His receptors worked better now with electronics than with human touch, probably thanks to practice. Touching the phone gave him a flash of an unexpected helpful conversation. Very well. He picked up the receiver.

"I too wish to stop a man named Mikkel Nygaard," the voice on the other end said. The accent was heavy Danish and something else as well.

"Who is this?" Baldur appreciated bluntness but was hardly willing to trust a disembodied voice.

"I'm a Greenlander who was once a friend of Mikkel's. I'm a man who doesn't like what he sees and wants to stop further damage. Can we meet?"

Well, this was a pleasant surprise.

"Yes, I suspect we can and should. Tell me more."

******

It took Ariel a while to get through all the pages Toby printed out for her, but by the time she was halfway through she knew the premory of her agreeing to help now had a ninety-nine-percent chance of happening. Toby was right. He had compelling evidence Baldur was doing more than getting richer. He and d^4 had an advantage over the entire world of trading, and nothing in their ethical make-up obliged them to do anything but utilize it to its fullest. Would they stop short of destroying the societies that fed them? Ariel wondered how much restraint the group could or would use once their plans were nearly complete. Absolute power and all that.

Keeping her job with Ullow couldn't possibly be more important than putting a stop to d^4. She called Zane the next evening.

In the middle of an innocuous chat about life, work and weather, she interjected a message for a mutual friend. She would help any way she could and needed the friend to know about a programmer in her company who had evidence of his own to share. Same conclusion, but derived from different data. She could provide details.

Zane took the odd message in stride, leaving Ariel sure her brother was expecting something of the sort. At one time, Zane would have been more inquisitive. Two years ago his own job had put him in danger, though, and now he seemed willing to not pry.

He was a good brother and a good friend. Perhaps she ought to confide in him about her premonitions. As far as Ariel knew, the men in her family lacked the odd gifts bestowed on her, her mother and her sister, but Zane wasn't without his own unusual talents. As a child, he'd developed extraordinary control over muscles most humans never used, and as a result he could alter his body shape and facial features well beyond anything Ariel would have thought possible. A year and half ago, he'd given Ariel a demonstration. At Zane's request, she'd kept quiet about the information and hadn't brought it up since.

Ariel thought of Nell, and the premonition in which the woman appeared as a young man.

"Zane? Have you ever met anyone who can do what you can with your appearance?"

"No. I mean, it's not like I go around asking people, but as far as I know, I'm the only one. Why? Did you meet somebody like me?"

"I'm not sure. It would be one way of explaining something."

"Well, if you have, I'd like to meet him."

"Her," Ariel said. "At least, I think so."

******

Nell offered to buy lunch. Ariel had to smile when she learned they were meeting at one of the best Japanese restaurants in Dublin. Nell had done her homework; sushi was Ariel's favorite. Ariel wondered why her goodwill was being sought. What did a worker bee like her have to offer someone like Nell?

As the waiter fussed over them, Nell gushed about the beauty of spring in Ireland and Ariel nodded and agreed and waited. Something was coming.

"How are you when it comes to accepting things that are kind of, well, odd?" Nell asked. "Ireland is full of stories, you know, not just of the sidhe, leprechauns, and ghosts, but of all manner of spirits and magic powers. It's part of who we are."

"I like that about you."

"Most people do. They think it makes us charming, and we sell that image to the world. Tourism is a good bit of our economy, and we're not stupid. Dig deeper, though, and you'll find a dark collective unconscious. Our stories are filled with trickery, treachery, and great loss. The Irish love a tragedy far more than a happy ending."

Ariel nodded. She guessed this was going somewhere interesting.

"So it's no surprise our heroes are often tragic as well. Do you know much about Ireland's past?"

"No, I'm not much of a history buff. I don't even know much U.S. history."

"Real history is full of horrible things; darker stories than even the Irish could concoct. Our last thousand years have been particularly brutal. But I want to tell you about the time before then, when Irish kings and queens and monks and poets moved freely about the land and Ireland flourished."

"Okay."

"Around the year five hundred, not long after St. Patrick, there lived a great Irish man, a famous monk. He is still beloved here, probably third only to Saint Patrick and Blessed Brigid. His name was Cillian, although he was also called Colm Cille and Saint Columba."

"Our Cillian is named after him?"

"Of course, as are hundreds of Irish males. Ours is more than named after him, though. In one of those quirks common on this island, he *is* him. Not reincarnation, we don't go for that. I mean he embodies Cillian's powers. He's his spiritual heir. His parents had no idea when they named him, of course, but the saints must have guided them. Cillian's dad never learned what his boy can do or he might have appreciated him more. You see, Cillian is a prophet. He knows."

So that's where this is going. No wonder accepting this job in Ireland made my head spin. I'm fooking surrounded by people who see the future.

It prompted the question: was Nell trying to gain her acceptance or her silence?

"He knows what?"

"Like the Cillian of old, he can see a millennium ahead. There is a lot of darkness to come, a lot of horrible things in the future. Cillian is trying to use what he knows to do what he can for humanity. It's a hard road. There's a small group of us working with him."

"Supposing I believe you, why would you tell me this?"

"You've caused Cillian worry. He thinks you're too smart and too curious not to figure out there's more to his story. He's good at reading people and he believes you have a good heart. He hopes you'll leave him be to do what he needs to do. That's all we ask of you."

Ariel let a sigh come out, and it was a long slow exhalation. She had tales of her own she could tell, but should she? Responding with a confession of her own talents, or with what Jake and Toby guessed about Baldur, or what she knew to be true of Siarnaq, could lead to all kinds of complications. She could precall many of them without trying.

Cillian wasn't asking her for information. He was asking to be left alone. She could always volunteer information later, but she could never take back any mess she created by speaking up now.

"Does he get much in the way of detail? Closer in, I mean?"

Nell shrugged. "Some, but usually he only sees events tied to this other time. He's focused on it. He knows what he has to do. He often asks me to speak for him, because he hates to talk to others of his gift. We're both trusting you, Ariel. Please. Overlook the odd about him, and go on about your life. Okay?"

"One could suspect this seer thing was bullshit and you guys were running some scam you're trying to hide."

"True. But you'll find nothing to make you think we're causing harm to anyone. If you think you do, come to me and I'll explain. I've been asked to tell you all you need but no more. Now, can we count on your discretion?"

Nell reached her hand out and put it over Ariel's as she asked and for once Ariel didn't withdraw her hand. She needed all the information she could get.

"I promise," she said, as she noted a clear premory of a gnarled old man on a park bench waiting to deliver a message. The man was Nell. "I may be back with more questions."

"I'm sure you will."

d⁴

12. Things a Decent Man Won't Do

Eoin regarded Baldur with the same wariness he showed to his neighbor's Doberman. He kept his distance and never assumed a meeting would be friendly. When Baldur called to arrange an outing together, Eoin agreed because he had no other reasonable choice.

Baldur insisted they meet for a round of golf at an exclusive Dublin club. Eoin neither enjoyed golf nor played it well, and he was pretty sure Baldur knew that.

It was an overcast day with a brisk breeze. An impeccably dressed Baldur secured the golf cart. His state-of-the-art clubs and fashionable bag glowed with style. Eoin's old equipment slunk down next to it in embarrassment.

Baldur told Eoin this was the perfect opportunity for the two men to discuss d^4 and its goals. Eoin was sure more was involved, and it wouldn't be near as pleasant as Baldur made it sound. He was down two strokes after the first hole when Baldur mentioned the situation with Mikkel needed modification.

"I don't know how he's managed to do so well, but your leniency in allowing him access to my software upgrades has to stop. He's nipping at my heels, Eoin, and I don't want to share. At all. Ever."

"No problem. He has our best commercial products; he can do well with them. Why be so upset at his success, though? I mean, isn't there enough money out there for the both of you?"

Baldur stopped the cart and gave Eoin a hard stare. "That question should never be asked."

"Right. It's not enough to win. He must also lose."

"Everyone else must lose," Baldur said, as he pulled out a club and walked towards the tee.

"Try not to be such a charmer." Eoin muttered it just loud enough to be heard.

Baldur took a perfect swing. "I like playing golf with you because I don't have to pretend to be charming. I can concentrate more on my game."

Baldur was up five strokes at the end of the second hole, and Eoin thought about offering to caddy for him instead, but his instincts told him life would be worse if he did. He concentrated on how he'd been a decent athlete once, even if this hadn't been his sport. He picked his play up a little, and was down only six strokes by the end of the seventh hole when Baldur brought the conversation back to business.

"I need to know more about Mikkel. I'm told his training is in engineering, not economics and he goes by his middle name now. Is he hiding something?"

Eoin was rubbing sunscreen on his face and hands, being careful to keep it out of his eyes. Crying, no matter what its cause, would not enhance his stature on this already miserable day.

"Ariel pointed out Mikkel's background to me. It struck me as odd, but a man can change his interests and his image. Who knows why he did it. You don't ask Mikkel questions; he makes *you* look approachable."

"Yes, so I've been told. Nonetheless, I want you to learn more about him."

Eoin rolled his eyes. "Our arrangement does not include me gathering intel on other investors for you."

"Our arrangement includes whatever I want it to include. I expect you to learn more and update me."

By the end of the twelfth hole Eoin was down a dozen strokes and wanted to go home.

After the fifteenth hole, Baldur brought up his next concern. "I'd like to get to know that girl you gave me." Even Eoin recognized he had not *given* Ariel to anyone, and had no power to do so, but he wasn't about to correct Baldur. He went for a wary "What do you mean?"

"What it sounds like. You put a pretty girl on my project; I'd like to get to know her better. Surely you don't object?"

"What you do with your free time is your business, and what she does with hers is hers."

"Don't be ridiculous. Her boss can direct what she does and we both know it. I'm going to have my yacht brought over to Dun Laoghaire Marina next week. I'll fly over the week after and invite her out for a ride. I want you to make sure she agrees to go."

Eoin said nothing. He picked up his club and a ball and walked up to the tee. He took a deep breath and made the swing of his life. The breeze caught the ball and it rolled onto the green, tumbling to within a few feet of the hole.

He turned to face Baldur. "I don't mind encouraging Ariel to spend time with you. But know this. I will not make sleeping with you a requirement of her job. If you make doing so a requirement of mine, then Ullow will have my resignation. Period. There are a few things a decent man doesn't do, and pimping is one of them."

Baldur seemed amused, either by the surprising tee off or by the equally uncharacteristic bit of rebellion. Maybe both.

"Well then, let's hope Ariel accepts your encouragement."

In the end, Eoin lost by twenty strokes but felt he'd won something else. Even so, he was concerned this thing with Ariel was likely to turn into a disaster.

******

Ariel and Siarnaq were in touch often. He liked to send her little things to make her laugh, stories best appreciated by someone with her skills. She responded in kind and by June they had a comfortable long-distance friendship. He didn't bring up Mikkel for weeks, and she was grateful. Finally, the subject came up at the end of a text message.

"I have contacted another person who knows Mikkel and doesn't like what he's doing either. I won't lie to you. His name is Baldur and he's your client."

S. R. Cronin

What? Ariel was furious. How did Siarnaq know Baldur? Then she froze.

All that time lying side-by-side. She viewed the lives of the Inuit three centuries in the future while Siarnaq picked up on people that mattered to her. Of course he'd seen Baldur, and he could easily have gleaned animosity between Baldur and Mikkel.

"Not acceptable! This is my career you are fucking with!" Ariel was in no mood to use nice words as she typed with a staccato anger.

The words "This is humanity I'm trying to save," came back in seconds.

"Fuck humanity." Ariel muttered it as she started to type, then she stopped. That sounded horrible. Didn't she care if her species saw the year 3000? Of course she did. But a voice in her head pushed back.

So a bunch of strangers die. Is someone keeping score? Are we a failure as a species if we don't make it to the paltry fifty-thousand-year mark as a life form?

This was too much for Ariel. She went for a different response.

"Your enemy's enemy may NOT be your friend. Baldur could be more dangerous than Mikkel. Be careful."

"I will." It came back right away. "Thank you, sunset hair. I will try to cause you no trouble at your job."

******

Zane called the next night, and opened the conversation with the good news that all was well with their sister Teddie, who'd returned home from India.

"The need to be careful about what we say is no longer there, due to *her* situation." Ariel was pretty sure she heard the emphasis correctly. Okay, Zane didn't want her to jump in and start talking about Toby. Was the whole world getting paranoid, or what?

After more pleasantries Zane remarked he had a visit with an old friend who was happy to learn of Ariel's recent decision. This friend thought Ariel should be cautious, but any information was appreciated. If she could convey more about a colleague she'd mentioned, that would be helpful.

"He's an odd duck." Zane chuckled and moved the conversation on to how difficult law school was."

"Hang in there, Zane."

"I will. Uh, be careful out there. I'm not sure you and I grew up understanding how nasty some people can be."

"Yeah, I get that part these days. I'll keep an eye out."

******

Nell looked at the pile of clothes on her bed and laughed at the random inventory from second hand clothing stores. Well, she could hardly afford to dress in new clothes for all the roles she played. Cillian's generous allowance for costumes went mostly to looking the part of his sexy actress friend.

It had been a while since Nell Gallagher appeared in any theatrical production, and anyone who cared assumed her relationship with the rich Cillian McGrane was the cause. They were right, just not in the way they thought.

Cillian and Nell had the ideal platonic relationship between a man and a woman, the kind born of at least one person being attracted to their own gender. Nell didn't fancy men much, except as buds, while Cillian had plenty of potential bedmates but needed all the true friends he could find. Once Cillian offered Nell the role of her life working for him, and she heard why, she took the part.

She had three or four characters she resorted to often, and that made it easier. Most of them were used as couriers, delivering goods and information best not trusted to others. Her most important character, however, was not all that different from Nell.

Murna was a pretty Irish woman who liked women and made her living as a fake fortune-teller in Donegal. Murna was in town practicing her profession on a regular enough basis, so locals could vouch that Murna was real. The truth was Nell got a kick out of pretending to see the future, given the real fortune-teller she spent time with these days.

Murna's new age interests took her to fairs and conferences, many of which were in Reykjavik—considered a premier location for such things. They'd learned that Hulda, the unobtrusive receptionist for d^4, had a private soft spot for aura readings and crystal vibrations. A pretty fortune-teller from Ireland with a bit of a gypsy style about her was exactly Hulda's type.

Nell always did her homework, and after the second conference she landed in Hulda's bed, where she now was a frequent visitor. Away from the office, Hulda was smarter, funnier and nicer than Nell would have guessed, and the line between acting and enjoying was now quite blurred. Subterfuge worked best that way and Nell knew it, but the more she cared for Hulda the more she dreaded the inevitable end of her role. Ah well, that was a worry for another day.

Today's problem was sticky, too. She needed to be a young male and pick up some temporary work at the Marina outside of Dublin. Hulda had said Baldur was having his yacht brought over. Nell wanted to use the opportunity to learn what she could.

Then her sweet Icelandic lover had called, confiding to Murna how she was willing to ignore Baldur's ongoing conceit and arrogance, but was concerned about his fixation with taking some young woman out on his yacht. Hulda got the impression this lady would be forced to go on the boat ride and more, for business reasons, and that offended Hulda to her core. She'd called Murna to questioned her about the Irish police and their attitudes and whether this young woman would find the legal system helpful in the worst of cases. Did Murna think maybe Hulda should do something?

Nell, as Murna, listened and assured Hulda the situation couldn't be that bad. As soon as she heard the young woman's name, however, it had taken all the acting talent she had to sound disinterested. Why in the world would Baldur insist on taking Ariel out to sea?

Nell decided she had to be on board for the ride and so well camouflaged that Ariel could look right at her and suspect nothing. Nell tore into the pile of clothes, seeking just the right look.

******

Siarnaq was glad Baldur was willing to travel to Nuuk. Ariel had a good point. It was possible this enemy of his enemy was as untrustworthy as his own cousin, and more ruthless. Siarnaq thought if he could look this stranger in the eye, he could judge if he should align himself with this foreigner.

******

Baldur was sure he could gain the Inuit man's cooperation, one way or another. Eoin had been proof of how easy it was to gain the obedience of a good man, if you took your time. You needed to threaten the well-being of a loved one, and require the tiniest of infractions to remove the danger. Then, over time, the threats could grow less while the requests grew larger, until the good man was so complicit he harmed himself more than anyone by trying to get out of the situation.

Not that Eoin hadn't asserted a little uncharacteristic independence out on the golf course the other day. Baldur wasn't worried; he found it amusing. Pimping was such an ugly word.

Baldur had never been to Greenland, and would have been happy to keep it that way, but the Inuit man insisted they meet in person. So, what the hell? It was only an overnight trip.

Baldur exited the small plane and walked straight onto the runway at the tiny airport in Nuuk and laughed. This was a capital city? It was hard to imagine there was anything up here worth coveting.

******

Siarnaq reached out his hand without thinking. His experiences with Ariel were unique, as far as he knew, so he didn't expected the surge of electricity that left him confused and almost helpless as soon as his fingers were a centimeter away from Baldur's hand. Had he ever been touched by a stun gun, he'd have put the sensation in the same category.

******

Baldur responded to the reach for a handshake without thought. He usually wore gloves, but had removed them once the day turned balmy. He couldn't have been more surprised when a dull low roar vibrated through his body like an earthquake. He fought to keep his balance.

******

The two men eyed each other carefully. "We have to talk."
So they did.

******

Baldur returned home amazed he could have been so naïve. Not only was there a person who saw weeks ahead, there was another who claimed to see through the centuries. Why had these possibilities not occurred to him?

Baldur saw Ariel's gift as useful, but couldn't imagine what good Siarnaq's ability was. What a nuisance to walk around obsessed with the end of the world. No wonder the man seemed a little peculiar.

What mattered with this obsession was that it had led Siarnaq to some crazy crusade to isolate his people. Baldur could've cared less whether the Inuit retained their old ways or not, but Siarnaq's struggle led to a hatred of a cousin Siarnaq wished to stop. Sensibly enough, he'd sought out the man's enemies.

That was excellent because the cousin was none other than the tagalong investor Mikkel.

Baldur supposed Mikkel's money was being funneled into his modernize-the-far-north campaign, which did seem like a colossal waste of resources. Not that humanity hadn't already found endless ways to take perfectly good money and piss it away. Baldur didn't like waste, and he would have thought more of Mikkel if the man were doing something productive with his money, like using it to grow more wealth. But not all humans were as rational as he was.

What mattered now was he knew what Mikkel was up to and he could go after his pet project. Sabotage could drain Mikkel's resources to the point of leaving the man with no need to carry on.

He promised Siarnaq to stay in touch, and to work to bring Mikkel down. Siarnaq, for his part, promised to pass along more information.

Baldur wouldn't go so far as to say they parted as friends, but they'd parted as two men with a common objective. Baldur admitted he felt a little sorry for the guy. What a burden to live with all that doom. Poor man.

******

Siarnaq said farewell to Baldur, amazed he could've been so naïve. Not only was there a person who saw events from her own life, there was another who saw seconds into the future. Why hadn't this possibility occurred to him?

Siarnaq saw Ariel's gift as useful, but couldn't imagine living with Baldur's ability. Maybe it could help you avoid having something fall on your head, but what a nuisance to walk around obsessed with the next few seconds. No wonder the man seemed a little peculiar.

What mattered was this obsession with the immediate had led Baldur to some investment strategy that had become his reason for living. Siarnaq had almost confided in Baldur about his relationship with Ariel, but in the end he held the information back, being vague about how he'd learned of the competition between Baldur and Mikkel. Better to wait and learn more.

The good news was his cousin had become a thorn in Baldur's side, and Baldur was anxious to put a stop to him. Siarnaq didn't care how rich Mikkel got, but if Baldur could stop him from reshaping Greenland by stopping his flow of money, then a good end would be achieved.

He promised Baldur to stay in touch, and to pass along new information. Baldur assured Siarnaq he'd find a way to bring Mikkel down.

Siarnaq wouldn't go so far as to say they parted as friends, but they parted as two men with a common objective. Siarnaq admitted he felt for the guy. To be forced into being so shortsighted all the time. What a burden. Poor man.

13. On a Yacht

Eoin tried to be direct. "Yes, he told me he wanted to take you out on his yacht and get to know you better. Come on Ariel, you're a big girl. He's a big client. Go and be friendly."

"I don't like boats. Could I just have dinner with the man somewhere in town?" Ariel was angry at Eoin for pushing her into this but didn't know how to explain why. Eoin's request for her to spend time with a client was justified.

"He wants you two to enjoy a boat ride together. Look, do you want to bring a friend along? If that's the problem, I'll send Jake, our giant teddy bear, with you, although I'd think at your age and with your looks you've figured out how to say no gracefully."

Ariel considered the idea of bringing Jake. She felt stupid requesting a chaperone. She could take care of herself.

"It's okay. There'll be a whole boat full of people. I'll be fine. Sorry to be a problem, but I'm just not fond of the man."

Eoin gave her a sympathetic look. "I doubt his own mother is fond of him."

In the middle of a misty Saturday afternoon, Ariel arrived for a dinner sail wearing sunglasses, a large hat, and baggy clothing covering every inch of her skin except for her face. Her body language as she strode on deck must have said as much as her clothing, because Baldur greeted her with a raised eyebrow and an "Oh my."

He avoided touching her while he gave her a tour of the boat, keeping doors open and others in sight as he did so. *He's trying to put me at ease. Maybe he isn't such a bad guy.*

Talk was light until they settled into deck chairs and a waiter brought drinks and fancy snacks.

"Word is you like a good mojito." He smiled.

"Yes. I do." She gave him a small smile back.

"Ariel, I'll be honest with you. I manipulate numbers well, but I'm not good with people and my English is not as good as you may think. I'm poor with nuances in Icelandic, and worse in other languages."

She nodded in sympathy. She'd bought software to study Icelandic and gotten through four lessons before she gave up in frustration. She couldn't imagine learning a second language, much less the several managed by many Europeans.

"Besides that, you surprised me and I don't surprise well. Perhaps you understand?"

Ariel did.

"I was drawn to you when I touched you. It was so unexpected that I reacted poorly."

"You told me you wanted to take over the world and use me to do it."

"That's where language and nuance may have been a problem. I wish to make lots of money, but so do all of Ullow's clients. There is nothing evil about that."

"You have an unfair advantage. You sense the future, don't you?"

"Yes, you've learned my secret."

Ariel appreciated hearing the truth.

"High frequency trading gives all your clients an unfair advantage, and you know it, so don't claim high moral ground with me," he said. "What's more, I'm not completely accurate. I make mistakes and I've lost large sums."

"When you touch me, you can see further than you normally do, can't you?"

Baldur nodded. "That's what surprised me so much."

"When you touch me, I see closer in. We interfere with each other's natural frequencies."

"That's a good way to put it." Baldur seemed delighted to hear it explained so well. "From the interference comes new information. What I'm trying to say is if you would work with me, I think I could become better at investing and perhaps train you as well. We'd both benefit. Surely you don't want to work for some company all your life? I could help you get started, even give you some seed capital, and in return you help me be more effective."

Ariel was wary. "I thought you said humans never really helped each other, they just pretended they did." She took the glove off of her right hand with a deliberate motion. It was time to gather information. "Have you developed a higher opinion of humanity over the past couple of months?"

"I misspoke." Her approaching hand was making him nervous. "I think cooperation is possible and you and I could aspire to it."

"Really?" Ariel was having trouble accepting his changed worldview. As her fingers wiggled towards the open V-neck shirt exposing his throat, he took a step back from her.

"Don't touch me!" He said it more sharply than he intended and she looked at him, surprised.

"Why? Is there something in our immediate future you don't want me to see?"

"I'm offering you the chance to be richer than you could ever hope to be. I would think your response would be gratitude and eager acceptance."

"Assuming I want to be very rich, and I'm not sure I do, exactly how would you envision a partnership between us? I'm prohibited from using my company's software to make trades."

He laughed aloud when he heard her concern. "I rather assumed you'd quit your job. That would allow me unlimited access to you, physically, and in return you'd no longer have any ethical constraints."

"So not a partnership, but more of an apprenticeship. Are we talking about a sexual relationship?"

"I don't know. Holding your hand might be as effective as anything, in which case I d ask for nothing more. However, I've developed some theories of my own about how this works. Did you know atoms are almost all space? I read somewhere you could fit the entire human race inside of a sugar cube! So I figure, with all that space, our boundaries are less clear than it appears on a macroscopic scale."

Ariel agreed. "Electrons get shared all the time between atoms. In the subatomic world they jump all over the place and have no sense of belonging to me or you or the chair I am sitting in. They go where they go."

"Exactly! The past is done—where those electrons have been is decided. But the future is possibilities, and because of that I think the fuzziness of the boundaries between me and you matters. When I see the future, my edges aren't so well defined. I touch you, or my keyboard, and there's fluidity."

"You think more skin contact gives better results?"

"It makes sense. I also notice changing the contact area helps. It's like after a while you've exploited all the overlap and if you introduce new surfaces, the information flow stays strong. To answer your question, I'd require sufficient and varied skin contact with you, as I experiment with ways to be more effective with longer term trading. There would need to be some trial and error and you'd have to be open to that."

"So I'd be your girlfriend?" Ariel persisted with the questions. "And your student?"

"Others would likely consider you my girlfriend, yes. What we consider each other is up to us and matters little to me as long as I have access to as much of your body as I need."

She wiggled her fingers towards his neck again. "And I get as much access as I need, too?"

"Of course. It's a mutually beneficial arrangement. It could possibly include pleasure and affection. I understand those are frequent byproducts of intimacy.

This one was a charmer with ladies. "What if one of us tires of the arrangement?"

"We'd revert to the initial terms of teacher and apprentice. When the teacher believes the arrangement is done, the student leaves with new skills and, in this case, money as well. I'd want my seed capital repaid with interest of course, but the profits you make will be yours to keep and they'll likely be considerable."

Ariel knew the next question would be the sticking point.

"What if the student decides she no longer wishes to continue her training?"

Baldur shook his head. "Once a teacher invests a great deal in an apprentice, he's understandably reluctant to have her quit the arrangement too soon. The teacher is expected to be reasonable, however, and to take the needs of the student into account."

"So, if I agree to your proposal, you can send me on my way any time, but as long as I'm making you money, you don't have to let me go anywhere. Do I become your prisoner?"

Baldur considered. He wanted to give her the best answer, because he was starting to get disturbing flashes every time his hand brushed against anything on the boat. It was rare for him to have premonitions about anything but money. These were so faint they were almost unnoticeable until a few minutes ago, but he suspected they were increasing in probability because of the conversation he was having.

"You'll have no reason to be unhappy with the arrangement."

"If I choose to decline your generous offer?"

He noted the sarcasm. "It would be an irrational choice. Don't you want to know what we are capable of together?"

A black fuzziness was beginning to form on the periphery of Ariel's vision, and she felt a little dizzy. Baldur noticed how she steadied herself in her chair.

"I'm sorry Ariel, but I couldn't take the chance of you declining to participate in my experiment today. For my own planning purposes, I must know if this thing between us is effective for investing, and if so, how well it works."

"You put something in my drink?!" Ariel was outraged.

"It's only a mild sedative. You'll be fine. I think you have to be conscious to be of use to me. Now, I'm going help you out of your chair, and remove that terribly ugly jacket you found to wear today. We'll enjoy the sunset while I put my arm around your bare waist and I gather information for both of us. You may not be as useful as I think, in which case we part agreeably. I'll keep your secrets and you keep mine."

That seems like my best hope.

"If it looks like I'm right, however, then you'll come below deck with me and please don't be childish about it. Everyone on this boat works for me. The New York Stock Exchange is open for two more hours. We'll try a few test decisions and see what happens. If it goes well, then we'll face the thorny question of what comes next."

It almost seemed reasonable. Ariel stood up, took off her own jacket, and grabbed Baldur's arm and placed it around her waist, thinking she'd rather get this little experiment over with.

However, as soon as the skin touched, the flash of premory hit her hard. It was an almost certain tilting of the yacht as it made an alarming turn to the right. She saw the boat approach a dangerous list as chairs and people slid across the deck. The image gave Ariel enough warning for her grab onto a rail behind her and be holding on tight when the incident began a second later.

Baldur had already seen the possibility of his boat making an unexplained extreme turn, but when Ariel put his arm on her waist, his mind went straight to the wonders of the weeks ahead and lost its connection with the immediate future. The sudden tilt took him by surprise and he slid between the slats of the outer guardrail and hung over the water yelling for help as he tried to keep his feet out of the icy bay. It was not a dignified experience.

By the time the boat righted itself and an angry Baldur was hauled to safety, two patrol vessels were along side, making sure all was well. A disturbed Ariel accepted their offer for safe transportation back to shore.

The agitated crew thought one of the two local hired hands had been serving as helmsman on the calm bay while the captain tended to other business, but only one of the locals could be found, and he'd been below deck. The crew guessed the other had tried to swim to shore rather than face the consequences of his actions. The police watched for him, but he was never found.

******

Ariel called Zane the next night and she was in a foul mood.

"Tell your friend his worst assumptions about our mutual acquaintance are correct and I need to find a way to tell him more. Zane, you know how you morph your appearance but you don't really want people to know about it?"

"Right. I don't want it to be public knowledge, at any rate, but my close friends all know. Why? Did you tell somebody else?"

"Oh no, nothing like that." Ariel hesitated. "Zane, I have a secret like that, too. Only in my case, nobody knows."

"That isn't healthy," Zane said, worry in his voice.

"Well, two people know now, but they aren't my family and it turns out they aren't my friends either. In fact, these people are both part of my problem. I could be in over my head."

Ariel could feel her brother searching for the right response.

"Can I pass along any sort of request for help for you?"

"Maybe. Tell your friend—tell him the thing he thinks our mutual acquaintance can do—he's right. The guy can do it. But I need you to tell him that I can do it, too. Only differently. I'm sorry, I know this is confusing and not the best way to let your brother in on your troubles. Tell him maybe I should have told him right away but for god's sake I'd never told anybody before and I didn't see at the time how it was going to turn out to be so important."

There was more silence on the other end of the line.

"Ariel, what sort of thing does this mutual acquaintance do exactly?"

Ariel shrugged. She was tired of being paranoid. If Baldur had her phone tapped, he did, and he wasn't going to learn anything new from this conversation.

"He sees the future, Zane. He's a client of mine and he's wreaking havoc in the world of investing, and your friends are worried about the ramifications."

"Oh. That does explain several things. What about you?"

"I also have a way of remembering what could happen, but it's not, like, about things that would help me make money. It's, I don't know, it's mostly a nuisance, but now this head case thinks he can harness what I do to get even richer."

"Should I try to get somebody over to Dublin to get you back to Texas?" The worry in Zane's voice was growing.

"I don't want to overreact. I think I'm okay for now. I just want your friend to have all the facts. I'll find a way to get him Jake's research too and more specifics about my own, uh, abilities. I'll find a way to put the information somewhere out there on the internet where only you can access it and pass it along. All this background in IT, I ought to at least be able to do that."

"Ariel, I know you're not one to ask for help," he said. "But if things get weird, I mean weirder, don't wait too long, okay?"

"I promise I won't."

******

When Ariel called Siarnaq the next night, she was calmer but more determined. Once Siarnaq learned of Baldur's horrible fixation with her, surely he'd back off of his idiotic plan to align with Baldur. However, Ariel didn't get a chance to confide in Siarnaq. He started talking first.

"I'm so glad you called, beautiful sunset lady with sky blue eyes." His good humor and joy at hearing from her were clear. "I've been wanting to call you and share my wonderful news about your client from Iceland. We talked and he's not a bad man at all. He's going to look into the information I gave him. He says putting a stop to Mikkel will solve his problems as well as mine."

"Oh no."

"Aren't you happy for me? You of all people, you've seen the lives that will be because of this alliance. Don't you wish these distant descendants the joys you and I have shared?" When Ariel said nothing, Siarnaq said, "Or perhaps you value them less because they are not going to be people like you."

"That's ridiculous, Siarnaq." Ariel was annoyed at the accusation. "You should understand me better than that. I want you to succeed and I want people, any and all kinds of people, to live on. But this is more complicated. Baldur is using you to accomplish some nasty short-term plans. You don't want to be helping him."

"I doubt that's true, or you would have seen scenarios in which he causes harm. Have you?"

"No but I don't see everything. I can't touch him like a normal person and get information. He's got some variation of what you and I have." Ariel wasn't sure how far she wanted to go with this line of thought.

"I know this already!" Siarnaq's voice was filled with excitement again. "We discovered it when we met. It is one of the reasons I trust him. I do not think those who can see ahead do harm to others lightly. They know the consequences."

"Did you two spend much time in contact?"

"We could barely touch. It was painful when we did. I think it's because what he and I are is so different it can't be melded like it can between me and you. But we both felt each other's power."

Well, he and I *can* meld," Ariel said. "He was aggressive about trying it with me, and he made it clear he intended to gain my cooperation."

"So cooperate with him. This man is on our side."

"This man is on no one's side but his own," Ariel answered in frustration. "He wants to stop Mikkel from making money so he can make more, god only knows why. He's totally selfish and I can't believe you are so naïve you can't see that."

"You suspect anyone who didn't grow up in your sophisticated society is naive, don't you?" Siarnaq shot back. "This man is my ally. If you're my friend, you'll help him."

"Then I guess I'm not your friend, because I sure as hell don't intend to help him."

Her goodbye was as cold as Greenland had been when she and Siarnaq first met.

14. A Stupid Virus

Over the next week, a disgruntled Ariel spent her free time figuring out the best way to send information to Toby. She'd walked away from Siarnaq, a man with whom she had a unique relationship, in part because of Toby's assurances Baldur was hell-bent on taking over the world's economy.

She'd heard nothing from Siarnaq since she bade him a cold goodbye a week ago, and she missed their ongoing dialog. In spite of her irritation, she worried about him. She was pretty sure any collaboration with Baldur only ended well for Baldur.

On a whim, she typed d^4 into her search engine to see if it had some secret meaning. Up came products and a few links to the Icelandic investment company. She tried the calculus notation d^4/dt instead, and found what had to be the meaning of the name.

d^4/dt is short for the fourth derivative of where you are versus where you'll be. The first derivation is your speed and direction, and the second is how fast you're speeding up or slowing down. Most people know about these two. The third is how fast you change how fast you're speeding up. It's called jerk, and if you have too much of it, you probably puke. So jerk matters.

The fourth derivative is called snap and it's beyond human detection. People don't know it exists. They don't care, either. It's change under the radar. Baldur and his plans.

Ariel was glad she'd hadn't heard from Baldur since a patrol boat took her back to Dun Laoghaire Marina a week ago. She'd had time to ponder whether she was exaggerating how much of a threat Baldur was.

He'd drugged her, but assured her it was a mild sedative. He told her he was awkward in her language. Did he sound like a creep because of bad social skills and poor word choice? Doubtful, but she kept playing the conversations over in her mind.

Eoin was out sick all week with a nasty flu he caught from his kids, and she'd taken the opportunity to fill up her thumb drive with documentation from Jake about his study on Baldur. She looked it over. Jake was right. He'd proven Baldur had minute-to-minute insider information on entire market sectors.

She began putting together her own information for Toby. It ended up with bullet points about her own premories since childhood, her experiences with Siarnaq, Siarnaq's quest to prolong humanity's survival, his hatred for Mikkel, Siarnaq's new allegiance with Baldur, and finally Baldur's threats and/or offer of collaboration with her. Oh wait. At the last minute she went ahead and added in Nell's information on Cillian's alleged powers of distant prophesy, and her own premonitions of Nell as other people.

Zane was right; it had probably been therapeutic to write it down. It did read a little like the script for a bad comic book series, but she sent it on to Toby anyway. He could believe her or not, and do with the information as he saw fit. At least someone out there would know everything about the situation.

Now that she thought about it, she felt a little weak and feverish herself. Surely she wasn't coming down with what Eoin had. Getting sick was the last thing she needed.

Ariel spent the weekend in bed. Her mom video-called Sunday afternoon to check on her, apologizing that she kept picking up general misery from her daughter and was getting worried. Ariel made a concerted effort to think about anyone but Baldur and Siarnaq while she assured her mother it was only a virus, and she'd see a doctor if she didn't get better soon.

Her mom played along, chatting about life in Texas and how hot it was already and how her magazine article would get published next month and she was so excited. As the conversation wore down, her mother began to fidget.

"I'm not sure how to say this, honey. I can't tell what you're trying so hard not to think about, but I *can* tell that's what you're doing. I know you're capable and independent so I'm not going to pry."

"Good," Ariel said, but of course her mom hadn't finished.

"Please understand we all need help sometimes. If you get in over your head, I've got resources. Some of them live near you and would be happy to back you up."

Ariel hadn't thought of that. There *was* the old guy from London with the canoe paddle. Actually, between Mom and Teddie, there were quite a few others with skills that could be useful against an evil tyrant trying to take over the world. The ladies in her family did have connections.

"You're right, mom. I'm not in a situation where I have to call for help, but I promise if things go there, I'll yell. Thanks for offering."

By Monday morning her fever hadn't broken and she called in sick, and by Tuesday she started looking for healthcare options in a foreign country. By afternoon she was in a crowded clinic waiting room, eying two dozen other sick people who sat next to her sneezing and wiping their noses.

"This is insane," Ariel told the busy middle-aged Irish woman who was her new doctor. "I can fling a hundred gigabytes of data around the globe, have text translated into over two hundred languages as I read it, and pull up satellite photos of your parking lot on my cell phone. Why the hell can't we wipe out the flu?"

The woman laughed. "Because it's more difficult than the stuff you're describing. You don't fight anything, your machines cooperate. Well, at least they have so far." When Ariel raised an eyebrow the doctor laughed again. "Don't mind me, I read too much science fiction. When I'm not reading, I do battle with an enemy with the sense to keep changing and the foresight *not* to destroy its habitat. I can't say as much for the human race."

"Wait, we are talking about a virus here, right?"

"We definitely are. If a virus doesn't adapt, we *can* eradicate it. We say the virus is mutating, kind of a pejorative term, actually. The poor thing is just trying to exist as long as it can. It's the prime directive of life."

Ariel sniffed to hold back a sneeze. "I never looked at it from the virus's point of view."

"Well, looking at it like a virus, we're big lumbering habitats it has to keep alive to survive. Good thing, too. You get a stupid virus like Ebola, and it kills off its host before gets to a new one. Dumb, dumb, dumb."

"So a smart virus causes mild symptoms, so its habitat will go out and launch it everywhere?"

"That's right, but you need to be sneezing and coughing to launch it. The one you've got isn't a genius because it made you sick enough to stay home. I'll prescribe some drugs to make you feel better and you'll be out spreading it everywhere by morning." She gave a wink. "I'm a virus's best friend."

"You're mine, too, if you can make me feel better,"

Ariel was back in the office Wednesday, and a still sick-looking Eoin sought her out early in the day.

"You're back. Good. Baldur came down sick last week, but he called to convey his disappointment your outing ending so poorly. They never caught the lad who sabotaged your ride. The police are blaming it on some fringe Irish independence group that tries to scare off foreign money." Eoin shook his head. "So many kinds of idiots out there."

Ariel nodded without comment.

"He wants to try for another get-together. The man is determined to get to know you better. But relax. He's not only invited me this time, he s gone so far as to invite our other two Dublin-based clients. Sort of the walrus hunt idea you had back when."

"I wasn't going to hunt walruses," Ariel said. "Isn't this out of character for Baldur? Friendly and generous all at once?"

Eoin considered. "Yeah, it is. Maybe he's smitten with you?"

"I don't think so."

"Offer another explanation. You can hardly say no under the circumstances. He's hosting a day at Iceland's famous Blue Lagoon geothermal spa, which is one of the most amazing things in that country. A Friday in two weeks. He's reserved an exclusive lounge for us for the whole afternoon, and then dinner in their famous LAVA restaurant built into the side of a cliff. You can fly home the next morning or stay on and sightsee for the weekend. I'm thinking of having the missus come over on Saturday if she can get her mum to watch the kids."

Once Ariel sighed in resignation, he couldn't resist adding, "Do they wear clothes at that spa or not? You never know with those Scandinavians." Then seeing her pained expression, he laughed. "Don't worry. I checked. Swimsuits are required, and they'll let you wear a burqini." Eoin couldn't resist giving Ariel a wink. "I hear that some of those burqinis are kind of cute, if you want to go that route."

Ariel glared at him as he continued to chuckle.

"Wear what you fooking like, Zeitman, but clear your calendar for the trip. Your presence is required."

Ariel had options. The most obvious was to do her job, go to Iceland, have a good time, and let Baldur get his answer about how much use she could be to him. It was a sensible option because it didn't involve overreacting and making a situation worse. It made sense for any woman who didn't see her own future.

Only a fool would take such a chance, however, when touching items on her desk related to Baldur produced faint premories that were all over the place. Somewhere out there was a future where Ariel and Baldur became lovers in Iceland. In some scenarios, he destroyed her in months. In other futures, they ruled the world together like despots, their greed growing like a tumor. Alternatives existed in which she killed him when she had the chance.

Other futures spoke of Ariel locked away, kept barely alive and used by all of d^4. In the worst of those, they used her not only for the touch of her skin but any other way they saw fit. Alternatives existed in which she killed herself before it could go on any longer.

Some possibilities were less dire. Baldur could find her to be useless. In some scenarios, he didn't get his answers as their game of cat and mouse wore on past when Ariel could see. Some alternatives had her pacifying him for months, aiding him a little to keep him at bay. It was clear this had many ways to go, and some were bad. She concentrated on various responses, struggling to weave her way through the filmy threads created when she focused on different choices.

Inaction on her part now made the worst alternatives brighter. Doing anything at all dimmed them. Excellent. For once this damn gift was of some use. So what action did the best job of bringing the best outcomes to the forefront?

Talking to Cillian. How odd. That one had been low on her list. She was curious about how foresight worked for a true prophet who saw ahead a millennium, but Nell had said Cillian didn't like to talk about it. Ariel understood.

Cillian also didn't know what Ariel could do, or what Baldur could do, or what kind of danger the two of them could produce together. She doubted their little events affected the big things he saw, but maybe not. The man should be told.

As a courtesy, she'd email Eoin that she was setting up a meeting with Cillian. As she turned to her computer, the images began to morph and darker outcomes began to grow. It was the whirling, dizzy sensation she got when probabilities shifted. She froze.

For some reason, including Eoin was a poor choice. What about Nell? That seemed neutral. She thought about asking Brendan if he had anything scheduled with Cillian soon. Maybe she could piggyback onto his meeting?

Dizzy twirling took over. It seemed things were best with Brendan. Decision making 101. She picked up her phone. "Brendan? You got a moment?"

Cillian was happy to make time for her, if she'd travel to his place. With light in the sky till ten now, she didn't mind driving an hour for a late meal and was even happier when Brendan offered to take his car.

Cillian greeted them with his brown hair still wet from the shower. Conversation focused on business while drinks and appetizers appeared.

"Let's walk through the gardens," Cillian said, and Ariel assumed the man didn't trust the household help. Perhaps one or more reported back to Mr. McGrane on his good days?"

Once the three of them were far from the house, Cillian's tone changed. "Nell says you either accepted what she said or pretended you did. You know I don't like to talk to about this, but she told you to come forth if you had questions. So something is bothering you."

The breeze and the mist in the air had worked together to churn Brendan's bright hair into a froth of butterscotch, but underneath it, his serious face nodded like this all made perfect sense. Ariel guessed he was in the loop. Of course he was.

Ariel opened her mouth and then had a better idea. Hadn't Siarnaq told her he and Baldur felt each other's psychic abilities when their hands were close? She reached out her arm and placed the inside of her right wrist against Cillian's bare arm. He jumped back and yelled like he'd been burned.

"I'm sorry, I'm so sorry," Ariel said holding her own arm in pain as the slow throbbing began to subside. "I had no idea it would be so strong."

"What are you?" he asked in horror.

"I'm like you. But different. You need to know. Let me explain."

An hour later their drinks and appetizers were long gone and Ariel was sure the staff was waiting to serve dinner. Ariel had described everything from learning about her gift as a child up to her odd reaction at being offered the job in Dublin, and the amazing experiences she had with Siarnaq.

Cillian and Brendan encouraged her, offering few opinions and asking few questions. It was clear Brendan was more than a programmer; he spoke like he was Cillian's confidant and friend.

"We thought someone like you couldn't exist," Cillian said once Ariel had finished. "We've known about Baldur for a while. His high frequency foresight isn't that uncommon really; people who have it often don't fully notice it. A second before the phone rings they know who it is, a second before the song comes on the radio they know what's coming. That kind of thing. For some reason Baldur developed his ability as a child, and early practice strengthens any talent."

"Why don't more people use it like he does?"

"Well, the small percentage who even recognize their gift usually lack the resources and training to use it on the stock market. Baldur is a confluence of events, and now he's found and trained a small group like him. They've all gotten good at using their skills online. In a world without electronic stock exchanges, he's just someone who can avoid a punch better than most. In this world, he's a problem."

"He wants to use me to become more of one," Ariel said. "He's being helped by the one man who knows too much about what I can do. Why did I sleep with Siarnaq?"

S. R. Cronin

Cillian smile was gentle. "I don't throw stones. Foresight makes it harder to connect; we take the opportunities we get. I do already know about Siarnaq's talents, by the way."

"How would you know of him?"

Brendan answered. "Cillian sees the effects of Siarnaq far down the road. What he's trying to do could matter."

"He could succeed?"

"He could. In some scenarios his name is remembered."

"You've seen him become famous?" Ariel was happier at this news than she expected.

"I have. Ariel, before the entire kitchen empties out to find us, I need to tell you two things. Three actually, but I think you've guessed the third, which is we don't speak of this once we are back in the house."

"Of course."

"Good. Another is that while people with Baldur's skill aren't uncommon, history has also produced a fair number of prophets, like Siarnaq and myself, who see far ahead. Of course it's also produced a lot of charlatans who claimed they could. However, nobody thinks you could happen. What with the myriad of possibilities and the emotional burden of seeing those probabilities evolve in one's own life, well, we guessed nature would block out your frequencies, like a notch filter. You're rare, and possibly unique. We need to look out for you."

"There you are," a flustered woman's voice came from the other side of the hedge. "The roast is nearly ruined, Mr. McGrane. Please do come inside and let us serve you dinner."

"We're on our way, Maeve." As the threesome made their way around the shrubbery, he whispered to Ariel. "The last thing I wanted to say was that we've got your back at this Blue Lagoon thing in Iceland."

"You're going?"

"Are you kidding? Given the guest list, Nell, Brendan and I wouldn't miss it."

******

Mikkel didn't want to waste two days in Iceland at a spa. He was overwhelmed with the amount of work he had to do, even though he knew he needed some playtime. He'd once loved hiking, skiing, climbing, and relaxing with a few cold beers afterwards. He wondered sometimes what happened to the young man who enjoyed the outdoors. He hardly left his computer screen now.

There had also been a day when he enjoyed his work. He'd sped through a Ph.D. program, powered by his love of the subject. How could anyone not be fascinated by learning to fly through the air, or by figuring out how to hurl things into space? The young boy who stared at the never-ending night sky of winter wanted nothing more than to fly to the stars.

Only now that man was tired. The hours were long, and managing people was not his forte. He wasn't well suited to all the hand-holding and encouraging it seemed to take to get people to work together.

He needed to be at this shindig in Iceland. He, Baldur and Cillian were linked together, three men dragging each other along in a bizarre sack race with the fate of the human race at stake. The innocent software company Ullow served as the sack binding them together. Mikkel shook his head. How in the hell had he gotten into this mess?

He thought of the guest list. The young American woman, Ariel, would certainly be there. Eager and curious, she'd been the last thing this situation needed. Eoin should send her back to London before she managed to really muck things up.

Yet, the mental image of spending two days in a spa with Ariel, with her bikini clad body possibly sitting next to him, brought him a certain amount of unexpected pleasure. *Oh good grief.* He supposed it had been too long since he'd had any of *that* sort of relaxation either.

Stop it. Lusting after business contacts is a bad idea. In this case, it's an awful one.

Which brought to mind the obvious question. What sort of game was Baldur playing? Socializing was not a tool in the man's arsenal; so why this? The image of Baldur sitting next to Ariel in a hot tub, telling her stories while she listened in fascination, disturbed Mikkel, and he scolded himself again.

Don't let this competition thing take over your brain. The young lady is not a prize to fight over, she is person who needs to go home before she gets hurt.

Mikkel puzzled over that last thought. He thought he wanted Ariel gone so she wouldn't dig into his affairs and cause problems. Could it be he was also worried for her safety? He supposed so.

He went back to what he'd been reviewing. Numbers flashed on his screen as he scrolled, and yet he couldn't get rid of the mental image of a certain support engineer wearing a swimsuit far skimpier than any real woman would wear on a business outing.

What did they call those things? Thongs? He gave himself a mental head slap and went back to his numbers.

July 2012

15. The Blue Lagoon

Toby didn't surprise easily. He'd come across his share of oddities, not the least of which was Zane Zeitman. Zane's ability to change the shape of his body and the look of his face was nothing short of remarkable. If he had the right wig and clothing, he could resemble any one.

Toby considered Ariel's story about remembering events from the future. A shape-shifting brother with a clairvoyant sister? Had these kids grown up next to a radioactive waste dump? He supposed Ariel could be making the whole thing up, driven by childhood competition with her brother, but from what he knew of the young woman, he doubted it.

She'd written him from her heart, telling him stories she probably had never shared with anyone. He'd read of little Ariel sorting knowledge in her brain into memories and premories, like a child in a bilingual household learning to separate words into two languages.

She'd told him of her encounter with the Inuit man and how his prophetic abilities had merged with hers. Toby read of the man's quest to isolate the people of Northern Greenland. Toby was fascinated by Mikkel, a former aeronautics professor now doing something secretive. He'd earned the Inuit man's hatred, forging an alliance between the Inuit and an Icelandic investor named Baldur. That brought the whole mess squarely into Toby's world.

Baldur's threats to Ariel, or at least his determination to use her skills to amass more wealth, had bad implications for the young woman and the world economy. Casinos in Vegas threw out gamblers who could count cards well. They had no qualms about doing so.

Were stock exchanges capable of accepting that investors could gain a similar advantage by using a psychic ability most people would scoff at? Toby was guessing Baldur could do a lot of damage before anyone believed the possibility enough to put regulations in place.

If Baldur was smart, and Toby was sure he was, Baldur would move slow enough not to set off alarms and quick enough to become a force of his own before anyone could prove anything. Ariel would make him faster, and more difficult to stop.

Toby didn't know what to make of the prophet Cillian and his dire predictions. That part of Ariel's narrative struck him as far-fetched, conjuring up images of bearded men in rags holding up signs saying "The end is near." Toby admitted thinking a thousand years ahead wasn't his strong suit.

Plus, the present held plenty of its own problems. y[1] had watched Baldur long enough to be sure he was a crisis in the making, and Ariel had confirmed their suspicions and added more urgency. They needed a plan for stopping Baldur now.

******

Ariel was surprised at how hard her heart pounded when she saw the incoming call was from Siarnaq.

"Hello, pretty sunset hair," he greeted her like they'd never quarreled. "We shouldn't be strangers."

"No, we shouldn't," she agreed, searching for a neutral follow up. "How are things for you?"

"Pretty good. I know you don't want to hear more, unless you've changed your mind about the means I'm using. I called only to see if you're okay, and to tell you I remain your friend, no matter what."

"Thanks, Siarnaq. I appreciate that. I'm your friend too. I still don't think much of your new partner, though, and I worry you've made an alliance with a snake."

"A snake. That's some sort of tropical reptile, right?"

Ariel thought he was joking, then it dawned on her Greenland may not have snakes. "It's an animal with a reputation for biting others, even those who help it. It means someone you can't trust."

"I see."

A few seconds of silence followed. Ariel said, "I'll be at a company event next week in Iceland, spending a day in Baldur's company. Because of my job, I have to be nice. I'll try to think better of the man and give him the benefit of the doubt."

"This I would appreciate. At least use your open mind, not your closed one. Already he's doing my cause so much good."

That's another problem. "You know, if he bankrupts one of my clients, that's not good for me either."

"Perhaps this other client, the real snake, will wise up and put his money elsewhere, given all the troubles he now has."

"Lots of problems, huh?"

"Baldur is good at creating trouble," Siarnaq said. "It will only get worse. Can you advise Mikkel to move on to other interests?"

"I don't tell my clients what to do with their money. My job is to help them make the stuff, and lots of it."

"I see. Well then, I will simply hope you and Baldur have a *very* nice time next week." Something about the way he said *very* made Ariel's skin crawl.

"Surely you're not hoping I jump into bed with him?"

"He's mentioned to me that if you two worked together, he could be more effective. I wish him to be as effective as he can."

"You don't care what our working together entails?" She knew it was an unreasonable question. She and Siarnaq had made no promises. Hell, they hadn't even spoken in a month.

"This man is my ally. If you're my friend, you'll help him anyway you can."

"I'm not *that* much of a friend." As Ariel disconnected the call, she realized this was pretty much how their last conversation ended, too.

The trip from the airport to the spa was less than half an hour by limo. The Ullow group consisted of Ariel, Eoin, Brendan, and Jake, traveling together. Cillian and Nell would arrive later by chartered jet.

Jake and Eoin were checking out the bar in the limo, acting like college kids pretending to be movie stars. Brendan was lost in his own thoughts, and, judging from the look in his eyes, he was worried. He and Ariel would both be flying back in the morning, while Jake and Eoin were making a holiday of the outing.

Ariel knew the less time she spent in Iceland the better. It was a shame, because the country was gorgeous and the people outside of Baldur's boardroom were welcoming.

When they arrived, they were taken to an ultramodern lounge to shower privately and change. Ariel studied the famous murky turquoise water as they walked, and the combinations of blues and greens in the mist created a feeling of wonder. She marveled at the small geysers shooting into the air and at the sheer size of the stunning lagoon.

She'd already been told there'd be a catered lunch, time to relax in the healing waters, and individual spa treatments before the group headed to a lavish dinner. Under other circumstances, this would have been the best day at work ever.

Bloody Marys and pretty little snacks greeted them, along with Ulfur and his apologies that Baldur had been detained and would arrive later. Several board members were already enjoying the private lagoon, and he suggested the Ullow group join them.

Ariel headed off to the mandatory shower, her most business friendly one-piece in hand. She'd just stepped under the hot water, eyes closed as let her muscles relax after travel, when her skin jumped. The touch was electric and familiar. She opened her eyes to see Baldur's arms circling her from behind, his right hand moving up to cover her mouth.

"Don't scream. You'll embarrass us both. Hold still and let me concentrate. I'm not going to hurt you. I just want information."

Ariel turned enough to see Baldur had on swim trunks, and true to his word he kept his arms and hands at her waist, leaving her bare breasts alone. His eyes were closed. He pressed his entire body hard against her back. Although he had the expected response to holding a naked woman in a shower, he made no move to do anything about it.

She was annoyed he'd chosen to run his little experiment while she had no clothes on, and she considered several moves she'd learned in self-defense classes. Coming down hard on his instep with her heel seemed like her best bet. Oddly enough, his touch gave her the ability to see how effective that and other moves would be. She hesitated.

There wasn't much she could do about being naked, so why not gather intel of her own? If her experiences with Siarnaq were a guide, Baldur was now seeing weeks ahead. He'd be getting flickers of the information he was most used to handling. She bet he was seeing fluctuations in stock prices.

She, on the other hand, wasn't a helpless woman. For all Baldur took, he couldn't help but give back to her as well. Touching him, she saw the near future. She saw him walking out of the stall in less than a minute, with no harm done. He'd be silent, too engrossed in trying to remember the information to apologize, thank or threaten. It was the most likely and the least messy alternative.

As she realized that, it became a near certainty. Then the wave of time washed over the moment and the soon-to-happen became the now and it then it became the past. Ariel found herself standing alone and naked in a shower stall. She reached for her towel.

******

Mikkel arrived at the Blue Lagoon a little after 3 p.m. The last reports from Peary Land had been so bleak, he'd almost changed his mind. In the snow-free desert north of Greenland, where the daylight lasted twenty-four-hours well into August, this should have been the most productive time of the year for his project. But problem after problem plagued the operation. Insufficient or poorly made materials arrived. Workers quit unexpectedly. Everything was going wrong. The situation cried out for him to get up there and find out what the difficulty was.

He suspected sabotage, but for the life of him he couldn't imagine why. He'd come to Iceland figuring if something other than a string of bad luck was occurring, there could be more information at this little fluff of an outing than in the middle of his assembly room floor.

It was possible Baldur was annoyed at him for piggybacking on his success, but everything about Baldur indicated he was logical and obsessed with making money. He was making plenty of it, so why waste profits to stop another man from doing well? Perhaps there was an illogical side to Baldur. If they met, maybe Mikkel could tell more.

Plus, this outing would give him a chance to see Cillian, and it had been too long since he and Cillian had talked. Maybe they could find a way to have a private word or two. If he told Cillian about the suspected sabotage, Cillian might have some ideas.

Mikkel accepted a cold beer from an attendant in the private suite, and decided on a short soak in the healing waters before he tackled any difficult issues. He was told Baldur hadn't arrived but others from d^4 were outside enjoying the amenities and looking forward to greeting him.

A few more questions established that Cillian and his girlfriend were having a private couple's massage and two people from Ullow were out in the lagoon somewhere. The redheaded woman was getting ready for a facial and one of the men from Ullow was in the sauna. Cocktails were being served at five, so would he please be kind enough to return by then.

******

Ariel had no idea if Baldur learned all he wanted, or what his next move would be. She looked for a quiet spot in the lagoon where she could regroup. As her body sank into the thick warm water, she was amazed at the strength of its calming influence even under the circumstances.

Minutes later the Icelandic woman on the d^4 board waved to her through the mist. Ariel considered ducking under water to hide, but it was too late. The woman was making her way over.

"There you are." She spoke in a heavy Icelandic accent.

"I was going to close my eyes for a few minutes." Ariel intended to ask the woman to leave.

"Oh, I can't let you do that. You and I have a facial and algae wrap scheduled. Baldur thought us women might enjoy that. If he'd known the man from Ireland was going to bring his girlfriend along, he'd have scheduled one for her, too. I don't understand people assuming they can bring a guest without asking."

"I suspect Cillian is used to doing what he wants without asking permission."

"That's what Baldur thought, too," the woman said.

Ariel got out of the water and followed the lady through the cool breeze into one of the many small, windowless rooms used for spa treatments. As she stepped into the room, it occurred to her. The comment about what Baldur thought meant the woman had talked to Baldur in the last hour or so.

There were no attendants in the room, only Baldur and two older men sitting in front of three computer screens arranged around a single treatment bed. They were all typing away.

"Thanks Gróa," Baldur said without looking up from his screen. "Stay if you like."

"No, that's fine." Gróa left with a wave.

"Lie down," Baldur told Ariel, pointing towards the thin massage cot, without even looking up as he said it.

"Shit no." Ariel turned to follow Gróa out, but the door had shut and, of course, it was locked. The two men who stepped out of the shadows looked like hired muscle, and they had bulk and surprise working in their favor. Ariel was strapped to the table in under a minute, in spite of her attempts to use every self-defense move she knew.

"You want us to stay?" one of them asked Baldur, rubbing his Adam's apple where Ariel had landed a painful punch.

"No, wait outside, but don't go far. We need to keep her alert, so she could be trouble."

"Yeah, this one's a fighter," the other one added. He'd taken a knee to his groin, but Ariel hadn't gotten enough force or aim to make it as damaging as it should have been. "We'll stay close."

Ariel tried to breathe calmly and clear her head as she determined what parts of her were restrained. What did she have to bargain with? They needed her conscious, but did they need her to cooperate? Perhaps they didn't know.

"Don't you think we should remove her clothes?" the older of the two men asked. She hadn't met him before, and he spoke with a British accent. While the front of her brain jumped in fear at his question, some distant part reasoned he was why everyone was talking in English.

"No," Baldur said, with a firmness that quelled Ariel's rising panic. "There's plenty of skin there, and no one needs that distraction. Do what I said earlier. Get information. Buy and sell futures; buy and sell options. We need lots of them, but make sure each has a high probability. I know for a fact she's never certain about what she sees, so we need lots of trades. We get one chance to test this out. Let's make it count."

The other older man ran his hand up the inside of her bare thigh and smiled. Ariel's considered spitting in his face.

"Don't waste time, Valdi," Baldur said. "Gróa will be back for an algae wrap in thirty minutes. So focus."

So that was his plan? He'd segue this bizarre experiment into a spa treatment and pretend like it never happened? Like hell he would.

She pushed against the plastic ties binding her hands and feet, trying to work any of them loose while the three men ran their left hands absently over her body and their right hands typed orders onto a screen. In minutes all three were in trancelike state, not noticing when a hand grazed the top of her boob, and moving their fingers off her swimsuit whenever they touched it.

Flickers of their precollections made their way to Ariel. Her mind was filled with the Brit looking into commodities, and thigh man going to small cap companies and emerging markets. Baldur was moving on to complicated option strategies. She supposed she was getting this information because there was no other kind to get. That was good news; it meant the men posed no threat to her.

She wondered if they were getting anything from her besides stock information. She generally learned about family and friends, dating, clothes, her job, things that mattered to her. She didn't get sports scores or investment advice. She'd never wanted it.

Was there a sort of muscle memory involved? It was the human brain after all, and a mind tended to do what it was used to doing. These men all spent much of their time investing online.

Ariel studied the faces of her captors, each illuminated by the glow of his own backlit screen. They looked only part human as they typed, willingly becoming nothing more than organic interfaces between her premories and the machine that could turn what she knew into gold.

I'm Rumpelstiltskin. No, wait, I think I'm more like the straw. Or the spinning wheel. I guess it doesn't matter because those stories never end well for anyone, do they?

A faint chime began to sound. "Two minutes," Baldur said without looking up.

"Finishing now," Valdi said.

"I'm out," the Brit added and his screen turned dim.

Baldur finally looked at her.

"It'll be weeks before we see the results of today's work. I'm not used to having such patience, but I will, because the potential rewards are enormous. Thank you for your help, begrudging though it was. Now relax, and have a nice spa treatment."

He waved something in front of her nose and she felt dizzy, then groggy, then sleepy.

She woke up and still couldn't move. She could feel the plastic restraints gone from her wrists and ankles, which was great, but now her arms were held tight and useless at her sides with her body completely encased in some kind of body cast. What the hell? Her eyes flashed open but she was blindfolded too. Shit. She tried to scream but her whole face was held immobile by what felt like glue. They had buried her in something? They were going to kill her? Why?

She squirmed in panic, and heard a reassuring woman's voice speak in Icelandic.

"I think she only speaks English." This second voice sounded like Gróa.

"You're awake," the pleasant voice said in English, as Ariel watched two slices of cucumber being lifted off her eyes. "They help so much with the little fine lines," her beauty therapist added. Ariel looked down at her body. She was wrapped in a cocoon of gauze, and coated in a thick casing of mud. The same mud appeared to coat her face, and Gróa was covered in it too.

"I'll get this off of your face so you can talk," the woman said, reaching for a warm washcloth. "I think I used too much aromatherapy on you at the beginning. You got woozy, started saying a lot of odd things. I was worried we'd have to stop the treatment."

"Your skin looks prettier now," Gróa said. "I hope you didn't have bad dreams."

So that's how they were going to play it. Ariel was pissed. The beauty therapist had to be in on it too, otherwise Baldur couldn't have pulled off the switch.

"Fuck you both," she said.

"I'm sorry, I don't understand English so well," the therapist replied as she moved on to sponging the mud off of Ariel's legs.

"I think you're recovering from the reaction to, what was it again? Lavender and peppermint. Perhaps you should avoid those two when used together, yes?" Gróa said.

"I have no problem with lavender or peppermint. I have a problem with lying assholes."

The therapist looked at Gróa and Gróa nodded. "Perhaps I need to keep you here longer? For your own safety, until you calm down?"

Right. She had to calm down to get out of here.

"That won't be necessary. I'm feeling calmer by the minute."

"If that's the case, once she gets you cleaned up, you run along," Gróa said. "They need an incident report about your reaction to the aromatherapy, but don't worry, I'll fill it out. You just sign the blank form before you go."

"Take it easy this evening while you enjoy dinner," the therapist added.

"Trust me. I'm going to be really careful for the rest of my visit."

16. Plenty of Daylight

"Of course you're not making this up," Nell said. She sat on the edge of the lavish bed in the suite she was sharing with Cillian. Brendan was pouring Ariel a cold beer to calm her nerves.

"A shot of good whiskey would do her better," Cillian said.

"Didn't bring any. She'll have to calm down with this."

"I'm calm already. Really, I'm fine. It was creepy, but they didn't harm me. Waking up in that damn algae wrap was the worst part. Now I'm just pissed they got away with it."

How about telling Eoin?" Nell said. "He should know what happened."

Ariel held still a minute and tried to premember. "There's something odd about Eoin. If he shows up in my premories, it's always to make matters worse. My guess is his loyalties lie with Baldur, which is sad."

Brendan shook his head. "I don't believe that. Eoin cares about his job, but he's not willing to see you harmed."

Ariel shrugged. "Maybe not, but what do I say to him? 'By the way, did I mention I'm clairvoyant?'"

Cillian agreed. "We're better off keeping the cards closer to our chest. I say we get ready for dinner, and all show up looking marvelous. Ariel, until you get on the plane home, Nell goes with you everywhere. She's a resourceful body guard."

"No. They've no reason to bother me any more. I'll need Nell's services in a couple of months when those options expire."

"You'll have them then, too," Nell said. "Tonight, we keep an eye on you in case someone remembers an investment category they didn't try and wants a repeat feel session. You've had enough trauma; you deserve a sound night's rest."

Ariel decided to accept the help and say thanks. A good sleep sounded wonderful.

Ariel opted for the squash soup. She sat alone at the end of the table, enjoying the hot puree and marveling at how soup was always soothing, no matter how humble or fancy.

The rest of the guests were mingling as they nibbled on appetizers. Ariel watched Baldur make his rounds, greeting everyone with apologies for having been detained in Reykjavik. She guessed he'd greet her last and put on his most effervescent show, daring her to counter him. It would be a victory lap, making her play along, and she was looking for a way to avoid giving him the satisfaction.

She was also studying the membership of d^4. Eight of the ten board members were there. She'd already met the four from Iceland. Gróa was the only woman in that group, and Valdi appeared to be their leader. Both halves of a Lithuania couple were members, and they and a younger Japanese man chatted.

True to her word, Nell was never more than ten feet from her. As Baldur moved away from Eoin, Ariel turned to Nell to start a conversation. She was surprised when Mikkel stepped in and asked if he could join her.

They'd only met once months ago, and hadn't spoken since their less-than-friendly phone conversation after Ariel's trip to Greenland. Work updates were handled by terse emails, and Ariel expected to have nothing to do with Mikkel here other than to exchange a polite hello.

"Of course. Please have a seat." So now was the time for the hello.

"I've been wanting to talk with you." His manner was cordial, even perhaps apologetic "You've been doing a fine job. I should have been glad to have you on the team from the start. Sometimes I don't adjust well to changes."

Even at a business function, Mikkel sported an outdoorsy look in his grooming and his clothes. His light brown hair was too long to be stylish and too short for a ponytail. His beard and moustache were well trimmed, but they made it hard to read his facial expressions underneath.

"It's not my strong suit either," Ariel said. "We talked about that last April." She let a few seconds pass.

"Yes, well, since I met you I seem to be acquiring enemies faster than I can deal with them. Making more on my own is a poor plan."

"I'm not your enemy," Ariel said, as Siarnaq's quest to stop Mikkel jumped into her mind. She pushed the thought of Siarnaq away. She'd severed all loyalties there; she had no reason to feel guilty about a conversation with a man Siarnaq disliked.

"I was hoping to elevate our business relationship to slightly better than 'I don't hate you,'" Mikkel said. "What I'm trying to say is I could use..." he searched for the word. "I could use your buy-in on what I'm trying to accomplish."

Ariel noticed Baldur had glanced her way twice, looking for his chance to greet her but not wanting to approach until Mikkel moved on. How convenient.

"Please, tell me more," she said.

"Would you take a walk out to the deck before the main course arrives?"

"I'd love to. Let's just pass by Baldur, so I can give him a wave hello as we go by."

******

Cillian had never met Baldur before, and he was surprised. The man was younger than he expected, and somehow more fragile. There was an intensity in his light blue eyes that made Cillian think of a candle burning too brightly, exhausting itself before its time. He was also quite slender, giving Cillian the impression he'd blow over in a strong wind.

Cillian remembered how painful touching Ariel had been and was glad his hands were full when he and Baldur met, so he didn't have to shake the man's hand. Cillian could have sworn he felt a faint buzz of electricity even standing near him.

******

Ariel's baked cod topped with langoustines was almost cold by the time she and Mikkel came back inside, and Baldur's refusal to look their way told her how miffed he was at having his fancy dinner snubbed and showy welcome spoiled. She enjoyed irritating the man who'd caused her such fear. Better than that, she sat down to dinner with a better understanding of her most mysterious client.

Mikkel Nygaard was on a mission to put human beings on Mars in a decade or so. Sure, other entrepreneurs were trying the same thing, but Mikkel's approach was unique and his background was perfect. For vague reasons, he wasn't working with others and needed his project to remain secret for now. His work was based out of a small arctic desert in Northeastern Greenland. The dry air and low temperatures were crucial to parts of his manufacturing process, and the long summer days were an asset as well. He wasn't trying to bring technology to anyone, but rather to fund and achieve a life's dream, away from prying eyes. His investments were his main means of funding.

He deferred a lot of her questions until later, and once Ariel bit into the wonderful dinner she was glad they'd come indoors. The important thing was he trusted her, and because he did, she could better help him accomplish his dream.

The deep black irises of his eyes glowed like coals as he spoke, and Ariel realized the man was not only committed to his project, he lived and breathed it. He sat next to her at dinner, and the animation born of speaking about what he loved carried through conversations about more mundane matters.

He's an interesting man. One who knows and does things most guys are clueless about.

She enjoyed Mikkel's company, and as the banana mousse and warm chocolate cake was served, she noticed Nell was giving her more private space. Ariel smiled. She hadn't been planning on doing anything tonight requiring privacy, but she *was* hoping to get to know this client better.

******

Eoin was looking forward to the weekend with his wife. How many times had the two of them been alone in a bedroom lately without a small child? Not many. He wasn't happy when Baldur tapped him on the shoulder as he was loading his luggage into the hired car.

"We need to talk before you leave."

"My wife is flying in, Baldur. She doesn't travel much; I have to meet her."

Baldur looked as if his dog had refused to do a trick. "She can wait for an hour."

He was going to show up for his wife's flight an hour late? That wouldn't be a good start to the romantic night Eoin was hoping for. What choice did he have? He followed Baldur inside. Something about the man, a certain intensity, was making Eoin uncomfortable.

"Have a seat."

"I'll pass."

"I insist." Baldur gave Eoin a meaningful look. "You need to be sitting down for this."

Eoin sighed and did as he was told. Baldur stayed standing, and began pacing as he talked.

"My relationship with Ullow may be coming to an end soon."

Eoin's mouth dropped open. "Oh no." If he lost a client this big ...

"I hope to move on to options and futures, so I need to close this window of opportunity behind me. Can't have others getting as rich from it as I did. Which reminds me, have you told those boys working on Mikkel's stuff to stop copying my software?"

Eoin looked down.

"I didn't think so. I want it done, Eoin, even though I'll be working to see HFT becomes so regulated it won't be lucrative enough to bother with."

"Why would you do that?"

"You know d^4 has a skill most people deny exists. What you don't know is, we aren't unique. Other such companies *will* spring up. It may take years, but it'll happen."

"Now you think there are lots of psychics like you? And you're worried about them?" Eoin thought it was almost funny. Almost.

"Not lots. A few. But a few are all it will take to remove my unique advantage, so I've found another. It's one I don't think can be duplicated."

Baldur looked pleased and Eoin wasn't sure he wanted to hear more.

"It's your girl, Ariel. She's no mere technical liaison, you idiot. She's a black swan, a living thing none of us thought was possible. That girl sees next week. She sees next month. When I touch her, I see it too."

"Wait. Now you're saying Ariel is psychic?"

"She's powerful, Eoin, more powerful than she knows. I believe the two of us will form an alliance soon, and our amassed wealth months from now could be staggering. The trick will be strategy, as always. Stealthy movements. Multiple accounts. You and your staff could be useful as we implement specific tactics. Not everyone would remain in their current roles, of course, but if you wish to retain my account a while longer, your company can play a part in this transition."

"Ariel wants to do this?" Eoin felt protective of his young employee.

"Not yet. But once I establish with certainty that her skills and mine combine the way I suspect, I'll find ways to convince her. You know I will."

Eoin did know.

"Don't worry. You've served me well and you'll find I have a sense of gratitude. As the wealth of world shifts over the next few years, you and your family will have a better berth. There will always be less unpleasant jobs for workers."

Eoin's raised eyebrow made it clear he was starting to questions Baldur's sanity. The man responded by giving Eoin a friendly punch on the arm.

"Cheer up. Go, enjoy the weekend with your missus. I think, in a few years, extra money for things like vacations will be a fond memory for working men like you."

******

Toby knew his solution was about as unsexy as a plan could get. Who thinks its cool to write a report?

However, it would get the job done. Several influential members of y[1] had pulled strings to fund a study looking into the fairness of high frequency trading. The report would be widely publicized.

Toby hoped Baldur's response to being watched would be to curb his advantage until the study was over. That would keep him in check. What wouldn't be public was how the investigators would also look at data from the past. He hoped the contrast between d^4's earlier performance and its results while under scrutiny would be striking enough to warrant a closer look.

Toby didn't wish to cause problems for Ariel, but he knew questions about Ullow's complicity would arise. Once d^4's success rate became known, people would assume Baldur was doing something illegal, and Ullow had helped. Over time Ullow's innocence would be proved and he hoped Ariel could ride out the storm.

Most of the world would be bored with the story by then, but a small group would care about how Baldur *had* managed success beyond all odds without breaking the law. Once all other possibilities were eliminated, psychic abilities would have to be considered. In the cynical world of economists, Toby had no idea what would happen next.

******

No one was in a good mood after the trip to the wonderful Blue Lagoon Spa. Eoin came back irritable. Fergus and Ronan were annoyed they hadn't been invited. Ariel and Brendon began avoiding conversation with everybody.

Morale dropped further when Eoin told Fergus and Ronan to cease duplicating Jake's work immediately.

"But, doing what Jake does *is* our main assignment," Fergus said. "What do you expect us to do?"

"I expect you to stop inconveniencing d^4, and keep Mikkel happy. If you can't do both, I suggest you start polishing your CVs. Understood?"

Jake wasn't pleased either.

"I gain something by bouncing ideas off of these guys. Even if Baldur doesn't get it, d^4 benefits from our collaboration."

"Baldur doesn't agree. He wants complete confidentiality point forward. So find a way to collaborate with yourself."

A few days later Eoin had a more disturbing directive for Jake.

"Some group of economic professors has gotten a wild hair up their arse to study HFT. They want to look at whether the rules are fair. It's important we don't look too successful."

"I'm not willing to lie."

"Oh for god sake, grow up," Eoin replied. "I'll repeat. This is a stupid academic study, not a government investigation. Handle it any way your scruples dictate, as long as you make these clowns go away. Understand?"

Jake sighed. He understood.

Later Jake invited Ariel to join him for one of the cigarettes she didn't smoke.

"I overheard your conversation with Eoin," she said. "You should know you're one of the reasons for this study."

"What? How could I be?"

"Remember when you gave me your data on Baldur to give to my brother's friend who runs an economics think tank?"

"Yeah. You told me the man would find it fascinating."

"Well, Toby did, and he already had similar suspicions."

"Toby of y^1?"

"You've heard of the guy?"

"I've more than heard of him. I'm a huge fan. He's a legend. You really gave my research to y^1?" Jake looked proud.

"I did. They were impressed. So impressed they came up with this study so they could uncover what you and Toby already know."

"That's too funny. My work set in motion a study I've now been told to deceive, so it won't reach the same conclusions I did."

"Yeah. It's a bizarre universe. What are you gonna do?"

"Well, I sure as hell won't disprove my own work, will I?"

Ariel felt bad for Jake and the pickle she'd put him in. "I didn't think Toby would do something like this."

"Don't worry. I'm glad you told me."

"How are you going to handle Eoin?"

"Screw Eoin. I can get another job. Lucky for us, Baldur doesn't run the world."

******

Baldur planned to run the world well.

Even if the ten psychics he'd trained didn't grasp it, Baldur knew this was about more than making money. People had done that before, then frittered most of it away. The very rich had all the usual vices, plus they were prone to trying to shape the world to their liking. Because none of them had the same vision, they squandered their power like gods throwing lightning bolts at each other. Why didn't they understand it was all about keeping the money?

Retaining great wealth required having politicians on his side. Luckily money could buy that; it always had. He'd need public opinion, too, or enough of it so detractors would be ignored. These days, buying journalists who'd twist the truth was as easy as buying politicians. Maybe easier.

He needed the poor. Only a fool thought otherwise. Hell, they did the work, and they bought the products. They had to be solvent enough so advertisers could coax away their bits of discretionary income for whatever frivolities were being sold.

He needed the rich. Someone had to support the restaurants, arts and entertainment that made wealth enjoyable. No one in this shrinking upper class could have the means to challenge him, of course, but they could run corners of the world Baldur had no interest in.

The others were the difficulty.

The middle class had enough free time to grow restless, yet lacked the rich's attachment to the status quo. They were always trying to make things more fair, so they could get more. Yet society required managers, physicians and educators. The answer was to keep them scared. Wasn't it lucky humans gravitated to leaders who peddled fear, then promised safety in return for loyalty? Baldur would encourage those leaders.

He'd expected to need at least ten years for his slow but steady draining of wealth out of the system and was prepared

S. R. Cronin

for the wait. However, scrutiny was coming in spite of his caution. Perhaps he was making too much of a small thing, but little nuisances spiraling out of control had brought down others. This study looking into the fairness of HFT concerned him. It was well funded, fast-tracked, and had come out of nowhere. Like a storm brewing on the horizon, it carried potential for destruction.

His best hope was his redheaded black swan. He'd been a little heavy-handed with her, but if she'd been more cooperative he wouldn't have needed such drama. He and two of his most capable cohorts used the best they got from her to put numerous complex trading strategies in place. Most wouldn't mature until September, but after a week it was already looking good. Would the young lady in question be willing to assist him?

Did she have to be willing? That was the latest twist. She didn't have to want to be present, as the incident at the spa proved. She'd been curious about the investing, though, and paid some attention while the men worked. Baldur noticed her attention mattered. When her mind wandered, the quality of the information dropped.

He'd kept quiet about the observation, but left the session certain Ariel had to be somewhat engaged. He knew she'd find a way not to be if he kept her in a cage. She needed to be persuaded not forced.

Baldur shook his head at his own bad luck. Ninety-nine percent of the people in the world would have cooperated with him for the money alone Ariel fell into the other one percent.

Unfortunately, he'd approached this all wrong in terms of gaining her affection. So how about capitalizing on her affection for another? Would she cooperate for the sake of someone she cared about? Who did she care about? What did she care about?

In order to run the world, Baldur needed to know more about Ariel.

140

17. Summer Secrets

Ariel could tell she was being followed a lot of the time, and whether it was by friend or foe she was getting tired of it. Her first guess was Baldur was making sure she didn't bolt for Tierra del Fuego while he waited to see how useful her investment guidance was. Her second guess was Cillian was trying to look out for her. She supposed other reasonable options included Toby, also being protective, or Mikkel, making sure she didn't betray his confidences.

What a mess. No, what a clusterfuck. She needed to get some normal friends.

On the plus side, her family was having no troubles at the moment. She really should call home, and tell her mom about the depths Baldur sank to last month at the Blue Lagoon. Mom would be livid, and worried sick, which was why Ariel hadn't made the call already.

It made sense, though, for her family to help each other. Mom had telepath friends in Europe. Maybe they could learn more about Baldur and his plans. Teddie had told Ariel if she never had another out-of-body experience again it would be too soon, but hadn't Teddie stayed in touch with those who did that kind of thing all the time? Could these people help strangers? Ariel figured she ought to learn more in case her situation turned worse.

Dad didn't have anything odd about him as far as Ariel could tell, and Zane's talents were only helpful if Zane was right there with you. He—

Ariel spun around as an elderly Hindu woman who'd done a surprising job of keeping up with Ariel's fast pace ducked into a doorway.

Oh hell, enough was enough. She stormed back to the tiny woman, glaring down into her eyes. She swore she could see Nell somewhere inside.

"Nell?"

As soon as Ariel said it the woman's wrinkled features began to relax and her body filled out as she stood taller.

"Hey, just a little practice to keep the old acting skills sharp." The woman who looked more like Nell every second gave a nervous giggle.

"No, that is more than acting. Stop pretending, Nell. I know, because my brother can do what you do."

"No way." Nell didn't argue the original point. "I spent my whole life learning to do this. You have no idea how many great roles it got me. Need someone older, younger, larger, smaller, whiter, browner, thinner, fatter. I go way past acting—I become. No way another actor does this."

"My brother Zane is no actor. At least, not in the theatrical sense. Come on. Let's go get a beer. We'll compare notes."

As the first Guinness was downed, Ariel learned Nell used her talents on behalf of her friend and current employer, Cillian. Her role as his part-time girlfriend was one of the many she'd adopted; she and Cillian had never been lovers.

"Not my type." Ariel got it.

"Zane's gay too. I don't think it's related to what you guys can do, but it's interesting. You're like mirrored twins."

"Well, we've had to work harder at blending in than you, so maybe it's a little part of it. Not that you don't have your own issues. Speaking of which, why are so many people following you these days?"

"It hasn't all been you?"

"Hardly. Cillian asked me to check in on you occasionally after the thing in Iceland, so I did. Once I noticed I wasn't the only one, I upped the frequency. You're pretty much a full-time job now, lady."

"My guess is my other fan is Baldur."

Nell agreed. She didn't know about Toby, so her other guess was Mikkel.

"I couldn't help notice the two of you had your own private dinner that night at the lagoon." There was teasing in her voice.

"We had a nice time together. He's more interesting than I realized, at least when he isn't pissed about me butting into his business. He even talked to me a little about it." Ariel had no intention of telling Mikkel's secrets to Nell or anyone else, but Nell didn't push the point.

"You could consider filling him in on this odd premonition thing of yours, you know. It might ease his mind if you shared, too."

"Are you crazy?" Ariel had spent a lifetime guarding her secret. She was hardly going to start blurting it out to everyone she met.

"I'm just saying. Confidences exchanged go a long way. You could use a friend, and so could he. Think about it."

******

Toby was pleased at the responses to his study. His cheerful assessment of the information coming back was interrupted by a call from Zane.

"I'm getting to talk to you a lot lately."

"I know. Look, I don't mind being a courier, but I have to tell you some of this stuff is starting to scare me. I talked to my sister last night and she's upset because some guy is planning on amassing the world's wealth and she figures into his plans for global domination. This creep tied her to a massage table and tried to suck away her powers or something. You know about this?"

"Yeah. I'm involved. I'm trying to look out for her, although she's pretty good at taking care of herself. Plan A is to bring this guy down soon."

"Can someone really take over the world? I mean, like, the whole world?"

"You wouldn't think so," Toby said, "but then again you wouldn't think people could alter their appearance or see the future, now, would you?"

Zane ignored that. "Ariel says your study caused a lot of turmoil in her office, and to tell you she's posted more information in your secret place online. There's also more there about another client, who's trying to save humanity from something else. How many catastrophes are we talking about here?"

"I only know of two," Toby said. "Did she say which client?"

"The secretive one. Something about sending people to Mars. I'm to remind you it's for background only. You sure we're not going to be wiped out by an asteroid next week?"

Toby chuckled. "No, I'm not sure, but your sister doesn't think so, and I'll go with that. Tell her I'll keep whatever it is secret and I appreciate everything she tells me."

"One more thing. She met someone who can do what I can. Can you believe it? Ariel says the lady is really good."

"I'd have bet you were unique. Does knowing about this other person bother you?"

"Hell, no. I've got to find a way to meet her."

******

Ariel didn't have a boyfriend back in the U.S, nor had she found one in London or Dublin, according to Baldur's sources. So, no lover to hold hostage. It did leave open the possibility of igniting a romance convenient for Baldur's needs.

He reconsidered courting her. He *had* planned to find a wife over the next few years. It was a social convenience. An Icelandic woman who shared his native tongue and culture seemed best, but Ariel was attractive and smart and would do fine. What better way to control both her and her assets?

He'd be the first to admit his sales technique probably needed improving. Were there coaches he could hire for this sort of thing? There must be. He should look into the males Ariel was attracted to over the years. Baldur read somewhere everyone had a type. Maybe, at first, he could be more her type. He'd ask his people to look into Ariel's past.

A few days later Baldur was told Ariel's most recent romantic involvement was with none other than Siarnaq, his Greenland ally. How in the world had those two crossed paths? At the airport in Nuuk, according to his sources. There were those in town still talking about the Inuit man and the girl from Ireland standing in the middle of a restaurant rubbing their arms against each other.

Well, Ariel did have reason to go to Greenland, and there weren't that many people in Nuuk. The two of them could have touched each other somehow and experienced some variation of what he and Ariel did. Intimacy could so easily have followed.

Sources reported the girl came back to Greenland for a second visit a month later. She and Siarnaq spent most of their time in a hotel room in a town on the east coast. No visit since.

Had they been too busy to schedule a third tryst, or had they broken things off? It sounded like Siarnaq and Ariel may have gone their separate ways about the time Baldur and Siarnaq joined forces.

Baldur studied the calendar on his desk. He'd met with Siarnaq three months ago and Siarnaq had been vague about what alerted him to Baldur's rivalry with Mikkel. Wasn't Ariel the perfect source for that information?

Over the last few months, the two men had communicated as they worked together to sabotage Mikkel's project. Baldur had the resources to make things happen, and Siarnaq provided insight into the land and the people. Together they'd done well.

Baldur had told Siarnaq about Ariel and his hopes for gaining her cooperation. Siarnaq had chosen to remain mute about his own time spent with the girl. Interesting. Perhaps he could reignite their relationship and use Siarnaq as leverage over Ariel?

Did the two of them still have contact? Did Ariel know what he and Siarnaq were doing? Did she disapprove? Of course she disapproved if she knew about it.

Come to think of it, she and Mikkel spent a lot of time together at the Blue Lagoon. Did Ariel know about Mikkel's space project? Did she liked the idea? Did she find Mikkel attractive? Perhaps her affections had moved on from Siarnaq to his hated cousin. Wouldn't it be less messy to push the woman to have more feelings for Mikkel? That seemed easier.

He could even carve out a small financial niche for Mikkel and his pet project, if doing so bought Ariel's cooperation. How compliant would she be if she discovered helping Baldur was the only way for Mikkel to succeed? She'd need to care more about Mikkel. What could Baldur do to move things along?

Hulda brought him in an afternoon cup of tea.

"You're a woman. What can a man do to get a woman to like him?"

"You could send her little gifts. Everybody likes presents." Hulda smiled as she thought of the beautiful crystal sun catcher hanging in her window at home, a gift from an Irish fortune-teller who'd stolen Hulda's heart two years ago.

"I misspoke. I don't want to get her to like me. It would be easier to get her to like someone else."

"Oh." Hulda looked puzzled. "Well, I guess you could send little gifts from him, then."

"You're right." Baldur looked more pleased with Hulda then he had in weeks. "I could conduct a damn fine courtship for him. Probably a better one than he could for himself."

"Why would you want to do such a thing?"

"For the same reason I do anything," Baldur said in the tone an adult would use to instruct a child. "It's the best way to get what I want."

******

Eoin avoided Ariel after the trip to Iceland. He couldn't accept the quick-thinking young woman had any of the faerie about her, but there was no doubt Baldur thought so, and he meant her harm for it. It was one thing to cover for Baldur, to keep his secret and direct the staff in ways that made Baldur happy. It was another to be part of a plan hurting an innocent young lady.

It also crossed one line too many to ask his own staff to lie. How could a man keep any self-respect after that? He couldn't. Well, at least that part of the problem could be fixed.

Eoin called Jake into his office. The young man squeezed his big frame into the little guest chair, eying the floor as if he expected more unwelcome instructions. Eoin explained his change of heart.

"Mind you, I'm not going to defy Baldur. That would piss him off, and he'd come after me and our company in ways we can't imagine. So, I'm asking *you* to defy *me*. Don't worry, I'll cover for you, and get you everything you need. You make sure you nail the bastard. I want those study people to be positive something funny is going on with d^4."

Jake looked relieved, but he had more on his mind. "I'm happy to do this, but what if I told you I suspected the man of

146

worse than cheating? Don't think I've lost my mind here, but I'm worried he has some ability to predict the market."

Eoin was impressed. "You figured that out, did you?" At Jake's surprised look, he added, "You're not crazy; you're correct. I've known it for a while, only because Baldur told me. He promised to take good care of me, too, if I guarded his secret."

"I won't tell anyone you gave me the okay to do this."

"Thanks, but that won't matter much to Baldur, if Ullow brings him down."

Brendan poked his carrot-topped head in the door. Jake and Eoin both turned his way nervously. "Did I interrupt something?"

"Not at all. Jake and I were talking about this nuisance study. I wouldn't even give these guys data, except it could make us look guilty and who needs that? Brendan, you need to make sure Cillian knows we're participating, too."

"Ariel is paying him a visit to fill him in. Cillian won't care."

"True. Do you know if she's informed Mikkel?"

"He's coming to town in a couple of days. He's having issues with some project and they were going to talk about both things."

"Good." Eoin was glad to hear the young lady at the center of all this craziness appeared to be taking care of business.

******

Mikkel and Ariel exchanged warmer emails after the outing at the Blue Lagoon Spa. He was arriving Friday to discuss business, and Ariel was looking forward to the visit. It was nice to be dealing with an uncomplicated man.

She was dismayed when she walked into the office Thursday and found a huge bouquet of lilies and white roses occupying half her desk. What the hell? She touched the flowers and got a quick premory of a young florist's happiness at something. Never mind. She reached for the card instead.

"Can't stop thinking about you," it said. Her first fear was the flowers were from Baldur, but it would be even worse if they were from Siarnaq. She was sad when she saw the card signed Mikkel. Damn. Her one simple relationship had gone complicated.

Before the day was out, every guy in the office had made unwelcome guesses about the identity and intentions of the sender.

Ariel endured the comments as she grew more irritated. Damn him. Why did he have to do something like this? Now she dreaded his visit.

She'd offered to pick him up at the airport. He gave her a funny look the next morning as he got in her car and she gave him a cold hello.

"Did I do something wrong?"

"That was embarrassing and inappropriate."

"What was?"

Out came the story of the showy white flowers. The ensuing ride was filled with Mikkel's denials followed by his anger someone would do such a thing in his name. Ariel countered with disbelief and then ... she stopped. She realized she was annoyed with the wrong person.

"Who did send the flowers?" They asked it in unison then laughed.

"Who wants me to hate you?" she asked.

"Who wants you to like me? I get why you're embarrassed, but guys generally send flowers because they want to be liked."

Neither of them could think of a plausible reason for such odd behavior from anyone.

Mikkel and Ariel spent the morning in one of the conference rooms, strategizing over ways to provide full disclosure on Mikkel's financial dealings with minimum attention drawn to how he was spending his money.

"We need to be able to explain how you have the same tools as all of Ullow's other clients and yet do measurably better than all of them, except for Baldur," Ariel said.

"It's no secret I've piggybacked on his innovations. I've no reason to hide that."

"Yeah." Ariel was bothered by something and she finally put her finger on it. Baldur's innovations worked because of his short-term psychic abilities. How was Mikkel using the same tools almost as well? Surely he wasn't like Baldur? Ariel took a deep breath, reached out and put her hand on Mikkel's arm. He raised an eyebrow, but said nothing.

She closed her eyes. There was nothing. No electricity, no change in her abilities, nothing but his warm skin underneath her. He certainly was no visionary. Did the man have no future? Then it came. A premory from months ahead—distant, small and vague. Maybe a one out of three chance. Mikkel on a beach, relaxed and laughing. Ariel next to him. It was a pleasant scene, warm and happy. All was well. Ariel searched for other possibilities, but she could find nothing else.

She opened her eyes to see Mikkel smiling at her.

"Do you mind if I ask what you're doing?"

"Not at all." She made a quick decision. "I have something I'd like to tell you about me, but I'd rather do it out of the office. Lunch?"

"Lunch."

Mikkel wasn't a big fan of sushi, but he agreed to Ariel's favorite place as long as he could order something else. Once they were settled in with food and drinks, silence took over.

"You wanted to tell me something?" he prompted. When she didn't say anything, he added, "Something you don't usually tell people?"

"How'd you know that?"

"From the way you're acting. I've shared my secret project and now you want to exchange confidences but you're having trouble doing it. Come on. How big a secret can a straightforward young woman like you have?"

"I see the future." Ariel blurted it out, and Mikkel didn't even look surprised. "It turns out other people do too, just not like I do." Mikkel continued to smile and say nothing.

"You know this already?" she asked with irritation.

"Only the last part. I suspect you're referring to Baldur, and I figured out a while ago the man has some uncanny advantage in predicting the market. I've been trying to mimic him ever since. So you do, too?"

Ariel explained the ways she and Baldur were alike and different, and before she knew it the story of their ability to combine what they could do came out as well and Mikkel was hearing about the whole awful spa incident. She saw the anger growing in his eyes.

"That's just wrong. Tying you up like that, doing that to you."

"He was desperate to get an answer; I don't think he does stuff like that usually."

"Ariel, don't make excuses. That's seriously disturbed behavior. What's going to happen if he discovers you give him the advantage he hopes for?"

"I suspect he'll try to bribe me with wealth beyond my wildest dreams."

"If you don't agree to the partnership?"

"I think things will get ugly."

"So do I. This nonsense has gone too far. I've got to find a way to stop this guy."

"I'm already on it." She told Mikkel about Toby and y^1 and how the study had gotten started. "It's my fault, really. I needed help in bringing Baldur down, and I didn't consider how the scrutiny would affect your project. That's why I wanted to meet with you in person."

Mikkel was smiling again.

"Now what's so funny?"

"You've got the world's worst creep planning to handcuff you to his computer for the rest of your life, and you're worried about me? It's not funny. It's charming."

"I'm glad you're entertained."

"Don't be that way. I meant it as a compliment." He reached out his hand until it almost touched hers. "Do you risk destroying the space-time continuum if you touch me and tell me what you see?"

"It doesn't work that way. I see probabilities, not certainties, and telling someone only alters the landscape a little, sometimes."

"Okay then..." He brushed his fingers lightly over the skin of her hand. "What does my future hold?"

With the light touch she felt a soft wind blow, and smelled coffee, freshly perked. She premembered Mikkel lying in a hammock, enjoying the morning breeze coming off the sea as he took the hot coffee from a freckled hand Ariel was sure was her own. Seriously? She was going to bring the man a cup of coffee?

"You seem to have a beach vacation in your future," she said.

"That's all? With everything I've got going on in my life, I'm going to the beach?"

"It is a ways in the future, months from now. That's as far as I see. It's not a given, one of many possibilities, really."

"So what are the other possibilities?"

"That's just it, I don't know." She tried to bring up more premories, those closer in. A few snippets came. There were some fine dinners, an unusually good night's sleep, and a few orgasms which were kind of embarrassing. It was a collage of the short but happy moments of a healthy life.

"For some reason, I seem to get only the good times with you. It's not like you have a lot of them," she added.

"Odd. Well, I guess I ought to be glad I have anything in store for you to see."

"I'll try again later."

They left the restaurant and started the walk back to the office.

"I don't usually do this for people. I mean, I never have. But given the problems we share, I want to try again to see if I can help."

"Can't you do this for yourself?"

"It doesn't focus as well when it's about me. I get a lot of junk, like the odd things you remember from a year ago. It's interesting, but not as useful as you'd think."

"Have you seen alternatives for this thing with Baldur?"

"Yeah and some really weird ones. The most likely one right now is a game of cat and mouse that goes on as long as I can see."

"I bet you play a fine game of cat and mouse if you have to."

Ariel shrugged. "Honestly, I'd rather be the cat."

By the time they left the office late in the afternoon, Ariel knew she was going back to Mikkel's hotel with him. Mikkel understood why without asking.

"It works best if I relax, and we lay next to each other without any clothes," she said once they were in his room. He began to unbutton her blouse.

"Do I mess anything up if I undress you?"

She sighed with pleasure. "No, but you might interfere with my concentration."

"I'll take my chances."

They stretched out together and she wrapped her arms around him, steeling herself for whatever premories came. It took a few seconds, and then there they were, lying together in sand still warm from the afternoon sun. There was a bit of dusk left in the sky. In the privacy of the near-darkness, their naked bodies were pressed together, enjoying the closeness. His hand was stimulating her, she was stroking him and then, as the surf pounded, they started to make love.

Ariel realized she and Mikkel were in fact doing the same in real life. She supposed she was responsible, probably acting out her premory as it came to her. Now what?

Ariel of the future savored the growing fire inside until she threw her head back with a moan of ecstasy and let her pleasure unfold. Not to be outdone, Ariel of the present closed her eyes and let her body embrace the joy of the moment as well. Then, as her breathing slowed, she savored Mikkel's enjoyment too, while the couple on the beach dissipated into nothingness.

They held each other until their heartbeats were back to normal. Mikkel broke the silence.

"I won't complain if you didn't learn anything new, but if you did, I'd love to hear it."

She smiled. "All I got was that you continue to have the distinct possibility of one hell of a nice beach vacation coming up. It's all I'm getting from you. The good news is it already seems more likely than it did at lunch today, and, well, I get to be there too."

He didn't say anything for a few seconds. "I like the idea of you being there. How about we keep tabs on these odds, and do what we can to improve them?"

"Okay. Any future with a beach vacation in a few months has got to be a pretty good one. We'll check on it every so often."

"I was thinking we should check on it once a day," he said with a straight face. The she noticed the bit of a grin hidden by his facial hair. "Some days maybe two or three times, you know, just in case."

August 2012

18. Odds of Survival

To Ariel's surprise she spent most of the weekend with Mikkel, but by Sunday afternoon she had to excuse herself. She'd agreed to drive Brendan out to Cillian's estate so they could tell Cillian about the y^1 study. After she explained to Mikkel where she was going, he asked if he could ride along.

"I don't think that's appropriate." Ariel was irritated he'd even ask.

"Ariel, don't be mad. I asked for a ride because I'm already invited and planning to go."

"Why would you be invited?"

Mikkel sighed. "I know Cillian better than you think. I know he has things he wants to tell you today, and he's asked me to be there. I didn't mention this earlier because they're his things to tell, not mine. I'll take a cab if you insist, but I won't explain anymore."

"Fine." Ariel's tone was colder already. They waited in silence while the valet got the car.

"Was this whole weekend just so you'd have something to do while you waited for this meeting?" she asked as she pulled out into traffic.

"Don't be ridiculous. I brought plenty of work with me." The words tumbled out before he realized this wasn't the best response.

"Ariel, these have been the best two days I've had in a long time. I had no idea this was going to happen when I told Cillian I'd be there."

He gave her a helpless look but she ignored it, turning her music up loud enough to prevent conversation.

Brendan was in good spirits as he got in the car, his normally serious face creased with a seldom seen smile. He acted like being picked up by the two of them was the most natural thing in the world. He made a couple of tries at friendly conversation, but when Ariel didn't turn the music down and Mikkel didn't respond, he gave up. They rode in silence through the outskirts of Dublin and into the countryside.

It was mid-afternoon by the time Nell met them at the McGrane Manor door, steering them out to the backyard grounds. "Cillian's got us set up in the gazebo. He's put together a picnic and given most of the staff the day off. Isn't it gorgeous? Look at that blue sky."

So this was going to be another conversation Cillian didn't want anyone in the house to overhear. Of course it was.

Cillian had a stout in his hand as they walked up the steps to the gazebo, but Ariel noticed his glass was full. He seemed older and sadder as he reached out to Ariel with his hand.

"Just barely touch it," he said. "Carefully."

Even grazing his skin, she was startled by the painful zap.

"See how much stronger it is since you touched me two months ago? Our visions are connecting, even though what we see is drastically different."

"How far do you see?" she asked, rubbing her hand.

"My clearest information comes from several hundred years from now, although a lot of the time I don't know exactly when I'm seeing. I get quite a range. It's a good bit further than Siarnaq sees." She noticed he was rubbing his hand as well.

Ariel looked around and saw Nell stuffing her face with dolmades and Mikkel pouring himself a stiff glass of whiskey. She turned to Brendan.

"Is there anything I should know about you?"

Brendan chuckled. "Nothing. I swear. I really do write code, and otherwise I babysit these three. Here, let me get you a Guinness. You're going to want one."

As it happened, Ariel drank three while she listened to Cillian.

The last time she'd been here, everyone wanted to know about her. This time, Cillian wanted to talk about him. He looked into her eyes as he talked, his faded soft blue meeting hers while he ignored the other three people.

He described how his deepest childhood secret had been seeing the far future and as a boy he'd been mostly confused by what he saw. As a young lad, he'd struggled to shut the visions out. He couldn't, though, and they made his parents' obsession with wealth seem increasingly inane.

He'd played the role of an irresponsible lad because it explained the substances and distractions he embraced to shut out what he saw. Once he settled down with Lara and had children, he tried to learn more specifics. Lara knew about it, and she encouraged him at first, but eventually the things he understood made him crazy.

"When it all clarified, I realized there was only one vision. I'd see bones of people, see birds and plants living in decaying buildings, and occasionally rotting human flesh. There was always a haunting feeling that brought me to tears. I knew humanity was gone. The extinction of my species filled my dreams, and everything I touched spoke to me of the end. By the time I was in my early thirties I was depressed and becoming suicidal."

He told Ariel he regretted not handling it better, but he'd been overwhelmed. Lara had done him the favor of letting the world think she'd become fed up with his drinking and womanizing. She'd taken the children far away where neither Cillian nor his family could find her.

Ariel noticed Brendan and Nell listening with sympathy, even though they'd certainly heard the story many times before. Mikkel was looking down, lost in his own thoughts.

"After she left, I had a lot of time on my hands. I tried to work backwards, to see shorter, to learn more. I believe the future isn't set and there had to be alternatives, but finding a vision of a different outcome took me a long time, and it was faint when I found it. I knew the world I'd been seeing was a near certainty."

Ariel interrupted. "So you four are working to strengthen other, better visions. Are you going to tell me what happens?"

"He doesn't know," Nell said. "Although, as he gets more information we've eliminated some pretty awful options."

"Obviously, Mars is involved," Mikkel said, "but not as a substitute for Earth. It's more like if Earth starts to recover, Mars helps with the process. It becomes a center of stored knowledge, an avenue for communication, maybe even the seat of a temporary government. It gives humanity hope."

"It seems as if recovery on Earth gives Mars hope as well. Two planets on the buddy system," Nell said. "What matters is we've shown that, within a mere decade, we *can* affect the odds. Every so often they get worse, but mostly they get a little better with everything we do. Until you showed up."

"What? I'm a problem for humanity?"

"No, that would be easy. We'd just shoot you," Brendan said. Ariel thought he was kidding.

"Then what?" As she asked the question, her mind went to the vision she'd had back when she'd taken this job. This conversation was the one she'd premembered. They were having it now!

Cillian said it. "You're capable of taking a remote chance for survival and single handedly making it more probable."

"How?"

"I wish we knew," Cillian said. "Like the rest of this, it's complicated. One good place to start would be to ask what you've been doing over the last twenty-four hours?"

"Why?" Mikkel asked.

"Because whatever the young lady was doing seems to have nudged up the human race's chances of survival."

Mikkel and Ariel exchanged a glance. Nell giggled. Then everyone started talking until Mikkel insisted it was time to let Ariel ask questions. She was grateful; she had plenty.

Through their answers she learned Mikkel had been persuaded to get involved when a barely sane Cillian approached him in 2009. Mikkel was a young professor then, and listened because Cillian had narrowed down the year of the catastrophe to the same year his cousin Siarnaq insisted would be the beginning of the end.

From Mikkel's point of view, he'd heard a crazy prediction twice in his life, and the odds of both people randomly choosing 2352 were ridiculous. When he agreed to learn more, Cillian saw the odds of survival go from almost nothing to a little better.

Cillian cleared the cobwebs out of his head once he realized his ability wasn't a useless predictor of doom. Rather, it could serve as a compass, showing when he was on the right track. His gift reminded him of a children's game, where one child seeks an object while others tell him if he is getting warmer or colder.

"I realized I was going to need a lot of money if I wanted to make a difference. So I stopped scoffing at my parent's greed and cleaned up my act. I got my dad to give me a real job at his company. I took as much play money as I could weasel from my parents and pretended to play while stuffing it away."

Cillian paused to have a long swallow of beer.

"Pretty soon I had a sizable nest egg, and I did some research on investing. I stumbled on HFT. One more way for the wealthy to siphon off money, I thought. Then I remembered; I was wealthy. A discrete way to make money pennies at a time was perfect for funding secret projects. Once I started using HFT, I discovered the uncanny success of an Icelandic investor and his new company d^4. So I became an investor in the same office, with the intention of copying d^4's success. That's how I met my good friend Brendan."

"So Baldur is the reason you picked Ullow?" Ariel asked.

"That's right. I figured they could do for me what they did for him. They have. I'm making a lot of money, but survival odds aren't going up. I was about to get out of HFT when I figured out I'm dealing with two variables here and their effects are cancelling each other. More capital must be raising humanity's chances of survival, but Baldur is an increasing threat. I think the man actually wants to take over the world economy, and his growing wealth is cancelling out everything positive I'm doing."

"The man is *not* a significant player," Brendan said with irritation. "Even with his most successful reign, you've said Baldur is a flash in the pan. You've never seen a survival scenario in which he's remembered."

"He matters because his success weakens us as a species," Cillian corrected him. "Once things right themselves, he leaves us more vulnerable. That's why I think our landing at Ullow was the best piece of good luck we've had. It made us aware of Baldur and the need to stop him. Yet, you have to appreciate the irony that Baldur's ability to make money has also given us a leg up in financing our projects. Baldur is both a threat and a useful tool."

"Except he now hopes to lock Ariel in a closest and use her like a cash machine," Nell said. "Please tell us that's not what needs to be done."

"Just the opposite. I m concerned Ariel's capabilities could allow him to do enough damage fast enough to shut Mikkel and me down. We can't let that happen."

"Yes, but don't you need to let him keep going so you all can bring in the money, too?" Ariel asked Cillian.

"Not for much longer. I've figured out how much we need to have so our investments will finance us going forward. We're only a year away from this tipping point. After that, we want to shut him down.

"There is a problem with that timing," Ariel said. "y¹ wants to shut him down now. They don't know about you guys. Was my turning to Toby a mistake?"

Cillian chose his words with care. "We didn't bring you here to blame you, or to tell you what to do. We brought you here to make you fully aware of the situation and to ask for your help. We want you to understand why it's vital Toby does *not* succeed. At least not until we're ready."

So the conversation came full circle to what Ariel thought it was about, and it ended with a plan for Cillian and Toby to meet.

******

She probably shouldn't have given her mom such a tough time about Santa Claus, but Ariel had never liked the idea of a large group of people knowing something she didn't. It was embarrassing. All these people dressing up in costumes and conspiring to make her believe a story, with her own parents complicit in the deception. Who cared if she was only nine? She felt like a fool when she found out.

It was much the way she now felt about the entire Ullow office. What a crock. Brendan, pretending to amuse a wayward client who was arguably the most responsible man in the world. Then there was secretive Mikkel, who was really a gentle intellectual sucked into a scheme to save the planet by acting like a greedy investor. No wait—Mikkel was more than *just* a gentle intellectual, at least under the right circumstances. Ariel smiled as she remembered their weekend together.

She had learned at the meeting that Cillian and Mikkel seldom talked. Cillian had started out funneling what money he could to Mikkel, until he opened his own account at Ullow to better preserve secrecy and accelerate the process. Now Mikkel focused entirely on Mars, while Cillian used his money to fund other promising projects.

The rest of the office wasn't what it appeared to be, either. Baldur, the brilliant young investor, was a man with a secret talent few people would believe. Big Jake, who handled his coding, was no friend of Baldur's, but someone in the office must be. Ariel pondered the dynamics, and decided her boss Eoin must have sworn allegiance to Baldur and his cause years ago. Why else would talking to Eoin continue to be a bad idea?

Ariel realized her boss was one enemy she hadn't counted on. Yet, she now had several friends she hadn't known about either.

Her first problem was delaying Toby. Another crisis loomed once Baldur's stock options expired on September 22. After that, she had some sort of role to play in humanity's survival, and the more she learned about it, the less it made sense.

Okay. Being lied to about Santa Claus was the least of her problems.

******

When Baldur's people reported back to him about the do not disturb sign on Mikkel's hotel door in Dublin, and the redheaded woman seen with him the few times he did emerge, Baldur was delighted.

"Thank you, Hulda," he said with uncharacteristic warmth as he walked into the office on Monday. "It's useful to know women can be bought for the price of flowers."

Hulda looked up from her desk like she was considering whether she should say something or not. Her better judgment lost the battle.

"Men," she replied "can be had for no price at all."

Baldur stared at her in disbelief, then burst into a laugh.

"You're right! You may be cheap, but we're free. It's true!" He was not at all offended. "This is good, or I'd be out the cost of two lavish bouquets instead of one."

He walked into his own office in the best of spirits, and Hulda wondered what had gotten into the both of them.

******

Ariel had put off a conversation with her folks for weeks. It was easy to avoid topics in emails and text messages, but her parents were making it clear they were worried and wanted to see her face. So, she placed a video call home on Labor Day. Her father and sister were out, but Mom was fooling around on her computer and took the call.

"How are things there?"

"Okay. Work is fine and our health is good and Teddie has settled into her senior year in high school, but—"

Ariel recognized a cue when she heard one.

"But what, Mom?"

"I got my magazine article published."

Oh damn. She'd forgotten about that.

"That's great. You should be proud."

"You'd think, but I'm getting flak for it from a news outlet getting a lot of mileage out of making fun of me."

Oh dear. "What idiots. I'm sure it will die down soon."

"I suppose." Her mother looked discouraged. "It gets worse. See, I've got this daughter I love and I know she's in trouble. I can feel her worry but she won't talk to me. It's driving me crazy."

"That's cute, mom."

"I try. Come on, Ariel. Please tell me what's going on."

So Ariel did. Out came more than she'd intended, really. Toby and y[1] and Baldur and his creepy experiment, and fear and psychics and extinction events, and Siarnaq and Mikkel. Her mom was quiet through most of it, and at the end she looked more relieved than worried.

"I'm going to email you contacts, sweetie. I know you've got allies and that's great, but you can use more. These people I know, they know others. They'll all help you, no questions asked, if you tell them who you are. Don't hesitate."

"Thanks Mom. It must be hard when your kid's in danger. I promise I'll reach out to your friends if I need to." Ariel was relieved her mom was handling this well, but her mother wasn't done.

"I need you to understand something else. I stay out of your head, but I can't keep from feeling your anger or fear or sorrow when it's strong. I ignore it, because every mom has to learn she can't make everything right for her children. But if you're ever really in trouble, like unexpectedly and you can't call anyone for help, you should know you *can* call me. Feel the problem, visualize information and concentrate on the fact that it's okay for me to get involved. I'll have no way of letting you know I heard you, but I will you get help. Do you understand?"

"I do, Mom. Thanks. I hope it never comes to that."

******

To test Ariel's usefulness, Baldur used investment strategies involving options. They offered more reward, and he wanted the timeframe Ariel was best at seeing. Options expiring in September and October were perfect, so Baldur split his money between the two dates. If September went well, October's results would confirm Ariel's success was not a fluke.

In two weeks, he'd have his first answers. Many of the investments were favorable already, but they were the ones any keen investor could have made. It was the outliers that interested him. Before he risked big money on Ariel's guidance, she needed to be over seventy-five percent accurate with trades he'd never have chosen.

If only he had more time to push Ariel and Mikkel into a relationship. How could he speed up the process?

Fear pushed people together. Perhaps this infatuation would move along faster if there was a physical attack. Nothing serious, just a couple of thugs to scare Ariel and get her to turn instinctively to Mikkel.

Then, Baldur could surprise her with his reasonable offer. In return for giving Baldur a bit of willing help, Mikkel would reap serious financial benefits. With no help, his inane space project would run into bigger problems. Once she cooperated a little, his demands on her could increase slowly. Realtors boast how location is all that matters, but they're wrong. Baldur knew the rate of change is everything.

Once his financial empire was thriving, he'd weigh his choices for ensuring her ongoing cooperation. A wife? A partner in the firm? Perhaps both, if she was that good. Mikkel would be disposable by then, and Baldur could decide what was in his own best interest.

First, he needed to up the fear factor, then follow it with another romantic gesture on Mikkel's part. Mikkel must have taken credit for the flowers the first time around; hopefully he'd show the same good sense again.

September 2012

19. A Small Red Fox

Mikkel and Ariel talked often, and with each phone conversation secrets evaporated. He learned she had met Siarnaq, and been close to him before they disagreed and parted ways. She kept the details sparse.

Mikkel told Ariel of losing contact with Siarnaq years ago. Ariel realized he had no idea how much he'd hurt his cousin. She made sure he understood Siarnaq's hatred of what he was doing now.

"I didn't mean to insult him. I thought we just grew apart."

"What you're doing now upsets him more. It's why he's working with Baldur to stop you. They're the cause of many of your problems. Except for his misplaced hatred of you, he's a reasonable man. Why not make your life easier, and explain?"

"I wanted to bring him into this early on, but Cillian doesn't want too many people involved. Besides, Siarnaq has a role of his own to play and we don't want to screw it up."

"That could be a bad call. You're getting more trouble by leaving him in the dark."

"I think you're right. I'll fill Cillian in and, unless he has some new objection, I'll find a way to talk to Siarnaq."

Ariel told Mikkel how she wished he could attend the upcoming meeting between Cillian and Toby, but they both knew Mikkel could do more good tending to his own problems in Greenland. They comforted each other by comparing calendars and settling on early October for a getaway in Oslo, four long weeks away.

******

It was a meeting between two lions—men in the prime of their power, confident and passionate about their causes. Eoin watched them, expecting to hear one growl and the other, perhaps, to respond with a roar.

Cillian hadn't traveled far, in a physical sense, but he had in another manner. It hadn't been lost on Eoin that under the guise of entertaining, Cillian always met on his home turf. To be sitting in a conference room in Dublin was a compromise, a physical sign he was willing to cooperate.

Across the table from him sat Toby, who'd arrived this morning from Hawaii. A full day of travel should have taken its toll, but Toby's head of full thick dark hair was well kept and his flowered shirt and khakis looked pressed. His tanned, relaxed demeanor appeared unshaken.

Eoin was aware he'd almost not been invited. If Jake hadn't told Ariel about Eoin's late-in-the-game conversion to doing what was right regarding Toby's study, Eoin wouldn't even know about the meeting.

He looked around the rest of the table. Jake sat sprawled in his chair, taking up room for two people. Brendan scratched at hair the color of butterfly wings as he wrote on a pad. Nell amused herself by joking with Fergus and Ronan about how hard it was to tell them apart.

"I want to put a stop to this bastard and I want to do it now." Toby said it as he waited for the meeting to start.

"As do I, but there are complicating factors you need to understand." Cillian responded in a stage whisper as the conference room door opened. In came the creature destined to sit between the two lions and coerce them into an agreement. A small red fox, Eoin thought. One who could hold her own with two more powerful beasts, and who was leading this meeting by virtue of the respect she'd earned from both sides.

******

Ariel walked into the room holding a shillelagh, an Irish walking stick, in her hand.

"Planning to beat us into submission?" Cillian asked.

"Hardly." She smiled back. "We have a lot of complicated issues and I'm so not so good at yelling over those louder and more determined to be heard. So," she paused, looking for understanding, "I brought a talking stick. The only person who speaks is the person holding the shillelagh. Does everybody understand?"

They all shrugged and nodded.

"Toby, you start. Say your piece and pass it on."

Toby took the shillelagh with a grin.

"A fraction of one percent now controls about a third of the world's wealth. Much of this group builds their worth from stocks, using opportunities for making money that aren't available to others. Our system is designed to reward investors, not workers or those who save. This has some advantages for everybody, but it also has big disadvantages for everyone but these few. HFT pushes the advantages further in favor of very wealthy investors.

"Clear cheating, like insider trading, is banned the world over. However, Baldur has not only found a way to take advantage of this lucrative slice of legally privileged trading, he's also found a way to cheat that isn't illegal because most people don't think it's possible. We have to prove otherwise."

Toby started to awkwardly hand the shillelagh to Cillian, then he thought of something else and pulled it back.

"Not to mention that a young lady we're all fond of may be in danger because of Baldur. That's why my study of HFT *is* going to be released in two weeks. Here." He handed the shillelagh over to Cillian.

"I don't know where to start." Cillian looked at the shillelagh and shook his head.

"Ariel has given me advance info, so you can do the short intro," Toby said. Then he caught himself. "Oops."

"It's okay." Cillian chuckled. "Thanks for telling me. The short version it is."

The other eight in the room listened to Cillian's story of two disparate men seeing the same dark future. The newcomers to the story, Ronan, Fergus and Jake, had been warned by Ariel to expect bizarre revelations and hold their questions. Ronan couldn't resist

whispering to Fergus, "When she says weird, she means weird."
Ariel glared and pointed to the shillelagh.

Cillian had wanted to exclude the three from this meeting,
believing the fewer who were involved the better. Ariel argued that
each of the them had valuable information. Jake knew specifics
about Baldur's company and with Mikkel not attending, Ronan
and Fergus could offer perspective on his investing.

As Cillian described the plan to fund his various projects, he
told of finding the niche of high frequency trading, learning of d^4
and turning to Ullow.

"There was some plain dumb luck involved, I admit,' Cillian
said. "We've come so much further riding on the coattails of the
man you are compelled to shut down."

Toby started to answer, then stopped.

"Yes, we know he has to be stopped," Cillian said. "He's an
asshole who would drain all the world's resources and not think
twice. We don't want Ariel harmed, either. But this all comes
down to asking why you can't give us another year. There's a
tipping point, financially, and once we get past it, the Mars
settlement will happen. Then you can lock Baldur up for cheating
in the world's largest casino, and as far as I'm concerned you can
throw away the key."

"There's also a tipping point past which Baldur will control
too much wealth to be stopped," Toby answered, ignoring the
talking stick protocol. Then he remembered and raised his hand.
Cillian waved him on.

"I'm confused about something," Toby said. "If Baldur's
advantage comes from seeing seconds to minutes ahead, how in
the world are you people piggybacking on what he does? You
can't see what he sees."

Eoin raised his hand at the same time that he started to talk.
"It all has to go through Ullow hardware." He turned to stare at
Brendan. "Someone who is exceptionally competent must have
found a way to send every transaction Baldur makes straight on to
Cillian and Mikkel."

"I did," Brendan said. "And I slept like a baby after I did it."

"That's why Mikkel needed every software enhancement
Baldur had!" Ronan shouted it out like he'd just discovered gold.
"He could imitate Baldur precisely if he had exactly the same

enhancements." Ariel cleared her throat pointedly and gestured to the stick.

"Right. Sorry."

"You're correct," Cillian said. "I've had Doyle watching me like a hawk, so I've been limited in how much I could do. Mikkel's managed to stay on top of things, snagging at least fifty percent of Baldur's winning strategies while they were still in the money. Much of his success was due to these two lads."

Ronan and Fergus both grinned. "Geez, we helped save the world."

Ariel cleared her throat again. Toby raised his hand.

"I still don't get how you could be in place fast enough to mimic Baldur and his people," he said. "You had to know something about when they were trading. I mean, you couldn't be sitting by a computer all day every day."

Nell walked over to Cillian and took the shillelagh.

"I was wondering why you were here," Eoin said.

Nell gave him a sugary-sweet smile back. "I was wondering the same about you."

She told the group of Hulda, and how the woman had been persuaded two years ago by a fake fortune-teller she fancied to play the dangerous game of undercover asset.

"Most of the people of Iceland felt ripped off by their own upper class when the country went bankrupt in 2009. There's still a lot of anger; well, what passes for anger in Iceland. They're a pretty calm people. Anyway, Hulda had no trouble helping an Irishwoman trying to bring Baldur down. She views him as a traitor to his own. She's supplied us with the kind of intel you talked about, Toby."

"That's impressive spy craft," Toby told the actress. Nell shrugged.

"It's not so impressive when you learn to love her back, and all the more for the risks she's taken." Nell raised her hands helplessly. "I can only hope when she learns who I really am she'll find a way to forgive me and maybe..." The always composed Nell started to cry. The room full of men looked at each other in panic. Ariel rolled her eyes. She wasn't good at this either, but she stood up to offer Nell comfort. Jake beat her to it, and gave Nell one of his giant bear hugs.

"Baldur's a bastard, Nell, and I know so. Remember I work for the man, too. You did the right thing to help bring him down."

Nell nodded her appreciation and then laughed in embarrassment. "A good actress doesn't lose it like that."

Cillian took the stick back out of Nell's hands. "It is my plan to do right by Hulda when this is over, and by you, too. You've both played a dangerous game well". He turned to Toby. "We've all worked to slow Baldur down by sucking away as much as we can of his ill-gotten profits. We can slow him down even more if you can wait."

Ariel waved her hands up and down and Cillian passed the shillelagh on to her.

"Not anymore we can't," she said. "Baldur wanted a quicker approach. Now that he knows what I can do, he wants to use me to speed his agenda along."

"She's right," Eoin said. "He told me that. Ariel, I'm so sorry, he ordered me to get you on his boat that day, and then he insisted you show up in Iceland. I shouldn't have helped him, but you know how bad I need this job. I thought the man wanted a chance to seduce you. Nothing creepy, just a shot at it, you know. What was the harm?"

Ariel didn't say anything. She wasn't sure how much Eoin knew about what Baldur had done to her, but until she had more facts she was in no mood to be forgiving.

"Okay, then maybe coming after Baldur now only makes him desperate and more likely to hurt Ariel if she doesn't cooperate," Toby said. Ariel handed him the shillelagh. "But if she helps him, he gets what he wants even faster."

"Then why can't we do it faster too?" Ariel asked. "I mean, I give Baldur what he wants for a few months, and you guys soak up all the extra you can get. You get to your tipping point faster."

"I like that," Cillian said, taking the shillelagh from Toby as a broad smile crossed his face "Why can't we play with options too, and do a faster job of funding what we need? Toby and his group stay away from everybody just till the end of the year. It's a great idea."

He turned to Ariel, "We need to find a way to set you up as a barely coerced accomplice to Baldur, and then Jake and Brendan will find a way to use everything you two do."

"Ronan and I can help," Fergus said.

"Everyone will help. Luckily, the London office has little clue about what goes on here, so we can make this our top priority."

"I can do my part," Ariel said.

Nell gave Ariel a hard look. "It's a dangerous game you'll be playing, and don't pretend otherwise. Don't agree to this lightly."

"I know. There aren't a lot of other good options, are there?"

"It will be important to stay a step ahead of Baldur. We need to know what he's thinking," Brendan said.

"I do talk to the man. I can help with that," Jake said.

"Me even more so," Eoin added. He gave Ariel a weak smile. "You and I will be playing a dangerous game together. He still thinks he's got me scared enough to own me, and I'll let him believe that."

"Okay, okay. You've convinced me. I can bury my study for a few months," Toby said. "I did such a great job of ramrodding it through, too."

"What's Baldur's next move? He's not sitting around playing card games until those options expire," Eoin said. "Is he still trying to get into your pants, Ariel? I don't want you to have to take this charade that far."

"It sounds more like he's trying to get Mikkel into her pants." Nell giggled. "Hulda says he sent her flowers on Mikkel's behalf."

"Well, that makes no sense," Eoin said.

"Actually, it does," Brendan said. "He's decided his best bet is to have someone to threaten. Someone Ariel cares about."

"Okay." Eoin rolled his eyes and turned to Ariel. "No offense, but, if that's the case, will you play along and pretend you've let Mikkel in your pants?"

For the first time during the meeting Ariel turned a shade of bright red, and Cillian, Nell and Brendan all looked away and said nothing.

"I'm meeting Mikkel in Oslo in a few weeks."

"Oh. Right. Well then, it sounds like we need to be looking out for Mikkel's safety as well as yours. Let's roll him into the plan."

******

169

Ariel's guidance led Baldur to write puts on the Swiss company Weatherford International. Writing puts means you like the stock better than the person you're betting against. You think its price will be above a certain amount on a certain day. If you're right, you get to pocket the money you got paid for placing the bet. If you're wrong, you have to buy the stock from the other person at your higher price instead of the real price.

Baldur had been watching the Weatherford stock drop and feared Ariel was wrong about this one. Then on September 21, the Swiss stock exchange announced it was investigating Weatherford for infractions. The company's stock plummeted. A minute before the market closed, Baldur was facing huge losses. With seconds left in the trading day, the price shot back up and Baldur's profits were safe.

Baldur didn't care what caused the spike. It meant Ariel's abilities to predict an unexpected event were considerably more impressive than he dared hope.

20. In Combination

Ariel was walking home from the bus stop after work, when she noticed two guys following her. They mirrored every turn and loitered through every bit of window-shopping. A plump, middle-aged Irish woman was doing much the same, only further back. With any luck, she was Nell.

The two guys were probably in their late teens, skinny but tough-looking kids arguing with each other about something. As Ariel turned onto the more deserted street of her modest apartment, they followed more closely. She wished she still carried mace in her purse.

Damn, what was this about? Baldur had gotten what he needed for now, and no one else had any reason to harm her. Was she a random target? Had Baldur sent these guys to scare her? That idea pissed her off.

She spoke the truth when she told Mikkel she'd rather be the cat in a cat and mouse game. Maybe it was time to find her inner feline. She slowed down while she fumbled in her purse, putting her keychain in her right fist with a key sticking out between each pair of fingers. It wasn't a formidable weapon, but if these makeshift claws came out of nowhere, wielded with fury, they could damage someone's face.

As the young men caught up to her, she hunched forward in a fearful crouch that disguised the coiling motion her father had taught her years ago, when she learned to play tennis against those bigger and stronger than she.

S. R. Cronin

When they were right behind her, she turned and sprang like a cat, gouging the keys into the flesh of one thug's face while he screamed in pain. The other grabbed her left arm to pull her away. She jerked free, pulling against his thumb like she'd been taught, then went for a knee hard into his groin. She landed it perfectly.

As he screamed, she turned back to her first assailant, only to see the pudgy middle-aged woman clock him over the head with a huge purse that had to contain iron weights. As the first kid went down, the woman swung the purse like the weapon it was into the side of second boy's head. He staggered and fell back to the ground.

"Care for a cup of tea at my place?" Ariel asked the woman.

"If tea is all you've got," Nell's voice answered. The two women walked away fast, leaving the dazed hooligans unsure as to whether they should follow. One of them said something, the other nodded, and they left in the other direction.

"You've got to make some better friends," Nell said as Ariel reached to unlock her door. She stopped. There was a note taped over the keyhole.

"I let the florist in." The florist? Not again.

"Holy shit," Nell said as they walked inside. There were flowers on the kitchen counter. There were flowers on the little blue wooden table. There were flowers on the coffee table, flowers by the bathroom sink, more by the bed, and some on the floor. The place smelled like a hospital room and a funeral home.

"This might be creepier than getting attacked," Nell said.

Ariel saw a card poking out of the largest arrangement. *Can't wait to see you again. Mikkel,* it said in a florist's neat scrawl.

"Whoa. That man is smitten with you."

"No. That man is too smart, and too frugal, to have done this."

"So who do we know who sends flowers *for* Mikkel?"

"I'm glad Hulda told you about that. I can't believe he was dumb enough to do it again."

"From Baldur's point of view, it worked so well last time, these should really do the trick."

"He's an idiot. This day just keeps getting weirder." Ariel's left wrist was starting to hurt and her right hand was swelling. No one mentioned how self-defense moves took their toll on the defender, too.

172

"I think I could find a bit of Irish whiskey to put into that tea," she said in her best imitation of a Dubliner's accent.

"That would be lovely." Soon the two of them were sipping their own version of Irish Breakfast tea, which they much preferred to the original.

******

Siarnaq didn't want to talk to Mikkel. He ignored the messages, and didn't answer his phone. He'd spent years working up to the level of hatred he now felt, and he wanted no part of anything making Mikkel more sympathetic.

However, Mikkel wouldn't quit trying. He sent messages by phone, by mail, by dogsled and by computer. He left messages with the answering service in Nuuk, with every single one of Siarnaq's family members, and with local leaders in every village in Greenland. The messages got more urgent. "You need to hear what I have to say." "The thing you are trying to do is at risk. Please call me." And so on.

After a couple of weeks of questions from everyone he encountered, Siarnaq realized the only way to regain his privacy was to meet with Mikkel. The coercion made him angrier, but he'd do what needed to be done.

They scheduled an appointment through a family member. Siarnaq glared at Mikkel across a table in the same restaurant where he'd discovered how wondrous Ariel and her touch could be. The memory of what he'd lost did nothing to help this unwanted reunion.

"Speak," he said.

Mikkel knew Siarnaq's mind would be closed. He'd chosen his words with care.

Siarnaq felt his mind open a sliver as he listened. So, his cousin did the bidding of another, an Irish man who saw the same future. The exact same future. Siarnaq felt some relief at discovering he was not alone. This Irishman, who saw further and knew more, had cautioned Mikkel to let Siarnaq do what he must do without interfering. Siarnaq could accept that. Visions tended to work that way.

The rub came when Mikkel explained how his own role didn't interfere with Siarnaq's plan. "That's crazy. You can't put machines, computers, and modern facilities up here and think they'll have no effect."

Mikkel talked about the need for secrecy, spoke of the few Inuit who'd be involved and the role they and their families had agreed to play in a bizarre bid for the survival of the species.

"They interfere in no way. Cillian says what you are doing is important, truly important. What I do matters too. In the end, mine and yours will help each other, and *that combination* is what may save us. You and I, we don't need to help each other now. In fact, it's better if we don't. We do need not hurt each other, though."

So Siarnaq listened a little more, and for longer than he planned. In the end, he said words to Mikkel he never thought he'd say. "I'm sorry. I misjudged you."

Ariel taught Siarnaq about the surprising relationship between touch and seeing the future. It wasn't something Siarnaq would have discovered on his own, given the people he touched had no part in the future he saw. At least, no one had until now.

When he and Mikkel got up to say goodbye, having agreed to a truce, Siarnaq embraced his cousin, and shook his hand. As their skin touched, Siarnaq saw a possibility in which a mother told her child a story of how long ago two cousins helped save the world while working from the remotest reaches of the North. Their efforts made Greenland and its people forever important.

So his cousin spoke the truth. Someday, this could all work out, if Siarnaq could find a way to keep Baldur from destroying what Mikkel was doing.

******

Toby had his work cut out for him. The most active members of y[1] considered themselves watchdogs of the world economy. Some were very rich, others merely well off, and some struggling, but they all had one thing in common. They believed the rules governing money should be fair.

HFT had bothered many of them from the start, because the procedures for handling these split-second trades gave those using

HFT a slight advantage. Slight was all it took, when you had enough money from the start.

Once the suspicious watchdogs of y^1 honed in on HFT, Baldur was seen as a man enjoying uncanny luck within a system already rigged in his favor. A physicist in y^1 called the d^4 group "after jerks" and the name stuck as the fervor for investigating Baldur grew.

Now, Toby needed to cool things down, without explaining his true reasons to his colleagues. He focused on arguments he could use. There was another group doing more far-reaching analysis and they'd begged y^1 to back off until next year. They were equally devoted to helping humanity, and it was in everyone's interest to give them the time they asked for.

Toby practiced it in his head. He'd be fine, until he was asked the one question he was unable to answer. "What *is* this other group?"

Secret, he'd say. Extremely secret.

The fine folks of y^1 could conclude what they would.

******

Cillian had another matter he needed to tend to before events spiraled out of control. He explained it to Brendan; Brendan understood. Siarnaq and Cillian had to meet.

They would need Mikkel's help, even though Siarnaq barely trusted Mikkel after their brief meeting of reconciliation. The prospect of a trip to Ireland at the behest of a man he'd viewed for years as his enemy was not going to garner instant enthusiasm.

"Make sure Mikkel tells him what I can do," Cillian said. "One more thing. Mikkel may not know Ariel once shared an intimate relationship with Siarnaq. Tread carefully. All you need to do is make sure Mikkel tells Siarnaq it's important he and I exchange our visions."

"Siarnaq may not be open to the same kind of exchange he had with Ariel," Brendan said.

Cillian laughed. "I wasn't suggesting sex. For two other men, it could be the greatest joining ever, but Siarnaq and I aren't wired that way. We can strip to our skivvies and embrace as brothers. In

175

fact, have Mikkel tell Siarnaq we *are* brothers, and I wish to hug my brother, so I can see what he sees. That conveys the message."

"What do think you'll find out that you don't know already?"

Cillian took a deep breath. "Do you realize how many life-altering sacrifices I continue to ask of everyone around me? So many it's absurd. Were it not for Siarnaq, I'd have doubted myself long ago. Even knowing of him, I doubt. I need to know what happens. I need to know what I'm fighting."

"You're hoping that pressing your skin against his will let you see the missing pieces?"

"Of course I do. A year ago, I didn't know there was an Ariel, much less what happened if she combined her touch with others. I only know of one such muse I can tap into, and that's Siarnaq, my closest psychic kin. If our touch doesn't give answers to me, then maybe it will to him."

"We'd all like to know more."

"Sure you would. I'd be a fool not to try this and so would he. Let Mikkel know how important it is to convince his cousin to do this."

Siarnaq was on a plane two days later. When he agreed to come to Ireland, he hoped he could use the trip to see Ariel too, and maybe smooth over their differences in person. As soon as he saw his ticket he realized he'd been invited for this encounter only. Perhaps it was for the best. He had a purpose with Cillian that needed his full attention.

The thought of physical closeness with a stranger, and with a man, had given him pause, but in the end Cillian's reasoning was as clear to Siarnaq as it had been to Cillian. This needed to happen. Brendan picked Siarnaq up at the airport and drove him to the McGrane estate.

Views from around the world were available to Siarnaq on the internet, yet something on a screen isn't the same as being driven up a wide, rock-lined drive to an old Irish estate on a blustery autumn afternoon. The clouds were dark and heavy. The wind came in fast, strong bursts that warned of the storm to come.

In spite of the weather, Cillian had chosen to meet Siarnaq out at the gazebo, the best spot on the grounds for avoiding prying eyes. Cillian studied the mostly Inuit young man as he strode up the walk, determination in his every step.

He was taller, thinner and younger than Cillian expected, with a head full of shiny straight black hair, worn longish, and a seriousness on his face. He took a look at Cillian and he nodded. Then he pulled off his jacket, lifted a sweater over his head and a t-shirt after it. His clothes hid strong muscles that showed as he stood bare-chested in the cold wind and waited.

Cillian understood. Off came everything above the waist, while Brendan watched silently. As the breeze picked up and little pellets of rain began to fall, Siarnaq marched up to Cillian and wrapped his arms around the Irishman's sturdy torso and held on tight. Cillian hesitated for a few seconds, and then responded in kind. His long arms held Siarnaq's golden brown body against his.

The little roof of the gazebo provided scant protection from the rain that began blowing in hard as the wind picked up, but the two men seemed oblivious to the storm. Brendan got cold and wet as he stood guard, wondering how long this exchange was going to take. He turned at a sound and saw one of the housekeepers huddled under an umbrella walking towards the gazebo. She held three more umbrellas in her hand. "I brought you these." She handed them to Brendan, averting her eyes from the two men, then scurried back to the house with her head down.

Siarnaq and Cillian stepped apart, their concentration broken by the intrusion.

"Did you have enough time?" Brendan asked.

"I think so," Cillian said.

"I don't want to see more," Siarnaq added.

"Good," was all Brendan said as the three men hurried towards the main house in the rain. One of the older maids, who had always been kind to Cillian, met them with towels.

Doyle was standing at the window, holding his cell phone against the glass pane, trying to get pictures through the water drops. He stared at the two shirtless men as they came in the door.

"Now this? Haven't you broken your father's heart in enough ways?"

"You might want to do a bit of damage control with him," the maid whispered to Cillian. "He's such a prickly sort. He's probably headed upstairs to talk to your da, who seems to be having one of his good days."

S. R. Cronin

******

Nell looked for an excuse for her alter ego Murna to go to Reykjavik, but finally went without one. She told Hulda the truth; she needed the comfort of her lover's arms. Although no harsh words had passed between the two women, Nell had noticed less warmth in Hulda's voice, and less eye contact during their video chats. She mentioned it to Cillian. He agreed it was important Murna make the trip and reaffirm Hulda's loyalty.

Hulda cleared her calendar for the weekend and made Murna welcome in her home, but Nell could tell from the moment she arrived that something had changed. As the two women sat in Hulda's small, sparsely furnished front room, they exchanged pleasantries, but kept their distance from each other.

Nell realized she'd let the West Ireland accent slip since her arrival, and her gestures and manners were becoming more those of Nell, and less those of Murna. Finally, Hulda looked at her and asked, "Is this when you tell me who you really are?"

"I can't yet," Nell said. "This is when I tell you the real me loves you as well as Murna. No, loves you better than Murna, and I beg you to believe that until I can prove it to you."

There was a trace of sadness in Hulda's smile. "Really? Because I've grown fond of Murna over the past two years, and I'm not sure I'm inclined to be as taken with this other woman who sometimes occupies her body."

"Her reasons for misleading you are excellent. "How long have you known?"

"Suspected? From the beginning. Murna was a little too perfect to be more than fantasy. Yet why resist? I enjoyed myself, then after a while I played along to find out why this fantasy had targeted me, a mere secretary. As my boss became more powerful, more distasteful, and his whole company more suspicious, it was a fine surprise to discover this fantasy wanted me to play spy, to plant cameras and sneak information to bring down this loathsome boss. Why resist? It was that or quit in my disgust for Baldur. This way I had a lover, I had an honorable purpose, and I had a job." Hulda gave a satisfied shrug.

"Perhaps Murna underestimated how perceptive you are."

"Perhaps the imposter in Murna's body overestimated her own acting skills."

178

Nell had to laugh. "So, is this where you tell me you're tired of the charade and breaking up with me?"

"No, this is when I insist on getting some answers."

Nell thought for a few seconds. It was possible she would have to share more information with Hulda then she or Cillian had planned. "When did you go from suspicious to certain?" she asked.

"The day I called to tell Murna about Baldur's desire to get the American girl alone on his boat. When I shared my fears with Murna, I heard another woman answer. This woman knew Ariel, and she was too angry at Baldur and too fearful for her friend to remember to pretend. Since then, I've been sure there are two of you, and the woman I don't know has a life in Dublin. So this is also the day I ask you if you have feelings for this girl Ariel."

Nell let out a sigh of relief. "Is that what you've been worried about? My God, no."

"She's pretty, she's smart, I could see how it could happen."

"Well it hasn't, because we're both in love with somebody else," Nell said. "Rather, there's a man Ariel is falling in love with and he is a good match for her and she for him. As for me, as I might have mentioned already, my heart is taken."

Hulda didn't look convinced. She and Nell eyed each other for a long minute until Nell sighed for a second time and make an executive decision.

"Come here," Nell said, and she held her arms out to Hulda. Hulda hesitated, then came and sat on the couch next to Nell, and let Nell wrap an arm around her shoulder and stroke her hair. Her body softened a little, and she scooted closer.

As the two women curled together, Nell began to talk. "This is so much bigger, and about so much more than a gifted greedy man who threatens the wealth distribution in Iceland. Hulda, I'm part of something more important, and I need you to understand."

"So tell me. What could possibly be so important?"

Nell started to talk. Speaking the truth felt good, and Nell went way beyond what she'd intended. By the time the night was halfway through, Hulda and Nell had no more secrets. Then Nell did her best to convince Hulda she was not only Murna's lover, but she was Nell's true love as well.

Jerk and Snap

21. Awkward in Oslo

Ariel was really looking forward to the weekend with Mikkel, until the meeting in Dublin put a damper on her enthusiasm. The group decided she needed to play along with Baldur's attempt to push her and Mikkel together, and left it to her to draw the line where she wished. Now, she had to find a balance between her own desires and the best outcome for everyone.

Mikkel greeted her with a warm hug, and Ariel savored a premory of chocolate pudding enjoyed at some upcoming celebration. His mother's chocolate pudding, made from scratch.

"What do you see?" he asked, recognizing the look on her face.

"Not much. Dessert. You do like your desserts."

They flirted and talked as they made their way out of the airport and to the hotel. Once they were checked in and the bellhop sent on his way, it was awkward.

"We don't know each other all that well," he said, thinking he understood her unexpected shyness.

"No, we don't, and things have gotten more complicated since I played fortune-teller with you last time."

"What do you mean?"

Out came the story of the meeting between Cillian and Toby and the group's consensus that Baldur would be less suspicious if she appeared to be falling for Mikkel, and to reluctantly be helping Baldur on Mikkel's behalf.

"So you're not here to be with me? You're here to bait this creep?" Mikkel sounded disappointed.

"No, I'm here to do both. I mean, being with you was my first choice, but now it's like, I don't know. I've got Baldur watching me, probably gloating that he can manipulate me into your arms. There are eight other people cheering us on, more than half of whom I work with, and something that was private and really nice now makes me feel like I'm up here pole dancing for everyone. I don't know how to explain it."

"You explained it fine. I don't blame you, to be honest. This is bizarre. Are you good with this group's plan?"

Ariel nodded. "I helped create it. No one forced me into this."

"Okay. I'm not as wild about it as the rest of you. I don't mind you faking an interest in me..." Ariel started to object. Mikkel put up his hand. "Let me finish please. I don't mind you faking an interest in me in order to further the demise of a man who needs to be stopped, but this puts you, and me too, in a certain amount of danger. Let's not pretend otherwise."

"I don't think we have to get so dramatic about it."

"I think we do. Baldur is a dangerous man playing for high stakes. We're not fools. We shouldn't act like fools by developing feelings for each other right now. You need to keep a clear head. So do I."

"Well this sucks."

"Hey, once your gang of eight decided you and I were going to deceive Baldur, they dictated this." He looked at her, puzzled. "What, you thought that we could have a little fun on the side, no harm no foul, and part way through the weekend you'd give me the good news that we were also fulfilling a greater agenda?"

She nodded.

"Come on. Hearts often follow where bodies go. What if only one of us gets attached? We both have to keep up the charade. What if we both develop feelings? Two people with clouded judgement is a dangerous situation. You know I'm right."

Ariel hadn't given the situation such cold analysis, but she got what he was trying to say. He was looking out for their safety. She sat on the corner of the bed feeling miserable.

"It's not all bad, Ariel. We need to be seen doing things, so we get to go sightseeing in Oslo. We'll have some fun."

Of course we will. Just not the kind of fun I was hoping for.

They treated themselves to dinner at a wonderful restaurant and kept the conversation light. By the time they got back to the hotel some of the awkwardness had subsided. Mikkel looked around the room for an alternative to sharing the cozy double bed or sleeping on the floor. There wasn't one.

"We can share the bed," Ariel said. "I promise I'll behave."

"I think I know just the mood killer to make sure we do."

She gave him a puzzled look. "You've got a nasty communicable disease?"

He had to laugh. "Fortunately, no. But there's another painful conversation we need to have. I was going to wait, but under the circumstances, we may as well have this talk now."

Ariel's insides went icy cold. "You're married."

"No. I'm not. What you need to know is I don't have a potential future with anyone, including you."

"You're dying?"

"Sorry. I'm not doing this very well. I haven't had a chance to explain this to many ladies. Ariel, I'm not just designing a permanent manned mission to Mars. I'm leading it."

"What?"

I'm going. Sometime in the early twenties, I hope. It's not like it's tomorrow, but I can't make promises about the rest of my life."

"That's insane. Do you want to go to Mars?"

"It is not insane, and yes I do. More than anything. The truth is I've given my life to a cause, and I don't decide anymore what I have in my future. I willingly follow the premonitions of an Irish psychic who stares into space and decrees this or that will or won't keep my species from going extinct. If something is going to help the cause, I do it. If it doesn't matter, then I do what I want.

"It turns out my leading the mission is a huge factor, according to Cillian. So while I'm available as a boyfriend, or a fling or whatever you want to call it, any relationship with me has an expiration date of less than ten years."

"I could be okay with that."

"Maybe. I could have to send you packing well before, to make sure you don't tempt me to stay, or break my heart when I go. You see, there are all kinds of nasty issues with knowing your own future, even when someone else sees it for you."

"Yeah." Ariel stood up, walked over to Mikkel and embraced him in a bear hug. He stiffened, but he held still. Just as she expected, the premories of the beach vacation had receded into tiny fractions of a possibility, and there weren't near as many other pleasant moments either. Just the damn chocolate pudding.

Looked like dessert might be the highlight of Mikkel's life for a long while.

******

Cillian was staring out the window of the library on a late Saturday afternoon when Nell walked in. It was a stormy day, as gloomy as it had been a week earlier when he and Siarnaq had their embrace in the rain swept gazebo. Cillian had hardly spoken to anyone since the encounter, and Nell was worried.

"You have to talk to someone," she said. "It doesn't have to be me. Hell, find a therapist or a priest or even a bartender who will simply think you're are crazy. It doesn't matter who, but find someone, Cillian. I mean it, as your friend."

"Can't afford to be crazy." Nell noticed his words were slurred. "My dad has Doyle disinheriting me and removing me from this house. Who'd have thought I could be a drunk womanizer who gambled our fortune away and be forgiven, but catch me even half naked holding another man and I've crossed the line into sin."

"You've got to be kidding."

"My dad, if he did become responsive enough to make these wishes known, probably thinks I am penniless without him. Doyle knows better, but even he doesn't know how much I've stashed away, much less what kind of fortune Mikkel and I have made."

"You think Doyle is faking your dad's wishes?"

Cillian shrugged. "Doesn't matter, does it? I'll walk away with the plenty I've got and be happy enough to lose all these damn people tending to me all the time."

"Have you tried to talk to your dad?"

"Of course. It's the first thing I did. The man won't look at me, not even the little bit he used to. So who knows?"

"Did you try to explain to Doyle? Not that you should have to."

"No, I didn't. What would I say to him, anyway?"

He poured himself another whiskey and poured one for Nell as well. She took it and they sipped in silence.

"You know what pisses me off the most?" he said. "The end is so stupid. No alien invasion, no asteroid. Not even a computer rebellion, or climate change disaster, or nuclear war. It's nothing poetic, nothing we bring on ourselves, nothing we can avoid. It's random stupidity."

Nell took another slow sip and said nothing. Cillian didn't either. After a while, she had to ask. "Now that you know, can't you tell people? Warn Mrs. O'Leary her cow is going to kick over the lantern and burn down Chicago? Yes, you've told me how doing that kind of thing starts another timeline that could be awful, but what's worse than total annihilation?"

"No," Cillian barked. Then, with more gentleness. "No, there's no Mrs. O'Leary to warn. The stupidity comes from a creature that isn't human, isn't mammal, has no brain."

Nell looked at him with questions in her eyes.

"It's a life form that doesn't exist now. It evolves, coming out of the virus family, like we came from the primates. It's much like us, actually, in that it becomes more complex and capable than its ancestors in an extremely short time. Just a little experiment of nature, one more new idea to try as life keeps reshuffling the deck. Only this species is a particularly bad idea."

"How can a creature without a brain be stupid?" Nell asked.

"Because it kills off the hosts that give it life. Once it gets going, it's so contagious it destroys everything it needs to live until it goes extinct. It ends up having one of the briefest stints of any species on this planet, managing only months of existence. It's pathetic."

"Do we bring it on somehow? Experiments gone awry, biological warfare run amok?"

"No. It comes tearing out of nowhere all by itself. There's nobody to warn; the little fooker just evolves. It gets its time to be, and for whatever reason, that time is in 2352."

"How bad is it?"

"It attacks all mammals including humans, and leaves one creature alive out of every ten-thousand it infects. It's hard to imagine nature, normally so clever, could produce such a complex yet short-sighted, creature."

Nell did the math. The city of Dublin had about half a million people. "That leaves fifty people alive in Dublin."

Nell poured them both another whiskey.

"It wouldn't be so deadly," Cillian said, "except it lays dormant for over two weeks before symptoms start, allowing it to spread almost everywhere. Travel restrictions are put in place once we know, but they come too late. Only the most isolated regions survive and there aren't many of those left. A few island atolls in the Pacific, if we get global warming under control. A few remote places in the Himalayas, and northern Greenland, of course."

Nell understood. "After that it's a numbers game. Die off in a few generations or turn the tide and grow again as a species."

Cillian nodded. "You've got it. It's a tough road. I've been racking my brain for ideas. I could fund more medical research on communicative diseases. I considered advocating for a travel ban that year, but I can't see a future in which I'm listened to."

"Speaking out like that carries too many risks. You need to keep chipping away at those awful odds every way you can. There is no better idea."

"I suppose not." Cillian savored the last few drops of his whiskey. "I'll keep trying; of course. Tonight I'm sad I'll have to do it somewhere other than here." He gestured around the rich dark wood and the leather-bound volumes in the study. "This is my home. I wish I'd appreciated it more."

******

Siarnaq began to smooth away Mikkel's problems, but he didn't hurry. After the two of them met in the diner, his mind accepted his cousin was no threat, but in his heart a small sense of betrayal hadn't completely melted away. He was a man of his word, however, so he plodded along at putting things right.

After his encounter with the Irish prophet, however, Siarnaq felt more urgency. The horrible visions the embrace brought left him ready to help anyone working to make the future right.

Baldur hadn't contacted Siarnaq in over a month, and Siarnaq hoped the Icelander had moved on to money-making schemes that didn't involve Mikkel. He was visiting family in Nuuk when a polite email from Baldur confirmed his best-case scenario.

"I regret disappointing you, but a change in business strategy has made it impossible for me to continue with our arrangement regarding your cousin. Consider our collaboration over. I wish you success in your efforts to protect the natural way of life in Greenland."

That was helpful. Siarnaq sent back a note describing a recent family reconciliation resulting in his own change of heart. He now considered his cousin to be a harmless zealot causing no damage.

He was delighted Baldur was focusing his attention elsewhere and wished him and his money-hoarding all the best.

Siarnaq stared at the screen for a minute after he sent the message. With Baldur on to other matters, and he and Mikkel reconciled, what prevented him from reaching out to Ariel? She could remain miffed at his choices, but he hoped she wouldn't.

"Hello Ariel," he typed. "I hope this finds you well..."

******

Ariel had been back at her desk in Dublin for over a week, trying to carry on with normal life, when she was surprised to see an email from Siarnaq. He was in Nuuk, letting her know he and Baldur had gone their separate ways and her client Mikkel was safe from interference. She wondered what Siarnaq would think of her impending partnership with Baldur. Matters had gotten so much more complicated in the last few weeks.

In the email, Siarnaq told her he now knew the purpose of Mikkel's work, and Mikkel knew of his. Of course, Siarnaq didn't know of her recent intimacy with Mikkel. Frankly, it was none of his business.

On the other hand, Mikkel knew there'd once been something between her and Siarnaq. He'd never questioned her about it, and she'd offered little information. Well, those details weren't Mikkel's business either.

But ... they were cousins. Childhood friends. Sworn enemies. Now, co-conspirators in a mission to improve humanity's chances of survival. Yes, she'd slept with both of them and enjoyed it. Under the right circumstances, she'd sleep with either one of them again. Yet to say what she did wasn't either one's business .... well, she admitted that wasn't entirely true.

Mikkel and she had agreed to keep their distance while they pretended to be lovers. He'd be here in Dublin on Friday, and had invited her out to dinner as part of their performance. Ariel was pretty sure he wished the two of them could have more.

Siarnaq had now invited her to come visit him if she was interested and able. Probably he was hoping for more than dinner and conversation, too.

How to respond? What to do? How had this turned so damned complicated?

"Ariel?"

It was Fergus, or maybe Ronan. She thought the one with the pointier chin was Fergus but she wasn't positive. It didn't matter. She could hear the urgency in his voice.

"There you are. When did you get in? We've got Eoin on the phone and we're all in the conference room. We need you now."

Jake was leading a discussion as she and Fergus walked in, and Ariel was impressed with the math he was trying to explain. His wide body blocked most of the white board he was writing on, but he'd filled two other white boards with equations and there were spreadsheets open on three laptops.

"I do this for fun," he told Ariel, with a sheepish smile. "It's how I could be sure Baldur was beating the system."

"What *is* this?" Ariel stared at the equations on the board. She was no slouch at math, but this would make most humans dizzy.

"Black-Scholes calculations on the time value of the expiring options Baldur selected in July. They can guide our decisions as to what we sell. We can't mirror Baldur exactly. If you could offer any guidance…"

Ariel shook her head. "I don't get premories about the stock market, and I don't see anything in the few-day time frame you're are asking about." Something puzzled her. "How do you get so much info on what he is doing?"

Brendan walked in the room, cables and cords in his hand. "That's what I do. If it goes through any machine I care for, forget hacking. That can be traced. The hardware doesn't talk like the software does."

Ronan, or the one with the wider eyes, added, "Baldur's got a mole in his organization, too. Hulda gets word to us whenever she can. She plants a camera in the room, sometimes, if she thinks she can get away with it."

"The key here," Eoin chimed in on the speakerphone, "is we want Baldur to make enough money consider his collaboration with Ariel a success, but not as much as he hopes.

The person Ariel thought was Fergus nodded. "Mikkel says if we do this right, it'll only take a few months before he crosses his tipping point. We can let the wolves loose on Baldur after that."

22. Honor in Reykjavik

Baldur knew enough history to appreciate the irony of October being a bad month for the stock market. Tomorrow, on October 19, his options would expire. When he arrived at his office Thursday morning, he asked Hulda to see he had food but otherwise remained undisturbed all day and all of Friday as well.

"Doing some serious trading these two days?"

"No, important data-gathering. No one, I mean *no one,* is to walk through this door before Monday. Do you understand?"

"Of course. You have my word of honor."

Baldur snorted. "Hulda. I mean no offense, but it's my observation women don't have a sense of honor."

Hulda decided she was offended, whether Baldur had meant her to be or not.

"What I meant to say is a woman's honor consists of her willingness to keep men's paws off of her. It's not the same thing as a man's sense of honor, which involves loftier concepts."

"What you describe," Hulda said "is a *man's* definition of a woman's honor."

"Really?"

"Really," she said. "I've seldom met a woman silly enough to think honor has anything to do with who you sleep with, or for that matter, how you fight. I've met many men too silly to realize that."

Baldur considered for a minute. "Cleopatra. Helen of Troy. Salome. Guinevere. I think history proves women have no sense of honor."

"History proves a few women didn't, and they are the ones men remember.

"Okay," Baldur said. "History is full of honorable men. Where are the comparable women?"

"Not mentioned in history. There's a cliff in Bulgaria where forty women braided their hair together and jumped into the ocean to keep the Ottomans from invading their village to steal brides. If forty men had done something like that, they'd still be making movies about it."

"Maybe," Baldur conceded "but that's a single story."

"Do you have any idea how many more stories like that I could tell you?"

"No, I don't, and today I don't have time to find out."

"So how about you agree women are at least as prone as men to make sacrifices for the well-being of others? That, by the way, is what honor is about, for both genders. Not screwing or fighting."

Baldur looked at Hulda like he'd just met her. Then he shook his head in disbelief as he closed his office door. He settled in, put his newly argumentative receptionist out of his mind, and watched with fascination as the market began to respond to world news.

A telecommunications company in Mexico City announced it would offer high-speed internet service without a phone line. Ariel predicted it. The decision increased the Chief Executive's net worth by $1.8 billion and netted Baldur millions. That would do.

Next, General Electric, McDonald's and Microsoft stock all dropped when the companies reported profits slightly less than what Wall Street expected. Baldur smiled as Ariel's bets against the three brought him more money.

The real clincher was late in the day, when Google stock dived eleven percent because its third-quarter results were released ahead of schedule due to a human blunder. The company had revenue of $11.3 billion for the quarter, and not the $11.8 billion analysts were expecting. The two founders of Google saw their personal fortunes drop by over three billion because of the shortfall. Baldur, however, managed to make over $100 million before trading of Google stock was halted on NASDAQ.

He slept in his office that night, waking a few times to follow the investments on the Tokyo and Hong Kong exchanges. He rose early to check in on the other European stock markets. By the end of the day, almost every option Ariel had guided him to had moved in his favor. A quick calculation gave her an incredible success rate of over ninety-five percent.

He noted from the Bloomberg report that the 100 richest people on Earth added over twelve billion to their collective net worth during the past five days, while lower-than-expected corporate earnings wiped out most gains for average investors.

Baldur studied his chart of the 100 wealthiest humans. He wasn't listed, of course, and was doing his best to keep it that way. Let the press focus on those who headed conglomerates or had come into this world wealthy at birth. Much of Baldur's worth was hidden here and there. It would stay that way until he was too big to be scrutinized.

He needed to ensure Ariel's cooperation, now that he knew how successful she could make him.

Was her affection for Mikkel strong enough for Baldur to play that card? He thought it was his best bet. Time to contact her, and reassure her he was a reasonable man proposing a sensible arrangement.

******

Friday after work, Ariel greeted Mikkel with a business-like demeanor and no touch, as separate cabs let them off outside the trendy Dublin restaurant she'd picked for their performance.

"Not very convincing," he said as they stepped onto the sidewalk together. "This would be better."

He placed his hand firmly behind her head and gave her a deep kiss that spoke of longing and days of separation. She tried to back away at first, and then realized he was right. She kissed back with equal ardor.

"Much better. Now, we look like two lovers about to have dinner."

She was bothered by the unwanted emotions stirred up by the kiss, and by something else.

"I didn't see anything when we did that."

"Maybe you were too distracted," he said as they made their way through the Friday night crowd to the hostess stand.

"Don't flatter yourself." He responded with a wink.

Once they were seated, they kept the conversation light. They held hands as they lingered over liquor and dessert. Ariel suspected Mikkel hated to see their outward show end. She had to agree; it was fun pretending to fall in love.

"Ready to go check out late-night television at the hotel?" She asked because it looked like he was never going to sign the credit card receipt even though the waiter had been hovering.

"Sure." He put on his best business face. "Of course."

The nice room had two double beds, and Ariel placed her travel bag on one, then joined him, sitting cross-legged on his bed. She picked up the remote.

He scooted closer to offer her one of the chocolates on his pillow. Well, there was no need to be rude. She took the chocolate, and as she touched his hand she was back on the beach in a hammock with him naked. How had that premory got there? In it she was having the time of her life.

The Mikkel on the hotel bed looked puzzled as she crawled onto his lap, and the kiss they started on the sidewalk hours ago continued as though three hours hadn't gotten in the way. Soon the hammock memory vanished as the real Ariel enjoyed the real now. Mikkel not only didn't object, but before long he was an active participant.

They lay together in silence afterwards, neither wanting to break the spell. Ariel could only guess what Mikkel was thinking, but she suspected it had something to do with how they couldn't let this wonderful moment happen again. For her part, she was baffled but impressed by the premories floating through her head. Every one of them involved superb to incredible sex over the next several months. She giggled inside. This was a use of her abilities she wished she'd found sooner. Then she stopped. Every occurrence, every single one, was with Mikkel.

"Damn you."

She stood up, and the second time she said it she yelled it at him. "Damn you!"

"Hey, you started it, not me." He was instantly defensive.

"Of course I did. I don't mean that. I mean damn you because I'm not going to Mars."

"Of course you're not. You have no interest in going." Then he got it too.

"Oh no, this is so wrong. Ariel, I am not trying to rope you into my dream. I want you to have free will. I'm not ever going to ask you to go to Mars."

He was genuinely upset and Ariel appreciated it.

"I know you're not. But it makes sense, doesn't it? I come to Dublin and Cillian starts getting far-off vibes of a better future. What can I do that matters? I thought I was going to make a difference by bringing down Baldur, but I'm not sure that's the whole story. You and I have a fun weekend together and our favorite prophet sees humanity's chances of survival go up. We laughed it off, but Mikkel, part of this is about us. We roll around together, things look better. I bet you can call Cillian now and he can't explain why but his giant crystal ball in the sky suddenly shows everything has improved again."

Mikkel reached for his phone.

"Don't you dare."

"Why would you matter so much?" Mikkel was thinking aloud, she realized, and meant no offense at the question.

"Maybe having someone along who sees the future has a positive effect on the outpost's chances of survival? Here on Earth there's so much input, I hardly get anything useful. It could be different there."

"I don't know what to say. I don't even know how I feel about this. I sure as hell don't want to add to your issues, and I don't need you adding to mine."

"Okay. Short term problems first," Ariel took a breath. "Let's put a stop to Baldur. He's more than capable of adding to the world's misery now and of mucking up your and Cillian's plans. Do you think we can get through the next couple of months ignoring our future?"

Mikkel nodded. "I could support deferring this issue." He gestured to the pillow next to him. "So... how do you want to leave things for the moment?"

Ariel got up and moved to the other bed. "I'm not taking a vow of chastity here or anything, but for the rest of tonight I could do without all the sensual images I get every time I touch you. Okay?"

"Sure." He smiled. "Sensual images, huh? Don't want those to keep you awake."

She smiled back at him from her own bed before she turned away and tried to sleep.

Mikkel left on Saturday as planned, and Sunday morning there was a knock on Ariel's door. It would be someone sent by Baldur. She'd seen this possible future emerge and grow; as the options expired and she made Baldur a fortune. Now it was coming to pass. So be it. She'd play her part.

But first, she had an idea.

"Just a minute," she yelled as she opened an email from her mother. Mom had included a dozen telepaths in Western Europe on her note. Ariel hit reply to all and added Jake and Brendan. They'd be baffled, but would get word to others in the office.

The knock became louder. She typed as fast as she could.

"Will be in Reykjavik. My safety is in question. Check on me. My mom knows more."

Send, close browser, turn off laptop. This was going to scare her mom but it couldn't be helped.

"Coming," she yelled.

The man at the door identified himself as a limo driver, there to take her to Baldur's private jet, which was waiting.

"Let me grab a few things."

Once he was inside, he waited patiently. She wondered what his instructions were if she ran. She saw no point in finding out. Going to work for Baldur was exactly what she needed to do.

Once she boarded the plane, Ariel put her earbuds in, turned up her music and indulged in every snack in the well-stocked cupboard. She avoid the alcohol, though, tempting as it was. She needed to stay sharp.

Another polite driver met her on the other end. She wondered if she was going to a hotel in Reykjavik or to Baldur's house. The answer was neither.

"Welcome."

Ulfur, Baldur's lawyer and expert question deflector, greeted her as though she was an old friend come to visit. Ulfur's wife was close behind, ready to show Ariel to her room. So this was how it was going to be. She was the guest of a friendly middle-aged couple.

"Baldur asked me to tell you he'll see you tomorrow at the office. Your driver will be here at nine. Would you like something to eat before you go to bed?"

They couldn't have been more pleasant, but for once Ariel wasn't hungry. Alone in her room, she pulled on the sweat clothes she'd started sleeping as the nights got colder. She took a few minutes to run her hands over the bed, the dresser, and her own things hoping for a premory of some use, but it was the usual nonsense. She was starting to think being able to precall the next few hours or days would be more helpful. Maybe that was why no one seemed to have the ability.

After she crawled under the covers, she sent quick bland emails about an unexpected trip to Iceland to her folks, to Eoin, and to co-workers Jake and Brendan. They'd each figure out what was happening. Then she shut her computer off, put it under her pillow and tried to sleep.

Hulda didn't look Ariel in the eye the next morning, and Ariel wondered how much the woman knew. Perhaps the role she played as frosty gatekeeper was getting harder to maintain. She showed Ariel into Baldur's office and left. Once the door was closed, Baldur tried to give her his warmest smile.

"Our relationship has changed. I'm not your client, at least not for much longer. I propose a business partnership and I insist you consider it."

"The Google tip worked out well, didn't it?"

He nodded. "As did having a sense of the less-than-stellar earnings of three other big companies, not to mention the Mexican telecommunication intel. All around impressive and all it took was an hour of your time."

"I don't want to play the stock market. I don't want to risk being in violation of SEC rules. And I don't want to go into partnership with you." It was easy to say with feeling.

"I know. But I have an additional incentive to offer you. You have a new boyfriend, no?"

"I don't think I'd call him my boyfriend, but yes, I'm in the early stages of a relationship." Ariel tried to appear evasive.

"Yes. With one of your clients. Naughty girl." Baldur seemed to find this amusing. "But this can stay our little secret. You must know something about what your new boyfriend is doing with the millions he is making following in my footsteps?"

Ariel rolled her eyes and tried to look annoyed. "He has some stupid dream about Mars. The time and money he spends on it is ridiculous."

"Yes, that must bother you. He could be buying you lavish gifts instead. Did you know he's having to put so much time into this project because he keeps running into problems? Materials, labor, if anything can go wrong, it does. You do have the power to make his problems go away, because I have the power to do so."

Ariel tried for her best look of surprise mixed with a little outrage. "You're causing Mikkel's problems? Why?"

Baldur shrugged. "He got on my nerves. Always imitating my update requests. Then I found out how much he was making. I sure as hell don't need to let a newcomer take more of my pie."

"I see." Ariel didn't have to work to make her voice cold.

"That's all about to change. Given what you and I can do together, we've got whole new pies to go after. Lots of pies. I can afford to let Mikkel have a share, and a lack of troubles too, if it pleases my new business partner."

"Are you planning to tie me to a table again?"

"I told you I was sorry about that. I needed answers and you wouldn't give them to me. There will be no need for anything so barbaric in the future."

"What exactly are you proposing?"

"A day of your time, every month. Allow me unlimited access to your skin for the duration of the trading day. If I'm not rushed, I won't need others to participate, so I can guarantee no uncomfortable invasion of your privacy. As long as you cooperate, you'll be treated with the respect you deserve."

"I want a cut of it."

"I'm willing to allow your boyfriend" he said the word pointedly "a certain amount of leeway in copying my investments, as long as he becomes less greedy than he has been."

"What do you consider less greedy?"

He smiled at the question. "You, too, may profit, of course, as long as what you and your boyfriend make together doesn't exceed one percent of what I make."

"One percent is nothing!"

"One percent of the kind of money I intend to make is far from nothing. You have little knowledge of stocks. You've never seen events that could help you invest, have you?"

"I've never tried."

"Let me assure you, it's not as easy as it sounds. Even with a strong background, it's a difficult system to navigate. Your learning curve would be long and expensive. Ariel, one percent of what I'm going to make is way better than one-hundred percent of what you and Mikkel can do by yourselves. Consider carefully."

Ariel did, or at least she gave her best appearance of doing so, given that her decision was already made.

"A day every month. No creepy behavior. One percent of your profits. Things up in Greenland encounter no problems you cause. We have a deal."

"There's no legal way to enforce this arrangement, but luckily we're both better off adhering to it," Baldur said.

"Agreed. I trust your driver will take me back to the airport now." Ariel was all business.

"Good heavens, no. Today is the first day you owe me, and I need you until the New York markets close tonight. There's a couch for you to lie on, and I've taken the liberty of having Hulda purchase a swimsuit for you. I'm sorry it's so skimpy, but I've established the contact between us remains better if I move my hands around. I'll be watching the screen and can't afford to miss a crucial trade because I put my hand on your clothing."

"Okay." She guessed she should have expected this, and it was probably why Hulda hadn't looked her in the eye. "Is it okay if I read a book or something while you work? Maybe take a nap?"

A pained expression barely crossed his face, and Ariel realized she'd found his weakness.

"You need to be awake. I won't lie to you; it works better when you pay attention. I'll be talking aloud about what I'm doing, much the way my colleagues and I talked last time. I'll probably also run an investor's news program in the background while we work. You should do your best to keep the stock market on your mind. More profits for me means more profits for you."

She had to hide her delight. He not only needed her exposed flesh, he also needed her to pay attention, and to care about what was happening. That was a whole new kind of power, wasn't it? She couldn't wait to tell the others.

When Ariel got home from Reykjavik early Tuesday afternoon she was utterly exhausted. She knew she'd done well for Baldur, paying attention to the stocks under consideration. With her greater concentration, the constructive interference from their abilities was stronger. Ariel was pretty sure Baldur had put a lot more money on the line.

She sent a quick email to everyone who might care, assuring them she was home safe and in no mood to talk and would be at work the next morning. Ariel was in bed before 6 p.m. and slept until the alarm went off.

Mikkel was the first to call, and he caught her as she emerged from the shower. He was worried. She described the trip, and he had the sense not to over-react. He wanted her to know that more than one sticky problem had resolved itself already at his plant in Northern Greenland.

He was bothered nothing was in place yet to mimic the investments she and Baldur had made. Would she get with Ronan and Fergus and see what she could do? Also, they should plan another weekend together in a couple of weeks, to keep the show going. Maybe London?

Ariel didn't know whether to laugh or cry. Mikkel didn't realize it yet, but he was becoming emotionally involved in spite of his resolve. Ariel knew the symptoms.

As she hung up the phone, she wondered if she felt the same way back. She didn't think so. Ten years was a long time, far longer than any relationship she'd had. Still, knowing something had to end put a damper on it. She'd hoped for marriage and kids maybe, down the road, someday. No hurry. It wasn't her primary criteria for dating, but knowing it was impossible did change things.

As did knowing if the relationship went well, she could end up going somewhere she didn't want to go. She liked nightlife and cities. She liked the wind and the sky and the whole beautiful planet teeming with life. She didn't want to leave it.

She'd told Mikkel she wouldn't think about the future now, and she was trying hard not to. But putting on her mascara forced her to look into her eye in the mirror. Was it possible she could mess things up for the human race by having the life she wanted?

She felt sad as she drove into the office, and slipped into her cube unnoticed.

October 2012

23. An Autumn Night

Ariel had ignored the email from Siarnaq for longer than she meant to, and tonight she would respond. It was going to be tough. Beneath her anger at his alliance with Baldur, she felt affection for him and appreciation for what he was trying to do. She'd waded far enough into murky waters with Cillian and his cause to not throw stones at anyone trying to do right in this mess.

On the other hand, her life was complicated, and Siarnaq only offered more complications. She had neither the means nor the time to run off to Greenland for a weekend. Even worse, she could be developing affection for his cousin. It was best to end anything resembling romance, and offer Siarnaq no more than her friendship from afar.

She crafted the best response she could, and sent it off hoping it conveyed warmth and yet a desire to close the door on what they shared.

Siarnaq responded within an hour.

"When you did not answer me for days, I didn't expect to hear from you again. I found out why. Families talk. Imagine how sad I was to learn that my cousin, who I've only recently reconciled with, has been seeing a red-haired American girl who lives in Ireland and works with the computers for his investment company. Did you start a romance with him to spite me? My dear Ariel, I did not realize I had hurt you so badly."

Oh Siarnaq, What I did with Mikkel had nothing to do with you. But in Siarnaq's mind it did. Ariel wondered who Mikkel had talked to in his family, and why? Knowing Mikkel, she guessed he'd been trying to deflect unwanted questions about his love life. "I'm seeing someone, sort of." Easy to have said without thinking.

Siarnaq ended his email: "I can't believe we've grown so far from each other, after the intensity of what we shared. We need to talk; we need to touch. I've learned much about what lies ahead and I could use the comfort of your arms. Please find a way to come to Greenland."

Well that didn't work so well.

Ariel curled up on her bed and let a few tears of self-pity fall. Then the premory came. A likely one. Siarnaq was hugging her, wishing her well, and she had a sense things were good between them. It was a flash; but it felt important. She wiped away the tears, grabbed her laptop and opened her calendar for November. The first weekend was open, but it was in ten days. Eoin was giving her an unusual amount of leeway. Could she work out a business trip to Nuuk?

******

When Cillian invited the six employees of Ullow to his house for a business dinner, no one thought it was going to be about business. The cold dark nights of autumn made any outdoors gathering out of the question, but Ariel was surprised to see a table set-up in the main dining room, a peat fireplace lit, candles glowing and a full bar in plain view.

"We can visit inside?"

Cillian answered as a maid took her coat. "We're going to. I've given most of the staff the night off. Kaitlin here," he gestured to the maid, "is tending to our needs, and she's already acquainted with my situation."

Eoin, Ronan, Fergus and Jake gathered around Cillian, equally curious. Something had changed for him, and they all wanted to understand.

"I'll get to the point soon enough," he promised everyone. "Get yourself a drink and have a seat."

After a few minutes of shuffling around, Ariel sat down between Brendan and the young man she'd decided was Fergus. She held a whisky and soda in her hand.

"Isn't this a gorgeous house, Fergus?"

"It is, but I'm Ronan. Don't worry, everyone confuses us all the time. I'm the one whose chin is a little sharper, you know?"

"Right. Thanks. I'll remember that."

Cillian stood up to speak and all other conversation stopped.

"Doyle recently started legal proceedings to remove me from this house, claiming he is acting in my father's wishes," Cillian began. The Ullow group exchanged looks ranging from puzzled to knowing. "My father has become more catatonic over the last two weeks, and Doyle does have dad's power of attorney. My lawyers are advising me this could turn into a long legal battle and not end well for me. As you know, I don't need to find myself back in the public eye. So yesterday I agreed to vacate the premises by the end of November. This is, in essence, a farewell party to this lovely house.

"Doyle agreed to give me a month to make other living arrangements." He smiled a little at the objections from the group. "Please. The money to fund my projects is available to me, so I'll hardly be homeless. A few of the household staff have said they'd like to relocate with me, so I may not even have to learn to cook. I'm going to be fine." He said the last bit as though he was trying to convince himself.

"In some ways, you've become family over the past few months as we've shared our secrets, so I wanted to tell you this in person and make a toast."

Cillian raised his glass. "My friends are the best friends, loyal, willing and able. Now let's get to drinking! All glasses off the table! Sláinte."

The group laughed and drank, but the questions were far from over. As the soup was served, those who didn't know already were told about Siarnaq's visit two weeks ago, and of the embrace that brought more detailed visions to both men.

"I see no harm in sharing what we learned, although I suggest discretion with the information. I've seen no future in which public knowledge helps the situation, and several in which it causes worse to happen. Plus, you make your own life less pleasant if people think of you as a nut job."

He turned to Ariel. "The Irish have a saying that there's nothing so bad it couldn't be worse. I'm afraid what I'm going to tell you may test that theory."

The group listened as Cillian told them of the rapid evolution of a tiny, short-lived new life form that would render most mammals extinct and create the struggle for survival haunting his visions.

"Our efforts help," Cillian assured his friends. "I've seen no way to keep this critter from evolving, but there are ways in which less people die. There are paths providing a better world for those who survive. I've sensed the odds of these improvements inch upwards even in a short time, as both Siarnaq and I better understand what we're doing. Yes, of course, I'm looking into new ideas now that I know more. Yes, of course, I'll listen to every great idea each of you has no doubt had while I've been telling you this. But later. This is a party, and I'd like us to enjoy ourselves. So, just one really short business conversation on the more upbeat topic of how to build our nest egg before we stop Baldur."

"We do have updates," Brendan said. He turned to Ariel.

Ariel told those she hadn't yet spoken with about her quasi-abduction to Iceland as Baldur proposed a working relationship.

"It's basically extortion," she said, explaining Baldur was promising to ensure her boyfriend's space project didn't catch on fire as long as his girlfriend provided financial consulting to d^4 and never made more than one percent of what Baldur made from the consultation.

"That's excellent!" Brendan couldn't contain his enthusiasm.

"I didn't think one percent was enough."

"It's not about the amount," Brendan said. "Baldur is hiding his income and we're having trouble tracking it. He may not tell you about everything, but in order to hold you to one percent, he has to come clean about a good bit of the money he makes so you can calculate your take."

"Wait. There is more good news." With everything else going on, Ariel forgot Cillian and Nell didn't know the best part. "This mind-melding of visions thing works best for Baldur if I'm conscious and engaged in what is happening."

"This keeps getting better," Jake said. "Now he has to treat you well, and keep you in the know."

"Which brings us to exactly what Baldur does have in mind for Ariel," Eoin said. "As some of you know, Baldur is in the habit of viewing me as his pet. He may not play well with others, but he likes boasting to them. He's called me three times this past week to brag about how well he's doing."

"So that's why you're always on the phone when I try to talk to you," Ronan said.

"Yeah, well, yesterday I got to listen to a rather embarrassing recitation of Ariel's' various charms, physical and mental, and hear how Baldur was considering requiring her to break up with her space boyfriend in a few months. He thinks it would clear the way for her to realize what a team she and Baldur would make. He did refer to you two as a team, Ariel — that's something."

"It's not like Baldur to take on a partner," Jake said. "I'm pretty sure he'd never have trained the rest of d^4 if he thought he could do this alone. He needed their cash and skills to get started. I wonder what his plans are for them now? Probably not what they're expecting."

"Good point," Eoin said. "Baldur reminded me he wouldn't be needing Ullow soon and I needed to think about my own future. He was feeling quite magnanimous. He said d^4 would dissolve, once he got done cleaning up the regulations. I assume he hopes to get laws in place to ensure his old colleagues no longer have any kind of advantage."

"It does beat killing them," Brendan said.

"Not only less messy," Jake added, "but he doesn't have to play whack-a-mole every time someone who can see a few seconds ahead tries to use their gift in the stock market."

"So what does he have in mind for me?" Ariel was having trouble sitting still through this discussion.

"I got the idea he thinks he's going to marry you eventually," Eoin said. "He thinks his wealth will make him irresistible and he'll sort of make you his queen, and the two of you will run the world. He expects you to be no trouble at all, which shows how little he really knows you." Eoin gave her a friendly wink.

"Oh for christsakes."

"Have you seen any futures with Baldur?" Cillian asked. "It's okay if you have. All possibilities are out there."

Ariel nodded. "I know that. There's always odd stuff on the fringes." She turned to the group. "Don't get alarmed but I've seen flashes of aliens landing in New York and clones of Hitler rising to power when I've let myself go far enough. That's why I generally avoid the edges, they're disturbing and ridiculously unlikely. However, I do check the less fringy fringe. So while mostly I see me cooperating with Baldur again in late November, I've seen him kill me. I've seen me kill him. I've seen me lose myself and become what he wants. None of it's likely, but it's all there."

Cillian nodded in understanding. "Don't let Ariel's honesty disturb you," he told the group. "What she described is how real prescience works."

He turned to Nell, and asked about Hulda.

"She figured out more than we expected," Nell said, adding that after a recent visit Hulda was more informed than Nell intended. Nell kept glancing at Cillian while she talked. Ariel guessed Nell revealed more to Hulda than Cillian wanted.

"No harm's been done," Brendan told the group, defending both women. "Hulda can be trusted."

"We do owe Hulda a safe exit when this is over, somewhere Baldur's anger can't follow," Cillian said. Ariel saw the relief on Nell's face and hoped the safe place would be somewhere near Nell.

Brendan and Jake told the group how they were setting up hundreds of new accounts the world over, planning to grow each in secret, amassing the tipping point money. Ronan and Fergus had received field training in the shadowy world of hiding wealth.

"Once the January options expire, we'll consolidate these accounts, then give Toby's group the go-ahead. Some of his information will be outdated by then, but no less compelling. We should have clean, secure places ready for Mikkel and Cillian's entire purses."

"It's a dangerous game," Cillian said. "Ariel, do you get anything helpful?"

She shook her head. "Not about money. I do get a flash of Mikkel in a few months, feeling happy about how much he's stashed, knowing it's good enough. Better than even odds."

"Okay then. Time for brandy in front of the fire. Toasts are in order."

Once they were seated, Eoin raised his glass first.

"This is one of my favorites: 'May your home always be too small to hold all your friends.' Looking around, I have to say, I don't think the problem is that you need more friends."

Their host laughed in appreciation. "I agree. Seven true friends are more than any man has a right to ask for. Thank you Eoin. I get your toast and it's wise. I need a smaller house."

With that, the liquor went down smooth and the toasts flowed into the wee hours of the night.

"I have unfinished business," Ariel told Eoin as she marched into his office the next morning. "I need to go to Nuuk."

"Why? Is there is some reason Mikkel can't come here?"

"This isn't about Mikkel. It's about Siarnaq, Mikkel's cousin. He needs to talk to me."

"You?" Eoin rolled his eyes. "Could you please close the door?" Ariel complied and Eoin gestured for her to have a seat.

"How do *you* know Siarnaq, Cillian's kindred prophet, and why in the world does he need to visit with you?"

"He needs to touch me, Eoin, not visit with me. We've, uh, touched before. You could do me a favor and keep this between us, but Siarnaq and I do some variation of what Siarnaq and Cillian did. I'm the reason Cillian thought of trying it. Touch is different for us—I can't explain why—but it's a way to learn, a way to see beyond our normal frequencies."

"God bless us all, I've gone loony. You're not only making sense, but I believe you. So, you want me to send you off to Nuuk in the dead of winter so you can hug an Eskimo and learn more about the future?"

"No one says Eskimo anymore."

"Whatever. Can you write me up some plausible business reason?"

"You know I can. When the shit hits the fan in this office, your signing off on this trip will be the least of your problems."

"I know. Go, do whatever it is you need to do and hurry back. Even I can see the shit storm coming."

******

The only way to get from Dublin to Nuuk once summer was over was to fly to Oslo, then to Reykjavik, the last city on Earth Ariel wanted to visit. Worse yet, once she got to Iceland her flight to Nuuk was delayed due to weather.

She fretted and dozed at the Reykjavik airport for more than five hours before her small plane took off into a cloud-filled night, with pockets of warmer air causing it to bounce around.

The plane was chilly, and she shivered in her seat as she held on to her armrest. She forced herself to search for a happy premory, anything to assure her she'd be alive in a week and need not worry.

For the first time in her life, some of the far fringes returned nothing but blackness. Ariel felt her insides turn to ice as she realized those were futures in which she didn't exist. Faint, unlikely, but planes do go down in the icy waters of the North Atlantic.

She grasped for the more likely and saw herself helping Baldur, giving him what he needed to put his plans in place. Odds were it would go as expected. Wait. There was a whole family of futures in which Baldur and she were arguing as he worked. She felt her own anger that he knew. Knew what? Indignation. She would never. Never what?

The plane gave a strong lurch and Ariel wondered if planes still had airsickness bags.

She saw a smaller subset of futures branch off from the argument. In those Cillian came charging into Baldur's workroom. Cillian? He never went anywhere. What was he doing in Iceland?

The plane lurched again and Ariel rose inches out of her seat. She concentrated on reciting multiplication tables in her head. If she got to Nuuk in the next minute, it wouldn't be soon enough.

When the plane hit the runway the premories faded like the memory of a bad dream, leaving her with a vague befuddled feeling.

The Siarnaq who met her plane seemed older. He gave her a long hug through his parka and hers, the insulation sufficient to buffer any exchange. She knew his home was in Ilulissat, but he had relatives in Nuuk and stayed with them when he was in town. Not this time though, and he preferred not to go to the hotel. A friend of a friend had offered his apartment, and that would have to do.

As they drove away from the town's lights, the aurora borealis began its show. Often an undulating green curtain, tonight the northern lights reached high into the sky with the greens fading into blues, purples, pinks and reds and the curtain movements slowly giving way to what looked like multicolored feathered wings filling the sky. Siarnaq smiled as Ariel stared out the car window with her mouth open, and he reached across the front seat and put his gloved hand over hers. Once they found the friend's place, they stood together in the cold and watched the show until Ariel began to shiver.

Inside the apartment, the sights were not as pretty. The friend of a friend wasn't much for housekeeping. As the two of them eyed each other in the filthy little apartment, Siarnaq had to laugh.

"All the times I imagined a reunion with you, sunset hair, it never involved somebody so incapable of using a broom and dustpan."

"It's okay. You couldn't have known." Ariel shrugged. "I've missed you. I wish things had gone differently between us."

"Me too. Maybe we can close our eyes and pretend we're still outside."

She nodded, and they sat together on the couch, holding each other and remembering nature's incredible show.

The premories didn't come for a while, maybe because her own emotions from the day were so strong, leaving her unwilling to give her consciousness over to others. Finally, her thoughts stilled, and she saw the world through the eyes of those who made up Siarnaq's premories of things to come.

She watched their lives, felt their loves, cried their tears. Many lived before 2352 and some after. For those whose lives came after, there seemed to be more happiness this time around. She didn't have Cillian's knack for putting a number on it, but it was a sign things went in the right direction.

He seemed lost in her world, and several times he stroked her hair and mumbled things to her in a language she didn't understand. They fell asleep that way, half-dressed and holding each other, lost in other lives.

When she woke up he was gone. There was a pot of fresh coffee and a note.

"A bigger storm is coming. I've arranged a cab for you and moved your flights. You need to go. Fly safe, sunset hair, and stay safe in the winds ahead."

Oh. So this was all that would pass between them? Ariel was surprised at how disappointed she felt, but she had no desire to be stranded here or, worse yet, stuck in transit trying to get home. How like Siarnaq to help her this way.

As she made her way to the airport, she worked to recall the scenes she'd witnessed the night before in his arms. Was there anything in there of use? She didn't think so. Unless Siarnaq had seen something helpful as he moved into her wavelengths, this trip had been no more than a chance to see an incredible light show, and hug a kindred spirit good-bye.

24. For the Kittens

Hulda was careful when she first started to help Murna, but she wasn't scared. Nervous maybe. If Baldur caught her looking at documents she had no business handling or checking his schedule with no need, he could have been annoyed and, at worst, fired her. That would have been unpleasant, but for the first year, no one could prove her guilty of more than being nosy and talking too much to her new friend.

Then Murna taught her to use tiny cameras and recording devices because they would help bring Baldur down. Hulda knew if she was caught using these, no company in Reykjavik would hire her. Murna insisted it was important and begged Hulda, so she agreed.

Hulda was an honest woman, and surprised to find out how easily the devious can mislead the unsuspecting. She'd earned Baldur's trust early on; he'd watched her and concluded she was industrious and reliable. It was an artifact of Baldur's vanity that it didn't occur to him Hulda could change. He never imagined she could learn to dislike him so much she'd do things her own family would swear she was incapable of doing.

It became easier with time.

Murna coaxed her along, telling her Baldur used evil sorcery to gain advantage over others. Hulda balked at this last idea. It was true she loved her aura readings, crystals and astrology. It was all sparkly fun, and she hoped there was some truth buried in the entertainment. It was a large leap, however, to accept her boss used psychic powers to make money in the stock market. Over time, Murna convinced her.

Hulda knew Murna had come to her in disguise. She didn't question the need, not until she contacted Murna with concern for a young woman in Ireland working for Baldur. The conversation made it clear Murna knew Baldur's people in Dublin. How did she know them? That was when Hulda became worried she was the one being played, for reasons she couldn't imagine.

She'd expected Murna to lie to her, or at best to explain why Hulda was being tricked. Instead, Murna had become Nell, and had let Hulda see who she really was: an Irish woman playing a dangerous game intertwined with humanity's survival.

So. Hulda had not been tricked, not really. She was a small part in a far bigger plan than she realized. Nell, the real Murna, loved her and trusted her with secrets no human should have to know. Now, Nell needed Hulda to do more, because the stakes were becoming even higher. Hulda needed to become bolder on behalf of Murna's cause.

Unfortunately, Murna's message of importance didn't have the desired effect. Instead of feeling bolder, Hulda was now scared. In fact, she was could-hardly-make-her-muscles-work terrified, because it all mattered so much more than she'd ever guessed.

It was why she got sloppy, hurrying into Baldur's trading room to hide the device. She did such a poor job it practically fell into his hand as he brushed against a shelf. This particular one recorded audio and video, and he studied it suspiciously before he yelled for Hulda.

"Who's been in this room?"

He still trusted her, blamed her only for being a poor gatekeeper because he couldn't imagine her doing worse. Then he saw the fear on her face and he knew.

"What the hell is going on here? Are *you* spying on me? Why?" He was struggling to get his arms around the idea.

"No, it's not like that," she said, trying to force her brain to stop acting like it was drowning in molasses and to think of what it could be like. "I've been trying to learn something about investing. I opened a little account, for my retirement. I didn't think you'd want me in the room and I wanted to watch you work."

That was good. It flattered him. "See, the device doesn't transmit anywhere." It didn't. When timing permitted, she used cameras and recorders because they were harder to scan for and detect. She'd go transmit later from somewhere safer. It was the advantage of being an insider who could come and go as she pleased.

He studied her face, juggling what he wanted to believe with what he feared.

"Why didn't you ask me questions about investing if you were so curious?"

"I didn't want to bother you." Then, in a quiet, embarrassed tone, "I thought you'd laugh at me."

He smiled, that bit of condescension returning to his eyes, and Hulda knew he was back on ground he liked.

"Yes, yes I suppose I may have, just a little. So, the assistant wants to learn the master's tricks, huh? Very well." He threw the device on the ground and crunched it under the heel of his Italian leather shoe. "You won't be needing this again and I trust you'll never bring in anything similar. You may sit and watch today, as long as you say nothing. Two of my colleagues will arrive shortly."

Something occurred to him. "Have you photographed us before without our permission?"

"Yes." She'd read that including all the truth you could along with a lie helped. Her answer came out with conviction, but then she saw the anger grow on his face. "But the camera didn't work. I guess I didn't do it right. The instructions were confusing. That's why I wanted to try again."

He smiled at her ineptness. "Well, lucky for you there will be no need for you to figure out mechanical devices. I'm not sure how much you'll learn by watching us, but you may ask me a few questions after the others have left. Okay?"

"Thank you." The relief in her voice couldn't have been more real, and it served to satisfy Baldur he'd handled the crisis with all the magnanimity befitting a man as important as he was.

******

Toby was always surprised when people were reasonable. In his experience, so many people were drawn to making somebody else's life difficult because they could. He was pleased his group didn't give him a hard time with his about-face on the need to stop d⁴ immediately.

"You've never come to us before and said *please trust me,*" an economics professor from an Ivy League school said. "I'm inclined to think you must have an excellent reason."

Others echoed her sentiment, so ways were found to expand the study so results would take months longer to compile.

With that handled, Toby turned his attention to helping the inexperienced computer geeks at Ullow, who were in over their heads. They all knew how to invest money, but lacked any sense of how to hide it. Toby taught them to bend rules, to go far into the grey areas of regulations. It caused him some heartburn, but he was willing to bend his principles for the continued existence of his own species.

Actually, forget his species. Toby decided he was doing this for all the mammals. He thought back to his high school biology class. What kind of world would it be with only bugs, fish, birds, reptiles and lots and lots of different kinds of worms?

If Cillian's worst-case visions came to pass, mammals would become a short-lived experiment, simply because one hoity-toity species had figured out ways to fly around the globe spreading something deadly to every continent before it could kill itself off like nature intended. Toby didn't think the dogs deserved that sort of fate. Neither did the wolves, horses or squirrels. That's who he was bending the rules for. What kind of man would refuse to set up a few offshore bank accounts if it would ensure the survival of bunny rabbits?

On impulse, he found an incredibly cute picture of a basket of kittens and set it up as his wallpaper. Point forward, he was engaging in these shenanigans on behalf of the kittens. Who could argue with that?

******

After his mother died, Cillian looked in on his father at least once a day. He always made eye contact, said a few words to him, and made himself touch the old man's thin, dry skin because he read somewhere how human touch was important for emotional health. The truth was his dad had never done that, and most of their conversations had consisted of the father telling the son how to behave. Cillian supposed he felt love for the man, in the sense that children instinctively love a parent who doesn't harm them, and sometimes love a parent that does.

During most of Cillian's visits, the dad failed to notice his son, but occasionally there was something in his eyes that spoke of recognition. Other times, the man would mutter, or flinch at Cillian's touch. On rare occasion, he smiled when Cillian brushed his hand against his cheek. Cillian never knew what to expect.

Doyle oversaw the nursing staff and all things related to Mr. McGrane's care. There was always a nurse on duty, almost always a she. She could be found reading a book or watching television while the old man dozed. The nurses came and went so fast Cillian could never remember their names, but he would sometimes offer to sit with his dad a bit, to give the woman a break.

He saw no reason to change his habits once he was informed he was being ousted from the house. If it was the doing of the old man, and not Doyle, then the frail shell sitting before him now knew nothing of what his more conscious self had decreed. Cillian reached out to touch the parchment skin of his father's hand as Doyle came in the room, annoyed to see him.

"What are you doing here?"

"What I do every day," Cillian answered in a soft voice.

"So I've heard. I don't know why you bother. He has no idea who you are and he wouldn't like it if he did."

"Yes, I can see he doesn't know me now." Cillian crossed his eyes and stuck his tongue out at his father, who stared back without reacting. "Hard to believe he becomes so lucid he can give you clear directions." Cillian had always tiptoed around this issue, seeing nothing to be gained from challenging Doyle's claims. Now, however, Cillian had nothing to lose.

"I do your father's wishes," Doyle said, with a fierceness in his voice. "I'm more the person he wanted for his heir than you ever were."

"I agree."

"You do?"

"Of course. Any fool could see it's true. My father always liked you, and he never really liked me."

"You think so?" Doyle was perplexed. "You intend to fight me for your inheritance, don't you? Of course you do. So let me remind you, I have some video I could distribute from that day out at the gazebo. *Cillian McGrane, more deviant than thought.* It would grab a few headlines."

Cillian actually laughed. "Doyle, you've got to get out more. First of all, my having sex with a man on video would hardly interest anyone, much less my merely hugging someone. Have you been on the internet lately? Do you have any idea how many athletes, newscasters, musicians, actors and other famous people are openly gay now and hardly anyone cares?"

"That's not true in Ireland."

"Plaster your damn pictures all over the Irish press if you want. I couldn't care less. Not that it matters, but the man I was hugging isn't my lover. We were involved in a sort of, I guess a healing ritual is what you'd call it. So accuse me of engaging in New Age wackiness. That's hardly newsworthy either. You can't hurt me, Doyle. That's a terribly liberating thought."

"I can make you leave and take a good bit of your wealth."

"Yes, you can. However, I've received a fine salary and a generous living allowance for years, not to mention free room and board. I've been tucking away more than you know and investing it more successfully than you expected. There's easily as much in my name as in my dad's. So please, take his share and have a nice life."

"You are serious, aren't you?"

"I am. That lack of competitive spirit is why my own father was never so fond of me. I do hope you treat him well. Tell me, is he really this ill or is it just the heavy medication?"

"I'm outraged you would suggest such a thing."

"Does he ever have those lucid moments we all hear about, or do you just make them up?"

"I'm not going to dignify that with a response."

"That's what I thought. There isn't a nurse who's worked here long enough to accuse you of lying about either issue. Speaking alone, that is. But in aggregate, if one assembled testimony from the dozens of women you've hired and then fired, one could make a pretty strong case."

Doyle gave Cillian a sharp look.

"I was going to discuss this with you in a few days, but now seems as good a time as any. I spoke to my lawyers about fighting you for this house, primarily because I was annoyed at the way you were trying to force me out. My lawyers persuaded me that because you have his power of attorney, I'd lose the case. So instead, we decided to do one decent thing for my dad."

"You want to help your dad?"

"I do. We were never close, but that doesn't mean I shouldn't do right by him. So, you and I are going to draw up an agreement. I'll drop my persuasive civil suit accusing you of fraud and negligence in my father's care, and in exchange you'll do three things."

"What three things?"

"You'll place my father in a facility of my choosing, where he'll receive independent care that you won't oversee. I've chosen a place big on therapy and avoiding medication. Perhaps there's some life left in him and, if so, he ought to get to live it. This will be paid for entirely out of the funds you're keeping."

"Fine. Trust me, he's less alert than you think. If this gets you off my back, then I'll do it. It can't be more expensive than these damn nurses."

"Excellent." Cillian smiled. "A quarter of my dad's wealth is to go into a trust fund for my sister and her kids. She's to receive a monthly check from it."

"Hell no."

"I'm not finished. In return for this part of our arrangement, my sister will drop *her* civil suit against you."

"I see. Very well. A quarter to your sister. I suppose that's fair. What's the third thing?"

"I thought I wanted to keep this house, but I don't. A friend pointed out I'd be happier in a smaller place and he's right. I would however, like to keep the gazebo."

Doyle gave him a puzzled look. "Keep it?"

"Yes. It can be torn down and moved."

"Why? You can build a much nicer one yourself."

"I know, but this one has sentimental value. Do we have a deal?"

Doyle shrugged. "Medical care, a trust fund and a gazebo. Consider it done. How soon will you be moving?"

"In a week or two. Don't worry. I won't let the door hit me on the way out."

******

Mikkel and Ariel scheduled another play date for the weekend of November tenth, so they could show off their growing affection to anyone being paid to be Baldur's eyes. Mikkel had business to tend to in London and Ariel was happy to take the short flight over to join him.

She knew there was a conversation she needed to have with Mikkel, and the longer she waited the worse it would be. She planned it so she was waiting for Mikkel in the hotel room, not wanting to start this conversation off with the kind of kiss he'd greeted her with on their last visit. He let himself in the room, took one look at her and knew something was up.

"Did Baldur hurt you?"

"He hasn't been near me. It was a long day at the office. I'm fine."

"Is Eoin being unreasonable?"

"Mikkel stop it."

"Stop what? Being concerned about you?"

"No. Stop trying to guess what is wrong and let me tell you."

"Oh." Mikkel seemed surprised. "Of course."

So out came the details she'd never told Mikkel about the encounter with the young man connecting a computer monitor at the airport in Nuuk months ago, and all the ensuing closeness, visions, sex, fighting, and finally the reconciliation of the past couple of weeks.

Mikkel didn't say anything for a few minutes while Ariel stirred the ice in her whiskey and coke.

"I'm not surprised you two got close. Disappointed you didn't level with me, but ..."

"You're not angry?"

"I've no right to be angry. You did most of what you did before we knew each other. As to the recent stuff, I accept we're having a fake relationship and I've no claim on you. It's awkward because he's family and it would have been nice if you'd given me a heads up, that's all."

"I know. It's why I'm sorry I didn't tell you sooner. I hurt him too and I never meant to cause problems for either of you. I'm fond of both of you, you know."

He shrugged. "That's nice."

"Why did you say you weren't surprised? It's not like I've slept with every guy in Northern Europe?" Her tone had become a little defensive and he laughed.

"That's not what I was implying. You've given me no reason to think that. I wasn't surprised because you and Siarnaq together was the missing link. You know, put you and Baldur together and one thing happens. Put Siarnaq and Cillian together and another does. Why was nobody talking about putting Siarnaq and Ariel together? It occurred to me it probably *had* happened already, and everybody else knew about it but me."

Ariel blushed. "Not everyone. Cillian and Brendan knew, and I told Toby just because I told Toby everything."

"What did you see?"

"What I usually see. Everyday stuff, except it was the stuff of people centuries from now. With Baldur, I see everyday stuff from the next few seconds. It's kind of like, I don't know, using a telescope on one end and a microscope on the other."

Mikkel's fascination with the phenomenon was taking his mind off of Ariel's sex life. She was happy to continue the distraction.

"Baldur's trained himself to see stocks and the events that affect them. I'm a telescope for him. He sees the same thing but further out. Siarnaq focuses on life stories of people. With me, he sees those kind of life events, but from the present."

"So why can't you and Cillian combine, or whatever you call it?"

"I don't know. At some point our two ways of seeing seem so out of synch they can't meld. When I touch him, it's painful, like getting shocked."

Mikkel was thoughtful. "Do you think there's anyone out there between you and Baldur? A magnifying glass instead of microscope? I mean, like they see a few hours ahead? You can't do that, can you?"

"No, and there are times when it would be damn useful. I think there could be such people but Cillian thinks it would be hard to stay sane like that. The closest I see is maybe a week away. Never closer."

"That's too bad. What about someone between you and Siarnaq? A pair of binoculars seeing years to decades ahead?"

"I'm glad that's not me."

"Of course. No one really wants to know how they die, do they?"

"Cillian assumes there are zero people with that gift, but who knows."

"It sounds to me like you're Goldilocks. The woman with the perfect vision of the future, not too close, not too far."

"I guess," she said, stirring her ice around some more. Mikkel reached out and took the drink out of her hand.

"Come on, let me take my fake girlfriend out for a marvelous dinner at one of the best new restaurants in London."

"I'd like that." She picked up her coat and purse and realized she was looking forward to the pretending she and Mikkel were going to do for the rest of the evening.

25. A Day at the Beach

Hulda would never know why she said it. Maybe she'd listened to one too many insults from Baldur, or too many odd things had come at her lately and addled her judgment. Maybe she wanted Baldur to know he wasn't that important. Whatever the recipe, the critical ingredients came together Thursday morning.

It started when Baldur strode into the office whistling. He was in fine spirits, while Hulda had a headache. She'd always found men whistling to be annoying.

"How does it feel to be working for the most important man on Earth?" he asked as he walked by.

"I wouldn't know. Who is he?"

Baldur rolled his eyes.

"You're trying to make a joke. Not funny. I spent last night going over my books. Even I had no idea how fast this could snowball. By this time next month, I will have doubled my wealth. Doubled it. Do you have any idea how hard it is to do that when you're worth as much as I am?"

"Why does having a lot more money make you important?"

"You are so cute when you pretend to be naïve." He chucked her under the chin like one would a child. That could have been what did it.

"Being important means doing something to help others, like Mikkel or Cillian," she said. "They make boatloads of money too, but you don't see them hoarding it and bragging. They're taking their money, sending people to Mars so we don't all get wiped ou…ut." She froze before she could say more, but Baldur was staring at her with all the admiration she could have hoped for.

"You're not nearly as dumb as you pretend to be, are you?" he said, starting to get it. "You know some of the people over at Ullow, don't you?"

"I've visited with them once or twice, yes," she said while her knees turned into cold water. "While arranging things for you, I've gotten snippets about what else goes on there."

"Did it ever occur to you those snippets were useful to me? No, of course not. You know things you're not supposed to know, don't you? I want to know how you learned about them, now."

Hulda's instincts told her to go on the offense with Baldur. "I ask people questions instead of only talking about me. You should try it sometime. You can learn a lot that way."

"This makes so much sense." Baldur's mind was moving on from Hulda to the bigger picture "Why does a guy like Mikkel decide out of the blue to become rich and go to Mars? Sure, he could have a wild hair up his ass, but doesn't it make more sense if he thinks he's becoming the most important man who ever lived? That's what we are all after, isn't it? Us men, I mean. You women, you all want to be beautiful."

Hulda thought of several replies, but she kept quiet. She had already said way too much.

"So Cillian is in on this too, is he? And Ariel, of course. Is she the one who's predicted we need to vacate the planet? Or maybe … maybe she's in cahoots with the doom and gloom Inuit. Are there more of them? Maybe a whole collection of people wailing about the end of the world?"

Baldur had gone from angry to something else Hulda didn't understand. At least it didn't make any sense to her until he did the last thing she expected. He walked up to her desk and kissed her squarely on the mouth.

"Thank you, my silly, smart secretary. You've given me the greatest gift of all time. Do you know what it is?"

Hulda didn't want to guess.

"It's called leverage. Really. Great. Leverage. It's one thing to say to a girl, 'You better help me out or I'll hurt your boyfriend.' That's all well and good and it's worked so far. But it's entirely different to be able to say to her, 'Help me out or I'll mess up your boyfriend's plans to save the world.' Now *that* is leverage, isn't it?"

The cold water in Hulda's knees had turned to ice and the chill was making its way up her thighs and into her stomach.

"Would you actually prevent someone from saving the human race?"

"Oh come on. These people have no idea of what the future holds and no way of altering the outcome of any disaster if they did. All that matters is they believe in what they are doing, believe in it enough so they'll do what I want."

"But what if they're right?"

"Then they're right." Baldur laughed. "So what. We'll never know."

That was the moment Hulda knew she had to get as far away from Baldur as she could. She'd ceased to be effective as an inside spy. He wouldn't trust her going forward, and she'd lost all ability to humor him. They were at a philosophical impasse as large as the Milky Way.

She promised to be a good employee and tell him anything else useful she could think of, and then she finished her day at work. He mostly ignored her.

Hulda knew Baldur wouldn't keep an assistant he didn't trust. She also knew he'd never let such an assistant go where she could cause him harm. That didn't leave many pleasant alternatives. Hulda went home as normal, packed everything she could cram into two suitcases, and drove over to her cousin's house and begged for help.

Once her cousin was convinced Hulda wasn't running from bill collectors or the law, he agreed to take her out to his cabin in the country and let her hide there. It was close to winter, and the place wasn't exactly posh. However, it was hard to find and probably safe for anyone who needed to stay hidden. Was this creep at work so frightening that getting away from him was worth this?

"Yes," Hulda assured her cousin, "He is."

Early the next morning the two of them left his house hours before the sun would make its brief appearance in the southern sky.

******

On Monday, Baldur contacted Ariel to inform her he'd purchased a ticket for her to fly commercial on Sunday. He expected her in his office the next morning before the London Stock Exchange opened. She was free to arrange her own lodging, and needed to be available all day Tuesday also, as the approaching end of year offered more possibilities, and he wanted to tap into all of them.

She'd expected as much. They'd exchanged a few curt emails as November wore on, so this plan was no surprise. The coming week was Thanksgiving, and the rest of her family would be getting together without her. She was glad she had a ticket back to the U.S. for Christmas and made a mental note to let Baldur know her trip to see her family for the holidays was non-negotiable.

Tuesday Nell called, worried about Hulda.

"I got the oddest email from her cousin last night. He told me she's hiding at his cabin. Something happened late last week at work and she'll explain when she sees me. She wanted to make sure you knew she won't be there Monday when you arrive."

"Running away sounds extreme," Ariel said. "She knows how important it is to have her there, doesn't she?"

"She absolutely does. This can't be good. Maybe you shouldn't go."

"Whatever happened, Baldur's now more suspicious. I have to go"

Ariel stopped, took a breath, tried to precall anything from a week ahead.

"If I don't show, worse things could be set in motion." Ariel shuddered as the images flickered. "There's ugly stuff if Baldur tries to chase me down. Not to mention Toby has the Dublin office set up to capitalize on what Baldur does Monday. Mikkel says he could get to where he needs to be after this one session, especially if Baldur goes for two days of trading. So it's got to happen."

"Damn, I wish I spoke Icelandic better," Nell said. "Never mind. I'll find a way to get somebody on the ground to help you. I'll call as soon as I know more. Try to keep Baldur from figuring out we know anything has changed, okay?"

******

223

Ariel spent Wednesday explaining to her co-workers everything she knew about how the coming Monday was going to go. She'd been Baldur's telescope into the future twice now. She understood more about the process, and so did he. Much of the information he'd get would be useless, which is why it took so much time. He'd look for trades that were long shots, surprises on which he could safely bet a lot of money.

Baldur's best data would be in areas of interest to them both. That common ground centered on technology and business. His trades wouldn't be time-sensitive, at least as far as seconds were concerned. He'd be dividing his purchases into many small lots from numerous sources, and he'd space them out in time to avoid suspicion. That left room for the crew at Ullow to swoop in and get the same prices.

Jake had ideas for Ariel to try. She could focus on sectors Baldur had little interest in, like women's fashion. He might place a small trade, not wanting to risk much in an unfamiliar area. Ullow could trust the insight from Ariel and bet more.

Because touching Baldur allowed Ariel to premember possibilities over the next few minutes, Ariel could see trades Baldur considered and rejected. If she could remember a few, Ullow could make those trades once she got home.

"He told me he's going to make a fooking fortune off of what you two come up with next week," Eoin said. "If this goes the way we expect, he will have one hell of a lot of money come January and February. I mean, one hell of a lot more than he already has."

"What do you think he's worth? Hidden everywhere?" Fergus asked. "Does he have, like, a billion euros?"

Eoin laughed. "You don't follow financial news much, do you?"

"Not really. But a billion seems like a lot."

"Fergus, there are easily over a hundred people out there worth ten times that much. Their wealth fluctuates every day by tens of millions of euros. No biggie, when you are worth over ten billion. You've never heard of most of them. Unless Baldur is lying, and I don't think he is, he's got to be in the over ten billion group already. Probably hasn't been there all that long, though. If he can triple what he's got, then he gets into the thirty-plus billion category and he's playing with the big boys, the top eighteen richest."

"Wow," Ronan said. "I had no idea people had that kind of money. Does anybody clear a hundred billion?"

"Only if you clump siblings together. Otherwise, not yet. You know, Baldur's a goal-oriented kind of guy. I bet you he's aiming to be the first human worth a hundred billion euros and he's hoping this trading session will put him there. *That's* when he'll start to flex his muscles and go public. He's got to have the tax thing figured out, with citizenship in a nice tax haven somewhere. I guess he keeps Ariel around in case his coffers dip too low."

As soon as Eoin said those words, he knew. Ariel, who was sitting across the table, knew it, too. In fact, everyone in the room knew.

Baldur was getting far richer far faster than planned. At one point, back when he thought the process would be slow and fraught with mistakes, he probably *had* intended to keep Ariel around, surmising he would always need her. Maybe he had some old-fashioned idea of marrying her, in the best case, or keeping her loyal through threats and extortion in the worst.

But that had changed. Baldur's coffers were never going to dip too low, now. He was a man who wanted to ensure he not only became the richest person in the world, but that no one could ever follow him. That meant no imitator could utilize Ariel the way he had. Ariel could not live by his side. Ariel could not live anywhere. Ariel could not live at all.

"What was I thinking?" Ariel said it first. "Last July he used me to make sure this thing worked. I exceeded his expectations. Our last session resulted in a few trades that expired on Saturday. I'm pretty sure I did even better. If what you say is true, Baldur needs one more really good trading session with me and then he needs me dead."

No one said anything for a minute.

"You are not going to Iceland," Jake said.

"No shit," Fergus agreed.

"What about Cillian and Mikkel and all they're trying to do? My efforts next Monday are funding them, too. Toby will get Baldur shut down before this new wealth makes him harder to touch. That means Mikkel and Cillian won't get another chance to make the kind of money they need. I have to go to Iceland."

No one had an argument to the contrary.

"What can be done to make sure you get out of there alive?" Ronan asked. "Do you, like, see anything helpful?"

Ariel sighed. The trip to Iceland was in four days. She tried to look out a week for anything useful. She saw a fair bit of nothingness, more than she'd seen while riding the small plane into a winter storm a few weeks ago. This was real danger. The chance of her not surviving a week was bigger than it had been in her life, but the chance of other outcomes was greater.

It was most likely she became Baldur's prisoner for a while, while he considered alternatives. She looked ahead further. In one world, he was trying to stage a believable accident. In another he was pressuring her to let loved ones know she was with him by choice. Over there, she was escaping from Baldur, and there, she was attempting and failing. There were scenes that made little sense, brought on by turns of events she couldn't guess. Then there were some in which she was relieved, safe and happy. No information on how she'd gotten that way. But at least they existed.

"Nothing useful," she said, not wanting to elaborate. "I'll keep trying."

Thursday evening, she video-called her family to wish them a happy Thanksgiving across the miles. They were about to sit down for their feast. Pumpkin and pecan pies were visible in the background, along with a chocolate cheesecake that was probably her mother's doing.

For once, Ariel made no effort to conceal her concerns from anyone.

"Things have gotten shaky," she told her family. "I'm trying to do the right thing, to help out some people doing something important. I'm going to be in danger in a few days."

"You sure are." Zane and her mother said it at the same time. Ariel's eyebrow went up. Was everyone seeing the future now?

"I've been talking to Toby," Zane said. "He's working with your friends to think of better ways to keep you safe. They'll do everything they can, but if he's worried, he's got reasons."

"You are an unusually open book today," her mom added. "I wish I knew someone in Iceland. I don't but I'll see if any of my friends do. I'll do anything I can to help you be safe, dear."

"Thanks guys. I love you all," she said. As they waved and laughed and signed off it had a familiar feel to it, as if memories and premories of that particular scene filled her past and her future.

She decided to take Friday off work, and Eoin didn't object. "Any special plans?"

"No. Just preparing." He didn't ask for more.

The day turned out to be one of those unusual winter days when the sky is bright blue and the temperature climbs. Ariel smiled at her good fortune as she took the little car the company leased for her and headed north out of Dublin, planning to drive for as long as it felt good, and then to stop and do yoga along the shore.

Ireland doesn't have much in the way of sandy beaches, with a coast made from ancient granite and volcanic remains. She drove far enough to find a deserted strip of rocky shore, spread out her mat, and worked on clearing her mind. The poses came to her in a random sequence, without thought. The cat. The cow. The pigeon. The plough.

Her goal was to calm down, and gather her strength. Downward dog into a plank, then a cobra and repeat it again. Warrior poses, one, two and three. She had skills, she had advantages, and she had back-up. She finished her routine concentrating on balance, holding the pose of a strong tree while she gazed at the far horizon.

She was ready.

******

Saturday, Baldur paced around his penthouse apartment. It was particularly nice, one of the best in the city. He'd planned to buy a house soon, because men with money owned houses. Now, he was glad he'd waited. Who'd have thought someone like Ariel would come along and raise the level of what he did?

He looked around his place. There wasn't much he'd miss, and people could be paid to send him the few things he valued. He'd be leaving Iceland now, of course, and establishing residence in a place with far more friendly tax laws and no inclination to turn inhabitants over to the authorities of another country. These places all seemed to be tropical, and Baldur didn't care much for hot sunny beaches. For starters, he hated having to wear sunglasses and sunscreen all the time. But he'd adjust. Pick one and learn to like it. He wished he'd had more time to plan.

Baldur knew once the trades were finished Tuesday night, he wouldn't need Ariel, or d^4, or anyone else ever again. Except, of course, for the army of accountants, lawyers and security specialists he'd have to hire. His money would buy those people.

On the other hand, no one would need him either. Baldur didn't doubt for a minute that Mikkel, Cillian, and the entire doom and gloom chorus in Ireland would have all the money they needed when this was over. They weren't stupid; they knew this was a one-time opportunity.

So the remaining problem became Ariel and what to do with her. He'd struggled to come up with a plan he thought he could go through with. His latest idea was for the two of them to leave Wednesday morning for a spontaneous vacation in the Caribbean.

Once Ariel understood her choices, Baldur was sure she'd cooperate by assuring people she was heading off on a voluntary vacation with a man she was becoming fond of. Mikkel wouldn't be happy, and that was Baldur's own fault. He wished he'd known earlier that he didn't need to push Mikkel and Ariel together, but so it went. It hadn't cost him much.

Baldur thought he understood Mikkel pretty well. The man would stash his dollars away for his pointless goal. He'd be sad when his fling left him for the arms of another, but he'd get over it. Mikkel was a man obsessed with a cause.

The problem was, once they were on vacation, Ariel would need to die an accidental death. Baldur was sad when he realized the inevitability of that conclusion. It didn't matter how much Ariel came to like him, or hate him, over time. Her feelings for him didn't matter. She was a liability he couldn't afford.

Maybe some sort of boating or diving accident would work, provided he had an excellent alibi. He didn't need to start out this venture as a suspected murderer. Then again, something mimicking natural causes could be better. Finding a local doctor to help him would be a trivial problem. However it was done, it had to happen before the ever-resourceful Ariel or her friends found a way to get her to safety.

Baldur toyed with other options in his mind. Maybe he shouldn't take her along to the Caribbean. What was the most efficient way to kill someone and be nowhere nearby when it happened?

He saw Ariel in his mind as she'd first walked into his boardroom almost a year ago, her inexpensive blue blouse a perfect match to her eyes. She was a unique, beautiful creature. She deserved some kind of glorious ending. He needed to come up with an idea that was fitting.

November 2012

26. First Day of Trading

Sunday, Ariel kept busy. She packed a bag, sent Nell her travel details, and drove over to Jake's to drop off her key so he could water her plants if she was gone long. She played with Jake's puppy, who was almost full grown now, but still ridiculously cute.

She exchanged messages with friends and composed an email to Siarnaq, rewriting it until it was warm but not romantic, and didn't sound so much like a melodramatic goodbye. Then she video-chatted with her parents and Teddie, catching them as they started their day.

"Not a lot of well-developed telepaths in Iceland," her mother said. "We're everywhere, but Iceland is small. I'm looking into one lead. Meanwhile, okay if I keep loose tabs on you?"

"Definitely okay. Do anything you can to help me, please, as long as nothing gets in the way until Tuesday after the last stock exchange closes."

"You need to see this through," her mother said. "I understand."

Next, Ariel returned Mikkel's calls. He'd tried to reach her three times on Friday, twice yesterday, once while she was at Jake's, and again while she was talking to her folks. She felt bad ignoring him, but she knew what he was going to say, and she didn't want to hear it.

"Ariel, listen to me We can find another way to do this. You don't have to take this risk."

"I don't want to argue, and you know damn well it's why I haven't called you back. If it makes you feel better, my odds of staying alive don't improve much if I run from Baldur now. In exchange for a slightly higher chance of surviving, you guys get nothing instead of all the money you need. That's not acceptable."

"It is to me."

She ignored him. "Look, I'm not choosing death. I'm taking a risk in order to do the right thing. Don't try to talk me out of it."

She could hear Mikkel sigh over the phone. "I knew you'd say something like this. I suppose it's why I am becoming increasingly attached to you. Unfortunately."

This time Ariel couldn't ignore him. Her heart skipped a beat. "Yeah? Well, I'm unfortunately becoming fond of you too. My intention is to live long enough to make it a problem for both of us."

He laughed. "It's a good plan. I'll look forward to dealing with it."

Then it was time to go to the airport. Ariel thought for a minute of getting on a plane to anywhere else. Maybe a flight to Jamaica? Ah, rum and reggae. How long could she stay drunk and hidden at some all-inclusive in Montego Bay?

But no. That was not what she was going to do.

******

Monday morning Cillian decided to go to Iceland. Brendan was frantic trying to talk him out of it.

"I know if I could make Baldur see what I see, I could turn him. He'd let Ariel live. I bet you he'd even fund some of what I'm doing. Hell, he could do that and still be filthy rich. It doesn't have to go down this way. Why wouldn't he agree?"

"He won't," Brendan said. "He doesn't want to be reasonable, he wants to win. That's different."

"But I can make him see otherwise. I know I can." Cillian was adamant.

Brendan called the Ullow office for help, but in the end the argument was about who would leave with Cillian the next day.

Brendan insisted he should go, as Cillian's closest friend. Jake insisted he should be the one handling the meeting, as Baldur's Ullow contact. Eoin overruled them both. He'd go instead. It would give him a chance to stand up to Baldur in ways he never had, and he'd be delighted to do that with Cillian at his side. Maybe together they'd make amends for the damage Eoin had failed to prevent thus far.

******

Seven o'clock Monday morning, Ariel arrived at the stylish offices of d^4. It was still the middle of the night as far as the stars overhead were concerned. Ariel noticed the sky was as clear here as it had been in Ireland the last few days. The Northern Lights were taking a break for electromagnetic reasons of their own, leaving an almost full moon in the southwest glowing like a searchlight on the snow.

Ariel was surprised to find a receptionist there already. The small, dark-haired woman who greeted her spoke English with a heavy Icelandic accent. She introduced herself as Sigrun and showed Ariel into Baldur's trading room. Today the room contained several large screens attached to the fastest computers money could buy, and a portable massage table covered in a soft blue quilt. The table had a large, firm pillow for her head and a smaller pillow to slide under her knees.

"Baldur asked me to make sure you could remain comfortable for several hours." The receptionist said it as though it was the most normal request in the world for people interested in the stock market. "You're free to change in this room if you like, just lock the door when I leave and unlock when you're done."

Ariel wondered what Baldur had told this woman. Didn't matter. She pulled out the ugly grey gym trunks and oversize men's tank top she planned to wear this time around. It was show time.

Baldur greeted her like a friend when he came in, his eyes barely dropping to her clothes. A small smile crossed his lips as he took them in. He asked after her health and offered her coffee or juice. She declined but thanked him for the courtesy. She responded with pleasantries of her own about the unusually clear days they were having in Ireland and apparently in Iceland, too.

"If we're going to put in the kind of hours we both want, I'll need to take breaks to stay focused. You'll be more effective with breaks, too. Let's stop once the sun is up, get some fresh air, and maybe have a bite to eat."

Baldur nodded; he saw the sense in what she said. "I'll have Sigrun order in lunch. We can take it on the roof top." Ariel could have sworn she saw a trace of sadness in his eyes.

You're a self-centered son of bitch, but you're not a killer, are you? You'd rather not do it. If it just wasn't so damn necessary in my case, huh?

She said none of what she was thinking, of course. Instead she lay down, and a few minutes later when he came back into the room, he said nothing as he lay the inside of his left forearm along her bare thigh and they began.

There was something mesmerizing about the linkage. Ariel suspected Baldur experienced it, too. News reports and stock prices floated through her mind, and she considered the techniques Jake suggested.

She needed to think about something Baldur would ignore. Cosmetics. Estee Lauder. How was Ms. Lauder's company doing? How about her friend L'Oreal? Were things looking good for the hair and skin care business these days?

The hope was Ariel's concentration would tempt Baldur to chance a small investment in them, so Mikkel and Cillian could place a larger bet. Ariel remembered the entire Dublin office was tied into what was happening. Toby and Nell and even her freakin' mother were following along as best they could, ready to pounce in and help.

Breathe deeply. Think about feminine hygiene products. Bras. Playtex. How was Playtex doing? Wait, Playtex had been bought out by Energizer. Okay, bras, tampons and batteries. Ariel let her mind drift in ways she hoped would help her friends.

The break was friendly and the food surprisingly good. It was comfortable enough in the sunshine on the roof in a jacket. Sigrun had gotten an assortment of cold appetizers, and it wasn't until Ariel saw the little sushi rolls that she studied Sigrun more carefully. That thick black hair had to be a wig. Could Nell have managed to be here? Or was the inclusion of her favorite food a fluke?

"I love sushi," Baldur said, actually licking the sauce off of his fingers. "I wonder how this new girl guessed. And look. Greek dolmades. That's not something you see every day in Iceland."

The dolmades clinched it. Sigrun had to be a well disguised Nell.

Baldur gestured over to the stairs. "This girl's a temp, but I may have to keep her." Then sadness flickered across his face again. Ariel made a mental note to let the Dublin people know Baldur was closing his d[4] office once this session was over. He liked his office and was going to miss it. You never knew what piece of knowledge could be useful.

The second session of the day centered on stocks better traded in New York and on futures in the agricultural sector handled through the Chicago Board of Trade. Ariel changed her personal strategy to focusing on Jake's second suggestion, watching for trades Baldur barely passed on making.

"You're paying more attention than you were this morning," he remarked.

"Trying to keep my head in the game."

"Good girl." He murmured it as he typed. He'd gone to sitting on a bar stool using a laptop, and had rolled up his pants so that he could drape his bare leg over her exposed back as she lay face down. The change in position looked ridiculous, but it was doing them both good.

Mikkel made a good point. Not just about sex, either. Human touch brings people closer. She remembered her mother talking about the face painting booth at the school carnival. Hours of decorating the arms and faces of children had taught her mom about the common humanity of all on a visceral level.

Next time she saw her mom, she'd have to tell her how touch even softened your fear of someone contemplating you harm, if the touch was gentle, consensual, and bore no malice in the moment. Ariel hoped it worked two ways. Maybe the more contact they shared, the harder it would be for Baldur to hurt her.

"Where have you drifted off to?" he asked. "Who the hell is SHW?" He hit a few keys. "Sherwin-Williams? Why are you thinking about paint? Let's get back to the financial sector, please."

"Sorry." Ariel made an effort to focus on Baldur's favorite market sector. She didn't need him unhappy with her, and she wanted him to do well almost as much as he did.

She wondered what to expect when they parted for the night. One troubling possibility was all the touching had aroused him sexually. Then Ariel had a more disturbing thought. Intimacy wouldn't matter to a man used to killing, but with an amateur like Baldur, having sex could make it harder for him to kill her. She'd hardly be the first woman in the world to do that to stay alive, repugnant as it was. Should she?

But he was all business as the stock exchange closed at 8:30 pm in Iceland. Had he thought he'd made plenty of money already and could do away with her now, while no one was around and before he lost his nerve?

No. She was sure he wanted what he would get from tomorrow's trading. She could count on his greed, if nothing else. As he shut down the computers Sigrun knocked on the door and came in.

"I told you to go home at 6:30." Baldur was irritated.

"I know, but I wanted to be here to call a cab for the young lady." Definitely Nell, even though Ariel could barely detect her friend through the well-done disguise.

Baldur said something in Icelandic and Sigrun looked at him blankly for a second. Oh dear. Ariel jumped in with the first thing that popped into her mind.

"So do you need me here at seven, or will a quarter till eight work?"

"Seven thirty, no later," Baldur turned back to Sigrun and looked at her. She said something that sounded like "yeg ski" then turned to Ariel.

"Good night. Your cab should be here in a few minutes."

Baldur reached for his coat as well. "I'll let you change." He was half out the door when he added "I trust I can count on your desire to help your comrades, though I do have extra security assigned to you tonight. Wouldn't want anything to happen to you at such a critical point in our collaboration."

"I'll do as agreed." Then on a whim, she asked, "What are you going to do the day after tomorrow?"

"Prepare to be extremely rich."

"Obviously. We'll take our one percent, and part with no issues. It'll take a few months before we reap the benefits though. I'm guessing you won't need to do this again, will you?"

"I think you're right. Lots of money makes more money. Even with normal investing my wealth will now grow at a rate far greater than any country's economy. I have you to thank. Your success rate is higher than I hoped."

Ariel nodded. None of this was a surprise to her, and she couldn't see anything to be gained by pretending otherwise.

"I'll be busy," Baldur said, "spacing out how to best cash in on these trades without causing suspicion. I'll also be working to get the rules changed for high frequency trading, to make sure no one follows in my footsteps. You and I can part as two people who had a business arrangement."

He's thrown out all earlier thoughts of trying to include me in his life. Very well. After tomorrow I'm nothing but a liability and I know it.

"I do have a sense of honor," he added, and she heard defensiveness in his voice. "I've decided to uphold my agreement to not interfere with your friends' space project, or with anything else involving them, even if doing so is to my advantage. So there. You've bought your people shelter from me, and there aren't many who will have that."

"That's nice to know."

"The night watchman will lock up after you go. I'll see you in the morning."

Ariel was exhausted by the time she got to the hotel and could hardly stay awake until room service arrived. Matters were worse because all the prolonged contact with Baldur had created a new problem. She was now getting little aftershocks of short-term premories, snippets of the next few seconds that were nothing but a nuisance. She busied herself making handwritten notes about trades Baldur had passed on, and after a while the flickers stopped.

Baldur knew where she was staying, so communication through the hotel internet was easy for him to pay someone to access. She opted for a quick "I'm in Iceland safely and all is well" email, sent only to co-workers Baldur knew.

She fell asleep trying to premember anything from next week or next month. All that sunk in was how futures had split into two kinds. There was no longer an Ariel being held prisoner, no longer an Ariel working with Baldur, no longer any of the other odd variations. There was either a future in which she was safe and relieved as hell, or there was a future in which she wasn't at all.

Early Tuesday morning, Baldur made the call. He'd spent a restless night with the sensation of touching Ariel's silky skin drifting through his dreams. He recognized lust, and his own growing admiration for the young woman who'd so unexpectedly accelerated his plans beyond his wildest dreams.

Any alternative involving him spending a second longer with her than he needed was dangerous. For the first time in his life, Baldur wasn't sure he could do what was in his own best interest. Someone else would have to be told to do it, and they'd best be given those instructions before he lost the nerve to do even that.

His pilot didn't question the change in plans. Of course he could fly a couple of men over to some small town in Greenland Wednesday morning instead of taking Baldur to the Caribbean. As long as he was given an accurate weight for passengers and luggage, he didn't need to check the cabin. Yes, he could remain seated in the cockpit with the door to the cabin closed, no matter what he heard. He understood men such as Baldur sometimes needed extreme discretion. He'd fly the plane as directed and not leave his seat. But he balked at Baldur's last request.

"I won't fly without a co-pilot. That's stupid."

Baldur rolled his eyes. Okay, it probably was stupid.

"I have a compromise," Baldur said. "I don't want to involve any more people with this flight than necessary. Geirs, my head of security, will be one of men on board. I'll make a few calls and ensure his colleague has a pilot's license. I'll even make sure he's been checked out on a Hawker 800. Can you work with that?"

"If you can find someone like that, of course I can."

"The security company I use is quite accommodating. I'll call you if there's a problem. If you don't hear from me, it's wheels up at ten-thirty tomorrow. All you need to do is fly the plane."

******

Zane was jet lagged and still getting his arms around this whole telepathy thing his mother had explained to him before he left. He stared at the tiny ancient Icelandic woman with skepticism written all over his face.

237

"She doesn't speak English. I'm her grandson. I can translate for you," the teenaged boy said. He had driven his grandmother halfway across Iceland in winter to meet Zane at the cheery yellow and black Kronan grocery store on the south edge of Reykjavik. The three of them were standing next to the frozen pizzas.

"Her children played with Baldur's parents. She says she can find Baldur's brain for you."

Zane winced a little at the terminology but he got the idea.

"We need a sense of what Baldur is planning," Zane said. "We think he's going to try to kill my sister. I'm here to help her, but I need some idea of where to start."

The boy nodded, and he turned to the elderly woman and spoke in Icelandic. She listened, they exchanged a few words, and then she closed her eyes, leaned back against the freezer door, and started to moan and keen. Zane looked around in embarrassment, but nobody else in the store appeared bothered. This went on for several long minutes until finally the woman stopped, opened her eyes wide and yelled what had to be a pretty bad obscenity in Icelandic.

"Langamma!" the boy said, embarrassed. "I'm sorry," he added to Zane. "She's not herself when she comes out of these."

Zane thought this was a colossal waste of time on a day when he had no time to spare, but then the woman began talking to her grandson in rapid words filled with fury. She went on for two or three minutes before she quieted down.

"She says Baldur has become a very bad man. Selfish and greedy, and now he prepares to kill a red-haired girl he works with, she could be your sister. He is going to kill her to protect his money. My langamma knows details, and if you like she will give them to you."

Well, Zane had to admit it sounded like the woman had found Baldur's brain.

"Tell her yes, I'd like to know everything she can tell me."

November 2012

27. Last Day of Trading

Of course Ariel slept poorly. Early the next morning, she treated herself to all of the room service coffee she could hold while she fooled around on her computer and sent a terse email back to the office letting them know things were progressing as expected. Then she had an idea. She found a 12:45 a.m. flight out of Iceland that night and booked a seat, deciding to tell Baldur late in the day that she was leaving right after the two of them finished. Maybe if she caught him by surprise she could be gone before he figured out a way to stop her. It was worth a shot.

She didn't even bother with business clothes, but just pulled sweats over what she'd worn yesterday, crammed everything into her suitcase, and checked out of her room.

She took the cab through the dark streets of Reykjavik to arrive at the d⁴ offices by 7:30. Baldur was already in his trading room fooling with his screens when she arrived. Sigrun gave her a careful "Halo" and then reached across the reception desk and squeezed her arm. The silent, hidden gesture spoke volumes. *I'm here, on your side.*

Tears started to well up in Ariel's eyes, as fear, fatigue and gratitude mixed together to form something almost too strong to control. She managed to stop them before they flowed down her face, took a few breaths, and marched into the trading room.

Baldur looked up, glanced at his watch and said nothing. Ariel removed her outer layers of clothing in silence and crawled up onto the table as though she was preparing for a root canal. She looked at the clock. Twenty minutes until the opening bell. She should have slept later. She closed her eyes and tried to doze.

Twenty minutes later she was irritated when he laid his left hand just below her neck and started trading without so much as a hello.

"I'm here." she said.

"I can tell." He answered without looking in her direction.

"Fuck you," she said and felt his hand tighten slightly on her throat, though he said nothing. Then as he finished typing in something, he added "Fuck you, too."

Ariel changed her position twice after that and Baldur readjusted his, but neither of them spoke another word for the next four hours.

"I've ordered in lunch," Sigrun said as she walked in. "It's too cold on the roof today, so I set up food in a conference room. I hope that's okay."

"Sure," Baldur said. "We need to stop for a while anyway." He turned to Ariel. "Stretch your legs. It will help you stay alert."

"I am alert."

Sigrun tiptoed out without saying a word.

After lunch Baldur and Ariel again worked in silence, but Ariel had to stop twice in the afternoon to ask for coffee and go to the bathroom. Baldur looked annoyed each time, but said nothing.

In the ladies' room she stretched as well as she could, moving into her favorite yoga poses. It wasn't just for her own comfort. Although the windowless restroom offered no avenue of escape, and in fact the eighth floor office offered her no easy way to run, she had to assume she could need to sprint on foot or even try to fight, once the trading was over. She needed her body as well as her mind to be at its best.

They took another one-hour break in the early evening, and Ariel took an analgesic for a fatigue headache. Sigrun brought in sandwiches, insisting she'd stay in the office as long as they did, in case they needed anything. This time Baldur didn't argue with her. Ariel thought he was relieved not to be alone with her.

"I've changed my airline ticket. I'm flying home tonight," Ariel said as she lay down on the table after dinner. "There's a red eye over to Copenhagen. I can make easily if I leave here when New York closes."

Baldur shook his head. "You should have discussed that with me. I decided over dinner I'm going to need you to stay through the night tonight. We haven't made as many trades as I hoped, so we're going to work both Tokyo and Hong Kong once they open. We need to get some exposure in Asia anyway before you and I call it quits."

"I thought you said Asia was the place we were least effective. Why would you want to bother?"

"I did say that, but I've decided we need to use every avenue open to us. You'll stay the night."

"I will not," Ariel said, deciding she had nothing to lose by pushing back. "This wasn't part of our agreement and I don't do all-nighters."

"Yes it was and yes you do. The agreement was you stay until I decide we're done. We're not done. We're going to try the Australian Securities Exchange, too; I think we might do better there. You'll make more money and we'll stop at dawn. You can go home first thing in the morning."

Ariel was exhausted, and her muscles were cramping, and she was tired of playing games. "What if I refuse?"

"You won't. I learned more about Mikkel last week. I thought he had a childish dream about outer space. Useless, but he was entitled to it and if you wanted to help him, that was your business. However, my former secretary thinks your *boyfriend*," Baldur put extra sarcasm on the last word, "has some misguided idea about saving humanity with this. Clearly, we've moved beyond childish and gone into the realm of the deluded, don't you agree?"

"I wonder what gave Hulda such an idea?"

"I wondered the same thing. So I asked. Turns out she developed a social relationship with some of you over at Ullow. I was unaware of it. I found the omission odd. Don't you?"

"What happened to Hulda?" Answering an awkward question with a question of your own was one of the best business strategies Ariel had ever learned.

"I'd like to know, too. She's gone missing. Didn't show up for work Friday and I had to hire a temp. Yet, here you are, and so I have to conclude you're still interested in helping Mikkel. From what I understand, you're helping Cillian too."

"I am."

"What sort of girlfriend goes to these lengths to fund a project of a man she's dating?"

Ariel said nothing.

S. R. Cronin

"That's what I thought. You believe this nonsense, too, don't you? You wouldn't dream of doing this with me except you've bought into Mikkel's insane idea."

"It's not as crazy as you think. Mikkel's cousin Siarnaq..."

"I know all about Siarnaq," Baldur said, with no patience. "I've met him. He believes every bit of every gloomy outcome he's ever seen."

"That's not unreasonable. You believe what your abilities tell you. And mine, too."

"True. Because we can test them out. There's no way to test the sort of nonsense Siarnaq is worried about. Who knows what will happen in hundreds of years? Honestly, who cares? Why would a beautiful girl like you with a bright future throw away your own opportunities so you can protect people you'll never meet?"

Ariel realized the question made perfect sense from Baldur's point of view.

"If you drive by a building burning with no one around, do you stop and call the fire department?" Ariel asked.

"It depends. How busy am I? How windy is it? What are the odds someone else will call?"

"Suppose you know it's the worst combination of those."

"Okay. I probably keep driving, but once I get to where I'm going, I call."

"It's too late by then. There is an orphanage next door and the kids have all burnt to death."

Baldur laughed. "You do believe this nonsense, don't you? That's the best I could hope for. You're not here because you're being nice to a guy you like; you're here because you think you're making a sacrifice that will matter."

"That makes you happy because?"

"Because you're tired and you want to go home. Yet you will give me your absolute best all night long until because you think you're saving humanity and this extra trading will help. It's hilarious, but great."

He turned away from her and starting typing into his keyboard and said no more.

A couple of hours later Baldur moved his wrist off of her stomach and turned away from his screens. "Your mind is wandering; you need to get up and move around. I have to make some phone calls anyway." He nudged her in the ribcage with his elbow. "Take a break from saving the world and be back in fifteen."

His gesture was meant to be funny, she supposed, but as a fresh part of his body nudged into an untouched part of hers, it was all she needed. She saw him a minute from now, making a phone call, and she knew what the call was about.

He was confirming the change of plans he'd made that morning with his pilot. The plans were intended to result in Ariel's death. Her mind flew to the far outlying probabilities she'd seen a few weeks ago. She remembered a puzzling premory of her floundering in ice cold water, getting drowsier by the second as she fought to stay conscious while she knew there was no way rescue could arrive in time.

Baldur was going to insist she ride in his plane. The plane would go down over the ocean? Somehow she must survive the emergency landing and make it into the sea, where she'd die of hypothermia. She and someone else. Or he could live while she died. Or she could live while he died and that was incredibly sad, too. The slight probabilities she'd ignored were now approaching certainly. How could she change these odds?

Ariel headed to the restroom, hoping some cold water on her face would help her think. She saw Nell, disguised as Sigrun, leaving the ladies room and Ariel motioned with her head. Nell understood and turned around and went back inside.

I have an ally here. There has to be a way.

"Do you know anybody over here?" Ariel whispered once they were in the restroom.

Nell shook Sigrun's heavy black hair. "No, but Hulda does. She's in my earpiece listening to everything, giving me instructions, translating Icelandic for me. Any good actor can fake an accent, but I barely speak the language. They got her patched in so she can take phone calls, then tell me what was said. She's also checking in with your office every so often, letting them know you're okay."

That made sense.

"Can Hulda help you find a wetsuit this time of night? A really good one, with booties, gloves and a hood? I'll need tape for all the seams. Five millimeters thick at least, and six would be better."

Nell stared at her.

"I've done some diving; I know about this. I'm pretty sure I'm going to need one tomorrow. No, I'm going to need two. Somebody will be with me and I don't want him to die. So it's not Baldur. The pilot maybe? It's a he, so make the second suit sized for an average male."

Nell looked at her watch. It was almost eight thirty, so buying wetsuits from a store wasn't an option. "Hulda probably can figure out a way to do this, but then what?"

"Get the suits here and cram them into my luggage so I'll have them with me. Take out some of my clothes if you have to. How does the plane goes down? It can't be a crash. Maybe he puts a hole in the fuel tank?"

Nell started at her through Sigrun's face. "Look under the wetsuits for guns and knives, too. I think those might be more useful."

Ariel started to thank her, but they heard Baldur calling for Sigrun from the hallway. Nell put her finger to her lips and left the restroom.

As evening moved into night, Ariel insisted on a couple of bathroom breaks and each time she gave Nell a questioning look. The first time Nell shook her head, but the second time Ariel got a thumbs up and a nod.

It was almost three in the morning when Sigrun brought in more coffee and slices of cake. Baldur agreed to a break, saying he had to make a few phone calls. Ariel used her few minutes to check both exits and found a security guard posted at both. Of course. Running had never been a good option. She did a quick yoga routine in the ladies' room, begging her body to stay alert. On the way back, she saw Nell with her head on Sigrun's desk, sound asleep.

"Why didn't you have me come over for three days and do this in shifts?" she complained to Baldur as she entered the room.

"In retrospect, I should have. I'm wearing out as well, you know. But now that we're pushing our way through, let's be done with this and done with each other."

A few hours later, Baldur's trades began to drop to one every ten or fifteen minutes, and Ariel suspected they'd both run out of steam. The first glimmer of light appeared in the window around nine, although the slow sunrise was over an hour away.

"We're done," Baldur announced as he glanced up and saw the dawn, and Ariel thought he looked as relieved as she felt.

"Did you do it this way just to wear me out?" she asked as she stood up on shaky legs.

"It wasn't my plan, but I suppose it was an advantage. You're more cooperative when you're exhausted."

"So now what happens?"

"I put you on a plane. You're much too tired to fly commercial. I called the hangar late last night. My pilot is expecting you, and my driver will take you over. My head of security and I will ride along and make sure you get off safely."

Yeah. Of course you will.

When they left the office soon after, Nell was still sound asleep with her head on the desk. Ariel was surprised her friend could sleep in such an uncomfortable position, but then she dozed off herself as soon as she got in the car. When they got to the airport almost an hour later, she saw the sun above the horizon.

"It's been a pleasure," Baldur said as she took her bag away from Geirs and rolled it over to the plane. She looked inside the aircraft. The door to the cockpit was closed. Geirs was standing behind her, waiting to follow her up the steps. She looked at him puzzled.

"Geirs will be going with you. Ariel, I want you to know you've done your part and done it well." He gave a little shrug. "This is the best I could come up with for you."

Ariel willed her tired brain to think. Geirs was Baldur's trusted employee. Ariel doubted Baldur would do something as wasteful as killing Geirs, so maybe he hadn't sabotaged the plane.

She tried to focus on the future. Was there more emptiness ahead if she walked onto the plane, or less? There was a lot of it either way, but less if she put one foot in front of the other and went with this. Very well, onto the plane it was.

She settled into one of the soft cushioned chairs. Before the plane had taken off she'd fallen into a sleep far deeper than she intended.

******

Cillian and Eoin left on a red eye out of Dublin and it was late morning by the time they had their rental car in Reykjavik. Eoin had decided to wait and call Baldur once they were in Iceland, telling the man he'd flown over because he had to talk to him in person. Cillian's presence could be a surprise.

Their best hope was Baldur had allowed Ariel to return home already, opting to eliminate her later in a way less likely to raise suspicion. Or maybe Ariel was still tucked away in the offices of d^4. If Nell was there maintaining her charade, she could find Ariel for them. Ariel's family and y^1 were ready to help too, standing by, as far as Eoin knew, to do what they could once they knew more.

Baldur didn't answer his cell phone, and after a few tries, Eoin called the landline at the d^4 office. Nell answered.

"Thank God it's you," they both said at once, and then laughed. Eoin explained they were on their way to see Baldur.

"He's not here." Nell told them how she'd had fallen asleep at her desk and had woken up a bit ago to find Ariel and Baldur gone.

"Why were you all there in the middle of the night?"

Nell explained Ariel and Baldur had worked all night, so they could tap into Asian markets.

"I asked Hulda to let you guys know. She talked to Fergus and Ronan. They said you were coming and told her to sit tight. I didn't want to leave Ariel alone here with him, so I stayed, but I don't know how much use I was."

"Can you find out where they are now?" Eoin asked.

"That's the problem. Baldur left me a note saying he and Geirs left at 9:30 morning to take Ariel to the airport. He gave me her flight number, seat number, confirmation number, everything, you name it, and asked me to call Ullow to let them know she was on her way home. I called the office right after I woke up."

"That's great news."

"Not really. Someone at the hangar for Baldur's private plane called here after that, looking for Geirs. *He* was supposed to be there to take-off at ten-thirty."

"So? Geirs was going somewhere else and they dropped him off at Baldur's hanger."

"Not possible. Hulda is taking these calls, remember. She knows Baldur's private plane flies out of a small airport two hours in the opposite direction. If Geirs was supposed to be there at 10:30, there's no way they put Ariel on a commercial flight."

Eoin agreed. "Sounds like the three of them left on Baldur's plane instead. This isn't good. I wonder where Baldur would take her?"

Nell gave an audible sigh. "I don't know. Ariel had some kind of premonition about needing a wetsuit, and that's not exactly encouraging. Look, I've got another call coming in. Maybe it's Baldur. I'll get right back to you."

******

Stocks, newscasts, and prices floated through Ariel's dreams. She was lying on a table, uncomfortable, with strange hands touching her. She realized her leg was falling asleep and tried to move it, but couldn't. She woke up in alarm as she realized she actually couldn't move her leg. What the hell?

She turned behind her and saw her right wrist was held behind her back, attached to her left ankle with a plastic band. Geirs was studying her from the other end of the cabin.

"I'm sorry. Baldur told me not to restrain you, but I've seen you fight. This seemed to be a good idea."

"Un. Tie. Me. Now." She said it with all the fierceness she could.

The copilot poked his head through the door, and came into the cabin after noticing she was awake. He wasn't as big a man as Geirs, and she supposed that was lucky, because she bet they were working together. Could she take both of these guys out?

"Make. Me." Geirs responded.

"That was probably the wrong thing to say," the copilot said.

******

Eoin and Cillian drove towards town, discussing where Baldur would take Ariel. After a few minutes, Nell called back and Cillian took the call.

"Sorry it took so long. Baldur isn't taking her anywhere. I've found out Baldur isn't on his plane."

"That's worse. How do you know?"

"Because his pilot patched a call through to the office. He told Hulda he had to talk to Baldur immediately, and Hulda told him that was nonsense because Baldur was with him. He said no,

Baldur wasn't. Hulda and I figure the pilot knows who's on the plane. So she offers to relay a message, and he tells her there's been a lot of noise in the cabin and he hasn't seen the co-pilot in a while. Apparently Baldur ordered the pilot to stay in the cockpit, and now he wants permission to go back and check on things."

Cillian felt icy tendrils move throughout his body. "That's really not good."

"You think. Damn, the phone's ringing again. Let me call you back."

"A noise means a scuffle," Eoin said when he heard the news. "It means Ariel is alert enough to put up a fight." He was refusing to give up hope. "For all we know, she's got everybody but the pilot tied up in the back of the plane by now."

Cillian gave him a weak smile and they made nervous jokes until Nell called back.

******

Ariel wasn't sure why, but Geirs's childish taunt annoyed her. The position he had locked her into would have held most men and many women immobile, but it was barely a challenge for someone as limber as Ariel. She managed to bring the loop made by her two bound appendages past her hips and up over her other leg, and in a single motion she slammed her unattached foot hard into Geirs's stomach before she lost the element of surprise.

He doubled over but grabbed for her free leg. The adrenaline had started the aftershocks going again, so she saw his grab a fraction of a second before it happened. It was enough for her to know she had to latch on to his leg with her unfettered hand and do something to cause him a great deal of pain. She bit him in the ankle as hard as she could. It wasn't elegant, but he screamed and that's when the copilot pulled out a syringe.

******

"This could be good news," Nell said. "That was the hangar calling me. They found the co-pilot tied up in a supply closet sleeping off a dose of ketamine. Which is odd, because the man at the hangar told Hulda he saw the co-pilot board the plane."

"You might have lost me there," Cillian said.

"Me too, but then I remembered. Ariel said her brother has talents like mine. So if I can be a temp named Sigrun, why couldn't her brother have ended up as the co-pilot?"

"That's a little far-fetched," Cillian said. "We should call Toby or Ariel's family, and see if they decided to take matters into their own hands."

"Hang on, it's ringing again."

******

The co-pilot stuck the syringe in Geirs's arm.

"Thanks. I was wondering how I was ever going to get this into him," he said, and Ariel noticed the guy was looking more like her brother Zane every second.

"What the hell?"

"Ariel, you're doing a fine job of rescuing yourself, but I thought, you know, you maybe could use a little help. So I had the guy who was supposed to be the co-pilot take a nap for a few hours while I filled in for him."

"What about the pilot?"

"Oh, he's Baldur's man alright, but he's been instructed to stay in the cockpit and not come back here no matter what. He told me so."

"What are you thinking, Zane? I've seen this. This plane goes down in the ocean."

"No it doesn't." Zane kept looking at his watch. "We're flying at five thousand feet. Geirs and I are supposed to open the emergency exit and dump you out over the North Atlantic. Then the pilot takes us on to some bogus stop in Greenland where we lay low. You go missing; Baldur and Geirs insist they took you to the airport in Reykjavik for your scheduled flight. They imply your disappearance has to do with you embezzling funds and running off to the Caribbean."

"That asshole. So what's your plan?"

******

Eoin and Cillian were getting close to the city center when Eoin's phone rang again.

"That was Baldur's driver calling me this time," Nell said. "Guess what he wanted?"

"I'm not even going to try."

"He's new, and he didn't know I'm a temp, so he called me for advice. The driver said Ariel and Geirs both left on Baldur's private plane and Baldur did not. He said Baldur looked despondent and wouldn't talk after they left the hangar. He wanted to be driven over to Laugardalur, a big park east of city center. Baldur told the driver to park and wait for him. Baldur's there now, sitting in the hottest of the bathing pools and the driver is worried because he's been in there a while, staring straight ahead with tears running down his cheeks. The driver wondered if maybe he should call someone."

"Nell, you and Hulda couldn't have been more helpful," Cillian said. "We've got it from here."

******

"The plan is for us to jump out over the North Atlantic," Zane said. There wasn't much enthusiasm in his voice. "You've parachuted before, right?"

"Yeah, about twelve times," Ariel said. Her brother rolled his eyes. "It's easy to do things like that when you can see yourself having a happy life a month later."

"Yeah, well, I don't get to see myself safe like you do."

"Then why don't we make the pilot take us somewhere we want to go? That way you don't have to jump out of anything."

Zane shook his head. "I think that's a great idea but Toby says Baldur will be tracking the plane. Wherever we go, Baldur's men meet will us there. He says it's best to get you out of this aircraft altogether. So in exactly," Zane squinted at his watch "eight minutes and twelve seconds, we're going out that door."

"Why such exact timing?"

"At this low altitude, we need to open our chutes right away, and we need our ride to be down there waiting on us."

"Right. You don't last long in that ice water. How sure are you this pick-up is going to work?"

"Sure. Toby spent years at sea; he knows what he's doing. Plus, I've got a GPS tracker on me and our parachutes have these little inflatable things to crawl onto once we're in the water. We'll be fine."

Ariel finally understood. "No we won't. I'm such an idiot. The plane doesn't go down. What I was seeing was us jumping in the water and finding out Toby isn't there. By the time we hit the ocean we're too cold to inflate anything and we die. Or at least one of us does, because in the best of cases he can't get to us both."

******

Fifteen minutes later Eoin found a place to park, and a local store sold them both cheap swim trunks. They showered and walked over to the small, hot body of water that held Baldur and only two other bathers. Apparently public displays of grief worked well for emptying out a hot pool.

Baldur didn't look up as they got in, but the remaining two bathers decided this was as good a time as any to go.

"You need to let her live," Cillian said in his deep brogue as he climbed into the hot water.

"It's too late for that." Baldur replied without looking at him.

"Are you sure?" Eoin demanded.

Baldur shook his head and shrugged. "Maybe not. Maybe."

"Dammit man, then make a call." Eoin had his cell phone in his hand and thrust it at Baldur. "See if you can stop whatever nonsense you've started."

******

"What do you mean one or both of us die?" Zane asked, horrified.

"I mean I've seen this scene. You're the person with me, only I didn't get it. You're the person I'm so sad is dying, too. Or dying instead of me because Toby has been told it's more important I live. Only now, it doesn't have to go that way. Look."

Ariel pulled two garbage bags out of her roller bag. A couple of kitchen knives fell out. She handed Zane the bag Nell had labeled *his*.

"Get this on, quick. Here, tape it anywhere two pieces meet. It's gonna be cold going down so put your vest and scarf on over the wetsuit. Hat and gloves, too."

Zane looked at his watch again. "We jump in five minutes and four seconds. Better hurry. We have to get our parachutes on, too."

They pulled on the uncooperative neoprene fabric, then helped each with the clasps on the parachutes. With one minute to go they started to open the emergency door, thinking they had plenty of time.

******

"Can't do that," Baldur said. "If I stop it, I don't win. Can't do that."

"You idiot," Cillian said. "You don't win anything. You think what you do makes you special? Wise? It makes you short-sighted; that's what it does. You can't see past the nose on your face. Let me show you what this is about."

He reached towards Baldur and Baldur backed away, remembering the sting he'd felt when Siarnaq touched him.

"I don't care if it hurts me or you," Cillian yelled at him. "You are going to see. You are going to know. Here's what happens; here's what matters."

Baldur turned to climb out and an exasperated Eoin intervened. He grabbed Cillian's wrist with his left hand and Baldur's leg with his right hand and screamed.

******

It was a poor moment to discover the process of opening a door in a moving aircraft was more difficult than Zane or Ariel realized. It took them almost two minutes to figure out the mechanism. An extra minute at three-hundred miles an hour put them five miles away from a boat that would need ten long, cold minutes to travel the extra distance. At this point, there was no survival without the wetsuits. Unless the boat was well positioned, there wasn't much chance of survival with them.

******

The smell of searing flesh filled the pool as a crackle of electricity engulfed all three men and a whoosh of moving air made nearby birds take off in panic. Horrified bathers in the other pools looked over to see three bodies slump into the water.

One savvy guest picked up a phone and called for emergency help. Several others hopped out of their own pools to drag the bodies out. Staff came running from every direction as the most medically trained of the bystanders started resuscitation efforts on all three men, even though in one case there seemed to be little hope the man could be revived. Still, it was only right to try.

******

Ariel stood in the doorway of the plane wishing her brother would jump first, but he refused. As she took in the bright blue of the heavens, she searched for something to say to make sure he followed her.

"Jump and touch the sky," she screamed, struggling to be heard over the engines and the wind. She flung herself out into the azure nothingness, enjoying a second of incredible quiet before she pulled the ripcord on her chute and began to float down to the sea.

One of the best sights she had seen in a long time came into view above her a few seconds later, as Zane's chute opened and he gave her a wave. The other best sight was below, a large speedboat still a few miles away but moving through the water as fast as it could travel. She knew it was coming so those on board could pull her and Zane out of the ice-cold sea and take them home.

November 2012

28. Skyr in Seyðisfjörður

Thursday, November 29, news sources in Reykjavik reported one man was killed and two others severely injured when a freak lightning strike hit one of the small bathing pools in Laugardalur Park. The deceased was identified as Eoin Finn, an Irish manager from a software company who was visiting a local client. The injured included his client, Baldur, the well-known head of a local investment company, and an Irishman identified as Cillian McGrane who was also a client of the late Mr. Finn. Both injured men were reported to be in a coma, each in an intensive care unit at Landspitali.

******

Nell paced outside of the room where Cillian was being cared for. She was herself, not Sigrun, as the charade seemed pointless now. No one at the hospital questioned how Cillian's friend managed to arrive almost immediately while his other closest associate, a man named Brendan, was scurrying to get there.

The bereaved Mrs. Finn was known to be traveling to Iceland with Brendan, having announced her intention to speak in person with the *Ríkislögreglan*, Iceland's police force, to learn more about her husband's bizarre death.

Baldur's father arrived mid-afternoon from the countryside, and he and Baldur's chief counsel Ulfur remained in heated discussion in an adjoining waiting room. Nell did her best stay close, as the little earpiece transmitted to Hulda, who translated for Nell. The conversation centered around the fate of Baldur's considerable wealth if he remained unconscious indefinitely.

******

Ariel thought the beautiful Icelandic town of Seyðisfjörður would always be one of her favorite places on Earth. She'd never forget the wooden buildings glowing in the dusk, beaconing with the offer of comfort, as Toby's rented speedboat made its way to the barren, snow covered docks in the deepening afternoon twilight.

It had been difficult to hear each other as Toby sped them back to land, relying on expertise he'd gained from years at sea. Mikkel hadn't tried to talk to her. Rather, he placed his own dry, warm hat over her head and wrapped his arms around her, while fatigue and emotion took over and she cried in relief.

Rooms were available at the small hotel in town. Better yet, there was a liquor store, and—bless these fine people—it was open too. The thoroughly chilled, damp foursome received food and warm, dry clothes. They were asked no questions about why they rented a boat this time of year, or why two people had left the harbor in the morning and four had returned before nightfall.

Now, as they sat in the common room of the hotel, they enjoyed a snack of jam mixed with the local yogurt, called skyr. A waitress brought them Icelandic porters, while those in the kitchen worked to prepare something more substantial. Tomorrow they would resume their journey.

Zane and Toby were deep into analyzing Toby's intended takedown of d^4 when Mikkel reached for Ariel's hand under the table and held on to it.

Ariel gave him a smile. "Don't get too many ideas. I'm not going to Mars."

"I know. I'm just happy you're safe."

He hesitated, as if he wanted to say more.

"Ariel, this expedition isn't something you sign up for, like a field trip. You should know we expect to turn away a thousand candidates for every one we accept." He saw the storm growing in her eyes. "What I'm trying to say is please stop worrying about being coerced; it's not possible."

"I see." The smile was gone from her face. "Not possible because you don't think I'd make the cut?"

He pounded his forehead into the heel of his hand. "You could, Ariel. I don't know. I'm trying to take any feeling of pressure off of you, by pointing out this isn't something you can just agree to do. Let's save this for another time, okay. Tonight I'm glad you and your brother are safe."

"Have you had a word yet with Eoin and the people back at Ullow?" Toby asked. Ariel suspected she and Mikkel's voices may have gotten louder than they realized.

"No, I was going to call them as soon as we warmed up, to let them know everyone is okay." Mikkel pulled out his phone and looked. "Six missed calls. How did that happen?"

Toby wondered as well. He'd been more than happy to include the engineer on his maritime scurry, assuming Mikkel was handling communications with Ariel's company. Now, watching Mikkel and Ariel together, it was dawning on Toby that Mikkel's priorities were entirely with the young woman next to him. *She* was the reason Mikkel had wanted to be on the rescue boat.

"Let me check my messages now. I'll step outside," Mikkel looked flustered at dropping the ball. He came back a few minutes later. It was obvious something was wrong.

"We had it handled. I don't understand why Cillian couldn't have waited." Mikkel sounded angry at the man.

"What did he do?" Ariel asked.

"He went to Iceland this morning to confront Baldur. Thought he could change his mind about killing you, I guess. I don't know. According to Brendan, Eoin insisted on going with him and somehow they both ended up with Baldur after he put you on that plane to die."

"The meeting went poorly?" Zane asked.

"Much worse. Eoin is dead, Baldur and Cillian are both unconscious," Mikkel said. "We've got to get to Reykjavik."

"We can fly out before dawn." Toby reached for his phone. When Ariel looked puzzled, he added, "How do you think Mikkel and I got to this town this morning? I rent boats. I rent planes. It's a good thing I like rescuing people and I owe your brother a debt I can't repay."

"I'm ready to call it even after today," Zane said.

They were at the hospital by noon. Nell looked like she hadn't slept in days. Ariel realized that thanks to the woman's clever impersonation of an Icelandic receptionist, she hadn't.

"Any change?" Ariel asked. Nell shook her head. Brendan had been allowed to go in the room and they could see him through the window talking to an unconscious Cillian.

"The doctors say he has plenty of brain function; so they think maybe he just needs time. Do you think the electrical pulse between Baldur and Cillian was a more intense variation of what happened when you and he touched?"

"Probably. I saw a description on the internet. Everyone thought it was an electrical storm."

"Maybe the hot water, or the minerals in it, magnified the effect? Cillian always thought being closer to the North Pole made his powers stronger. Maybe it was being in Iceland?" Nell was trying to understand. "They'll let you go in to see him. Why don't you see if you can reach him?"

Ariel considered. The shock that had once passed between her and Cillian was mildly painful, but not dangerous. What would happen if she touched him now? When Brendan came out to talk to Nell, she went in. She stood next to Cillian's bedside, talking in a soothing tone she almost never used.

"You were trying to protect me, weren't you? You didn't want me to have to live in fear of Baldur for the rest of my life. I know you didn't. I'm going to try to help you Cillian, and I hope I'm right, because if I screw things up worse for you or for me I know it's a big mistake. Please... respond and be better."

She reached out her hand and stroked the skin on his lower arm. There was a hum of electricity this time as her fingers made contact, and a little tingle. She let her hand rest on his arm for a few seconds and saw Cillian give the faintest smile.

"Thanks. I needed a jumpstart," he whispered in his brogue. His eyes fluttered open. "Ariel?" Then with a little more panic in his voice. "It is you lass, isn't it?"

Ariel was puzzled. "I'm right here. Can't you see me?"

"I can't see anything. Just darkness, and the dozens of images that are usually in my head—more of them when you touched me." He shifted uncomfortably in the bed. "I think you better get the doctor."

S. R. Cronin

More tests would be run and experts consulted, but the initial conclusion was that Cillian's optic nerve was irreparably damaged. His hearing was fine, he was regaining muscle control, and he remembered events up through getting into the pool with Baldur. He told doctors he'd wanted to persuade the man not to harm his friend, and had no memory of the lightning strike. The physician explained this wasn't unusual in the case of trauma and the memory might never be regained.

Privately, Cillian affirmed what Brendan, Nell and Ariel had guessed. He'd hoped to make Baldur see the far future and understand the pain his actions could cause for countless humans not yet born. Eoin had accepted that such persuasion was Ariel's only hope for a safe life.

"Eoin made some bad decisions aligning with Baldur," Cillian said, "but damn it, the man died trying to find a way to do right. I'm going to miss him."

"I'm going to miss him too," Ariel said. "He didn't have to put himself in danger like that. There were other ways for me to be safe."

"Not really." Brendan disagreed. "I bet Eoin saw this as a way to redeem himself. He wasn't a bad mate deep down." Brendan turned away as the water began to well up in his eyes.

"Cillian, you had a great idea," Nell said. "Think how much help he could have been if you'd succeeded." She put her hand on his arm and squeezed.

"Yeah. Instead he's in a coma and I'm blind."

"Maybe you did succeed," Nell said. "We've got no idea what Baldur is thinking,"

"I say leave him be. As long as he's in a coma, the world is safer." Brendan was adamant.

"Maybe a tremendous resource for helping you guys is locked away,' Ariel said. "If I could jumpstart Cillian, why wouldn't my touching Baldur have the same effect? We could find out if Cillian succeeded. Maybe Eoin didn't die in vain. I should try."

Nell stepped in as the voice of reason. "Cillian, we need to know if you and Baldur exchanged any kind of visions. Before Ariel takes a risk like this "

Cillian shook his head. "I wish I knew. I have no idea what happened after we got into that water."

"Okay then," Ariel said. She marched out of the room before anyone tried to change her mind.

258

Ulfur, Baldur's father and Baldur's younger brother were in the waiting room next door, and they were going over piles of paperwork when Ariel walked in.

"He and I worked together closely. I'd like to go in to see him, please?" She knew Ulfur spoke English, and after he heard her request he turned to the other two men and spoke in Icelandic. Both men shrugged.

"They don't care. I'm puzzled, but go ahead. I'll be watching you through the window."

"I mean him no harm." Ariel opened the door, stepped in and closed it behind her, as Brendan and a nurse came into the waiting room, presumably to stop her.

She knew she didn't have much time. She walked up to the unconscious man she'd come to hate so much, took a deep breath, and lay the inside of her forearm against the inside of his.

"Come on. Wake up and do some damn good for once in your life."

The machinery hooked up to Baldur began to beep and whir in agitation, but the body of the pale man didn't move. Ariel pressed her other wrist against his cheek. The electronic responses became stronger but there was no physical response from Baldur.

The nurse made her way in, and barked something at Ariel in Icelandic. Ariel was willing to bet it translated as "What the hell are you doing?"

"Paying my respects," she said in English, hoping the tone would convey her innocent intentions. "And just leaving," she added, her hands up in a universal gesture of no harm meant.

Three doctors joined the nurse and as Ariel left Baldur's waiting room, they were gesturing at the readouts and shaking their heads. Next door, Cillian was trying to persuade the doctors to release him. When Ariel came back into his waiting area he was negotiating a move to a regular room and then a morning discharge, promising he'd get checked out once he was back on Irish soil. He wanted to go home.

Ariel considered going down to cafeteria to get away from everybody when Zane came by to say farewell.

"Where's Toby?"

"He thinks it's better if he isn't seen with us. He's headed back to his satellite office in Frankfurt now. He'll try to make sure Baldur and his estate will never see the money from the investing you two did together. He wants to keep claims of psychic investing out of the press, but there are regulatory bodies he'll have to level with privately. It's going to be a challenge."

"Can he keep Cillian and Mikkel out of it?"

"He thought he could, but that was before Cillian got into a hot tub with Baldur and got struck by lightning. It sort of draws attention to their relationship."

"I know. It's why I tried to revive Baldur before you got here."

"What? That asshole? Why in the world would you do something so stupid?"

"It wasn't stupid. Cillian tried to get Baldur to see the far future. He could have succeeded. Baldur could now be our biggest ally and Toby wouldn't have to do anything. But my touching him didn't work, so Toby better do what he needs to do."

Zane nodded, and started his goodbyes.

"Would you rather not hug me?" he asked. He understood his sister better these days.

She laughed. "It's a risk. I'll probably see things."

"I'll take a chance," he said and gave her a bear hug. She hugged back, but pulled away.

"Is everything okay at home?"

"Mom told me not to tell you. She's having some problems. I know she wants to talk to you about it over Christmas. Why?"

"Christmas isn't looking so good for our family. Mom is going to need help from both of us. Go. Catch your flight now. We'll talk more about it later."

Zane left wondering what it would be like to have normal relatives. Looked like he'd never know.

The next day Ulfur called Ariel, and they met in the hospital lobby. Ulfur told her he understood she'd had a complicated relationship with Baldur, both financially and emotionally.

"You should know Baldur took a turn for the worse while you were in the room with him. I don't blame you; I could see you didn't do anything. But the doctors say his brain woke up while you were in there and it's now fully functioning."

"So he's out of a coma?"

"No. His brain stem continues to communicate with his body, so he breathes and his heart pumps. Everything above the brain stem has lost its connection. The doctors don't think he can hear, see or experience touch, and he has no muscle control. He's cut off from the world, and they think he's conscious enough to know it."

Ariel shuddered. What a horrible fate. "Is there anything they can do?"

"Obviously they'll try all kinds of things, and no doubt chip away at his considerable wealth while they do so. There's no known cure, though. It seems they don't even understand it, so how can they fix it?"

Ariel tried to keep the look of relief off her face.

"I don't know if you two had any remaining financial dealings to iron out, but if you have claims, get in line with the others. I promise to give yours fair consideration."

Ariel shook her head. "No. Baldur was a client for my company and I have no remaining interest in his estate."

"He'll obviously be closing his account with Ullow. Do you think the Dublin office will stay open?"

Ariel hadn't thought that far ahead. "No, I don't suppose it will."

"So you'll be going back to London?"

"I doubt it." She realized it was true as soon as she said it. "I'll probably move into a different field. Something more about computers and less about money."

Ulfur looked relieved. "Good luck to you then. This planet needs more competent computer engineers."

"It does, doesn't it? Come to think of it, every planet does."

Ulfur gave her a funny a look as she walked out the door.

December 2012

29. Winter

Siarnaq knew he'd fallen in love with Ariel somewhere along the way. A romantic would say it happened at their first touch, but Siarnaq thought his feelings had sprouted as he watched her try to do the right thing under circumstances that would have challenged the finest of the gods.

Mikkel was kind enough to call Siarnaq the day after Ariel and her brother were pulled from the sea. The severity of the situation hit Siarnaq when he realized his relief at Ariel being alive was dampened by his envy at how Mikkel had ended up aboard the speedboat that saved her.

Siarnaq wanted to slap himself. Mikkel's part in the rescue was perfect. It was exactly what was needed. From such gestures grew deeper affection, and Ariel needed to love Mikkel. Well, she didn't need to, but her life would be better if she did, and Siarnaq wanted her to have a good life. Didn't he?

Of course he did.

It would not be good for her to wonder, even a little, if she and Siarnaq could have found a way to make a relationship work. His sunset-haired lover had important duties ahead, and she would need her heart, mind and soul in the game if she was going to take on the role fate would offer her. Siarnaq had seen it in full clarity, that last wonderful time he and Ariel lay together on the filthy couch in the messy apartment of someone Siarnaq knew. The lingering effects of Cillian's touch had combined with Ariel's to make it more clear than Siarnaq needed or wished. He'd known then he must say goodbye to her, and never see her again.

He swallowed his envy and his grief and thanked Mikkel for the news and wished Mikkel well with his projects. Siarnaq would go back to the purpose that drove him. He only wished it didn't feel so empty now.

Ariel had shown him more than her future, however. She'd also helped him see some of his own. There would be another love, eventually, and this one could end considerably better, if he wasn't stupid about it. He could end his days surrounded by affection, if he learned to move on.

So many ifs. At one time, the idea of a malleable future disturbed him, but now it brought him hope. It was perhaps the best gift Ariel had given him, this knowing that all these ifs determined what tomorrow would bring.

******

Ariel's grandfather had been a fireman, and attended more funerals than he would have liked. In too many cases, his relationship with the cause of death was complicated. Ariel thought of him now as she approached Mrs. Finn to pay her respects.

"All you say in a case like that is I'm sorry for your loss," he'd told her. "Don't say anything more."

Thanks papa.

Eoin's wife turned to her. "I'm sorry for your loss." She said it and meant it. The woman nodded.

Later, there were toasts and stories and tears and more toasts. Ariel noticed Eoin's wife and children stayed for only a few of them, while Eoin's mates and business associates were determined to spend the day drinking his soul into the afterlife.

The Ullow group sat together, trying to find the right balance between participation and sorrow. Rumor had it Ullow would close the Dublin office by the end of the year, so this was likely the last time they'd all be together.

Brendan didn't care about the office closing; he'd already decided to take time off from his career to help Cillian settle elsewhere. Ariel guessed Brendan would end up being Cillian's eyes, and his face to the world.

Ronan and Fergus were both going to work directly for Mikkel once the Ullow office closed. When there was a break in the toasts, Ariel turned to the one next to her, the one with the pointier chin.

"I wish you and Fergus the best of luck in Copenhagen."

"Thanks. I appreciate that, but I'm Fergus."

"Okay then, Fergus," she said looking hard into his eyes, "I hope learning Danish goes well for you guys."

"Thanks, but I'm Ronan," he said without cracking a smile.

Ariel grinned back at him. "It took me long enough. You guys have been doing this to me since I got here, haven't you?"

"We do it to everyone, don't we Ronan," one of the two young men said laughing.

"We've even confused our own mums, now haven't we, Ronan," the other laughed back.

"Does anyone know which of you is which?" Ariel looked around the table at the others. "What do the rest of you do?"

"We call them whichever name we fooking please," Brendan said, his serious face breaking into one of its rare smiles. Everyone laughed except Jake.

"Keep it down," Jake said. "We are at Eoin's funeral, you know."

Jake seemed to be the most lost member of the group, and Ariel wondered if he'd spoken with Toby about a job. Surely someone somewhere in y' could make good use of Jake's skills. Ariel made a mental note to check into it.

As for her, she planned to finish out the workweek, turn in her resignation, then use some of her remaining vacation to visit Mikkel in Copenhagen. Then she'd head on to Texas and deal with the future.

She went to the ladies' room and was surprised to find Eoin's wife standing at the sink, a lost look on her face.

"I thought you'd gone home," Ariel thought it was a dumb thing to say even as she said it.

"I did. My mum said she'd watch the children, and I should come back here and let friends console me. She was wrong. These people are celebrating his life. Me, I'm mourning his death, and I will be for a long while."

She gave Ariel a hard stare. "I need to know something. What happened to him? The police in Iceland, they were useless. My man didn't get struck by lightning, did he?"

"I'm sorry for your loss."

"Explain my loss," the woman replied. "He was doing something he wasn't supposed to be doing, wasn't he?"

"Oh no." So that's what his wife thought. "You can't put him to rest thinking that! I don't know exactly what happened; no on does. But I do know your husband went to that park to right wrongs. To save lives. He died trying to be a hero, not a villain, and you've got to believe it, because it's true. Nothing, nothing would have mattered more to him than your knowing that."

She studied Ariel's flushed face for a few seconds.

"You tell the truth. Thank you."

Ariel walked back into the room of drunken mourners, thinking even the wisest of grandparents occasionally got it wrong.

******

Toby had never handled negotiations as complicated or as delicate. Baldur had placed thousands of trades on over a dozen stock exchanges under hundreds of different names. His lawyer Ulfur was complicit, but dozens of other accomplices likely had no idea what they were part of.

The members of d^4 had been excluded from the real money; they just didn't know it yet. As these wealthy savants discovered they'd been cheated out of the top prize, they weren't happy.

Cillian and Mikkel had covered their tracks well. Toby tried to blur their association with Baldur, but they were connected through Ullow and through Eoin Finn, who hadn't helped the situation by dying a newsworthy death while literally linking Baldur to Cillian.

Toby was not a fan of claiming too much money was involved for justice to be served. He'd been scoffing at that assertion for the past four years. However, people with legitimate claim to trying to save the world did deserve special treatment as far as he was concerned.

So he worked harder at this than he had at anything in his life. Once he laid out the facts of Baldur's uncanny investment strategy and its upcoming success to the tune of nearly a hundred billion euros, a few key sensible people in power listened.

It was decided Baldur's considerable current wealth, already well into the billions, would be distributed among his probably undeserving family, his personal and professional staff, which included Hulda, and a large fund set aside for his medical bills. A sizable slice would go into an individual trust fund for Eoin's wife and five children. Once Ulfur realized he was being offered a sizable inheritance and a healthy fee to handle Baldur's affairs, he became not only cooperative but pleasant to deal with.

Loopholes providing an unfair advantage for high frequency traders would be closed, so no one in d⁴ could decide to go back into business and take further advantage of the situation. In return for making generous donations to local charities and then disappearing without complaint, no charges would be brought against d⁴ members for their irregular investments. Toby didn't like that, but he could live with it. He hoped nobody in the group would ever grasp the way Baldur had used Ariel's talents to circumvent even more of the system.

The final challenge was what to do about Baldur's many yet-to-mature options that were set to deliver over seventy billion euros if they went as expected. Finding a fair way to put that much money back into the world economy was going to be like putting toothpaste back into a tube.

Ronan advocated for distributing it evenly to every person on Earth.

"Are you nuts? So everybody gets ten euros, maybe five after shipping. I mean, it sounds like a lot of money, but we're a lot of people," Fergus said. "Not many lives get changed by ten euros. You take a fortune and make it insignificant."

"Think about that backwards," Ronan said. "If I could get every person on Earth to give me just ten euros, I'd be the richest man alive. There has got to be a way to do that."

Toby laughed. "Plenty of companies are trying that approach. It's tougher than it sounds. But you two have given me an idea that could work."

He explained how the profits of each little shell company could be handled separately. With over seven hundred of them, Toby could divide the world into as many groups, with about ten million people in each.

"Instead of everybody getting ten euros, each shell company take its hundred million and makes some kind of improvement in one part of the world. They can build schools, or parks, or hospitals. Maybe provide clean water or electricity. Each company figures out the best way to put money into its region."

Toby was delighted when Ariel mentioned Jake could use a job. It was fitting. Jake, the first person to figure out how d^4 was sucking up the world's wealth, would be in charge of putting the money back where it came from.

******

Brendan decided Cillian needed to move out of Dublin, so Nell set about finding a suitable house for the two men in County Donegal. That meant she had two houses she needed to find. Hulda had agreed to move to Ireland and try living with the person her former girlfriend Murna really was.

Cillian's outlook improved every day as he realized he had at least two dear friends willing to care for him. His contact with Baldur, Ariel and Siarnaq had left him with clearer visions than he had before. Perhaps the blindness helped the visions too.

Though he remained sad he'd never see his beloved Ireland again with his own eyes, he was determined not to lapse into the depression that claimed his own father. He had important work to do. There was research on communicable diseases to be encouraged, and libraries to be designed. Better long-life batteries had to be developed. Every day brought more helpful ideas.

It also brought him a certainty. They had crossed Mikkel's famous tipping point on money. Under anything but the most bizarre of circumstances, the Mars mission would be funded and Cillian's other, smaller projects would thrive and grow. Toby had done a magnificent job of protecting them.

Sometimes Cillian wondered how many people would deserve credit for saving the human race if he was successful. The growing number of candidates warmed Cillian's heart.

There was Mikkel, Ariel, and Siarnaq, and now one had to include Eoin. For that matter, Jake, Nell, Hulda and Brendan all deserved the accolade. Certainly he could add Ariel's brother Zane to the list, and an old woman in Iceland, and of course Toby. Yes, yes, it was a pointless thing to think about it, as nobody was ever going to be giving out awards. Nonetheless, it brought Cillian comfort to see the list of heroes grow.

******

Ariel was prepared to spend a week in rainy cold Copenhagen, but when Mikkel met her at the airport with tickets to fly on to a resort on the Turkish coast, she was delighted.

"I got great rates, and the place looks wonderful. I thought we could both use some pampering. I know you don't like surprises."

"I don't, but, well, it was about a forty percent chance you'd do this." She smiled at him. "I was hoping, but I couldn't risk packing for it."

He laughed at how easy it was to forget the ways she was different. "Buying you beach clothes will be no problem."

They held hands on the plane, and Ariel was pleased to discover she still got nothing from Mikkel's touch except happy premories. She didn't know why her mind filtered information about him, and only him, but she was willing to bet somewhere deep inside she had good reasons for it.

The best part was Mikkel seemed to have considerably more happy moments ahead of him than he used to. She let them drift through her mind as she closed her eyes and dozed.

Once they arrived at the resort, Ariel recognized the little bungalow with the hammock as soon as she saw it.

"This is the place. I knew it would be. I bring you coffee. We, we…"

"Do we now?"

"Yes, we do. A lot."

"Well, I'd hate to mess up the space-time continuum or anything by not behaving as expected."

"It doesn't work that way."

"Ariel, I know that. I also know you and I need to relax and for once not worry about the future. Let's enjoy now. Please."

"I couldn't agree more."

For the next few days, they had the time of their lives, living and loving like there was no tomorrow.

The Future

30. Christmas on Mars

Certain times of year always brought a touch of sadness, like a gentle brush across her cheek. Christmas was one, when the memories of Earth came rushing back demanding to be felt.

Each year, her family managed to video-call her on Christmas day, and she'd come to cherish seeing and hearing them all together again. This year, it mattered even more.

Not that her life on Mars was all bleak. Ariel stared out the window at the lonely red dust and was glad she didn't hate the sight of it anymore. Life had improved after the first year, when more people arrived and the tiny human colony grew large enough to banish her lingering claustrophobia and make her feelings of isolation more manageable.

Face it. It was never going to be like living in London or even Dubuque, but after a few years there was something of a town. They had a social life, a continuing education program and a tiny park with flowers in it. It kept getting better.

Ariel retreated to her small office where she could start the special call in private. Mikkel would join her at the end; he was understanding like that. Ariel peered into the Martian dusk, willing the call to come a few minutes early.

Mikkel had been one of the better reasons for going to Mars, even though Ariel knew no love for any man would have been enough to convince her to do this. It was lucky she cared for him, and he for her, and they'd built a life that mostly brought them joy in spite of the circumstances.

S. R. Cronin

She was safer here. Too many others back on Earth knew what she could do and how her peculiar talents could be harnessed to circumvent Earth's many forms of gambling. On Mars, she never had to look over her shoulder in fear. All the low-probability premories of being kidnapped vanished once she began her life on the red planet.

Maybe those she cared about were better off as well. With millions of miles of vacuum separating them, her family and friends had been able to live their lives without Ariel's always well intended, but not always productive, visions. She had a mantra before she left. *Better not to touch and know too much.*

Except it wasn't true on Mars. Here, she was needed to touch everyone and was listened to like the town oracle. It was an odd role, one not possible on a planet filled with the noise, skepticism and random actions of seven billion people. Once it became clear she wasn't faking it, everyone embraced it. Touch me and keep me safe. It was her main job, and everyone on Mars knew it.

After Eoin's horrible death years ago, Ariel considered disregarding Cillian's visions. But after a few years of blindness, Cillian was not only positive humanity required an outpost on Mars, where the ancestors of the deadly virus would never exist, he also was certain if this attempt failed, only three other serious attempts were likely. For various reasons, all three would probably be abandoned before 2352.

After that, Cillian decided if Ariel didn't go to Mars, there probably would be no humanity by the year 3000. Cillian believed it. Ariel believed Cillian. Therefore, there wasn't much more to think about. She went to Mars.

Once they'd been here a few years, Ariel allowed herself the one dream she refused to give up. She became the first pregnant woman on the planet. Once the pregnancy was found to be progressing well, her spirits lifted to highs she thought she'd never feel again. Mikkel was nervous. The other colonists had mixed reactions.

Damn it, who were they to judge? The rest of them had fought for the right to be here. She hadn't, and she would have this one pleasure before she got too old.

Her joy was short lived. A technician confirmed what Ariel had already precalled when he found a tiny opening between the upper two chambers of the heart of the growing fetus. Her brother Zane, now in medical school, assured her lots of people had this minor heart defect, and led normal lives. He promised her it would be okay, but she knew better. She put her hands on her belly every night and cried, knowing the likely outcome.

minor heart defect, and led normal lives. He promised her it would be okay, but she knew better. She put her hands on her belly every night and cried, knowing the likely outcome.

"I hate this gift!" She screamed it at Mikkel one evening as he walked in on her. "I'd cut my own brain out right now if I could." He turned away from her when the outburst started, and that angered her worse. She grabbed his head to turn him towards her and make him listen to her frustration. Then she saw the tears running down his cheeks.

Oh.

"He's my son, too," Mikkel said. Then they'd held each other and cried together.

They named him John, an Americanized form of Eoin, and the little boy could hardly sleep for all the time his parents held him after he was born. When the two doctors in the colony told them John was fighting a slow battle for his life, they already knew. The abnormality was larger than usual, and if John was to live into childhood, he'd need surgery not possible on Mars. If he was going to be put into cryogenic stasis and sent back, the best time to do it was now.

Ariel and Mikkel made the gut-wrenching decision to request the transport of a basically frozen infant back to Earth. This would be only the second ship to return, and modifications to the vessel needed to be started. Some objected to the frivolity of giving up cargo space to try to save a baby. The parents had known the risks, and needed to accept the consequences. Others knew Ariel's story and what she'd given up and why. They felt she'd earned this. Many rose to the technical challenge of getting the small parcel back safely.

Eight months later, nine-month-old John arrived on Earth, was brought out of stasis, and was given over to the care of Zane and his partner Afi. Ariel had seen the little boy having a high likelihood of surviving the journey, and the surgery. After that, she couldn't tell.

Ariel shook her head to clear the memories, and looked impatiently at the clock. The designated start time for the Christmas call had come and gone. A frustrated Ariel paced around her small office. How could they be late today of all days?

They'd sent tons of photos and video clips of him already, of course, but this was John's first real Christmas; being frozen on a spaceship last year didn't count. She should be seeing them all now, watching. Zane and Afi passing the squirming baby on to his Aunt Teddie and to her Mom and Dad, and dammit Ariel was crying again when the call finally came through. She wiped her eyes and did her best to smile as she answered.

"Sorry we're late, sweetie," her mom said. "Didn't mean to make you sad." She'd given her mom ongoing permission to check in on her. There were times when it was a nuisance.

"Yeah, somebody here took a world class dump five minutes ago to and needed a diaper change really bad." Zane laughed as he held up a squirming little boy. John looked happy and healthy.

As her family talked over each other, she concentrated on how her son was loved. She listened to news from each of them. Teddie was dating a telepath? Zane had been home with Afi when John took his first step? The video was coming. Her dad was excited one of his former students was being nominated for the Nobel Prize in physics. Her mother's organization was growing faster than she could keep up with it. So much good news. How she loved them all.

Mikkel knocked on the door. His questioning look said, "Ready for me?" She motioned him in.

"We've got some good news here too," she said as Mikkel put his arm around her. Ariel's mom gave a knowing smile but everyone else quieted down and looked inquisitive.

"We're expecting a baby in June. Everything looks good according to the doctor, and, more importantly, it looks good to me. John will have a sister, one who grows up on Mars."

Teddie gave a whoop and everyone else joined in. They were still carrying on when the ten-second warning chimed and they all began waving and blowing kisses and sending hugs through the air. Mikkel kept his arm around Ariel as she started to cry again.

"It's the hormones," she explained between sobs. "I'm fine, really I am."

"I should get back to the common room. It's almost time for dinner. You coming?"

Of course she was. This was her home and Christmas dinner was about to be served.

2046 - 2047

31. Life on Earth

If the return of the infant John sparked controversy, it was nothing compared with the decision to bring an adult settler back to Earth. The rules were and always had been clear. The journey to Mars was a one-way trip. But circumstances change, technology improves, and costs come down. Many on the engineering and medical side were curious if it could be done safely. There were those on Earth who thought Mars was pulling away, and who recognized the value of close ties. This goodwill trip would be financed by Earth. Who to bring?

The chancellor seemed like a logical choice. She was a fit woman in her late fifties, and a fine ambassador for the ten-thousand Martians she represented. There were humanitarian aspects. Her father passed away recently, and her family would delay the funeral until she arrived. The child she sent to Earth for surgery two decades ago had gotten his girlfriend pregnant. By the time the chancellor arrived, she'd be a grandmother. She could be photographed holding her earthling grandchild, providing endless touching symbolism of how the two worlds remained intertwined.

Ariel spent the early months of 2046 preparing for eight months in a large tin can, followed by a year in a stronger gravitational field. She delegated her responsibilities, said a two-year goodbye to her daughter and husband, and left her people with all the premories she could to ensure their safety in her absence. Even then she balked at the last minute, and spoke with Brendan.

"Nothing is changed since I wrote you. Cillian is positive. You have a window of over two years when all will be fine. He says the increased communication with Earth and the good will from the trip are positive for the future. He advises you to do it."

So she did.

She mourned her father while wishing she could have seen him one last time instead. She held her son's baby close to her heart, and each time she did, cameras turned towards her. John and his girlfriend had added to the media's infatuation with the child by naming her Trinity for her three lineages; that of her mother, of John's family on Earth, and of John's ties to distant Mars. Commentators loved the name.

Ariel attended meetings, functions and parades as required, but she also took time to play in the ocean and stare at the clouds. Why hadn't she appreciated clouds when she saw them every day?

She and her son John went on a picnic together, in a park with grass and trees. It felt like something out of dream. There was security around them, but her guards keep their distance to allow the illusion of privacy.

"Look at the colors and the curls in that cloud. They're amazing." When John didn't respond, she said "You have no idea, do you, what a gift it is to see a blue sky or to stare out to sea? I didn't realize how much I missed the color blue." She knew he found her odd. "It's just so different here."

"I'm sure it is. Please don't be mad, Mom, but I'm glad I live on Earth." At Zane and Aii's insistence, he called her Mom, while Mikkel had ended up as "Far," the Danish word for father.

"I mean, I love you and Far, but I like the life I have."

She'd expected this. It meant he was happy, and that was what she wanted. Right? She tried to rise to the occasion.

"Some days I don't like Mars either, and then they went and made me the mayor."

"I thought you were the chancellor?"

"That was Mikkel's idea. He thought Mayor of Mars sounded dumb, and we needed a title with more dignity. I'm more of a city manager than anything. Turns out I'm good at running things."

"Well, Earth is sure making a big deal about you. Don't you like it there sometimes?"

Ariel hesitated. This was a complicated question. Everyone in her family knew of her precognitive skills, though they kept it quiet. At Cillian's insistence, few knew of her real reasons for going to Mars. John wasn't one of them. It needed to stay that way.

"Far loves it there and it's home to your sister Bridget. We've made a nice life. I'm glad you're happy here." She gave him a quick hug to end the conversation, and was relieved when all she premembered was images of him playing with Trinity as she grew.

Ariel was on Earth for four months before she was able to make a trip to Donegal. The western coast of Ireland had formed its own nation a decade earlier, and English was rarely spoken in the new country. Relations with neighbors were strained and security was tricky, but Ariel insisted on the visit.

Nell and Hulda were setting out a picnic lunch on their deck overlooking the ocean when she arrived, her security detail in a separate vehicle behind her. Word must have reached her friends that Ariel couldn't get enough time outdoors looking at the sky or the sea, and late spring along the coast was beautiful.

"You didn't? Sushi and dolmades," Ariel clapped her hands with delight when she saw the food Nell was setting out.

"Old memories. The best kind." Nell was in her seventies now, and Ariel could see the years in her friend's face. She wondered if a lifetime of morphing her appearance had contributed to the many wrinkles. Hulda was weathering the passage of time better. They both seemed as much in love as they'd been thirty years ago.

"So are you going back to Mars?" Hulda asked once they had settled into the meal. Not when, but if. If hadn't occurred to Ariel.

"I have a husband and daughter there. I'm an elected official." Ariel gave the blue sky dotted with fluffy white clouds a wistful look. "I don't think staying here is an option."

"Have you talked to Cillian about it?" Nell asked.

"No, I haven't spoken with Cillian in years. Brendan handles his communication with me, but I'm am headed over there tomorrow morning. Have *you* discussed this with Cillian?"

Nell shook her head. "No, it's your question to ask. Hulda and I were talking about how you've made such a difference up there and we wondered if there was a chance they didn't need you anymore. I mean in the psychic sense."

Ariel tried on the idea. A sharp pang reminded her how much she'd miss Mikkel and Bridget. They might never understand such a choice. Then she thought of the eight-month journey back in the tin can and the recycled air for the rest of her life with never an ocean to swim in or clouds to watch. No more blue sky. Ever.

"I don't know. I don't *think* I'd stay if I could. I mean what kind of human would choose to give up everything they've built for the last two dozen years to go swimming and watch clouds?"

Hulda and Nell said nothing, and Ariel knew she'd ask Cillian the question.

She headed over to Cillian's estate the next morning, her security entourage behind her. Brendan had warned her the years had changed the elderly prophet.

"We haven't had a visitor in months," he said as he opened the door. Brendan's butterscotch mane was now more white than bronze and the entryway looked like it hadn't been cleaned in years. She spoke into the small mic she wore on her collar.

"All's well. I'm going in and I'll be shutting this off. No need to follow." She knew her security detail hated that, but she would have some privacy while she was here.

Brendan took her through the clutter, straight to the old man in a wheelchair seated by a window. A breeze was blowing through the opening, and the sunlight shown through the upper glass.

"I can still feel the sun on my face," he said. "And the wind."

"It's Ariel," Brendan said. "She's come from Mars to see you."

"I know that. You should touch me, Ariel. It won't hurt either of us now."

She obliged and put her hands on his papery skin. She stroked his arm softly and let her mind relax into the visions they shared. She'd forgotten the sensation of seeing so far ahead, and was disoriented until she began to make sense of what she saw and the knowledge that came with it.

"Oh. Wow. Things *have* changed, haven't they?"

"Yes. Better in many ways, and you and your family are part of that. But it's not better in all ways, is it?"

He was right. She understood why Cillian had become adamant about secrecy during the past decade. New probabilities had grown from tiny outliers to plausible outcomes. A solid rumor of an impending disaster spawned a wealth of unpleasant alternatives. Here, she saw fanatic political parties whipping fear into a frenzy of awful behavior. There, she saw a cautious medical establishment exacerbating the problem as it became frozen with its own dread of what might come. Cillian was right. All the best paths lay along the swath of a largely unsuspecting population. His growing insistence on secrecy was well founded.

"See. You thought I was going nuts, didn't you?"

Ariel laughed. "It sounded at times like you'd gone off the deep end."

"Well, I haven't. What happened is you, Baldur and Siarnaq left me with more clairvoyance than I started with. I'm sure you noticed how much wider the window I see into has grown. I still can't see a damn thing here, but I see every fooking thing likely to happen."

"It must be hard." She whispered it, more to herself than to him.

"The seeing is okay. The hard part is doing the right thing once you know. Did Brendan tell you I found Lara and my kids?"

"No! That's great. When? Where?"

"I found them in the late twenties. Wasn't a chance I could make their lives better at that point. Big chance I could cause harm. So I never spoke to them. I tell you, it's not the knowledge that kills you, Ariel. It's the having to do right by it."

"True." She knew what was coming. "I need to go back to Mars, don't I?"

"You saw it, I hope. Your biggest contributions, as a psychic, are yet to come. It does make your path forward more clear. No soul-wrenching decisions, huh?"

"It makes it easier. I'll go of course."

Cillian reached out, feeling the air, seeking her hand once again. He talked as he found it.

"If it matters, and I know it does to you, things look better now than they ever have. I believe it's going to be worth it in the end."

Something occurred to Ariel.

"Getting to see this has helped me. I know you don't want to communicate with me on Mars, but could you send me updates somehow? It would make such a difference."

He shook his head. "Too many people see and hear all your communications. Besides, you shouldn't know these things. No one should. You need to go back to not worrying about fluctuations in the probabilities. Accept that I won't be able to update you again."

Something in her balked at this last edict. She wasn't willing to accept it, not completely.

"No. You need to give me something here. A morsel. I have an idea. My mom is in her eighties and she's not doing well; she hasn't been since my dad died. Before she goes, would you give *her* an update? Just one."

"Your mother?" He tilted his head and thought. "I would, because I know how much she's given up, too. But I only talk in person, and I don't travel. She can hardly come here on her deathbed."

"Actually, she can. She's a telepath, remember? She can read your thoughts while you show her your most likely vision. What's the harm in that? I don't get to see it, but before she dies, she will. That'll be enough for me."

"There's some chance I die first, you know."

"Not much of one."

Cillian thought some more "She probably barely remembers me from back when. You told me telepaths can't find people they don't know. The last thing I need now is to make a new telepathic friend."

Ariel had expected this.

"You don't have to become friends. She won't know about your promise to me, and she'll have no reason to intrude on you. I'll ask my sister to take mom on a trip when her end is near. She'll bring mom's consciousness to your house."

"Right. I forgot about your sister. She can carry a telepath along when she does her out of body thing, can't she? But how will I know when it's happening."

"I'll contact you. All you have to do is bring on your best vision of the future and hold it in your head for a while. I know it's a long shot that it all works out, but I need this morsel."

Cillian was quiet for a minute more. "Right now, I see maybe a ten percent chance of having to deliver on this promise. I'm surprised it's that high. Okay, if Brendan gets a message from you saying "happening now" he and I will know what it means. I'll do everything I can to give your mum a good look at our most probable future."

Ariel said nothing, but gave him a kiss on the top of his head.

As her lips touched him, Cillian realized with a laugh that odds were good Lola Zeitman would recover from her health slump and live to be one-hundred and four. Thanks to the vow he'd just made, the probability of him living long enough to deliver on his promise had risen, too.

Ariel's last outing before quarantine was attending the annual Penthes celebration with her family in late July. The pharmaceutical company in Chicago had affected their lives in many ways, and now Penthes would supply the antidote to the senility taking over her grieving mother's mind.

She supposed it was inevitable someone would dig out the footage of her brother leading a conga line of dancers out of a hotel two years ago when he'd been the honoree at the Penthes event. His spontaneous display of joy struck a chord with the city, and thousands of people had joined the instant parade as media plastered the footage everywhere.

In spite of her efforts to avoid publicity before she left Earth, someone learned that The Lady from Mars was going to be in Chicago at the same event. DJs began extolling the public to show the red planet how to party by making this the best dance of joy ever. It didn't stop the hype that there'd only been two previous ones, Zane's unexpected parade and a small unsuccessful attempt to recreate it last year. Ariel didn't know whether to be horrified or amused when she saw a special report on how to choose one's costume for the event.

"Are you going to ignore this nonsense, or get out there and lead a conga line?" Ariel asked her brother once they were both in Chicago.

Zane shrugged. "Afi says do it, because nothing bad ever comes from dancing." She could tell her brother was weighing his options. He held out his arm to make a request he'd avoided throughout her visit. "I know you hate being asked, but this is a one-time deal, okay? What do you think? Dance?"

Ariel put her arm against his and hoped for nothing unwanted. She got her wish. The answer was simple. "Definitely dance."

"I will."

One could say Ariel came to Earth in a tin can, but to call the elaborate vehicle taking her back to Mars by that name was hardly fair. There were multiple rooms in a vessel packed with building materials, needed goods, and even luxuries for both the travelers and the Martians.

S. R. Cronin

Fifteen others would accompany her; all new settlers being sent on schedule. They brought added skills and youth. Thorough screening ensured they'd be decent traveling companions, so the months would pass faster with their company.

She told her young companions to consider her just another voyager, one who would do her chores and work as hard as everyone else to get along. They offered her no special treatment, but insisted on one courtesy.

"You take the com as we leave," a young woman said as she handed Ariel the communications apparatus.

When Ariel hesitated, the woman added. "Mars is a democracy, right? The vote is fifteen to one." She handed Ariel the mic. "You take the com."

So Ariel did.

The radio cackled: "Aries number 46. You are cleared for take-off. Proceed when you are ready."

"Copy that. We are initiating take-off procedure. Thanks for the great hospitality, Earth. It was fun. Now it's time for me to take my new friends here and head for home."

2064

32. How It All Ends

Lola knew she was at the end of her life. Her daughter held her hand and she was grateful Teddie had picked today to let her mother into her mind, and share a wonderful closeness. Lola was enjoying the warm sense of being loved when she heard Teddie think, *Okay Ariel, it's your turn.*

Really? What next?

She and Ariel had shared a secret for decades. Ariel wasn't fascinated by other planets, but knew her mother was. As Ariel made the difficult decision to settle on Mars, she'd offered her mother an incredible privilege.

"I know you'd love to come visit me, and it's not possible. I know you're going to worry about me, and communication will be limited. So let's make this easy. Drop in any time."

"Ariel, I don't even know if I can find you on Mars."

"I bet a telepathic mom can find her child anywhere in the universe."

"What if it's, you know, a private moment?"

Ariel giggled. "You've got manners. If it's not a good time, come back later. I trust you. When you *are* there, look around. See the two moons of Mars overhead and enjoy the stars in an alien sky. Reassure yourself I'm safe."

Practical Ariel. Lola took her up on the offer every so often, and it made her life richer and easier. She wished she could find a way to thank her child for this gift, but here she was in a hospice bed, barely capable of anything. Then she heard her daughter's voice in her mind. Ariel spoke with clarity.

"I need you to do something important for me, Mom. Please."

Lola flickered her eyes open and saw Teddie next to the bed, talking into the com on her wrist. Teddie brought her hand up to her ear to listen and nodded. She spoke to her mother in a loud voice.

"Mom. Listen to me. Ariel needs you to do something for her. Can you focus?"

Focus? Now? She'd try.

"You're going to ride with me again. It will be a shorter trip. An easier one. We'll go to Ireland where there's a man you met years ago. You have his permission to enter his mind. Go in and see what he sees."

That was it? See something? What good could that do?

"Ariel says this means the world to her. Will you do this?"

Lola nodded. Of course she would.

Teddie was right. The trip was quick, and the old man sat at a wooden table in a cluttered room, holding his head in his hands. She recognized him. A bottle of Jameson sat near his elbow and he looked like he'd consumed a good bit of it.

Lola moved her consciousness from Teddie into the elderly man. Once there, she lost her sight. That's right. This man was blind when she met him. She heard Ariel's voice coming over a communication device in the room.

"Mom, Teddie has left you, so she can go back to her body and talk to me. You met Cillian long ago. He's a prophet and my friend and you're hearing me through his mind. He'll show you the future now, the far future. Look at it for me. That's all I ask. That, and know I love you."

Lola wished there was a way to tell her daughter she loved her too, but there was none. The best way to show it was to do what Ariel wanted, so she turned her attention to what Cillian saw.

It was the year 2999. He knew it, so she knew it. They were in a city, but he didn't know its name, only that it was a new place built after the awful times six hundred years before. Cillian was happy, because the city was full of people.

Most of them were gathering into a queue, like they were planning to board public transportation. Were they going somewhere?

Of course. She knew it as Cillian knew it. It was nearly midnight on New Year's Eve. They'd kept the old calendar, and shared our fascination for watching the nines roll into zeroes.

On top of a distant stage she saw a flaming orange torch being passed from an elder to a child, as a chorus of sweet children's voices began to sing an ancient song to call for love and peace. The image was recreated on countless screens lining the street. As the song finished, the sound of chanting began, then it coalesced into what had to be a countdown. At the last shout, rhythmic music started to blare. There was kissing and yelling and jumping around, and people began to link their arms or hold onto each other by the shoulders or the waist.

What was this? Cillian knew. It was an old custom, from before the troubled times. One of Earth's oldest living traditions, the New Year's dance of joy. It was thought to have started in 2000, although the rumor was never confirmed.

Lola grinned as the healthy and happy bodies began moving forward, everyone boogying along in their own impromptu jig. It was a conga line, a giant conga line. She felt like she was dancing with these happy people and Cillian too, and they both agreed it was wonderful. It was the way every millennium should end.

******

The message came from Teddie.

"She died at 7:52 p.m. I was holding her hand. By the time I made it back to Cillian's place there was no Mom's mind to bring home. Cillian seems to have known it, too, because when I got there he was raising his whiskey in a toast. It was kind of sweet. I'm sending you what you asked for. I think she died happy, but you decide."

Ariel could hear the sorrow in Teddie's words. Even at 104, death was an ending, a loss. She watched the video Teddie sent.

There was her ancient mother, lying in a hospice bed with a cheerful grin spread across her face. When she started to twitch Ariel worried her mom was in pain, but in a few seconds it was apparent she was moving to a rhythm. She whispered something sounding like "dance for joy." Then her movements stopped, and her breathing followed. The smile on her face remained.

Teddie added in a quiet voiceover, "I don't know where she was, Ariel, but she looks to me like she was having a great time. How bad can the future be?"

Ariel agreed. Her mother died happy, and, against all odds, she'd done exactly what Ariel hoped. She sent word back from the future. Her message? It was likely to end well after all.

More

Flickers of Fortune is part of the 46. Ascending collection of interrelated novels about five family members who each discover they can do the extraordinary when circumstances require it. These books are designed to be read as stand-alone stories or in any order.

If you enjoyed *Flickers of Fortune*, consider *Layers of Light,* the story of Ariel's younger sister Teddie, as she uses her innate skills for out of body experiences to save her friends from a human trafficking ring. You might also enjoy *Shape of Secrets*, the story of Ariel's brother Zane as he uses his ability to alter his appearance to find a murderer in the South Pacific.

You may prefer to start with *Twists of Time*, the tale of Ariel's father as he learns to use his ability to warp time to protect the students at his high school or *One of One,* the story of Ariel's telepathic mother as she finds herself the unlikely hero in a rescue mission in Nigeria.

You can also go directly to *One of Two*, the last book in this collection, in which the Zeitman family combines their skills to prevail over the most dangerous threat they will face.

S. R. Cronin

Thanks

I have relied on many people and sources of information to weave this tale. I am particularly indebted to the following:

- my husband Kevin, my alpha and omega reader, who feeds me and loves me, and in this case introduced me to the Irish legends of Colm Cille, thereby shaping much of this story
- my sister June, who gives me witty page by page notes to aid my rewrites
- my son Casey who helps me see my writing in a larger context
- my daughter Emerald who knows what to say to keep me positive about this endeavor
- longtime friend John Ryan, a math professor who supplies links and catches plot holes
- Lenore Kaplan, a young engineer whose insights aided the plot, the accuracy and the wording
- Tyler Wight, new family friend who provided me with a fresh set of eyes on my stories
- Dhivya Balaji of India, who played a large role my fourth novel and proved how well her abilities to edit transcend cultures
- Shree Janani of India, who found me when she won a copy of my fist book and has been providing editorial expertise and encouragement ever since
- Deepika Anandakrishnan, friend of Dhivya and Shree, who volunteered to beta read and provided me with suggestions and corrections no one else thought of
- Steve Wilcock, an online word game buddy who's encouraged my writing from the start, served as a role model for my British telepath Tom, and now proved himself to be a highly capable beta reader as well
- Terie Beasley, who used her expertise as a retired English teacher to add extra polish to my words
- Margit Fernqvist of Denmark, a stranger who offered to share her expertise on Scandinavia and ended up teaching me about skyr, enticing me to write about the northern lights, and sharing her vacation photos of Iceland with me

- Michelle Willms, second time beta reader, who again provided the insights of a sociologist
- Faith O'Dwyer, first time beta reader who particularly helped with the beginning of this book
- Mickey Otterlei of Norway, who has encouraged me with this collection and added her Scandinavian perspective
- Henry Bourassa who lent his expertise on investing
- and Joel Handley, an editor whose abilities have grown with each novel.

Finally, and most significantly, my thanks go to my daughter Shenandoah. She has been there for me through this entire writing process. She has edited, commented, encouraged and involved others, and I appreciate it all. However, she played a special role in this novel.

The character Ariel is a work of fiction, but Shenandoah inspired Ariel. I thank my daughter for letting me borrow bits of her personality and her dreams to create this character, then providing me with ideas and expertise to make the character better, and then stepping back and allowing me the freedom to morph Ariel into the fictional person she needed to be to tell this story.

It takes a special kind of courage to let someone do that.

Additional Information

Written Material:

I love to research, and all my novels began by my devouring fact and fiction on subject matters of interest to me. I'd like to thank the following authors and acknowledge the contributions their books made to my thought process. It is my intent to be accurate, respectful of all cultures, and open-minded about various points of view. If I have fallen short, the fault is mine and regretted. Inclusion of a source below in no way implies that source's endorsement.

All About High-Frequency Trading (All About Series) July 26, 2010 by Michael Durbin. Publisher: McGraw-Hill; 1st edition ISBN-13: 978-0071743440

The Arctic: Enigmas and Myths September 9, 1996 by Simpson-Housley, Paul Simpson-Housley. Publisher: Dundurn Group; First Edition ISBN-13: 978-1550022643

Clairvoyance August 3, 2009 by Charles Webster Leadbeater. Publisher: Merchant Books ISBN-13: 978-1603862417

Lonely Planet Iceland, Greenland & the Faroe Islands May, 2001 by Graeme Cornwallis and Deanna Swaney. Publisher: Lonely Planet Publications; 4th edition (May 2001) ISBN-13: 978-0864426864

The Privatization of Space Exploration: Business, Technology, Law and Policy Paperback December 16, 2011 by Lewis D. Solomon. Publisher: Transaction Publishers; Reprint edition ISBN-13: 978-1412847568

The Problem of HFT - Collected Writings on High Frequency Trading & Stock Market Structure Reform January 18, 2013 by Haim Bodek. Publisher: Create Space Independent Publishing Platform; Reprint edition ISBN-13: 978-1481978354

Seeing Your Future: A Modern Look at Prophecy and Prediction March, 1990 by John E. Ronner. Publisher: Mamre Pr; First Edition ISBN-13: 978-0932945389.

The Story of the Irish Race A Popular History of Ireland 1921 by Seumas MacManus. Publisher: Devin-Adair Company; Forty-Fifth Printing edition (1992) ASIN: B001B1EI96

This Cold Heaven: Seven Seasons in Greenland January 7, 2003 by Gretel Ehrlich. Publisher: Vintage ISBN-13: 978-0679758525

Internet sources:

My research also included many internet sites. I have chosen the couple of dozen I thought would be of most interest to my readers and provided live links to them at the blog for this book, Touching the Sky to Save the World. Visit my blog at https://dtothepowerof4.org/

S. R. Cronin

About the Author

Sherrie Roth grew up in Western Kansas thinking there was no place in the universe more fascinating than outer space. After her mother vetoed astronaut as a career ambition, she went on to study journalism and physics in hopes of becoming a science writer.

She published her first science fiction short story and then waited a lot of tables while she looked for inspiration for the next tale. When it finally came, it declared to her it had to be a whole book, nothing less. One night, while digesting this disturbing piece of news, she drank way too many shots of ouzo with her boyfriend. She woke up thirty-one years later demanding to know what was going on.

The boyfriend, who she had apparently long since married, asked her to calm down. He explained that, in a fit of practicality, she had gone back to school and gotten a degree in geophysics and had spent the last 28 years interpreting seismic data in the oil industry. The good news, according to Mr. Cronin, was she found it at least mildly entertaining and ridiculously well-paying. The bad news was the two of them had still managed to spend almost all of the money.

Apparently she was now Mrs. Cronin, and the further good news was they had produced three wonderful children whom they loved dearly, even though to be honest that is where a lot of the money had gone. Even better news was that Mr. Cronin turned out to be a warm-hearted, encouraging sort who was happy to see her awake and ready to write. "It's about time," were his exact words.

Sherrie Cronin discovered that over the ensuing decades Sally Ride had already managed to become the first woman in space and done a fine job of it. No one, however, had written the book that had been in Sherrie's head for decades. The only problem was the book informed her it had grown into a six book collection. Sherrie decided she better start writing before it got any longer. She's been wide awake ever since, and writing away.

Places

Greenland

Kalaallit Nunaat: the native name of Greenland
Nuuk: the capital of Greenland, also known as Godthab
Qaanaaq: Greenland's largest northern village
Kulusuk: an island off of Eastern Greenland
Ilulissat: a common tourist destination in Greenland, located along
       the relatively mild Western Coast
Peary Land: A dessert region in the far northeast of Greenland

Iceland

Island: the native name of Iceland
Reykjavik: the capital of Iceland, also known as Reykjavíkurborg
Vatnajökull: Iceland's most famous glacier
Seyðisfjörður: a town in eastern Iceland
Laugardalur: a park in Reykjavik famous for its hot springs

Ireland

Éire: the native name of Ireland
Dublin: the capital of Ireland, also known as Baile Átha Cliath
Dun Laoghaire: a large marina outside of Dublin
Donegal: a city and a county on the far northwestern edge of
       Ireland

People

Ariel Zeitman: a young engineer who struggles with her memories of the future

Alex: Ariel's father

Baldur Hákonarson: an Icelandic investor who heads the company d^4 and is one of Ariel's three clients

Brendan: An Ullow programmer who handles Cillian's requests for new software

Cillian McGrane: Irish heir to a pharmaceutical manufacturing conglomerate and one of Ariel's three clients

Eoin Finn: Ariel's boss

Fergus: An Ullow programmer just out of university who handles Mikkel's requests for new software

Geirs: Baldur's head of security

Gróa: d^4 board member

Hulda: Baldur's personal assistant

Jake: head Ullow programmer for d^4

Lara: Cillian's ex-wife

Lola: Ariel's mother

Mikkel Nygaard: a Greenlandic investor, and one of Ariel's three clients

Mister McGrane: Cillian's father, a man who is usually barely conscious

Murna: Nell's creation, a fake Irish mystic from Donegal

Nell Gallagher: Cillian's friend, and an actress from Donegal

Doyle: Cillian's father's financial advisor

Ronan: An Ullow programmer just out of university who handles Mikkel's requests for new software

Siarnaq: a Kalaallit man who straddles two worlds and is plagued by visions of the far future. The Kalaallit are the Inuit of Western Greenland.

Teddie: Ariel's sister

Toby: friend of Ariel's brother Zane and head of y^1

Valdi: d^4 board member

Ulfur: Baldur's lawyer and right hand man

Zane: Ariel's brother